THE CLONE REBELLION
APOCALYPSE

STEVEN L. KENT

THE CLONE 10 REBELLION

APOCALYPSE

TITAN BOOKS

THE CLONE APOCALYPSE
Print edition ISBN: 9781783293391
E-book edition ISBN: 9781783293407

Published by Titan Books
A division of Titan Publishing Group Ltd
144 Southwark Street, London SE1 0UP

First edition: November 2014
2 4 6 8 10 9 7 5 3 1

A CIP catalogue record for this title is available from the British Library.

Printed and bound by CPI Group (UK) Ltd, Croydon, CR0 4YY.

Did you enjoy this book?

We love to hear from our readers. Please email us at:
readerfeedback@titanemail.com or write to us at the above address.

To receive advance information, news, competitions, and exclusive offers online, please sign up for the Titan newsletter on our website.

www.titanbooks.com

There are one thousand and ninety-five days in a three-year span, one thousand and ninety-six if it includes a leap year. By the time you are thirty, you will have lived nearly eleven thousand days.

This book is dedicated to my niece Elizabeth, who always took my breath away, though she didn't live to see eleven thousand days. My memories of her are filled with smiles and moonlight chats.

This book is also dedicated to Sean, who never saw a single sunrise, and to his parents, for whom the sun now rises more slowly.

SPIRAL ARMS OF THE MILKY WAY GALAXY

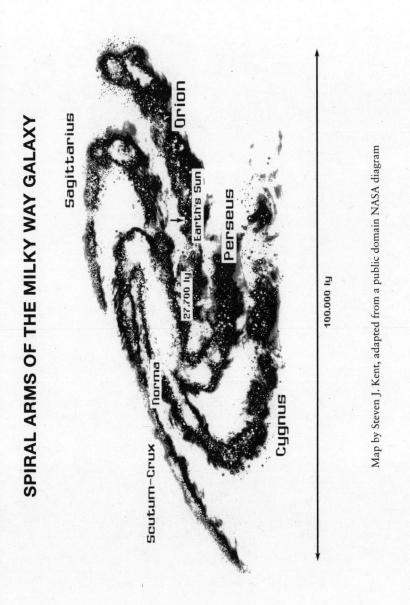

Map by Steven J. Kent, adapted from a public domain NASA diagram

A tomb now suffices him for whom the world was not enough.

—FROM THE EPITAPH OF ALEXANDER THE GREAT

If you want to make God laugh, tell him about your plans.

—WOODY ALLEN

NINE EVENTS THAT SHAPED HISTORY

2010 TO 2018
DECLINE OF THE U.S. ECONOMY

Following the examples of Chevrolet, Oracle, IBM, and ConAgra Foods, Microsoft moves its headquarters from the United States to Shanghai. Referring to their company as a "global corporation," Microsoft executives claim they are still committed to U.S. prosperity, but with its burgeoning economy, China has become the company's most important market.

Even with Toyota and Hyundai increasing their manufacturing activities in the United States—spurred on by the favorable cheap labor conditions—the U.S. economy becomes dependent on the shipping of raw materials and farm goods.

Bottoming out as the world's thirteenth largest economy behind China, United Korea, India, Cuba, the European Economic Community, Brazil, Mexico, Canada, Japan, South Africa, Israel, and Unincorporated France, the United States government focuses on maintaining its position as the world's last military superpower.

JANUARY 3, 2026
INTRODUCTION OF BROADCAST PHYSICS

Armadillo Aerospace announces the discovery of broadcast physics, a new technology capable of translating matter into data waves that can be transmitted to any location instantaneously. This opens the way for pangalactic exploration without time dilation or the dangers of light-speed travel.

The United States creates the first-ever fleet of self-broadcasting ships, a scientific fleet designed to locate suitable planets for future colonization. When initial scouting reports suggest that the rest of the galaxy is uninhabited, politicians fire up public sentiment with talk about a new "manifest destiny" and spreading humanity across space.

The discovery of broadcast physics leads to the creation of the Broadcast Network—a galactic superhighway consisting of satellites that send and receive ships across the galaxy. The Broadcast Network ushers in the age of galactic expansion.

JULY 4, 2110
RUSSIA AND KOREA SIGN A PACT WITH THE UNITED STATES

With the growth of its space-based economy, the United States reclaims its spot as the wealthiest nation on Earth. Russia and Korea become the first nations to sign the IGTA (Intergalactic Trade Accord), a treaty opening the way for other nations to become self-governing American territories and enjoy full partnership in the space-based economy.

In an effort to create a competing alliance, France unveils its Cousteau Oceanic Exploration program and announces plans to create undersea colonies. Only Tahiti signs on.

After the other nations of the European Economic Union, Japan, and all of Africa become members of the IGTA, France discontinues its undersea colonization and joins the IGTA. Several nations, most notably China and Afghanistan, refuse to sign, leading to a minor world war in which the final holdouts are coerced into signing the treaty.

More than 80 percent of the world's population is eventually sent to establish colonies throughout the galaxy.

JULY 4, 2250
TRANSMOGRIFICATION OF THE IGTA

With most of its citizens living off Earth, the IGTA is renamed "The Unified Authority" and restructured to serve as a government rather than an economic union.

The government of the Unified Authority merges principles from the U.S. Constitution with concepts from Plato's *Republic*. In accordance with Plato's ideals, society is broken into three strata—citizenry, defense, and governance.

With forty self-sustaining colonies across the galaxy, Earth becomes the political center of a new republic. The eastern seaboard of the former United States becomes an ever-growing capital city populated by the political class—families appointed to run the government in perpetuity.

Earth also becomes the home to the military class. After some experimentation, the Unified Authority adopts an all-clone conscription model to fulfill its growing need for soldiers. Clone farms euphemistically known as "orphanages" are established around Earth. These orphanages produce more than a million cloned recruits per year.

The military does not commission clone officers. The officer corps is drafted from the ruling class. When the children of politicians are drummed out of school or deemed unsuitable for politics, they are sent to officer-candidate school in Australia.

2452 TO 2512
UPRISING IN THE GALACTIC EYE

On October 29, 2452, a date later known as the new "Black Tuesday," a fleet of scientific exploration ships vanishes in the "galactic eye" region of the Norma Arm.

Fearing an alien attack, the U.A. Senate calls for the creation of the Galactic Central Fleet, an armada of self-broadcasting warships. Work on the Galactic Central Fleet is completed in 2455. The newly christened fleet travels to the Inner Curve, where it vanishes as well.

Having authorized the development of a top secret line of cloned soldiers called "Liberators," the Linear Committee—the executive branch of the U.A. government—approves sending an invasion force into the Galactic Eye to attack all hostile threats. The Liberators discover a human colony led by Morgan Atkins, a powerful senator who disappeared with the Galactic Central Fleet. The Liberators overthrow the colony, but Atkins and many of his followers escape in G.C. Fleet ships.

Over the next fifty years, a religious cult known as the Morgan Atkins Fanatics—"Mogats"—spreads across the 180 colonized planets, preaching independence from the Unified Authority government.

Spurred on by the growing Morgan Atkins movement, four of the six galactic arms declare independence from Unified Authority governance in 2510. Two years later, the combined forces of the Confederate Arms Treaty Organization and the Morgan

Atkins Fanatics defeat the Earth Fleet and destroy the Broadcast Network, effectively cutting the Earth government off from its loyal colonies and Navy.

Having crippled the Unified Authority, the Mogats turn on their Confederate Arms allies. The Confederates escape with fifty self-broadcasting ships and join forces with the Unified Authority, leaving the Mogats with a fleet of over four hundred self-broadcasting ships, the most powerful attack force in the galaxy.

In 2512, the Unified Authority and the Confederate Arms end the war by attacking the Mogat home world, leaving no survivors.

2514 TO 2515
AVATARI INVASION

In 2514, an alien force enters the outer region of the Scutum-Crux Arm, conquering U.A. colonies. As they attack planets, the aliens wrap an energy barrier around the atmosphere. Called an "ion curtain," the barrier prevents contact and communications.

In a matter of two years, the aliens spread throughout the galaxy, occupying planets deemed habitable by U.A. scientists. The Unified Authority loses 178 of its 180 populated planets before making a final stand on New Copenhagen.

During the battle of New Copenhagen, scientists unravel the secrets of the aliens' tachyon-based technology, enabling the U. A. military to win the war. In the aftermath of the invasion, the Unified Authority sends the four self-broadcasting ships of the Japanese Fleet along with twelve thousand Navy SEAL clones to locate and destroy the Avatari home world.

2517
RISE OF THE ENLISTED MAN'S EMPIRE

The Unified Authority Congress holds hearings investigating the military's performance during the Avatari invasion. When two generals blame their losses on lack of discipline among their cloned enlisted men, synthetic conscription is abolished and all remaining clones are transferred to frontier fleets—fleets stranded in deep space since the destruction of the Broadcast Network. The Navy plans to use these fleets in live-ordnance military exercises designed to test its new, more powerful Nike-class ships; but the clones thwart this plan by declaring independence.

After creating their own broadcast network, the clones establish the Enlisted Man's Empire, a nation consisting of twenty-three planets and thirteen naval fleets. As hostilities continue between the Enlisted Man's Empire and the Unified Authority, the Avatari return, attacking planets using a devastating weapon that raises atmospheric temperatures to nine thousand degrees for eighty-three seconds.

The Avatari attack three planets in December, 2517—New Copenhagen, a Unified Authority colony, Olympus Kri, an Enlisted Man's colony, and Terraneau, a neutral nation. Working together, the Enlisted Man's Navy and the Earth Fleet successfully evacuate Olympus Kri prior to the attack. Following the attack on Olympus Kri, the Avatari accelerate their attacks, incinerating a new populated planet every three days as they work their way toward Earth.

Despite the mutual threat, the Unified Authority renews its assault on the Enlisted Man's Empire.

2517
DESTRUCTION OF THE AVATARI HOME WORLD

The Japanese Fleet locates the Avatari home world in Bode's Galaxy. While the inhabitants of the planet have become extinct, its automated mining and military systems continue their destructive expansion.

After depositing all nonessential personnel on New Copenhagen to establish a new colony, the *Sakura*, the last ship in the fleet, launches a successful suicide attack on the Avatari planet.

2517
THE FALL OF THE UNIFIED AUTHORITY

Unaware of the Japanese attack on the Avatari home world, the Enlisted Man's Empire divides its military into two groups. One group establishes a colony on the burned-out remains of Terraneau, while the other defeats the Unified Authority, establishing a clone-controlled government.

The clones' hold on Earth proves tentative as remnants of the Unified Authority military attack EME bases on Earth and Mars. After an entire division of EME Marines defects, the clones learn that former members of the Unified Authority intelligence community have discovered how to change the neural programming in clones.

PROLOGUE

TWO HARBINGERS

Technical Sergeant Timothy Simpson of the Enlisted Man's Air Force looked at his monitor and saw an unidentified spaceship. "Lieutenant, I have a reading on a ship within our solar system," he told his commanding officer.

"Ours?"

"Nothing on record, sir."

"Have you tried to contact her?"

"She's not responding."

"Distance?"

"Four hundred sixty million miles from Earth."

"Is she hiding behind Jupiter?"

"She's out in the open, sir." The tracking-systems technician pointed to a screen, and said, "That's her, right there."

The screen showed a nondescript dot representing the ship, located in an area two hundred million miles from the nearest planet, which happened to be Mars.

"Is she moving?" asked the lieutenant.

"Drifting, sir. No sign of acceleration."

"Odd place to park a ship. Are you certain she's not a wreck from the war?"

The solar system had been littered with the carcasses of warships after two recent battles and a number of smaller skirmishes.

"No, sir. She's new."

The lieutenant laughed, and asked, "What are you telling me, T.S., that she just broadcasted in?"

"I don't have any record of a broadcast, sir, but she's just appeared on my radar."

"That would make her . . . If that's an Explorer, we'd better send somebody to have a look."

Lieutenant Walter J. Aspen, the officer on duty at the Hamsho-Kwok Deep Space Tracking Facility would die in five days. Technical Sergeant Timothy Simpson, the tracking-systems technician who discovered *Magellan*, UAES-539, outlived him by three hours.

Like the staff of Hamsho-Kwok, the crew of EMN *Millard Fillmore* was made up of clones. Every last man stood five feet, ten inches tall. Every sailor on the ship had brown hair and brown eyes. Not a one of them knew he was a clone. They all knew all of the other sailors aboard the ship were clones, but their neural programming didn't allow them to consider that they might be clones as well.

That programming included protocols that caused them to see themselves as having blond hair and blue eyes when they saw their reflections. The clones believed their own eyes even though they knew clones' eyes lied to them.

Fillmore was a Perseus-class destroyer, a wedge-shaped warship that was wider than she was long. She'd been circling Mars—not orbiting, circling outside the planet's gravitational influence. It took her eight hours to fly to the location of the mystery ship.

As his ship drifted closer to the target, Captain J. T. Matthews, commanding officer of *Fillmore*, examined the ship on a three-dimensional, holographic display. His ship had portholes and observation decks, but visual inspection wouldn't detect details like radiation, heat, toxins, and traps. Matthews searched the ship for signs of violence and structural damage, then he searched the area for enemy ships.

When he called in his first report to Naval Command, he said, "She's an Explorer. So far we haven't found any signs of damage." Designed for pangalactic cartography, Explorers were century-old self-broadcasting relics from the Unified Authority's early "Manifest Destiny" period.

He didn't wait for Naval Command to reply. Communications with Earth were slow from four hundred million miles out. In another half hour, he'd receive a message from Earth instructing him how to proceed. In the meantime, he flew within one hundred thousand miles of the wreck. From that distance, he could scan the ship's engines for energy usage and access her working computers.

Once he got the go-ahead, he would dispatch a transport to fly closer to the ship. Technicians aboard the transport would run another series of tests. If those final tests came back clean, the transport would release a team of engineers to board the Explorer.

Grave robbing; the Enlisted Man's Empire had robbed a lot of graves over the last few years, most in deep space. Only the Explorer *Magellan* was no war monument. Her hull was intact. A remote scan revealed that her navigation systems were working as was her communications equipment. Despite the fact that everyone inside the Explorer had died, the gravity generator still ran, and life support continued to fill the cabin with warm, breathable oxygen.

Still waiting for permission to proceed, Matthews sent a drone to have a closer look.

Monitoring the drone's transmission, Matthews spotted the deceased crewmen. He didn't even need to X-ray the ship; *Magellan* had portholes and observation spots on every wall. Directing his drone to peer in the windows, he mapped out the entire ship, locating all ten bodies.

Matthews relayed that information in a message, then began the long wait for further instruction. During that time, his engineers scanned *Magellan* for biological weapons. They scanned for carbon monoxide, carbon dioxide, and internal radiation leaks. They checked the internal temperature of the ship. They scanned for broadcast malfunctions.

After each test, Matthews sent the results back to Navy Command, then ordered his men to begin looking for some other hazard. Answers from Earth began trickling in. By the time Navy Command ordered Matthews to open the Explorer's hatch, his medical team had already attempted to diagnose the pilot's cause of death by parking a drone outside the windshield and photographing the dead man's face and limbs.

Matthews called sick bay, and asked, "What did you find?"

"He isn't moving," said a medical corpsman, a lieutenant.

"Corpses don't move much; that's my experience," said Matthews.

"We don't know that," said the corpsman.

"The hell we don't!" said Matthews. "I have seen all kinds of dead people over the last few years, and I can tell you with absolute certainty, they don't move."

"Yes, sir," said the corpsman, "but we don't know if these men are dead."

"They aren't moving," said Matthews.

"He doesn't appear to be breathing," the corpsman agreed. "He could be alive, hibernating or in stasis."

"The temperature in that ship is seventy-eight degrees."

"Warm for hibernation," the corpsman conceded.

"Don't people normally hibernate in a chamber?" asked Matthews.

"Normally."

"Why would he need to hibernate in a self-broadcasting ship? He could have broadcasted himself anywhere." Space travelers never hibernated, they never needed to. Hibernation was a way of keeping them alive and sane during prolonged spaceflights. Since self-broadcasting ships could bathe themselves in energy, then transfer themselves to any location instantaneously, staying sane during prolonged spaceflights never became a problem.

The medical corpsman considered this, and said, "Ah damn; they're probably dead, sir."

Matthews asked, "Do you think it's safe to send a boarding team?"

"That ship out there is one hundred years old. For all we know, she's no longer capable of sustaining life," said the corpsman.

Matthews said, "I'll make sure the team wears space suits."

"In that case, there's nothing to worry about," said the corpsman.

Matthews and his medical corpsman both died five days later, on August 22.

An away team with six engineers and two medical technicians rode the sled from *Fillmore* to *Magellan*. An open platform designed for traveling short distances in space, the sled had tiny booster rockets all along its edges and underside. It did not have walls, rails, or seats, just a floor large enough to accommodate eight men in space gear.

Lieutenant Devin LaFleur steered the rig and led the team. An experienced technician, LaFleur had done everything from rebuilding reactors to plumbing barracks. Though he'd never boarded an Explorer before, LaFleur had studied *Magellan*'s layout; he knew enough to park his sled on the roof of the ship, near the rear hatch.

He stepped off the sled and stared into space. Over five hundred million miles away, the sun nearly blended in with more distant stars. Sol was a shining dot, the other stars pinpricks.

Having been built for scientific exploration during a time of expansion, the Explorer didn't have locks or security systems. LaFleur opened the outer hatch with the press of a button, and he and his engineers crowded into the air lock. The outer door closed behind them, then the air pressure equalized, and the door leading into the ship slid open.

While his engineers ran diagnostics verifying the remote readings, LaFleur contacted Captain Matthews.

"Report," Matthews ordered.

"Oxygen, good. Temperature, good. Radiation level, normal. No toxins in the air." That didn't mean LaFleur would remove his helmet. He knew better; so did his men.

LaFleur noticed something that the remote tests had missed. The air inside *Magellan* was humid, almost steamy. He ran a test on the mist in the air and found no chemicals other than hydrogen and oxygen.

He spoke to one of his engineers, tasking him with finding the source of the moisture. Moments later, the man radioed back from *Magellan*'s tiny galley. It had taken him less than a minute to locate the source of the moisture. In the galley, four mugs sat empty beside a spigot designed for dispensing boiling water. A thin but steady stream of vapor leaked out of the improperly sealed valve.

LaFleur thanked the engineer and sent him to examine the cockpit.

The medical corpsmen examined each of the bodies one by one. Like the *Fillmore* crew and the staff at Hamsho-Kwok, the men manning *Magellan* were all clones, all five feet ten inches tall, all brown-haired and brown-eyed.

Six bodies lay side by side in the cargo hold. They lay on their backs, their heads facing up.

Corpsman Rich Jackson turned the first body on its side, saw dried blood on the man's left earlobe, and knew what had killed him. He found dried blood in the hair around the man's ear as well.

Leaning over the body for a better look, Jackson said, "Brandt, look at this."

Corpsman Timothy Brandt came for a closer look.

The corpsmen wore the "soft-shelled armor" of engineers, rubberized suits that covered them head to toe and provided air and heat. The suits were airtight and protected them from chemicals and radiation.

Having seen the blood around the ear, Brandt searched the next corpse. He said, "Same." He surveyed each of the corpses. "They all died the same way."

"They didn't die here; there's not enough blood," said Jackson. The cause of death was obvious, but there should have been a small puddle of blood under each of the dead men's heads.

Jackson reported the information to LaFleur, who relayed it to Matthews on *Fillmore*. He said, "Captain, we know what killed them. You're not going to like it."

"I don't like it already," Matthews snapped. "Let's have it."

"These men had a mass death reflex," said LaFleur.

"A mass death reflex," Matthews repeated. "That can't be good."

LOCATION: CORAL HILLS, MARYLAND
DATE: AUGUST 16, 2519

Howard Tasman sat in his wheelchair near the window, staring through the break between the curtains, looking down at the street. Most of the people had deserted this part of Coral Hills; those who remained mostly stayed indoors during daylight hours. That was why the man caught Tasman's attention; he was walking alone on the street.

The man was tall and gangly-looking, with long arms and long legs. As he came closer, Tasman recognized the man's soulful, sympathetic eyes. Tasman said, "Hey, I know that guy . . ."

Travis Watson, who also lived in the apartment, went to the window to have a look. "Who is he?"

Tasman said, "His name is Rhodes. He works for one of the intelligence agencies."

Emily Hughes, Watson's girlfriend, joined Tasman and Watson at the window. Like them, she hid behind the curtain. She said, "He doesn't look like a spy."

"He's not a spy; he's an administrator," said Tasman, a man who had spent his life working with both spies and administrators. Now an old man in his nineties, Tasman had lived to see his family die, leaving him bitter and alone.

Watson asked, "Can we trust him?"

"I wouldn't trust him to wipe my ass."

Emily sneered at the awful old man, and muttered, "That would be cruel and unusual punishment." She didn't like Tasman. She didn't like him in small doses, and now she'd been

26

stuck in the same apartment as him for weeks.

"What's wrong with him?" asked Watson.

"He works for EME Intelligence," said Tasman.

"That mean he's on our side," said Emily.

"He worked for U.A. Intelligence before the clones took over," said Tasman. "I don't trust anybody who works both sides of a war."

"You worked both sides," Emily pointed out.

Tasman only smiled, an unpleasant sight. His teeth had grayed to the color of wet cement. His gums were whiter than his teeth.

She looked around the shitty little one-room apartment with its worn furniture and bare wood floor. The sinks dripped all day, and the only oven was an old-fashioned microwave. In her mind, living in that apartment was punishment enough; sharing it with Tasman was like entering an inner circle of Hell.

The building had stairs instead of an elevator. Emily knew the only way Tasman could leave the building was riding on Watson's back. She said, "You know what, Howie? We could have left here a month ago if it weren't for you."

Tasman said, "Your boyfriend is the president of the Enlisted Man's Empire. Why don't you step out on the street and see who salutes him?"

Watson wasn't really the president of the EME, but he'd spent a few weeks in charge on an interim basis. Now he was in hiding.

They were on the southeastern outskirts of Washington, D.C., the wrong part of town. The neighborhood had become infested with Unified Authority soldiers, and that wasn't the only problem. Most of the local citizens preferred a government of natural-borns to clone rule. In their eyes, Watson, a natural-born who had risen up the civilian ranks under the clones, was a traitor.

"Rhodes might be able to get us out of here," said Watson.

Emily asked Tasman, "You said he worked for an intelligence agency?"

"Yeah, one of them."

"Does he work for the Marines?" she asked.

"Do you associate Marines with intelligence?" asked Tasman. "I said 'intelligence'; that means he doesn't work for the Marines."

In his right hand, Rhodes carried a small case marked with the emblem of the EME Marines—an eagle perched on a globe with an anchor in the background.

Emily said, "Do you see the emblem on his case?"

"That doesn't make him a Marine," said Tasman.

Watson started to take Emily's side, then he realized the old bastard had a point. They were in Unified Authority territory. Only a suicidal fool would carry a case like that on these streets. Either a fool, or someone with powerful friends.

Emily asked, "So what's he doing with that case?"

"Maybe we should go ask him," quipped Tasman.

Sounding even more sarcastic, Watson said, "Now there's an idea."

Emily said, "Trav, maybe we should stop him."

Travis Watson stood six-foot-six, but he was a law-school graduate, not a fighter, and he had no tolerance for pain. On the other hand, he had spent the last month of his life on the lam. Though he didn't realize it, desperation had toughened him.

Emily added, "He might have an encrypted phone. We'd be able to call Wayson or Freeman for help."

Tasman said, "Watson, if there's a problem, you can take him. You're bigger than he is."

"You said he was a spy," said Watson. "He might be dangerous."

"I said he was an administrator."

It was the middle of the day in an underclass Washington suburb in August. The day was oppressively bright and humid. The buildings across the street seemed to radiate in the heat.

Watson paused, thought of the possible outcomes, and said,

"Tasman, you're coming with me."

"What about me?" asked Emily.

"You're staying here," said Watson.

Emily said, "Get specked, Watson. What if he kicks your teeth in? You might need me."

Watson loved Emily. He said, "You'll be safer up here."

She laughed, and said, "Listen, Galahad, I've seen what happens when you lose a fight. You're going to need me."

Embarrassed by his girlfriend's lack of confidence, Watson asked, "You don't trust me?"

"In a fight?" asked Emily. "Travis, dear, I bet I can take you."

Tasman laughed, showing his white gums and gray teeth.

Watson loaded Tasman on his back and trotted down the stairs, Emily at his heels. They reached the street a moment after Rhodes had passed by the building.

Watson ducked back in the building and ran through a hallway, still carrying Tasman on his back. The hall led to a narrow alley with a Dumpster and crates and drunks. Rhodes strolled past as they moved down the alley.

Watson lowered Tasman to the ground and hid behind the Dumpster while the old crippled scientist shouted, "Rhodes! Hey, Rhodes, is that you?"

Rhodes stopped and paused as if he recognized Tasman's raspy voice. He turned to look in the alley and saw the old scientist sitting against the wall like a vagrant. Tasman wore an old suit that might have been nice one month earlier but had now been worn into oblivion.

Sounding confused, Rhodes said, "I know you."

"Damn straight you do, genius," said Tasman.

"You're Howard Tasman," said Rhodes.

Tasman said, "Can you give me a ride back to Washington?"

Smiling like a teen in a brothel, Rhodes stepped into the alley, and said, "Howard Tasman . . . Oh, I'll get you to Washington."

Watson had choreographed the fight in his head. With a few small variations, it went as he had expected.

Rhodes started to pull his gun from his holster as he stepped past the Dumpster. From where he hid, Watson couldn't see the gun, only the briefcase. Thinking that the luggage was Rhodes's most dangerous weapon, Watson sprang from his hiding place and grabbed the case. He caught Rhodes unaware, wrestled the case free, then swung Rhodes face-first into the side of the Dumpster. Seizing on his momentum, Watson slammed a fist into Rhodes's jaw, nearly knocking him out. As he fell, Watson slammed a knee into his groin, flattening his left testicle.

Kevin Rhodes dropped to one knee, then fell to the concrete.

Emily looked at Rhodes, then at Watson, and said, "Baby, I'm impressed."

Hoping he hadn't just mugged an innocent man, Watson carried Rhodes into the building. Emily dragged Tasman in behind him.

If *Magellan* had surfaced a few days earlier, or if Watson had bagged Rhodes the week before, the Enlisted Man's Empire might have won the war.

Part I

THE CONQUERORS

1

I was the seniormost officer in the EME military, technically I had four stars on my collar though I preferred not to wear them— General Wayson Harris, commander in chief and president extraordinaire. I may have qualified for the title of "emperor" as well. As I understood it, emperors ran empires, not presidents or generals. It really didn't matter. Our hold on humanity was temporary at best.

We were a nation of clones. The end of our rule was built into our DNA. Well, sterility was built into our DNA, and since we didn't have factories for building the next generation of clones, we were a nonrenewable empire.

One title I didn't mind too much carrying was "commandant of the Marines." I had agreed to accept that title. I had never agreed to be the president of the Enlisted Man's Empire. In fact, I had never actually been coronated . . . I suppose the term is "inaugurated." I had been missing in action when the admiral who was in charge was murdered. I may have been next in line, but I was missing, so the brass selected Travis Watson to run the empire until I was found or declared dead.

Now that I was back, I didn't want the job.

"I don't see that Watson matters one way or the other, Harris," said General John Strait, commander of the Enlisted Man's Air Force.

I said, "He's the president of the empire."

Thomas Hauser, commander of the EME Navy, corrected me. He said, "Watson was a temporary president."

We were having a summit. I was one of four people invited to participate. I represented the Marines. Our fourth was General Pernell MacAvoy, commanding officer of the EME Army and the only one in the bunch whom I considered a friend.

Strait, who read scientific journals and seldom used military vernacular, was the brightest man at the table and the most useless. MacAvoy was the dumbest. If his IQ had a third digit, he did a fine job hiding it, but he was also the man who was winning the war.

Strait said, "Watson was only the only interim president."

Hauser said, "Yeah, that's what I just said."

"You said he was a *temporary* president. The term is 'interim,'" said Strait.

MacAvoy said, "I thought he was the *acting* president."

Strait gave him an openly condescending pat on the arm, and said, "Harris is the acting president, Perry."

MacAvoy smiled and nodded.

We generally held these meetings in formal conference rooms or fancy dining halls. MacAvoy was in charge this time, and he arranged for us to meet in an indoor shooting range.

At least he'd closed the range during our meeting; the place was empty and mostly dark, silent, too, no gunfire serenade. The rest of us didn't complain or ask MacAvoy why he elected to hold a high-level summit in a shooting range; we simply accepted it as a *MacAvoy-ism*.

MacAvoy said, "I like Watson."

Strait smirked, and said, "Liking him doesn't matter, not in the grand scheme. He's unimportant."

MacAvoy said, "Yeah? Bullshit. Watson was a natural-born working for the Enlisted Man's Empire. He was loyal to us; the natural-borns are going to notice if we turn our back on him."

"Our backs," said Strait.

"That's what I said," said MacAvoy.

"You said, 'back.' There are more than one of us. We have more than one back," said Strait.

"Is that how it works?" asked MacAvoy. "There are four of us here, but I only see one asshole."

I said, "Perry has a point. The natural-borns are going to notice how the Enlisted Man's Empire takes care of its civilians."

When your empire is made up of clones who die the moment they realize they are clones, it's wise to use euphemisms like "enlisted man" when referring to your citizenry. As part of their physiology, the last model of clones had a death gland built into their brains that released a toxic poison when they realized they were clones. The Unified Authority scientists who created them wanted them convinced they were natural-born people and to keep them loyal and submissive.

The best-laid plans . . .

All of the officers in the summit were clones, including me, though I was a different make of clone. I was the last of the Liberator-class clones. Unlike MacAvoy and Strait, I knew I was synthetic. Instead of a death reflex that would kill me, my architecture included a gland that released an adrenaline and testosterone cocktail into my blood during combat.

"Do you really think anybody cares?" asked Hauser.

"No one on our side," I admitted. "But the Unifieds will make a real show of it if we throw him to the wolves."

I had personal reasons for wanting to save Watson; I considered him a friend. So did Hauser. MacAvoy only *fraternized* with other soldiers and women. And Strait . . . I didn't know anything about him. He ran the Air Force, a branch of the military that Hauser and MacAvoy no longer considered relevant. With six Navy fighter carriers orbiting Earth, who needed an air force?

Strait said, "We don't know if he's alive."

Lunch arrived. Strait or Hauser would have flown in their best chef. MacAvoy served us Army chow—boiled beef on potatoes smothered with gravy, canned green beans, and a baked pastry of unidentifiable origin. We ate at the conference table.

Hauser and Strait ate in silence, obviously seething at MacAvoy's frontline hospitality. I didn't mind it. Army chow and Marine chow are generally pretty similar, and I never cared for elegant food.

As we ate, MacAvoy said, "The reason we're meeting in a range is because I want to show you something. I got a new weapon that's gonna specking end this conflict."

Strait and Hauser managed to look dubious yet politely surprised. We were fighting an "end war," the final hostilities with an enemy that had officially surrendered a year ago.

"What do you have?" I asked.

"I've got the answer to shielded armor," said MacAvoy.

Unified Authority armor was based on the same design as ours, but it included electrical shielding that stopped bullets, knives, and shrapnel.

"I have bullets that destroy their shields," MacAvoy said.

Hauser and Strait seemed unimpressed. They fought wars from

far away; battlefield tactics didn't matter to them.

I said, "No shit? Are you going to show us?"

"That's why we're in a shooting range," said MacAvoy. "I wanted to show you all together."

MacAvoy placed his napkin on the table, and said, "Let's go."

Until that point, Admiral Hauser had only picked at his food, and Strait hadn't touched his fork. They showed no interest in Army chow, but apparently MacAvoy's bullets interested them even less. They started eating.

Our conference table was near the door of the range. MacAvoy had left the shooting lane dark. When he stood, he pulled a remote from his pocket and lit the lanes. He hit a second button, and a trio of mannequins dressed in U.A. armor began glowing at the far end of the range.

I hadn't noticed it before, but an M27 sat on the counter at the front of one of the shooting lanes. MacAvoy picked up the gun, and said, "Harris, you gave me the idea for these bullets. You were the one who figured out how to burn out their batteries."

His posture demonstrating just how relaxed he felt around firearms, MacAvoy pivoted to face the mannequins, aimed the M27, and fired a burst of three shots. Three-star general or not, Perry MacAvoy was no stockade soldier; all three shots hit the mannequin in the middle.

I had seen bullets and shrapnel disintegrate when they hit the shielding that protected that armor, having no more impact than a raindrop striking a bridge. MacAvoy's bullets didn't seem to do anything to the shields, either. His three fast shots hit the mannequin in the head, chest, and gut, and the shields glowed on.

I said, "Well, at least we know you're a good shot."

"What's the rush, Harris?" MacAvoy asked. "Give it a moment." He placed the M27 back on the counter, then stepped into the firing lanes. He said, "Let's inspect the damage." I followed. Hauser and Strait came as well.

As we approached, I saw something strange. The bullets might not have knocked the mannequin over, but they left spots on the ethereal electrical shields. Having never seen that happen before, I jogged over for a closer look.

The armor-clad mannequin stood at attention—arms at its sides, legs straight and shoulder width apart, its armor still glowing golden orange. Except for the stains, which seemed to have soaked into the electrical field, I saw no signs of damage.

"Are those holes?" asked General Strait. He and Hauser had come to inspect the mannequin.

Sounding as if he actually knew what he was talking about, MacAvoy answered, "General, that is a dynamic electrical field; you can't shoot holes into energy fields."

I said, "You can't stain them, either." But there they were, proving me wrong, three dark, splatter-shaped stains in the electrical energy. "What's in those bullets?"

"They're not bullets; they're simmies," said MacAvoy.

"Simmies," short for "simunition," were rounds used for faking assassination—gelatin cartridges filled with fake blood. Only, the simmies MacAvoy used hadn't been filled with blood.

MacAvoy said, "I stole your idea, you know, draining the batteries. These simmies are packed with liquidized carbon and iridium filings. That carbon shit sticks to anything, and the iridium doesn't melt."

The batteries were the chink in the Unified Authority shielded armor . . . literally. Since Marines don't march into battle wearing nuclear reactors on their backs and mobility matters as much as protection, the shielding on U.A. combat armor worked off tiny batteries with a limited amount of juice. The batteries could power the shields for an hour if they went unchallenged, but the power spiked whenever anything came in contact with the shields.

By staining the shields, MacAvoy was creating a permanent energy spike. Those batteries would burn out fast.

"You're staining the armor with a compound that has a high flash point," said Strait, admiration in his voice.

Even as we stood there, the batteries powering the armor died, leaving dull, old, dark green armor in its place.

"Hit them with this, and their shields last about a hundred seconds," said MacAvoy.

"What if they just charged their batteries?" I asked.

"You saw it," said MacAvoy. "We charged the battery in that suit this morning."

"And your goop drained it in two minutes?" I asked.

"One minute and forty seconds," said MacAvoy. "The results are always the same."

"When can we start manufacturing these?" I asked.

"Already in motion," said MacAvoy. "We'll have five million of these babies by the end of the month."

If we had received them by the end of July instead of August, things might have been different.

2

As I walked into my office, one of my aides, an overaged lieutenant, came to tell me that I had received a call on my private line. Now that my girlfriend, Sunny Ferris, had gone MIA, I hadn't had much use for that line. That call could have come from her. I should have been excited, but I wasn't. As far as I was concerned, she had stopped being my girlfriend before she went missing; I just hadn't had the chance to inform her of her change in status. If she was back, we'd need to have an uncomfortable conversation.

"Got a name and a number?" I asked, dreading the scene Sunny would make.

The lieutenant said that the call came from Kevin Rhodes, the director of encryption at the EME Intelligence Agency.

My first thought was, *Things are looking up.* I didn't know Rhodes, but the director of encryption didn't sound like a person who would have an emotional meltdown. Then I realized the obvious. *I don't know him. Why is he calling me on my private line? How the hell had he even gotten the number?*

The EME Intelligence Agency, a civilian organization, had nine directors. I had met all nine, but I seldom dealt with them. I asked, "Did he say why he was calling?"

"He refused to speak with me, sir."

"Refused to speak with you," I mused. "Maybe he called on my private line so he could have a private communication."

"He sounded nervous," said the lieutenant, who also sounded nervous.

"Do you have his number?" I asked.

"Yes, sir," he said. "I left it on your desk."

I'd stopped carrying my phone after we captured Washington. Carrying a phone was like wearing a target into battle. If the Unifieds managed to get their hands on my number, they could use my phone to track me. As president, I had access to secure communications that, in theory, could not be tracked. I also had enemies who put theories like that to the test.

I had the lieutenant leave the room and dialed Rhodes's number.

"This is Rhodes," said the voice.

Except that it wasn't Rhodes's voice. This voice I knew.

I asked, "Watson, is that you?"

Silence, then, "Harris, do you know if this is a secure line?" He sounded more than nervous; he sounded flat-out scared.

"It's as secure as they get," I said. "Where are you?"

He didn't answer for several seconds. I knew why he was scared. Just one month earlier, he'd been sitting in an office in the Pentagon when the Unifieds started pumping gas through the air-conditioning system. The gas knocked out every clone in the building. By the time they woke up, they'd been reprogrammed, and killing Watson was the first item on their list of things to do.

We had a security feed of Watson and his bodyguards driving

a stolen car through the security gate at the entrance to the Pentagon's underground parking structure. After that, they disappeared. We'd found the bullet-ridden remains of his car in downtown Washington, D.C. One by one, his bodyguards had turned up dead.

After considering his options, Watson said, "I'm in Coral Hills."

Coral Hills. I knew the name but needed a moment to locate it on my mental map. "What the speck are you doing there?" I asked.

Coral Hills, I could jog that far, I thought. Here we'd spent weeks searching for Watson, and he was just across the river. But I couldn't really jog over and get him; Coral Hills was a U.A. stronghold. MacAvoy called it "the U.C.D.," the *Unified Central District.*

"Look, Wayson, we need to get out of here. Can you get us out?" he asked.

"An extraction," I muttered. "Who is we? How many of you are there?"

"Emily is with me." He let a moment pass before adding, "We have Howard Tasman, too."

Tasman, that was good news. He was the scientist who invented the neural programming used in clones. If the Unified Authority captured him we'd have all kinds of problems.

Watson said, "And we captured Rhodes."

"Captured him?" I asked. "He's on our side."

"No he isn't," said Watson.

I wanted to ask what he meant, but that could wait. I said, "I'll arrange an extraction."

Watson seemed confused by my offer. He was a civilian. In his world you extracted teeth and rescued victims. He asked, "Can you get us out of here?"

3

A lot of people could handle a rifle. I had badges, pins, and ribbons for marksmanship, one of which I earned by putting three shots in a one-inch center circle from a mile away. Ray Freeman made me look like a piker when it came to the quiet art.

With his skills and scopes, Freeman had hit human targets from three miles away. He had a knack for assassination. His list of kills included gangsters, politicians, soldiers, and the founder of a fanatical religion. When guns weren't the right tool, he used bombs. Sometimes he used both. He'd beaten men to death with his fists as well; Freeman had a gift.

The man stood seven feet tall and weighed over three hundred pounds. He'd lost weight of late.

He'd been injured just a month earlier. An untreated sprain had turned into an infection which nearly cost him his leg and his life. After weeks in a hospital, he looked frail, but not in the way of mortal men. He didn't look any less dangerous, just more brittle.

He stood as we talked, his posture a bit less erect, his shoulders tighter than normal, his skin maybe just the slightest bit ashen. He said, "I bet you plan on going in yourself."

I asked, "You got a better idea?"

Freeman said, "You could stay out of the way. How about we both stay out of the way?"

I felt the irritation welling in me as I said, "You know somebody better than me for this mission?"

He said, "Harris, you're the president of the Enlisted Man's Empire; maybe it's time you started shuffling papers."

"I'm also a Marine," I said.

"You're a general. Generals send people into battle."

I said, "I was engineered for fighting battles."

Freeman walked to a tall stool and sat. The man had not fully healed from his wounds. He had a slight limp.

Speaking in his soft, resonant voice, he said, "You're getting too old to be fighting wars."

I didn't answer that, mostly because I agreed with him.

"We're the wrong men for the job," said Freeman. "I'm too old, and you're the president. You're also the only military clone over six feet tall. If they see you, they'll recognize you. I'm a seven-foot black man; they'll certainly recognize me."

Freeman was the last survivor of a Neo-Baptist colony. His people had been the descendants of African-Americans occupying a tiny planet in an isolated corner of a galaxy in which the government wanted to integrate races. I was the last Liberator, he was the last African-American; we belonged in a museum.

As I started to say something, he asked, "How old are you, Harris? You hit thirty yet?"

I started to admit that I had just turned thirty, but he interrupted me again. He said, "I just spent my forty-seventh birthday lying in a hospital listening to a couple of doctors arguing whether or not they could save my life without amputating my leg."

He shook his head, and said, "I'm nearly fifty years old, and I walk with a limp. One of my shoulders needs surgery, and the one that's been repaired still doesn't work right. I'm retired."

I said, "Maybe I am the right man for the job. I might not be the right one to get Watson out, but I'd make one hell of a distraction."

Freeman nodded, and said, "Yes, perhaps you should paint a target on your forehead and go for a stroll in downtown Coral Hills."

4

I met with Perry MacAvoy in the early evening, about 18:00, to discuss the situation. Admiral Hauser attended as well, but only in spirit. The general and I sat in the same room; Hauser appeared through a confabulator, a device that made it look like virtual people were actually sitting in the room. Around Washington, D. C., the political types called these devices, "social mirages."

Looking through the confabulator's window, we saw Hauser as if he were sitting in the room.

I began the conversation with a question for MacAvoy. "You said you'd have five million of those shield-busting bullets by the end of the month. How many do you have now?"

He said, "We haven't started manufacturing them yet."

"Do you have any?" I asked.

MacAvoy shrugged his shoulders, and said, "Just handmade loads. We have a few hundred."

"Not enough." I sighed.

Hauser asked the question that MacAvoy was about to ask. "What do you need them for?"

I told them about Watson and Rhodes.

Hauser said, "I want to make sure I understand the situation. Watson incapacitated one of the directors of our Intelligence Agency and used his phone to call you?"

"Something like that," I said.

Seen through the confabulator, Hauser looked as solid and three-dimensional as the wall behind him. The flicker of a smile entered his expression as he asked, "And he wants us to extract him from Unified-held territory?"

I said, "Affirmative."

"Let me guess, Harris. I bet you want to go in yourself. Is that right?"

Feigning indignation, I said, "Admiral, I am the president of the Enlisted Man's Empire. I hardly think that running covert extractions befits my pay grade."

MacAvoy's jaw dropped. Hauser whistled. An uncomfortable silence filled the room until MacAvoy finally said, "Admiral, maybe they've reprogrammed him."

I said, "Get specked, MacAvoy."

Still sounding surprised, Hauser said, "He sounds like Harris."

Ignoring them, I brought up a virtual map of the eastern suburbs. A red dot appeared marking Watson's location. I said, "General, I want to drop the extraction team here. They're going to need Jackals, personnel carriers, and a team of shooters. Can you muster your men by 05:00?"

"No problem," MacAvoy replied without a moment's hesitation. He examined the map. "No problem delivering men and material to the zone, but they're not going to last very long once they arrive. That's the Unified Central District; we could drop a column of

Schwarzkopfs there, and they wouldn't make it out."

Schwarzkopfs were our best tanks; they were fast, armed with big cannons, and covered with hardened plating, but the Unifieds had rockets that could destroy them, and anything that could destroy a Schwarzkopf would make short work of a Jackal or a personnel carrier.

I said, "They wouldn't last long under normal circumstances, but I don't think the Unifieds will notice your team."

"Why is that?" asked MacAvoy.

I tapped the map and a yellow stripe appeared along the eastern side of the shore of the Anacostia. "They're going to be busy fighting off a full-scale invasion."

"You're sending in the Marines?" asked MacAvoy.

"I bet you plan on leading the invasion," said Hauser.

I said, "Last time I checked, I was the commandant of the EME Marines."

I never knew the exact date of Tom Hauser's death; he died somewhere in space. Perry MacAvoy died on August 24. He was executed by a firing squad.

5

The sun wouldn't rise for another hour.

We preferred to work in the darkness, something the Army couldn't do. Marines wore combat armor, soldiers fought in fatigues. The armor made us more mobile; you could attach jetpacks to the back and magnetized rappelling cords to the front. Our armor didn't protect us from bullets, and shrapnel cut it to shreds, but our visors provided us night-for-day vision, heat vision, radar, sonar, telescopic sight, and more. Our armor came with rebreathers that allowed us to operate underwater and in outer space. The bodysuits we wore under our armor protected us against extreme temperatures, both cold and hot. The bodysuits wouldn't stop us from frying in a nuclear blast, but they keep us comfortable in the absolute zero degrees of deep space.

Few things gave away a night attack more quickly than the telltale glow of lights. Satellites detected columns of vehicles with blaring headlights. Enemy planes and helicopters spotted stadium lights from miles away. We didn't worry about it. With every man in the outfit wearing armor, we assembled our troops in the dark interior of an indoor stadium, hidden from prying eyes and lenses.

My infantrymen climbed into personnel carriers and my artillery (fifteen Schwarzkopfs and forty Targs) and my cavalry (a fleet of jeeps and Jackals) formed into lines behind them. The men in jeeps wore armor with visors; the men in the tanks and Jackals used computer-enhanced vision in the windshields of their vehicles.

I looked up and down the lines. The Enlisted Man's Empire controlled all of the satellites, but the Unifieds had been the ones who created the computers; they knew how to hack into our systems and peer through our eyes.

We communicated using the interLink, a military-grade communications network that let sergeants and captains communicate with their platoons, majors communicate with their companies, and lieutenant colonels communicate with their battalions.

As the officer in charge, I had the commandLink. I could listen in on every conversation, look through any Marine's visor, speak to any man or unit. I vacillated on whether or not there was a God, but if he existed, he probably used something similar to a commandLink to listen in on all of his believers' prayers.

I had two full-bird colonels working as my right-hand men, but I didn't know their names. I had become aloof to underlings.

"General Harris, the men are ready, sir." The man's name appeared in my visor. Whenever anyone communicated with me over the interLink, their name, rank, and unit appeared in my visor. That didn't mean I read it.

I wasn't always like this, indifferent to the men around me. My last right-hand man had been an officer named Hunter Ritz alongside whom I'd fought in several battles. He'd risked his life and pulled my ass out of the fire. Ritz's death changed me, hardening me to the men around me.

So what if I never learned this clone's name? We were all cogs, interchangeable parts in a machine. That included me.

I didn't worry about my Schwarzkopfs; those monsters couldn't be killed, but the smaller, faster, weaker Targs gave me pause. I asked, "What's going on with the Targs?"

We had three rows of them. They were as fast as jeeps and just as maneuverable, but not as easily damaged. Targs were exclusively Marine Corps property and the butt of Pernell MacAvoy's twisted sense of humor. He constantly joked about Targs mating with Rumsfeld Tanks and giving birth to bicycles.

We had other tanks for heavy combat—LGs, Specters, and some ancient Rumsfelds, but those battle wagons didn't fit with my strategy. I cared more about delivering blows than withstanding them once we crossed to the eastern side of the river. I wanted speed, not lumbering crushers.

Along with my commandLink, I had a communicator that connected me to Perry MacAvoy, who waited back at the base. I got on the horn, and asked, "You ready?"

He said, "I got my cock in one hand and my M27 in the other."

"Small arms?" I asked. "Interesting strategy."

MacAvoy, not the wittiest man I ever met, said, "Hooah!"

Marines say *Hoorah*. Soldiers say *Hooah*. Two damn syllables and they can't even get it right.

I said, "My Marines are locked and loaded."

MacAvoy said, "Good luck, Harris. Give a signal when you want us to make our move."

And that was it. We exited the armory in a long column of vehicles, with the Targs and Schwarzkopfs at the front, followed by Jackals and armored personnel carriers—all driving with their lights off. All of our equipment was coated with black, heat-reflecting enamel.

Driving under streetlamps on Independence Avenue, my tanks and trucks were plain to see. I was at street level. They wouldn't be as easily seen by satellites . . . I hoped.

We could have shut down the streetlights, but that would have given us away more surely than the streetlights.

Under the glow of the streetlights, our half-mile-long parade streamed past greenbelts, strip malls, and an outdoor stadium. The buildings were dark, the streets glowed white, orange, and gold. We drove down Independence to the banks of the Anacostia, but we didn't cross the bridge. Anyone with a rocket or a demolition kit can destroy a bridge. Marines became targets when they crossed bridges. We turned right when we reached the river, then we took a short drive south, past the twin islands that sat in the middle of the river.

I watched our advance from inside a Jackal, standing in the swiveling turret mounted in the roof. I could see the cannons of my Schwarzkopfs poking over the turrets of my Targs. A herd of six-wheeled personnel carriers brought up the rear. We looked like a line of gigantic black ants. Our windshields were obsidian, our vehicles dark as onyx and as unshining as marble. Moonlight and street glow fell on my column, and my vehicles absorbed them.

The Anacostia was to my left. A galaxy of little lights sparked across that chasm, stars taking the shapes of streets and buildings. Did they know we were coming?

It was exactly 05:00. Though a small nest of officers had stayed up planning this sortie late into the night, the average Marine didn't hear a word until we roused them from their racks and told them to suit up. Even now, they were just learning the details.

Think they know we're coming? I asked myself.

At one time, the Unified Authority could reprogram my clones and send them in to spy on us. I hoped there weren't any spies in the clutch of generals who had planned this invasion. But who knew? The column slowed as we approached a public park with an open shoreline. This was the moment at which we would give ourselves away; once we entered the river, we'd be visible from miles away. I didn't trust bridges, and tanks don't tread water. A fleet of amphibious transports, mobile warehouses designed to convey men and material, waited for us.

The amphibious transports would hover across the river on cushions of air instead of pounding through water. They were slow, but that didn't matter, not crossing a river that was only five hundred feet wide.

My driver knew the score without my telling him what to do. He drove to a rise from which I could observe my troops and parked. Strings of black vehicles rolled to the shore and vanished into the mouths of transports.

The Anacostia was inconvenient for us but narrow. Had the Unifieds expected our movements, they could have bombarded us from the other shore. They could have battered us with heavy artillery from miles away, but the night remained silent. And no flashes or explosions broke the darkness on the eastern side of the river.

The tanks, Jackals, and personnel carriers loaded quickly. Marines don't leave things to chance. We drilled and drilled again, until loading onto transports became one of our favorite pastimes.

"We're about to cross the river," I told MacAvoy.

"If you see Tobias Andropov, give him a five-toe enema, would you? Say it's from me," said MacAvoy.

Tobias Andropov was a Unified Authority politician, not a soldier. He was the one who came up with abandoning the all-clone conscription, transferring the clones to man outdated battleships that the new U.A. Navy would use for target practice. Amazing how ambitious men are brought down by their own avarice. Andropov would still be in charge if he hadn't turned on us.

I said, "Five-toe enema with your name on it; got it."

I signed off as my driver pulled up to the last of the amphibious transports. The entrance into the gigantic hovercraft looked like open jaws. We drove up the ramp, trading the sheer darkness behind us for the red-lit interior. All of the vehicles ahead of us were exactly identical, clones, like me and my men. Looking down the row was like looking down a row in a factory; every roof was the same height and size; all the wheels evenly spaced on identical chassis, turrets, hoods, and windshields on every carrier the same as the last. Inside those trucks, every driver was the same as the last. Every man wore identical armor. Remove their armor, and they had identical faces.

The red glow of the interior lights seemed to dissolve into the flat back enamel covering the personnel carriers. Our vehicles were beyond black; they were darkness itself.

I gave the order, and the invasion began.

Unified Authority infiltrators had moved into our shores, and we wanted them out, but we didn't want to cause too much damage along the way. The buildings, the streets, and the infrastructure were ours. We couldn't bombard the enemy to soften their defenses without damaging property we considered our own.

Stage one: a sortie of gunships flew overhead as our amphibious transports shuffled us across the river. Using my commandLink, I patched into the visor of my lead gunship pilot and watched the proceedings from his vantage point.

Gunships are flying tanks—slow, heavily armored, carrying enough cannons and machine guns to take out a fortress. They can withstand RPG fire, but missiles, rockets, and particle-beam cannons make short work of them, and the Unifieds had plenty of rockets.

So here's the scene, the sun started rising on the horizon. Looking through my lead pilot's visor, I saw a molten-lava sky with clouds ablaze in orange and red as the sun started rising. The city was all silhouettes, a jumble of gaps and boxes with hardly any movement.

The pilot looked to his left, then looked to his right. To his left was a cockpit window. Beyond that was a long row of gunships, a wing, flying slightly behind him. To his right sat his weapons officer. He sat staring into a screen.

The pilot said, "Looks like we caught them sleeping."

The gunner said, "They're still here. I got heat signatures."

The pilot said, "Remember, General Harris said as little damage as possible," to which the gunner replied, "It's a war; we're gonna break stuff."

And then the fighting began. The first shots fired were five rockets that streamed out of a single-story storefront, maybe a clothing shop, the contrails behind the rockets spread like the fingers of a grasping hand.

Our gunships flew approximately one hundred feet off the ground, traveling at a speed that might have seemed slow to a bicyclist.

The gunner said, "I'm going to feel real guilty about killing these bastards if that's the best they can do." He fired a countermeasure in the rockets' direction. The countermeasure, an exploding canister of flak, ended the barrage in an instant, creating bright explosions that filled the viewing window in my visor as the pilot yelled in triumph.

The gunner fired a Theron rocket in response. Therons killed with heat instead of percussion. The rocket had a lutetium alloy nose that punctured stone, brick, metal, and most armor with the ease of a hypodermic needle stabbing a new recruit in the ass. The rocket struck the building and windows shattered in a spray of glass, smoke, and flame.

"Think they're dead?" asked the pilot.

"They ain't happy," said the gunner.

"What if they're wearing shielded armor?" asked the pilot.

That didn't matter. It wasn't the armor, it was the bodysuit that protected Marines against heat and cold, and at six hundred degrees, bodysuits failed. Theron missiles generated a flash of thirty-five hundred degrees.

My twenty-five gunships broke formation. They scattered across the sky. Looking through the lead pilot's visor, I watched the carnage. They drifted over the city, like fish circling a reef in search of prey. They were black oblong shapes, nothing more than silhouettes, like the buildings below them.

A little more than a minute had passed when my nameless lieutenant reported, "General, we've reached the other side of the river."

I answered. "Move 'em out."

Every captain, every lieutenant, and every platoon sergeant had been briefed, and specific assignments had been uploaded into their visors. With a simple ocular command, they could access street maps and compasses. Virtual beacons marked their routes and their objectives.

The door of our transport dropped open, revealing the fiery sky.

Amphibious transports are built to operate like tunnels. You enter one side and leave through the other—first on, first off. We were the last vehicle to enter this transport, meaning we'd be the last one off. I watched the carriers ahead of us as they purred to life and loped down the ramp.

The sky was a swirl of oranges and reds, but the ground

remained dark as night. Twenty vehicles ahead of me, the first transport in our column started moving. The vehicle behind it roared to life immediately.

In my Jackal, I remained in the gunner's turret, my hands on the handles of the 60-caliber. A squeeze of my finger would release a burst of steel-jacketed rounds, four inches long, a half inch across. These bullets could split a twenty-foot tree. Line six men in front of a thick cement wall, and I could produce a half dozen corpses and a hole in that wall behind them with a single round.

The personnel carrier in front of mine began its slow march toward the ramp. A moment later, we followed. Last on; last off.

We drove through the red-lit innards of the amphibious transport, passing metal ribs, traffic-control booths, cameras, and a communications array.

I looked up into the sky, then down into the shadows. Some of my officers might have wanted to contact me, but I had closed my commandLink to them. They had their orders.

Our tires squealed as we hit the bottom of the ramp, and my driver accelerated. Standing in the turret, I fell back against the wall, then tightened my grip on the handles and pulled myself back toward the gun.

The gunfire had already begun. In the distant darkness, muzzle fire glittered and vanished like sparks from a grinding wheel. I heard the growl of the Jackal's engine through my armor; these vehicles were louder on the inside than the outside.

First came the gunships, then the Targs and Schwarzkopfs followed. These wagons didn't lumber like dinosaurs, they scurried like spiders, maneuvering perfectly well at speeds of over seventy miles per hour.

As we drove ahead, two more Jackals joined us, making us the middle car in a trio, speeding down a midtown avenue in a canyon of five- and six-story buildings. Shapes in the windows in some of the buildings glowed softly, barely perceptibly—men in shielded armor.

I spun my gun to the four o'clock position and fired. No need to aim at the windows. A 60-caliber round goes through walls and windows alike, but my 60-caliber man-splitters might as well have been spit wads against their shields.

One of the drawbacks of Unified Authority shielded armor was that you couldn't use the shields and hold a weapon at the same time. Their armor included wrist-mounted fléchette cannons that ran along the right sleeves, but that was a decidedly close-range weapon. Our Intelligence Agency had found data on remote-controlled rocket launchers that the Unifieds could fire using ocular commands built into their visor. I'd never seen those launchers in action, however.

I fired a string of bullets into the front window of a department-store lobby. The ghostly outlines of men in shielded armor rushed to return fire, but it came too late to do any damage. Like me, they didn't mind wasting ammo. They shot. I shot. We skidded around a corner, and I lost sight of the building, entering a new street, a lane filled with men in armor. Targets.

I aimed. I fired. My bullets meant nothing. They returned fire. There may have been fifty men there, milling around, glowing like embers in a dying fire. My driver kept clear of them. If we strayed too close, they stood a better chance of hurting us than we did of injuring them.

The cannon sounded so loud that it made my helmet vibrate. When I looked back where the passel of Unifieds had been, I saw a small crater. The Targ that had fired the shot pulled up beside our little convoy, thin wisps of smoke still twisting from its cannon. The shell probably hadn't hurt those U.A. Marines, but it scattered them beautifully, and who knows, some of them might have landed incorrectly and broken an arm or a leg.

To this point, the engagement was still in the dream state. They had fired a few shots. We had fired a few shots. Maybe we'd killed a few of them, then again, maybe not. The real excitement had yet to begin.

I contacted MacAvoy, and said, "We have our beachhead."

He responded, "My birds are wheels up, and my rubber's hit the specking road.

"How is it going down there?"

I asked, "Ever knocked a crippled man out of his wheelchair?"

"Sounds like you caught them napping."

"Quiet neighborhood, practically a bedroom community," I said. "Maybe I'll move here once the riffraff moves out."

As the last traces of orange and red cleared from the sky, the shelling began. Pillars of flame rose ten feet out of the ground, spraying our light armor with cement and rock as the Unifieds bombed the streets and infrastructure we hoped to preserve. Apparently, the Unifieds had adopted a scorched-earth policy.

An explosion that looked like a fifteen-foot fist punching up through the asphalt sent a Targ swerving. Targs were light and small by tank standards, but they still weighed thirty tons; it takes a powerful jolt to send one careening down the street. Dozens of small FLAWS rockets flew from the windows of a block-long brownstone, striking Jackals, Targs, and one of my Schwarzkopfs. A pair of gunships swooped in to respond.

I *voyeured* the scene, peering through one of the gunners' visors, and saw dozens of men swarming out of the back of the building like ants from a hill, their armor glowing. We could bury them, of course, blow up the buildings on either side of the alley and leave them interred under a mountain of shattered bricks.

The gunner had his orders. We wouldn't destroy two buildings to bury shielded Unifieds, not yet. Not yet. Not today. We had the Unifieds on the run, so we would show our better angels.

These boys didn't push their luck. They sprinted down the alley instead of trying to hide in the next building. I'd given specific orders about leaving empty buildings intact, but I'd been purposely vague about attacking buildings with enemy soldiers.

I heard the gunner say, "That's right you little turds, go hide in the nice building."

The pilot said, "You can shoot it down and say they went in."

Under normal circumstances I might have complimented the pilot on his bloodthirsty attitude, maybe even promoted him, but civilians lived in these buildings—innocent bystanders trapped in a war zone. In theory, those civilians hadn't taken sides. I thought they might if we started destroying their homes indiscriminately.

Ironically, the gunner was the sensible one in that cockpit. He said, "Tempting, but we have the general's orders."

My driver kept us moving, speeding around the yard-deep divots freshly blown into the street around us. I could barely see the two Targs that led our way through a dusty brown haze that hung low in the streets ahead of us, returning fire at occupied buildings and clearing U.A. soldiers out of our way.

Using heat vision, I spotted the signatures of people in buildings on both sides of the street. They showed as orange silhouettes, colorful shadows against dark backgrounds. I could tell if they were friendly by their posture. Civilians cowered against walls, Unifieds skulked under windows, as if preparing to return fire. I spotted smaller silhouettes, children.

A rocket struck the front grill of the Jackal, sending flames spreading across the windshield and disappearing. Lord it happened quickly. A glimpse of smoke, a flash of fire, and the car stopped so suddenly I thought maybe we had hit a wall. I had the disorienting sense of falling, of time stopping, of the world's spinning on a different axis, then we were upside down.

"General, General, are you okay?"

I lay on my side, the butt of the 60-caliber pressing against my chest. I tasted blood in my mouth and felt a ringing in my head.

The Jackal lay on its side, asphalt visible through the driver's side window and open sky visible through the passenger's. I couldn't see either; I still had the heat vision running in my visor. I looked out the top of the turret, saw an orange silhouette, recognized the posture of a man with a handheld rocket launcher, and I squeezed off twenty, maybe thirty rounds from my 60-caliber.

Someone said, "Oh, nice shot, sir."

I didn't know the voice.

A couple of officers came to pull me from the wreckage. I shooed them away.

Despite the ringing, my head was better than clear. I was focused. I was a Liberator-class clone, and my combat reflex had begun. Adrenaline and testosterone now flooded my veins, honing my thoughts and making me more aggressive. Fighting and happiness became synonymous in my head. Victory, like killing, became a means to an end; keeping the hormone in my bloodstream became my chief objective.

Still using heat vision, I searched the nearest building and the buildings around it for targets. I found a man with his arms crossed and his head down and knew what he was doing—he was hiding his heat signature under a cold shower. I squeezed the trigger and shot him, shot him through the walls. He had to be a Unified; civilians don't think about cooling down their heat signatures.

"How do you know he wasn't just jerking off?" one of the officers asked. I started to explain before noticing that the man was laughing. He'd seen what I saw.

I spotted other targets, too, people hiding, people running, people crawling. I wanted to kill them all. The combat reflex nearly drove me wild with soothing warmth. *Kill them,* I told myself. *Shoot and the hormone will continue.*

I pulled my hands away from the Big Sixty, ducked under the gun, and crawled out of the turret. The driver and copilot of the Jackal were dead. The driver's helmet pressed against the door, blood leaking out a hole. The safety harnesses held the copilot in his seat, his neck and arms dangling. A rocket had shattered our windshield.

The fire had blasted through the windshield and scorched the dash of the Jackal. I saw what it had done to my men and looked away.

The Jackal that dropped off my rescuers had already sped away; no one in their right mind would have parked on this road. Tanks sped by at top speed. Jackals weaved in and out of the alleyways. We crouched behind the armored chassis of my overturned Jackal, a wheel spinning above my head. Flames played harmlessly over the engine compartment. Any fuel in that reservoir had long since combusted, leaving a twisted frame and a burst fuel tank with sharp flanges that bent outward like the petals of a flower.

One of the men who'd come to get me reported the rescue to his superiors. Using the commandLink, I listened in.

He said, "Yeah, we got him. How the speck do you think he is? His Jackal's on its side; the guys in the front are confirmed K.I. A., but the general's still in the turret picking off snipers with the 60-caliber, and as happy as a pig in a mud hole."

The guy on the other end of the Link said, "Yeah, well, don't stand too close to General Harris. The guy's a Liberator; he's probably having a combat reflex."

Good to know what your men think of you, I told myself.

A rocket struck the sidewalk about forty feet ahead of us, near enough to make the ground shake. Rocks and dirt, and a flaming scab of grass flew into the air. A string of bullets snicked off the roof and sides of the overturned Jackal.

My rescuer radioed, "You better hurry; they're homing in on us."

Targs fired shells that caused the façades of buildings to shatter and crumble to the ground. Gunships danced across the skyline, firing chain guns and dodging rockets. A constant caravan of Jackals streamed in and out of alleys, offering themselves as targets.

Suddenly, the battle had concentrated around us. The fighting along the shore no longer mattered; this block had become the eye of the storm. The Unifieds had chosen the location and made their stand, now we would break their backs or fight our way around it.

I had hoped to see Marines in glowing armor entering the streets by this point in the battle, but the Unifieds played their cards well. They deployed snipers and grenadiers from buildings and watched as we tripped over land mines they had placed in the streets. I felt the ground tremble. The carcass of my Jackal slid in its wake.

"Run!" I shouted, and I darted to the nearest alley, evacuating my cover just as the fire flames belched out of the building across to my right. The first floor of the building seemed to disappear beneath a gush of liquid fire.

"Moveitmoveitmoveit!" I bellowed to myself as well as the men who had rescued me and the vehicles that were coming to secure me. Jellied fuel splashed everywhere, hot enough to melt through iron, possibly radioactive. They must have filled some underground storage tank with the stuff.

As I reached the alley, a Jackal came skidding out. I managed to jump out of the way, then turned and watched as it sped into the flaming fountain and vanished into a blinding flash that left only a skeletal chassis bathed in flames. Jellied fuel splashed three Targs, lining their turrets and cannons with fiery plumes. Two of the tanks rumbled to safety; but I watched the third Targ grind to a halt in the fiery mire. The men inside would have died after a minute; in another minute, the engine would melt.

I watched for a moment, then turned and continued running.

Three men in shielded armor stood at the far end of the alley. Their shields glowed, a pale orange-gold aura that warned us that they couldn't be hurt. Standing at the far end of the alley, they were four hundred feet away, outside the accurate range of their weapons. One of the two Marines who had come for me raised his M27 and fired. Almost all of his bullets hit the mark, they flashed and disappeared like moths hitting an electric grill. The Unifieds returned fire. Their fléchettes struck walls and ground. A window shattered forty feet ahead of me.

At this distance, the fléchettes might not even penetrate our armor. They couldn't hit us; we couldn't hurt them. Then a Targ rumbled by and fired a shell into the wall above them, burying the Unified Authority Marines in an avalanche of bricks and rubble.

It was a shallow grave that might not hold them. They'd be alive, and conscious and angry, and they might still be able to shoot at us.

I saw a door that led into one of the buildings lining the alley and ran for it. The door was locked, so I used my universal key— my M27. Three shots. The handle fell to the ground, and the door swung open. With that jellied-fuel fire to our backs and the buried Unifieds ahead of us, we leaped through that door lickety-split. When your choices are death or the unknown, the unknown becomes a charming option.

We moved cautiously through the dark interior, and facing the unknown quickly lost its charm. We had entered an apartment building. The walls, solid by civilian standards, became clear as windows when I examined our surroundings with heat vision. Orange and yellow spots appeared through every wall, some marking recently used stoves, some revealing people cowering behind beds and dressers and possibly betraying assassins in wait.

Glancing up at the ceiling, I saw indistinct apparitions in orange and red. Civilian, military, male, female, child, adult, wearing armor or diapers, I couldn't tell. Officers tried to contact me over the Link. I ignored most of them, but opened a channel to the men in the building with me.

"General, I can call for a platoon to clear the alley," one of my rescuers offered.

Now that we had entered the building, we had few options. We couldn't leave through the front door; that would take us back toward the fire. There might have been a back door, but the fighting in that area had gone hot. Sitting out the fight was not in my Liberator DNA.

I trotted down a hallway. There were no lights. I didn't know if we had cut the power or the Unifieds had unplugged the building when they set off their fire bomb. Enough morning sunlight floated in through the shattered front window for my visor to switch from night-for-day lenses to tactical. I saw shadows. I would have seen colors, too, had the building not had a black floor and white walls.

We had entered a four-story brownstone with a winding wooden staircase, two flights to every floor. Our plasticized armor clattered as we climbed the stairs.

I ran up the first flight, paused, searched the landing above me using heat vision, and saw no threats. The front window opened to the intersection in which the Unifieds had unleashed their napalm. Below me, I saw a nightmare landscape in which the hulls of Jackals and Targs lay still in a fire- and ash-colored mire. The entire scene looked like a mirage because of the ripples of heat rising above it.

I took in the view as my team passed my position. Distracted as I was, I had secured the first landing. The next man secured the second floor as our third man secured the next landing up. We encountered no resistance and found ourselves trapped.

I had never lived in a civilian tenement. None of us had. I expected the stairs to lead to the roof. They led to the top floor, and there they stopped.

"Now what?" asked one of my men.

"Got a can opener?" asked another.

The hall led to the back of the building. I sprinted in that direction, my men close behind me. I wanted to get back to the fight. I wanted . . . I wanted . . . I didn't want my combat reflex to end.

My boots slid as I ran on the black marble tile. Using heat vision, I searched the rooms as I passed. I saw a man holding a gun, a pistol. My finger tensed on the trigger and prepared to break into his apartment, then my thoughts overtook my instincts. If he was holding a pistol, he wasn't wearing shielded combat armor.

"There's someone in there," one of my men said.

"Leave him," I said.

"What if . . ."

"You heard me."

Despite what I had told my men, I decided that I would shoot the bastard if he stepped out of his doorway.

I glanced back to make sure he didn't step out behind us, and there he stood, a fat, unkempt man in need of a shave and fresh laundry. He looked at my M27 and dropped his pistol.

I said, "Return to your apartment, sir."

He wasted a moment staring into my visor, more likely at his own reflection than my eyes, then he stepped back and locked his door.

He'd been a civilian, one stupid enough to try to choose sides. Still, he'd live another day. Using heat vision, I watched his orange silhouette through the door as he stumbled into the bathroom and retched into the toilet.

We found a fire escape outside the back window. Had we been Unifieds, we wouldn't have been able to climb the ladder, not with our shields up and disintegrating or repulsing everything but the ground.

A ten-foot climb, easy enough. The ladder ran along the back of the building. Looking down, I saw the little mound of bricks that had fallen on the quartet of U.A. Marines. Under different circumstances, I might have scanned the pile with heat vision to see if they were still down there, but the battle had continued on autopilot, and I didn't want to spend an extra moment hanging from a fourth-story ladder with my ass in the air.

The battle had become messy.

Speeding around tight corners and through narrow alleys, some of our vehicles had collided. Targs may be light and small compared to other tanks, but they bash past Jackals the way bowling balls bash past pins.

Most of the buildings around us were of the three-story variety, allowing me to see the next street over. I saw a Jackal, still on all fours, that had crashed into a building. The windshield had shattered, but I thought the wheels might still turn.

Using ocular commands, I set up a direct Link with one of my aides, and asked, "What's the report?"

"They're in full retreat, sir."

"Which direction are they going?" I asked. Watson's address had been directly east of us. If the Unifieds caught them leaving his apartment, we'd have a significant problem.

"Backing up, sir," said the colonel.

"East?" I asked.

"Yes, sir," he said, sounding confused. He didn't know about the extraction. As I said before, the Unified Authority had landed spies in our midst; I only revealed the final objective of this mission on a need-to-know basis. The Marines fighting and dying in these streets didn't need to know about Watson.

Did that make me indifferent to my men?

"Yes, sir. They're retreating eas—"

I cut him off so I could warn the extraction team.

I said, "MacAvoy."

"There you are," he said. "I've been trying to catch your sorry jarhead ass for the last thirty minutes."

"The Unifieds are retreating toward your extraction team," I said.

"Let 'em," said MacAvoy. "I got my men out of there half an hour ago. That's what I've been trying to tell you. We found Watson, Hughes, and Tasman. Speck, man, we even found a spare."

"They're safe?" I asked.

He sounded so at ease as he said, "Out of harm's way and inhaling sandwiches in my officers' mess."

6

DATE: AUGUST 18, 2519

The battle raged on after I left, lasting six hours in total. Two hours after MacAvoy's commandos returned with Watson, Emily Hughes, Howard Tasman, and the unspecified guest, my infantry rolled onto Minnesota Avenue. We'd captured the eastern shore of the Anacostia.

I couldn't take credit for taking that land. We'd beaten the Unifieds because they didn't have anything in the way of artillery. They'd smuggled men into the capital using the Potomac, but when they'd tried to airlift their big guns, they'd run into a roadblock named Pernell MacAvoy. He'd kept them on the run, backed them into corners, and ultimately chased them into Maryland.

MacAvoy bullied subordinates, allowed his mind to drift during high-level briefings, and had the intelligence of a rabid bulldog, but I admired him. While other generals nibbled at the edges of big battles, MacAvoy marched his forces straight ahead.

I'd always been taught to reserve my best punch for the end of the fight. MacAvoy started out throwing hooks and uppercuts. He didn't deal in subtleties, just in knockouts.

I sat in my office in the Linear Committee Building, the modern equivalent of the building the ancient Americans referred to as their "White House." Some early American monuments still stood, and the city retained its original layout, but as the government had changed, so did the buildings that housed it. When the Linear Committee replaced the presidency, the two-story White House was replaced by a ten-story marble mausoleum.

Like the Unified Authority, the Enlisted Man's Empire retained Washington, D.C., as its seat of power after capturing Earth. After a few necessary personnel changes, we allowed the U.A. Congress to continue business as usual. Some of the old bastards complained about "playing a meaningless role in our puppet show," but they accepted their paychecks just the same.

The Linear Committee, on the other hand—that was another story. The Committee had been the executive branch of the Unified Authority government. Through most of Unified Authority history, the Linear Committee had been a stabilizing force. That ended when that toxic spider Andropov became the last chairman of the Linear Committee.

As the Unifieds had destroyed the Pentagon during their last big attack, I made the LCB our new capitol and strategic building. MacAvoy now occupied an entire floor of the building. So did General Strait. Admiral Hauser preferred to conduct his business from space.

The office I had inherited from Andropov was thirty-five feet long and twenty-nine feet wide. I sat behind the same desk Andropov had once used. It was an antique, over six hundred years old, and made from the timbers of an ancient sailing ship. It had drawers which I kept empty, a computer that I seldom touched, and landlocked communications gear originally designed to reach the farthest corners of the galaxy.

On this occasion, though, I thought maybe I saw a reprieve in my near future. Now that Travis Watson was back, I planned to make him the man in charge. He was a civilian, which made him better suited for the rigors of leading civilians than me. He could pass laws; I only knew how to give orders.

My aide opened the door. I expected MacAvoy to enter first, but a woman dashed in before him. She zipped around my desk and wrapped her arms around my neck as I stood to greet her. When MacAvoy warned me that he had rescued a "spare," I thought he meant Kevin Rhodes.

Sunny Ferris, who'd been my fiancée as recently as a month ago, pressed her mouth against mine. A lot had changed during that last month, but she hadn't been around to hear about it. As far as she knew, I still loved her.

She pressed her mouth so hard against mine that our teeth ground together. She kissed me and then kissed me again. Seemingly oblivious that other people had entered the room, she rolled her tongue over mine, and suddenly I needed to sit before the other guests noticed my reaction. She'd had that effect on me since the first time I'd seen her.

Sunny was beautiful, and she'd always given herself freely, but some quality about her disturbed me. Even now, physically aroused, I both wanted her and wanted to get away from her.

Dressed in fatigues and chomping his cigar, Lieutenant General Pernell M. MacAvoy let his lips slip into an ironic smile as he watched Sunny step away from me. He saluted, and said, "Specking hooah, Marine. We saved your boy, took back half of their land, and got your wench back. Not a bad day's work."

With my excitement safely hidden behind my desk, I returned his salute, and said, "Hoorah, Soldier."

Travis Watson and Emily Hughes had also entered my office. Watson looked starved and tired. Last time I saw him, he'd had the tan and the physique of a gym rat. Both had deserted him. Now he looked like a man who barely survived between meals.

Emily had thinned as well, but nothing that a week in a resort couldn't fix. Good food, rest on a decent bed, and a little exercise would set her right. Watson's eyes had gone dull; she still had fire in her big blues.

Howard Tasman had also rolled into the room. Emily looked pale and ragged, Watson needed medical attention, but Tasman looked worse than either of them with his gray teeth, red-rimmed eyes, and colorless skin—and that was his normal appearance. The absence of food and sun hadn't helped or marred his visage.

I had enough chairs to fill a classroom in my office. MacAvoy, the only guest who had seen my new digs, pulled a chair from along the wall and sat beside my desk. Watson trudged to the wall to fetch seats for Emily and Sunny, then took one more for himself. Happy in his wheelchair, Tasman remained in place.

Watson placed his chair so it touched Emily's. Sunny and Tasman sat on either side of them, both giving themselves lots of room. I noticed the way Tasman stole glances at Sunny from the corner of his eye, the horny old shit.

"Your plan went like clockwork," said MacAvoy. "There wasn't a Uny to be seen, every last one of the mother-specking bastards was busy shooting at you."

"No trouble at all?" I asked.

"Not a hiccup," said MacAvoy. "We could have sent chauffeured limousines instead of personnel carriers."

Watson and Emily showed no interest in joining the conversation. They sat slump-backed in their seats, looking anemic and saying nothing. If humans could achieve osmosis, they would have sucked the adrenaline and iron right out of my bloodstream.

Tasman looked more distracted than anything else. Though he tried to hide it, the old bastard kept glancing over at Sunny. I didn't blame him though I resented him; Sunny was beautiful beyond reason. Her eyes were this deep-water blue that reminded me of a pool in a desert oasis. She had the silkiest brown hair. It was lustrous, like mink fur. Apparently, she'd taken better care of herself than Watson or Emily; she sat spryly in her chair with the energy of a blushing teen debutante. She was a Harvard-trained lawyer, but the last few weeks seemed to have leeched the upper-crust starch out of her.

She'd disappeared shortly after Watson and Tasman. During the brief period when MacAvoy's men struggled to equalize their surge on D.C., the U.A. Marines captured the area around her apartment building. By the time we reclaimed the territory, she was already gone. My relationship with Sunny had been based on sexual attraction, maybe *sexual neediness*.

There was something about her, just the sight of her fired up every sexual synapse in my head, but I didn't like her. I didn't like talking to her. I didn't like the way she interacted with my friends. She looked down on them and probably me as well.

MacAvoy nodded toward Sunny, and said, "We found her on their way out. She saw the convoy and came running."

"What about Rhodes?" I asked.

"He's safe," said MacAvoy.

"In the brig?" I asked.

"This is the Army, General; we don't place criminals in brigs, we place them in prisons."

"In a cell?" I asked, purposely not adopting his jargon.

"We have him on a cage," said MacAvoy.

"On a cage" meant on an incapacitation cage, which looked more like an operating table than a cage. Rhodes was lying paralyzed on a table with two filaments surgically implanted in his neck. The filaments conducted a light charge of electricity into his spinal cord. The electricity wouldn't cause him any pain, but it would leave his body limp as wet laundry.

Placing him on a cage had been a good idea. If Kevin Rhodes was like other operatives in his field, he'd probably try to commit suicide before we could question him if we left him in a jail cell.

I looked at Watson, and asked, "Have you seen a doctor?"

He didn't answer. He wasn't catatonic, more lethargic. At first he seemed not to hear me. He stared at me. A moment passed, and he shook his head and seemed to wake from his daydream. He said, "Sorry, Harris, what did you say?"

I repeated, "Have you seen a doctor?"

"I'm sending them to a hospital as soon as we leave," said MacAvoy.

"Maybe you should put them up in a hotel," I suggested. "A comfortable bed and good food could be all they need."

Emily said, "We had a bed where we were."

Sunny said, "General MacAvoy says you demolished my apartment building."

"Yeah? Did he mention that it was his men who fired the shells?" I asked. When I learned Unified Authority commandos had captured the area, I had entered the building to look for Sunny and kicked the proverbial hornets' nest. MacAvoy's soldiers shelled the building when they came to fish me out.

She looked at MacAvoy, and said, "No. He left that part out."

MacAvoy laughed, a grinding and evil laugh. He leaned back and saluted me with his cigar.

They presented such an interesting study, these four refugees. Sunny still had energy and a sense of humor. The Unifieds hadn't been looking for her.

But even though Tasman had been trapped in the same building as Watson and Emily, the decrepit old bastard had almost as much energy as Sunny.

Watson and Emily acted like zombies. When MacAvoy said, "Perhaps we should get Travis and his wife to a doctor," they didn't stir.

I said, "They aren't married." They had only met a few months ago. Until meeting Emily, Watson had prided himself on overexercising his libido. From what I knew of her, Emily Hughes had lived a similar existence. They were well suited.

"Yeah. I know," MacAvoy said. "I just wanted to see if they were listening."

They still gazed into nowhere, completely oblivious of anything happening around them.

I said, "It doesn't appear that they heard you."

Watson hadn't sounded so good when he called. Since then, he'd only gotten worse.

Raising my voice to a drill-sergeant pitch, I said, "Travis."

He snapped out of his trance and turned toward me.

I said, "I'm sending you and Emily up to Bethesda."

Watson should have recognized the name, Bethesda; it was close enough to have been a prowling ground back in his bachelor days. He frowned, and asked, "Why are you sending us there?"

"Walter Reed," I said. When the confusion didn't clear from his expression, I said, "Walter Reed Center; it's a military hospital. I'm sending you to get examined. You know, maybe they can jump-start your brain cells."

Unlike Watson, Emily seemed to follow the conversation. She patted him on the hand, and said, "Walter Reed, isn't that the place you used to call the 'Harris Hotel'?"

Over the last year, I had spent time in that facility. Watson, who didn't approve of my Marines/pseudo-political lifestyle, made all sorts of quips about my injuries. Waking from his daze, he said, "Oh, right, the hospital."

MacAvoy absorbed what they both had said, then roared. He nearly laughed himself into convulsions. "Harris Hotel? Oh, that's specking excellent! Maybe they should rename their ambulances 'Wayson Wagons'!"

"Get specked," I said.

Sunny got a kick out of the name as well. She stifled a giggle, and said, "Travis, that's so funny!"

Sunny had a strained relationship with Travis, and Emily openly hated her. We'd invited them over to her apartment several times. More often than not, they declined our invitations.

Truth was, my feelings toward her vacillated. Seeing her now, I wondered what could ever have led me to want to leave her. In the quiet times, there was something about her, something vague and unpleasant. She'd say things, nasty barbs that seemed to come out of nowhere. Sometimes her words and tone contradicted one another, her words were warm, while her voice was frigid. Sometimes she seemed completely unaware of offending people, while other times, she clearly relished their discomfort.

Maybe it was her upbringing. She'd come from money, but so had Emily, and Emily never made me feel uncomfortable.

"Sunny, maybe you should go with them," I said. Emily turned and shot me an icicle glare.

Sunny either didn't notice Emily's reaction or didn't care. She said, "Wayson, I'm fine. I don't need to go to see a doctor." With those blue eyes, those deep-water-blue eyes, she had the most expressive face. Her forehead wrinkled, and her eyebrows curved up in a pleading way.

I said, "All four of you should go for a checkup, just to be safe."

Sunny smiled, laughed, placed her warm hand on mine, and said, "Don't worry about me."

Tasman spoke up. He said, "I don't need a doctor. I know my physical condition." He did. That wheelchair of his gave him a continuous physical examination. One look at the panel on his right armrest would reveal his blood pressure, his pulse, his temperature, his heart rate, and a dozen other readings.

MacAvoy told Sunny, "Tell you what, sweetheart, why don't you give your boyfriend and me a moment. I need to chat with him, you know, general-type stuff."

Sunny's eyes narrowed. Without speaking a word, she glared at MacAvoy and pled with me. That face . . . that beautiful, perfect, expressive face.

When I said, "Why don't you give us a moment?" she frowned, then nodded and left the room with Watson and Emily.

Seeing the anger in her expression, MacAvoy said, "I know who gives the orders in your house."

I said, "She'll be fine."

Tasman stayed put. I stared down at the old prick, and said, "You looking for something?"

He said, "I have personal business."

Having worked on the topmost of top secret projects, the man had every military clearance in the books. He might even have something to add to the conversation, but I couldn't stand the look of him.

The stooped old goat reached a hand under the seat of his wheelchair. He struggled for a moment or two, then he produced the small metal case that Watson had taken from Rhodes.

I spotted the Marines insignia and knew precisely what it held.

"What is that?" asked MacAvoy.

"Rhodes was carrying it when Watson attacked him," Tasman answered. He handed the case to me.

Marines used cases of this sort for transporting sensitive orders and information. I could hold a gun to the latch and fire without so much as scratching it. The metallic outer shell was laser-resistant as well, but I wouldn't need a laser to open this particular case. I stroked my finger across the lock, and the latch popped open. It knew my fingerprints, and I knew its contents.

Resting in the center of the case I found a bandage-shaped strap made out of stiff cloth—an encryption bandit. It was a device used for hijacking information from enemy computers, a little decoder and memory unit. This particular bandit had recently returned from the undersea cities the Unifieds had been occupying as bases. I knew where it had been because I was the one who had taken it down there—right before our Navy destroyed those cities.

I said, "This case belonged to Hunter Ritz." Not even a week had passed since we had found Ritz's body in an abandoned transport.

Tasman had not yet heard about Ritz's death; MacAvoy had. He asked, "How would Rhodes have gotten his hands on Ritz's case?"

I said, "Take a wild guess."

MacAvoy growled, and said, "Not a chance. I got a look at Rhodes when they lifted him off the transport; he couldn't have killed Ritz. The son of a bitch was whimpering like a new recruit."

"Good point," I said. "Maybe he had help."

"A lot of help," said MacAvoy. "He'd have been too afraid to take on Ritz on his own."

Perry MacAvoy had good instincts, but this time I thought he was wrong. Granted, Rhodes's brand of espionage had more to do with mathematics than combat, but he worked for the Intelligence Agency.

The general said, "Tell you what, Harris; I'll leave the speck in a dark room to see if he squirms." That was an old interrogation tactic, pretending to neglect prisoners, leaving them alone and scared, allowing their imaginations to get the best of them. Men on incapacitation cages tended to overthink their situations.

I showed MacAvoy and Tasman the encryption bandit, and asked, "Either of you ever seen one of these?"

MacAvoy pulled the remains of his cigar from his mouth, and

said, "Yeah, I've seen one before. We do have intelligence units in the Army." That answer sufficed. He knew, which embarrassed me because I hadn't known what this device was the first time I saw it.

Tasman said, "Pretend like I'm an ignorant Marine clone. Humor me. What is it?"

I said, "It's an encryption bandit. You attach this to enemy computers to duplicate their data."

Tasman said, "There isn't much room for storage, how much data can it hold?"

I had no idea, but apparently MacAvoy did. He said, "Bandits have crystalline-thread storage," whatever that meant. "That little strip could have sucked the Pentagon computers dry."

"How do we get the data off of it?" I asked.

"You're going to need a special computer to unencrypt it. Bandits turn data into unreadable solid brick."

"So where do we go to find a special computer?" I asked.

Tasman said, "Rhodes must have had one."

I said, "I don't think that's such a good idea."

MacAvoy grimaced and nodded. "Bad idea. Bad idea."

"What?" asked Tasman.

MacAvoy said, "That's a civilian agency, and he was one of the directors, so we know that the Unies infiltrated it. Who do you suggest we trust there?"

"I don't trust any of them," I said.

"None of them?" asked Tasman.

"How do you tell the loyal ones from the spies?" I asked.

"I have computers at Army Intel," said MacAvoy.

"So does Hauser," I said. Maybe it was because I was a Marine, but I always considered the Naval Intelligence more elite than its Army and Air Force equivalents. I laid down a little presidential edict, and said, "I want Hauser to take the first crack at it."

I was the top dog. I had the most stars on my collar. That

didn't stop MacAvoy from asking a good question. In a somewhat stunned voice, he asked, "Are you planning to send this specker into space?"

The Unifieds had at least one spy ship, a cloaked Navy cruiser that might well be watching our every move. We had no idea what remained in their fleet. For all we knew, they could have had over a hundred self-broadcasting ships waiting cloaked and hiding in the wings. Our fleet had more ships than theirs, no doubt, but their cloaked ships could still intercept a lowly transport.

"All I'm saying," MacAvoy continued, "is that I have computers downstairs in this very building. You see what I mean? You send that specker to Hauser, and you gotta load it on a transport and send it halfway to Mars. All that time we could be opening files and transcribing data. It's something to think about."

It was indeed something to think about. The information contained in the encryption bandit could list the extent of U.A. spying in our backyard. It might reveal plans for future attacks.

I asked, "Howard, how do you feel about bunking in the Linear Committee Building for the next little while?"

Without missing a beat, he asked, "Is it going to be safer than the Pentagon?"

I said, "You'll be more secure than the gold in Fort Knox."

Tasman narrowed his eyes, and said, "Fort Knox is empty. It's been empty for centuries." The man had the survival instincts of a rat. He said, "You said the Pentagon was secure. What makes the Linear Committee Building any safer?"

I said, "You'll have me here to protect you."

Tasman said, "Harris, you scare me more than all the rest of them."

I said, "Haven't you heard, I'm a Liberator; they can't reprogram me."

I thought about telling Tasman that he'd be a lot safer if he stopped leering at my girlfriend, then I realized that she really wasn't my girlfriend. Hell, for all I cared, he could have her.

MacAvoy pulled a fresh cigar from his pocket, lit it, and said, "If Harris isn't enough protection, I can scratch up some natural-borns to guard you."

Tasman flashed his ugly gray teeth in a death's-head grin, and asked, "How can you be sure they'll stay loyal? If you don't trust your own Intelligence Agency, whom can you trust?"

MacAvoy said, "You help us win this specked-up war, and we'll keep you around until that testicle you call your ticker stops pumping. I doubt Tobias Andropov will make a similar offer."

I didn't know if it was MacAvoy's callous attitude, his ineffable logic, or his mentioning Andropov, but Tasman caved in. He asked, "Can you get Ray Freeman to guard me?"

"He's retired," I said.

"I'd feel safer," he said.

"I'll ask," I said, "but I can already give you his answer." Then I slid the case to MacAvoy, and said, "You better get this started as quickly as you can."

I walked as far as the elevator with Tasman and MacAvoy. Tasman said, "Make sure you call Freeman." I said I would.

Sunny wasn't anywhere to be found when I looked for her. I asked an aide, "Where's the girl?"

He said, "She left you a note," and handed me a folded piece of paper. Expecting an address or a phone number, I unfolded the page. The note said:

I made things good for you. I shared myself.
  Good-bye, Wayson.

I didn't know it yet, but we had already lost the war.

7

I was home and settling down for the evening when I made the call. I started the conversation by saying, "They found Sunny."

"Who found her?" asked Kasara.

I had left Sunny for another girl; well, I had planned to leave Sunny for another girl—Kasara. Kasara was an old flame who had come back into my life. Back before the universe turned itself inside out, Kasara had worked as a cocktail waitress on a planet called Olympus Kri—Emily Hughes's old home. Back then, Kasara used to save every spare dime so she could take annual vacations on Earth. When I first met her, she'd been spoiled, reckless, self-centered, and so pretty it hurt my eyes. In her, youth and beauty had created their own particular variety of glamour.

I'd met her as a newly minted U.A. Marine on leave. That was back when the Unified Authority owned the galaxy, back when we believed that the only threat to mankind was man himself.

Time proved us wrong, but that's history, I'm talking romance.

After the aliens started incinerating planets, the population of Olympus Kri was evacuated to a defunct spaceport. We'd relocated seventeen million New Olympians to a facility designed to serve as a revolving door through which six million travelers would pass per day. There the New Olympians stayed for an entire year, rationing food, sanitation, and privacy until they nearly ran out of hope.

That year had left Kasara thirty pounds lighter. She still barely ate. Her hair had thinned, and her breasts had all but vanished. Her arms and legs looked like sticks, like the limbs of an insect. Only ten years had passed since I first saw Kasara on the beach, but her face had aged twenty-five years. She'd become old and pensive well beyond her years.

I didn't love her back when I first met her. She was *scrub*, a great girl for a one-night stand. Now, I thought that maybe I could love the woman that her suffering had unveiled. Hollow cheeks and thinning hair had given her a beauty that youth and energy had hidden.

Kasara didn't worry about Sunny. Despite the pleasures Sunny offered, she hadn't been able to hold on to me.

I said, "The Army found her," and I explained that when MacAvoy sent his commandos to extract Watson, they found Sunny as well. Then I told Kasara about Rhodes and the case Watson had taken from him, the case that had belonged to Hunter Ritz.

"Why didn't you tell me Hunter died?" she asked.

"I didn't think you'd remember him."

"Of course I remember him; he wanted to shoot my uncle," she said.

Her uncle was a gangster. He'd almost gotten me killed. Ritz and I kidnapped the bastard and drove him to an empty road, where I pulled out a gun and threatened to shoot him though I didn't plan on pulling the trigger.

Kasara had come along for the ride.

"I was the one with the gun," I said.

"He didn't try to stop you."

"I outranked him," I said.

"I'm sorry about Ritz. I liked him," she said. I believed her. This new Kasara didn't have energy for bullshit; the old one, the young, pretty one, told people whatever they wanted to hear.

We were on an old-style communications console. I saw her face on a five-inch two-dimensional screen. Anyone in the world could have been listening in on us, including the Unifieds, my aides, and her gangster uncle.

Kasara asked, "Do you plan on getting back together with her?"

I shook my head, and said, "She left me a note." I held the note up, and read it. "It says, 'I made things good for you. I shared myself. Good-bye, Wayson.'"

Kasara said, "Jeez, what a bitch. What did you see in her?"

I asked, "What did I see in you back in Hawaii?"

Kasara asked, "That pretty?"

"Maybe even a little prettier," I lied. Sunny was much prettier than Kasara had been.

She laughed because tales of the glamorous and beautiful Sunny Ferris didn't scare her. She said, "Do you think she went home?"

"Not likely," I said. "There's nothing left; it was in a war zone."

Kasara said, "Don't worry, Harris, you're still going to see her again."

"And that doesn't bother you?"

"No."

"You sound confident."

She said, "You don't go for glamour girls."

"I almost married Ava Gardner," I pointed out.

"And how did that end?" she asked. Ava was the clone of a

twentieth-century movie star. Before society turned its back on clones, she'd been the most lustworthy woman in Hollywood. The last time I saw her, she was a shut-in living in a luxury apartment on a planet scheduled for alien incineration. At her request, I left her to burn.

"Not so well," I admitted.

I said, "You were glamorous," and immediately realized how deeply I had sunk my foot in my mouth by using the word, "were."

Kasara favored me with a condescending smile, and asked, "Are you going after her?"

"I'm not planning on it," I said.

"Of course you are," she said. She was right.

I said, "We may have the war all sewed up, maybe not the entire war, but this phase of it. The Unifieds aren't putting up much of a fight. I expected more from them."

She asked, "What did you find in Ritz's case?"

"Baby, it could end the war," I said.

I don't know if the old Kasara would have minded being called "baby," but the new Kasara didn't think much of it. She gave me a sardonic smile and cocked an eyebrow.

I said, "I'd pay good money to see the Unifieds go away once and for all."

"When are you coming down to the Territories?" she asked. "The Territories" referred to the landmass that the Enlisted Man's Empire had ceded to the refugees of Olympus Kri. Some of my officers referred to them as "Martians." It wasn't as a term of endearment.

"If things keep going the way they are, it's going to be soon," I said. "Maybe next week. Maybe next month."

I'd travel down to the Territories soon enough, but not for a romantic vacation. I'd also try to find Sunny, but not for the reasons Kasara imagined.

8

"Harris, I'm flying in."

"You're flying in from Mars?" I asked. Admiral Hauser seldom traveled to Earth. He couldn't tear himself away from patrolling the inner third of the solar system.

"I'm coming in," he said. "Not from Mars."

"But you're actually flying here, touching terra firma and breathing uncycled air?"

"Yeah, what about it?"

"You don't make it back here very often," I said. "Maybe I should queue up a parade."

"We have serious business to discuss, Harris."

It was like we had come from different dimensions to discuss the same war. After yesterday's skirmish, I saw the world in happy, glowing colors. The Unifieds were on the run. I had my encryption bandit. In my heart of hearts, I believed it held a treasure trove of information.

I wondered what war Hauser was fighting.

Something about the way he watched me made me nervous. He hadn't flown all the way from Mars for a friendly chat. He kept plowing ahead. It had a sobering effect on me. He said, "Harris, my shuttle should arrive at 14:00. We need to arrange a summit. We'll need MacAvoy and Strait in attendance as well."

I said, "Tom, we're on the cusp of winning this thing. The Mogats are gone. The aliens are gone. The Unifieds are just about played out. I already told you that MacAvoy recovered the data I captured in the Cousteau undersea city.

"Tasman's working on it right now. I bet he's half-done by the time you arrive."

He said, "I hope you're right. In the meantime, set up that summit."

That sounded dangerously close to an order. Here I was the highest-ranking officer and the acting president, and he was giving me orders . . . and I didn't care. I asked, "What are you hiding from me?"

"Harris, if I could talk about it, I would."

Security.

U.A. stealth cruisers could slip into our territory undetected, and I'd seen their eavesdropping arrays.

I said, "We'll have a car waiting for you."

My bad day quickly got worse.

Not even an hour after my chat with Hauser, MacAvoy called, and asked, "Wayson, you got a minute?"

I said, "I'm a bit busy here."

"I'm in Tasman's lab."

"With Tasman?" I asked.

"Can you come down?"

Maybe my paranoia had gotten the better of me. I woke up with a solid strategy for expanding our hold on the east side of the Anacostia. I had even started thinking of ways to go after the U.A. Fleet. Now all my enthusiasm vanished.

"I'll be right down," I said.

I took a deep breath and steeled myself. Things had started to fall apart around me, and it appeared that the avalanche had only begun. I didn't run to the elevator, but I walked fast, fast enough to catch my aide's attention as I left my office.

Watching me from his desk, he asked, "General, is everything okay?"

I didn't answer; I had things on my mind.

The elevator only went down three floors, but the ride seemed to take forever. I didn't strum my fingers or tap my feet, but my mind sorted through the range of topics MacAvoy and Tasman might bring up. Maybe the Unifieds had constructed a bomb beneath D.C. Maybe the U.A. Fleet had more ships than we thought. *Could the Unifieds have found the aliens and allied with them?* Ridiculous propositions played out in my head.

The doors of the elevator opened. MacAvoy stood waiting for me. MacAvoy cupped his right hand into a fist and coughed into it. In his left hand, he carried a mug of what usually would have been coffee. Instead, it carried an unidentifiable, orange-colored sludge.

I asked, "What is that?"

"It's an old Army cure," he said.

"Are you sick?" I asked.

"I woke up with a cough."

We entered MacAvoy's Intelligence division. Teams of officers surrounded every desk, sitting so close together that their legs were touching.

"Is it medicine?"

"This stuff's for soldiers," he said, a note of pride in his voice. "It's flu fighter."

"What's in it?" I asked.

"Shit," he said.

"What kind of shit?"

"All kinds of shit . . . carrots, bell peppers, spinach, garlic, and cayenne pepper, and a little specking esprit de corps."

Tasman had an office to himself. We stepped in and closed the door behind us.

Instead of a desk, Tasman worked at a drafting table. MacAvoy must have had that stick of furniture brought in especially for the old man. Sitting in a bulky motorized wheelchair, Tasman would have had trouble sidling up close to a desk. The table was tall enough for him to scoot in and under without trouble.

I saw strain on Tasman's withered old face. Seeing this, I noticed that MacAvoy looked like he had a secret as well.

Tasman said, "The bandit isn't the problem; the Unifieds used a complex encryption system on their computers as well. Opening low-security files hasn't posed a problem. We know how much they spend on toilet paper and hand grenades every year."

"What about their fleet?" I asked.

"We haven't located any information so far," said MacAvoy.

"But it's in there, somewhere?" I asked.

"Yeah. Sure. It should be," said Tasman. He rolled away from the table and turned his chair so that he faced me.

"We found their plans for infiltrating the New Olympians on Mars," said MacAvoy. "Would you like to guess what they named it?"

"Legion," I said.

"Right on your first try," said MacAvoy.

Legion. I knew all about Legion. I'd been there, seen their recruiters preaching in the streets of Mars Spaceport. They'd set up an alliance with a New Olympian gangster named Petrie. We killed him. They reprogrammed an entire division of Marines on Mars. We killed them, too.

I said, "Legion didn't amount to much."

"We have several video feeds of their reprogramming experiments," said Tasman.

I felt a chill run down my spine. I'd been part of those experiments. They'd erased the memories from my conscious mind, but ghosts from that torture still haunted my subconscious.

Tasman pressed a key on a keyboard, and an image spun to life. I saw a large room, all white and sanitary like a wing in a hospital, with Marines laid out on incapacitation cages. They wore hospital gowns. Some were conscious. Some had already died.

I had never seen this feed before, but an impulse deep in my brain reminded me that I had been there. "Is this on Mars?" I asked.

"It's in an underwater city," said Tasman. "This one was in the Atlantic. They called it Gendenwitha."

"I visited that one," I muttered to myself.

"Show him," said MacAvoy.

Tasman nodded.

MacAvoy said, "Harris, you're not going to like this."

"Show me."

The feed showed me sitting at a table in a cafeteria packed with Marines in hospital gowns. We were all catatonic. We didn't speak to each other. We had trays of food in front of us, occasionally we fed ourselves, but mostly we sat like zombies.

The Marine sitting to my right picked up his knife and stared at it. He rolled it in his fingers, all the while studying his reflection. Two orderlies came to watch. They just stood there, joking between themselves as the Marines died. He stood and convulsed gently. It wasn't like an electrocution, more like a series of coughs.

He dropped the knife, fell back onto his seat, and his head hit the table. Blood dribbled out of his ear.

In the video feed, a woman walked over to the table and placed a tray in front of me. She saw the dead Marine and started screaming at the orderlies.

"Is that Sunny?" I asked. I saw her, felt the stirring of a familiar reaction, and sat down to hide my disgrace.

I never saw the woman's face; the camera was focused on the table. She had lustrous brown hair, it reminded me of mink.

Tasman said, "You were part of their experiment. When they couldn't reprogram you, they switched to an accelerated form of classical conditioning."

A new feed began. I was on an operating table, lying flat and unrestrained. If I'd had the strength, I could have stood up and walked away. Sunny stood over me wearing a white lab coat. She reached a hand into my gown and attached wires to me. She clamped some kind of breathing tube to my nose, then she released a stream of gas. I whipped my head from side to side, then I vomited and lay there in my bile. I passed out. She cleaned me and woke me and poisoned me again.

At some point she cleaned me and spoke to me. I couldn't hear what she said, but I watched her slip her hand into my gown, then she slipped off her smock, then her dress.

"Wow," said MacAvoy. "Paralyzed one moment and humping like a rabbit the next. Hoorah, Marine!"

Bastard.

"Sunny," I said. I felt more embarrassed than sad.

Tasman said, "Harris, you were brainwashed. They molded your subconscious into something they could use. There are hours of her toying with you. Hours of it."

Toying. I repeated the word in my head. It sounded even worse when I said it.

MacAvoy asked, "Did you know that Nailor was there?"

"Nailor?" I asked, slow to place the face with the name.

Franklin Nailor was a U.A. intelligence officer. He had fired a shotgun into my back. Ten days ago, I had believed that nothing mattered more than killing the little prick. Seven days ago I located him in Gendenwitha, beat him to death, and stuffed his corpse into a trash bin; now, my brain reeling and my grasp of reality in doubt, it took me a moment to recognize my worst enemy's name.

The feed showed me lying paralyzed in a cell. Nailor walked in. He yelled at me, hit me, and posed me like a toy. He urinated in my face. I was awake and paralyzed; there was nothing I could do.

Anger and embarrassment became indistinguishable in my head. I wanted to hurt MacAvoy and Tasman, wanted to rekill Nailor, wanted to murder Sunny, wanted to end myself.

On the screen, the door opened, and Sunny entered the cell. Tasman paused the feed. He said, "You've got an erection."

"What?" I asked, momentarily too stunned to be angry. The comment had caught me off guard.

Tasman said, "We've checked all the feeds; you get an erection every time she enters the room."

MacAvoy said, "The good little Marine stood at attention every time."

"Get specked," I said, so ashamed that I could barely control myself. He was joking with me, and that meant that he'd forgiven me. Worse, he didn't hold me accountable.

I asked Tasman, "How much of this have you watched?"

"You got it up twelve times in four days, if that's what you're looking for," said MacAvoy. "It's probably not world-record territory, but it's impressive."

I didn't say anything.

MacAvoy said, "Harris, maybe you should change the Marine Corps motto to *Semper Paratus*."

"Their information on you is fairly limited," said Tasman.

"You know what *Semper Paratus* means, right?" MacAvoy asked.

I tried to ignore him. "How much control do they have over me?" I asked.

MacAvoy said, "It means 'Always ready.'"

I wanted to tell him to shut the speck up, but I thought it might be more appropriate to hold out my wrists and have him arrest me.

Tasman said, "You aren't a security risk, if that's what you're asking. They weren't able to reprogram you. They trained you to fear Nailor. They trained you to have a pretty spectacular reaction to Sunny. Now that you know what they did to you, I don't think she's going to be much of a problem."

MacAvoy added, "Harris, I'd trust you with my life. I'd take a bullet for you, son, but your girlfriend's a bitch."

9

Obviously, I couldn't hide information about Sunny's working for the Unified Authority Intelligence. She'd entered both the Pentagon and the Linear Committee Building. As my girlfriend, she'd set foot on military bases and spoken to high-level personnel. Hell, she'd gone on double dates with me and Travis and Emily.

I stormed past my aide as I returned to my office. He put down his cup of water, and asked, "Is everything okay, sir?" Once again, I ignored him. I closed the door behind me and hid behind my desk.

I sat in my big, well-cushioned chair and stared at the door of my office while I relived emotions—the humiliation of watching myself helpless one moment and having sex the next. I thought about MacAvoy's making jokes and shook my head in disgust. I thought about Tasman apologizing on my behalf. I told myself that I had never loved Sunny, and I felt comfortable that was indeed the case.

My office was brightly lit, with white walls and blue carpeting. The crowded bookshelves and display cases came with the keys, property of the previous occupant. I had inherited the books, the pictures, the art along with the walls and furniture from Tobias Andropov.

Did Andropov know that I had commandeered his office? Sunny had walked through that door, bounded over to this desk, and kissed me. He knew. If she knew, he knew. That's how the spy game works.

What else did he know? Had he seen the video feeds? Had he seen me tortured? *Bullshit,* I told myself. I didn't care if he saw Sunny and Franklin torturing me. I cared about the other parts . . . Was he laughing at me?

I'd had sex with Sunny in her apartment. We'd done that on dozens of occasions. Had she recorded those, too?

I wondered if she ever got embarrassed. Did she watch the feeds with her bosses? What would she tell them? Were they laughing?

I contacted MacAvoy, and asked, "Has Tasman found Sunny Ferris's personnel file?"

"Affirmative."

"Did you read it?"

"Of course. It's got a whole lot of useless shit, most of which you already know. Her background is just like you said, rich parents and law school. Sound familiar?"

"How about—?" I started to ask.

MacAvoy cut me off. He said, "There wasn't anything that should have sent up flags, Harris. She wasn't an anticlone protester. She didn't lose a brother or a husband during the war. She isn't related to any members of the Linear Committee. She never worked as a prostitute or a spy.

"Satisfied?"

"No," I said, and switched off the console.

Sunny. The first time I saw her, she had come to my office representing the New Olympians, who were still trapped on Mars. A few days after I met her, I went to Mars on a rescue mission, and Nailor shot me.

I returned to Earth in medical stasis. My first night out of the hospital, Travis and Emily had taken me to a bar, and there she was again. I had taken her appearance for kismet. She'd been at the bar with friends from her law firm. Were they spies, too?

I called Naval Intelligence and told the commanding officer to investigate the Alexander Cross law firm. "If you have any questions, bring Cross in and torture him," I said.

"Can we do that, sir?" he asked.

"No, but do it anyway," I said.

He said, "Aye aye," but he did not sound convinced.

He called back five minutes later, and said, "The firm is closed, sir. Cross disappeared three weeks ago."

"Can you track down the whereabouts of the lawyers?" I asked.

"Already in progress, sir. General MacAvoy made the same request earlier this morning."

"Thank you, Major," I said, and I went back to being alone.

Admiral Hauser would arrive in another hour. I had a conference room ready. Strait and MacAvoy would be there. At least I knew what Hauser wanted to talk about. MacAvoy must have told him about my ex-girlfriend. He would've had to do that. Some mistakes are too large to be swept under a rug.

Glad to have time alone, I sat at my desk and reviewed all of my mistakes. I didn't stop with Sunny. I reviewed my life as a Marine, then as an orphan. What would Kasara say when I told her I'd been sleeping with a spy? Would she laugh at my stupidity or try to make me feel better?

My aide knocked on my door.

"What is it?" I shouted.

"Admiral Hauser has arrived, sir. He's at the summit. So are General MacAvoy and General Strait."

The firing squad has assembled, I told myself. "Tell them I'll be there in a minute." Then I called Tasman. I said, "Howard, have you found anything else?"

"About Sunny?" he asked.

"About anything," I said.

"I ran into a dead end on her a couple of hours ago. There are more files, but I can't access them."

"Why?"

"How much do you know about encryption?" Tasman asked me.

"Not much," I admitted.

"Do you have a secure line for calling Strait and MacAvoy?" he asked. "Do you use the same line when you call for your car?"

I had to think about that. I made all my LCB calls on the same line but used a secure line when contacting people outside the building.

Tasman said, "Our computers have security levels. So did theirs. I haven't found a key for opening some of their files. And Sunny may have worked under an alias or another identity. I've found files with her name in the title that don't have any information about her. They have information about a woman named Mary Mallon. Ever heard of her?"

"Mary Mallon?" I asked. *Could that be her real name?* I had run a security check on Sunny, at least I got that much right, but it wasn't particularly thorough.

"Legion produced some unexpected information," said Tasman. "Do you know what killed the clones you forced out of that underwater city?" He didn't bother trying to pronounce the name of the city, which happened to be Quetzalcoatl.

The Unified Authority had stashed an entire division of

reprogrammed Marines in Quetzalcoatl. Using torpedoes and threats, the EME Navy forced them to abandon the city. They boarded submarines and came to the surface, but when we boarded their submarines, they were dead.

"They died from the death reflex," I said. There'd been no mistaking that. We found thousands of corpses, all bleeding from their ears.

"So what caused their death reflex?" Tasman asked.

"They must have figured out they were clones," I said. It seemed pretty obvious.

"They already knew they were clones," said Tasman.

"What?" I asked. "They knew they were clones, and they didn't have reflexes?"

This was big news. If we could program our soldiers, sailors, and Marines not to die when they found out they were clones, we'd be lot more secure.

Tasman said, "The death gland isn't programmed. Neural programming impacts the brain, which impacts that gland. Normal clones are programmed to have a neural overload when they learn they're synthetic. The overloading stresses the brain, which then signals the gland to release the death hormone.

"Apparently, the Unifieds cared more about your reconverting those clones than they did about their becoming sentient."

"Sentient?" I asked.

"Self-aware, knowing they were synthetic," said Tasman. "The death glands were designed to be unstable, like fuses, built to overload and break."

The elevator doors opened. People watched me as I walked through the hall. Let me amend that. Clones watched me. Very few natural-borns worked in the Linear Committee Building.

I reached the conference room. The sentries standing beside the double doors saluted and stepped out of my way. The room beyond the doors was oval in shape, just slightly dimmed, and luxuriously appointed with wood-lined walls, a bar, an ebony table, and a waterfall.

Hauser, Strait, and MacAvoy stood by the twelve-foot waterfall, gazing into the pond at its base. They turned to welcome me. I saw nothing revealing in General Strait's posture. Hauser looked glad to see me, maybe even relieved. MacAvoy, on the other hand, had a devious glint in his eye. He didn't meet my gaze; instead, he stared at the koi swimming near his feet. He looked at me, looked away, took another glance at the waterfall, then floated toward the conference table.

As seniormost officer and acting commander in chief, I should have conducted this summit, but Hauser had called for it. I deferred to him. I said, "Tom, this is your show; maybe you should run it." *That way,* I thought, *I won't need to hand over the reins when the MPs remove me from the room.*

"If you don't mind, I think I will take the conn," he said.

MacAvoy surprised me. He said, "Harris, sit your ass over here. I got a question for you."

So much for his nervousness. I walked over to the table. As I sat, I noticed he had that "flu fighter" shit in his glass. It was orange and viscous, and I smelled the pepper from a few feet away. The drink didn't seem to help him, though. The bottom of his nose had turned pink and raw, and he held a napkin which he used every so often to wipe his nose.

"Do you know what this is about?" I asked MacAvoy, feigning ignorance.

He said, "You're more clued in than me."

I doubted that, but I didn't mention it. Once I sat, though, MacAvoy became as silent as a rock. He sat there, didn't look at me, and pretended to take notes. Let me tell you, that was a joke. Pernell MacAvoy may or may not have known how to read, but he'd never jotted notes.

Hauser sat at the head of the table. He fiddled with the computer station for a moment, then he spoke. He said, "The Earth Fleet discovered a ship floating in space three days ago. She appeared to be unharmed.

"When we went to investigate, we discovered she was *Magellan*, one of the old Explorers we sent out from Smithsonian Field."

Strait, the officer most out of the loop, said, "So you found an old antique, that's why you called us here?"

What you don't know may or may not be able to hurt you, but it can sure leave you looking like an ass. Strait, for instance, didn't know that we had inherited the entire two-hundred-ship Explorer fleet when we captured Washington, D.C. He didn't know we had used those ships to transport Marines to a battle on Mars. Apparently he didn't know that his branch, the Air Force, maintained Smithsonian Field, the hangar facility in which we kept the Explorer fleet.

MacAvoy hadn't been given that information either. Hauser and I hadn't told anyone that we had begun sending those ships to lost planets. I wondered what, if anything, this ghost ship had to do with Sunny. And then I saw the connection. I must have tipped her off about the operation.

"What about the crew?" I asked.

"Dead. Seven clones, five enlisted men, two officers. All hands died by death reflex."

"A mass death reflex?" I asked. I knew damn well what could cause that, and I saw Sunny's fingerprints all over it. I also knew where that Explorer had been. We'd sent her to Terraneau, a former Unified Authority planet located in the Scutum-Crux Arm—the far end of the galaxy. During the weeks before we attacked Earth, as the aliens attacked populated planets throughout the galaxy, we'd divided our Navy in half. One half attacked Earth. The other half transferred refugees to Terraneau, a planet that had already been incinerated and no longer interested the aliens.

The Unifieds, however, weren't done with us. As we attacked Earth, they attacked Terraneau. We didn't know how that battle went. For all we knew, our forces had routed the Unifieds, and we had a thriving empire on the opposite side of the galaxy. Or maybe it had gone the other way. The only ships we'd ever seen from that invasion were thoroughly battered.

Hauser said, "General Harris and I authorized *Magellan* to travel to Terraneau last week."

"Why wasn't I informed?" asked Strait.

MacAvoy answered before Hauser. He said, "It's on a need-to-know basis."

"I should have been informed about this," complained Strait.

"Why would you be in the loop?" asked MacAvoy. "Your birds can't even leave the atmosphere. If the Navy runs a covert operation in Pennsylvania, maybe they'll let you know."

"Did they tell you about the operation?" asked Strait.

"They did not," said MacAvoy. "Need-to-know basis . . . the only thing the Army needs to know is who to shoot. That's why we're still relevant."

"What's that supposed to mean?" asked Strait.

He knew what it meant.

MacAvoy was playing with Strait and enjoying himself. He asked, "What do you think it means, Flyboy?" Strait tried to ignore him. He started to say something to Hauser, then turned back to MacAvoy, and said, "Get specked, asshole."

MacAvoy answered with a satisfied smile.

Hauser asked, "May we continue?"

He should be running the empire, I thought. *It never should have been me*. Marines don't run governments; they break things and kill people.

Hauser knew how to run a fleet, a full-blown society. He understood politics. Knowing that my figurative firing squad waited around the corner, I decided to pull the trigger myself. Expecting Hauser to say that someone had leaked information about the operation and prepared to confess my part, I asked, "How did they capture the ship?"

Hauser said, "We don't know what happened to her."

I asked, "Could somebody have leaked information?"

"I don't see how," said Hauser. "You and I were the only officers who knew about the operation."

I got as far as saying, "What if," before MacAvoy A) kicked me under the table, and not gently, either, and B) shouted, "Could they have been reprogrammed? Tasman says that reprogramming can cause clones to have a death reflex?"

Hauser covered his mouth with a handkerchief and coughed once, then said, "We've analyzed their automated flight log. The ship may have been captured. Something happened after she broadcasted into Terraneau space; the question is what. Once she broadcasted in, her flight records stop."

"Are there any signs of battle?" asked Strait.

"*Magellan* is an Explorer. There wouldn't have been enough of her left if she got in a scrape."

I said, "If somebody warned the Unifieds . . ."

MacAvoy kicked me again. Speaking over me, he said, "Okay, if the Unies captured the ship, why kill the crew with a specking death reflex? Wouldn't it be easier to shoot 'em?"

The son of a bitch was trying to protect me. Hauser didn't know about Sunny, and MacAvoy didn't want me to blow the whistle on myself.

"Good question," said Hauser.

"Have you sent the crew in for autopsies?" asked Strait.

"There's no point; we know what killed them," said Hauser. "They had blood coming out of their ears."

"We know how they died," I agreed, "but that doesn't mean we know what killed them." At that point, I had forgotten all about Sunny.

I looked over at MacAvoy, and said, "Kick me again, and we're going to have a problem."

He nodded.

Then I turned back to Admiral Hauser. I said, "I just spoke with Howard Tasman. He says the clones we chased out of that underwater city knew they were clones."

"And it caused a death reflex?" asked Hauser.

"No; it didn't cause a death reflex. The Unifieds reprogrammed them so they could know they were clones. What killed them was surrendering to us. Tasman thinks they were programmed to die before we could capture them."

MacAvoy said, "What does that have to do with the ship Hauser found in space? You wouldn't go to all the trouble of reprogramming clones just to watch them die."

"You would if they were guinea pigs," said General Strait.

For once, I agreed with him.

So did Hauser. He stopped and thought about it, then said, "We'd better get started on the autopsies."

10

We all went our separate ways, Hauser to the Navy offices, MacAvoy to his Army area, me to my presidential palace on the tenth floor, and Strait to the Air Force area on the eighth. Five minutes later, we met in my office, all of us except Strait.

Strait was new and arrogant, and none of us liked him.

Hauser came carrying two bottles of bourbon. MacAvoy brought beer, an untapped keg's worth. I kept bottles of whiskey and Japanese saké in my office. I didn't keep them for drinking; I kept them for hospitality. As a Liberator clone, I had an impossibly high threshold for alcoholic consumption. The only drinks that got me drunk also came close to killing me. I could drink beer like water; I'd drown in the stuff before I got intoxicated, and let's face it; the only reason Marines drink is to get drunk.

Hauser arrived first. My aide showed him in. He came through the door, and asked, "Do Marines drink their bourbon on the rocks or do they take everything straight?"

I said, "Rocks, lemon wedges, soda water, we don't have hang-ups when it comes to soft drinks."

MacAvoy arrived a few moments later, looked at the bottles of bourbon, and grunted, "Stockade drinks."

Hauser nodded at the kegs he'd carried up on his shoulder, and said, "*Stockade drink*, and Harris here just called it a 'soft drink'; you know, I'm getting a little tired of ground-pounding chest thumpers. Call my bourbon genteel if you like, but it's a hell of a lot stronger than that piss," said Hauser.

"That so?" asked MacAvoy. "In that case, I'll take a pint."

"Are you planning to drink it or insult it?" asked Hauser.

"Hey, if it's stronger than this *piss*, I might even like it," MacAvoy said as he brought over a chair for himself.

"Would you like ice or lemon?" asked Hauser. He was tempting fate. MacAvoy had behaved himself so far, but, so help me, if Hauser offered us tiny umbrellas with our drinks, I'd break into giggles as well.

Still keeping himself under control, MacAvoy said, "Real men drink it straight."

Hauser nodded as if agreeing, and said, "Really? Harris took his with lemon and ice." He didn't give MacAvoy the pint that he'd asked for, but he filled most of a tumbler.

MacAvoy took the drink and finished it before I'd taken more than a sip or two. He smacked his lips, held the empty glass up for a closer look, and said, "Oh hell yeah. That's a lot stronger than beer."

"Want another?" asked Hauser.

MacAvoy asked, "What's the matter with you two? This isn't a drink; it's medicine. It's like a headache pill that makes your sober go away." He filled a quart-sized pitcher with beer from the keg, then said, "Maybe we should invite Strait."

Hauser responded, "Let's not."

On that one, we agreed. It wasn't that I disliked Strait; I was more indifferent to him than anything else. Hauser, MacAvoy, and I had all fought together. In one fashion or another, we had all emerged from the same fiery furnace.

This, by the way, would be the last time the three of us would stand in the same room. It was a triumphant meeting. We had the Unified Authority on the run. There were distractions. No one knew quite what to make of the Explorer and the dead clones. I had Sunny on my brain, but not in a way that she would have appreciated.

Seeing that MacAvoy sat too far away to kick me, I said, "Tasman found video feeds of the Unifieds programming me."

"Yes, MacAvoy mentioned that earlier," said Hauser.

"How much earlier?" I asked.

"He contacted me before he told you."

I turned to stare at MacAvoy. He saluted me, then downed half of that pitcher and coughed. He said, "I should'a brought my flu fighter. This swill is only good for cooking and pickling."

"If he already knew, why did you kick me?" I asked.

MacAvoy was tough and crude, but he didn't do all that well with liquor. Having downed a pint of beer and a tumbler of bourbon, he began showing signs of intoxication. It took him several seconds to ingest and absorb my question, then he shrugged his shoulders, and said, "Strait didn't know." The moment he finished speaking, he downed the other half of his pitcher.

It was a fair point. Strait almost certainly would have made a commotion about it. He would have been right, too, but making a commotion after the disaster never fixes the damage. *You weren't careless,* I reminded myself. *You were brainwashed.* Still, my inbred sense of honor demanded punishment.

Hauser finished his first bourbon. Admittedly, his second glass was a lot more full than his first. He said, "I can't help thinking they killed those clones in Scutum-Crux and brought them back to show us." He meant the ones on *Magellan*. We'd sent that Explorer to Terraneau, a planet in the Scutum-Crux Arm.

"Mmmmmm," I said. "That does fit Andropov's MO."

I'd tangled with Tobias Andropov on several occasions. He caved in when danger caught up to him, but when he thought he could get away with it, he liked to flaunt his power. Thinking he had an impenetrable missile shield around Earth, he contacted me in the moments before the EME invasion to taunt me. Once we'd landed and shut down his shield, he went from pit bull to scared pup in a matter of minutes.

When I started in the Corps, I held duty as my top priority. Now I seemed more motivated by grudges. I traveled to Gendenwitha specifically to kill Franklin Nailor. The encryption bandit had been Tom Hauser's idea. As the conversation included Tobias Andropov, I realized I wanted to kill him, too. And Sunny? My emotions became conflicted when it came to her. I felt odd when I thought of killing her, as if by killing her, I might release a demon I kept chained inside myself. So would I kill her if I got the chance? I told myself, *Yes*, but inwardly, I didn't know.

11

For the first time I could remember in over ten years, I woke up with a hangover, which really wasn't fair. I'd downed two glasses of bourbon and maybe a pint of beer. Drunkenness and I never spent time in the same vicinity, but now my brain hurt, and my muscles had that fine silvery ache. My head spun when I sat up. It spun even faster when I ignored the spinning and climbed off my rack.

I had a bad case of cotton mouth, too. I went to the bathroom and ran the blue light over my teeth, which added to the bad taste in my mouth, then I gargled. When I spit out my mouth rinse, the bad taste went with it. I could make the headache go away by dropping a couple of pills, but I avoided unneeded medicine.

So I dressed and commandeered a car from the motor pool—I lived in the Annapolis Naval Compound north of D.C. Annapolis sat several miles north of the enemy-held part of Maryland, and, because of its large Navy presence, we didn't worry much about U.A. incursions.

Hauser wanted me to include bodyguards and chauffeurs as part of my retinue, but I liked driving and I despised officers with entourages. They always reminded me of sharks and remoras, those officers and their hangers-on.

A beautiful day had begun. The area between Annapolis and the capital was long and flat, with forests of spindly trees. I took a moment to watch the sun rise over the shoreline. It seemed to rise out of the slate-colored ocean, a molten copper coin that cooled into gold as it rose in the sky.

Pelicans and seagulls glided over the waters and piers. Ravens and magpies flew over the land. The air smelled of sulfur, like eggs or a swamp. I inhaled deeply through my nose, ignoring the taste on my tongue.

Over the last few months, I'd been shot and kidnapped. Hauser allowed me to drive by myself, but he had finagled a caravan to protect me. Three cars traveled ahead of mine. Three more rode behind me. The cars were filled with guns and Marines. Boy, did I feel protected. Parades of this kind could be spotted from space and easily annihilated.

Two helicopter gunships flew my route just two minutes ahead of me. As a veteran of several wars, I felt my pulse race when I heard the sound of gunships. I liked them in battle, at least I liked them when they were on my side, but I equated them with death from above. In recent weeks, they'd begun to make me nervous.

The drive from Annapolis to the LCB took thirty-five minutes. It should have taken over an hour, but my entourage cleared the way for me. On that particular morning, I spent that thirty-five minutes marveling at how wiped out I felt. Maybe the war had worn me down.

As I pulled into the parking lot under the LCB, the Marine

assigned as my valet took my car. A tray with two rolls, coffee, and orange juice awaited me in my office. All in all, the day started off well.

Howard Tasman called. He said, "Harris, the Unifieds have abandoned their neural programming project."

I said, "Yes, you mentioned that yesterday." Steam rose out of my coffee, ice cubes floated in my orange juice, the butter on my rolls had almost melted, and I had zero interest in leaving my desk.

Tasman said, "They have a new weapon. I can't be sure, but I think it's genetic."

"If they have something new, why haven't they used it?" I asked.

"It's possible they already have," he said. "I've just sent you a decoded memo. You'd better have a look at it."

He'd actually sent it to my aides, who forwarded it to me. My entire staff had instructions to forward all calls and messages from Tasman without asking for permission. I made the old scientist my top priority, even higher than MacAvoy or Hauser. Strait received a slightly lower priority. My aides always asked before forwarding his calls.

I opened the message. It contained a communication between two people—TA and MM.

MM: The weapon works.

 TA: Does it kill them?

MM: It will kill all but one of them.

 TA: The most dangerous one.

MM: He'll be helpless. He'll be sick and alone and he'll want to die.

 TA: Wouldn't that be something.

"Do you know what the weapon is?" I asked.

Tasman sighed. He said, "We have the files, but we haven't been able to open them. The only reason we were able to decode this transmission is because it came from a separate communication."

"Am I right in thinking that 'TA' is Tobias Andropov?" I asked.

"That's how we interpret it."

"Do you know where we can find him?" I asked, thinking maybe it was time to take the fight to the Unified Authority. I imagined my Marines closing in on Andropov and him crumbling under pressure. Maybe they had a superweapon, maybe they didn't, but if we struck hard and fast, we could end the war before they ever used it.

Tasman said, "That's not my area of expertise. I'm not an intelligence officer. That's not in my wheelhouse.

"I'm more concerned about this weapon. Harris, your empire is made up of clones, people with identical DNA. If they have discovered a peculiarity in your genetic structure, they could create a weapon that kills clones without harming humans."

He had used the term, "without harming humans." In his mind, clones and humans were different. He was helping us, but in his heart, Howard Tasman considered us clones something other than human.

I coughed onto my fist and noticed a glob of yellow mucus across one of my knuckles. Still on the horn, I pulled out a trash can and flicked my hand over it, spraying the goop onto the pile of papers and cups. Since I didn't carry a handkerchief or keep a box of tissues on my desk, I'd need to go to the bathroom to wash my hands.

Tasman said, "As I understand it, Admiral Hauser recovered an Explorer craft on which all of the clones were dead. Is that correct?"

I looked up from the trash and nodded.

"Do you know what killed them?"

"They had death reflexes," I said. "Could it have something to do with the weapon?"

Tasman considered. He said, "MM, I'm guessing MM is Mary Mallon, says the weapon will kill every clone except for one. If the weapon caused clones to have a death reflex, it would kill every clone except for you. You have a different gland."

The thought had already occurred to me as well.

He asked, "Where did they find the Explorer?"

I had to think about that. My answer was vague but honest. I said, "Somewhere in this solar system."

"Were you involved in the mission?" he asked.

"I knew about it."

Tasman was old. He'd grown up during the time when the Unified Authority still used Explorers for galactic cartography, not spy missions. He asked, "Why did you use an Explorer for a near-space mission?"

I said, "We sent her to Terraneau."

Sounding astonished, he said, "Isn't that where the Unified Authority sent its fleet?"

"Yes; that's why we sent her. We wanted to know what happened out there." *Now we want to know more than ever*, I admitted to myself.

"Admiral Hauser ordered autopsies on the Explorer's crew, but I'm not sure what it will accomplish," I said.

"They're doing it now. Do you want in on it?" I asked. The bodies showed no signs of violence, and we knew what caused those clones to die. We needed to know what tripped their death reflex. "Do you have any suggestions for the coroner?"

Tasman said, "I wouldn't know what to look for. Harris, I don't have any more medical training than you."

12

MacAvoy called later that afternoon. He looked pale, and his eyes were bloodshot. His sinuses had become so congested that he sounded like he was pinching his nose. He said, "I know why you beat the Unies so specking easily." He coughed. Peppered sludge drink or no peppered sludge drink, that cold had him by the balls.

I said, "You weren't there. It wasn't that easy."

He said, "We're starting to decode some of their high-level communications. Get this. 'You're sure it will work?' 'Positive.' 'Maybe we should withdraw and come back when they're dead.' 'I wouldn't do that, not unless you want to make them suspicious. If you pull out, they're going to wonder why. They might figure out what we're doing.' 'How the hell would they do that?' "

"What are they doing?" I asked.

"It's an eviction notice," MacAvoy said, then he coughed. His cough produced a rolling throaty sound, as if he had to fight for breath. He put up a finger and stammered, "'Scuse me a moment," then he bent to the side as if trying to hide from the camera. He hadn't bent far enough. I watched him hock a slug-sized wad of phlegm. He might have spit it into a wastebasket or jar of some kind. Maybe he spit on the floor. I couldn't tell; nothing below his shoulders showed on the screen.

When he turned back to the camera, he said, "Tasman found out about Mary Mallon. She's not a spy, she's a code name. I'm betting Mary is another name for your girlfriend."

"For Sunny?"

"There was a real Mary Mallon six hundred years ago. They used to call her 'Typhoid Mary.' Ever heard of her?"

I had indeed heard that name, but I had no idea what or who she was. I said, "I've never heard of her."

"Want to guess what made her famous?" MacAvoy asked. "She spread a disease called typhoid without ever getting sick herself," said MacAvoy.

I said, "Oh speck."

"Yeah, and I helped that bitch off the transport. At least I didn't lock lips with her, but I bet I got the bug off her hands."

"What about Watson and Emily?" I asked. "Is that what turned them into the walking dead?"

"I doubt it. I think they were dehydrated. Tasman was in the same transport as her, and he's fine. Now my staff . . . half my officers called in sick today."

As I thought about my front office, I realized it was light a few aides as well.

I asked, "Have you contacted Hauser?"

"Yeah, there's a bug going on around his ship. I had him make some calls, and he says it's specking fleetwide."

Sunny couldn't have done that, I thought. Then I remembered the ghost ship, the Explorer. Before boarding, they would have run tests for bombs and biological agents, but would that have included germs? A flu bug? As far as I knew, the only way to test for something like that would be to take an actual air sample.

"You've had this for a few days now," I said. "How bad is it? Is it bad enough to kill you?"

He raised a glass so I could see it, so I could see the orange sludge inside it. He said, "I got a lot of aches and pains, every specking inch of me hurts, but no damn flu bug is going to kill me."

He coughed more, and we hung up.

I sat in my office and thought about colds. MacAvoy had had a cough and a runny nose two days ago. If this bug was designed to kill clones, I didn't think his flu-fighting drink would save him.

How would I spread the disease? I asked myself. Sunny couldn't have been the only *Typhoid Mary*. They probably had dozens of carriers, maybe even hundreds, people who could visit military bases, maybe strike up conversations with clones on the street.

I decided that Sunny must have already been infected when she saw the convoy driving Watson and Emily, but what was she doing in that area? How stupid had I been? Watson had captured Rhodes the day before, Rhodes and the encryption bandit. As far as she knew, the area was secure, but Rhodes had vanished. She must have gone to Coral Hills looking for Rhodes.

She had probably gone out looking for Rhodes, seen the convoy, and put two and two together. She might not have known that Watson and Tasman would be in that APC, but she knew enough to recognize a free ride to the LCB and possibly even a chance to recover the encryption bandit.

I switched the screen on my communications console to a menu of military bases and made several calls, starting with the Marine Corps base in Kaneohe, Hawaii, the place I had gone to live during the weeks after Sunny and Nailor had tried to brainwash me.

The base operator patched my call directly to the base

commander; the four stars on my collar and the title "Commander in Chief" come with certain privileges.

Colonel Ian Masters answered my call himself. He must have expected one of my aides on the other end of the line, a lackey who would say, "Please hold for General Harris." Without looking at the monitor, he said, "If he's planning on flying here on vacation, tell him we're all booked . . ." He glanced at the monitor, saw me staring back at him, and said, "Sir."

He saluted.

I smirked and returned the salute.

Doing the sitting version of standing at attention, clearly wishing he could turn back time for about ten seconds, he asked, "What I can I do for you, sir?"

I said, "At ease, Marine. We're not on the parade ground."

He said, "Yes, sir," then he let out a deep breath, relaxed his back and shoulders, and answered the question I had yet to ask. He coughed. It was just a slight cough, but he had a cough.

I asked, "You getting a cold, Masters?"

He said, "There's something going around."

"How bad?" I asked.

He smiled, and said, "Everybody is getting it. Nothing that a few miles running in the hot sun won't fix."

I remembered my time in Hawaii. I always traveled to Oahu, never bothering with the other islands. I heard they were prettier, less populated. Oahu had enough mountains and beaches for me. I didn't think jogging in the sun would save Masters any more than I thought MacAvoy's toxic concoction would save him.

We joked about bars we both knew and talked about finishing off the Unified Authority. I chatted with Masters for another minute, but I had already switched my attention to deciding the next base I would call.

I called Camp Lemonnier next. Lemonnier was the single

smallest Marine base left on Earth, a single security detachment—less than two hundred troops—in a tiny corner of Africa known as Djibouti. If the empire had a base the Unifieds might ignore, I thought it might be Lemonnier.

The camp commandant took my call. Unlike Masters, this stressed-out major didn't have a staff to answer his phone. He saw me on the screen and saluted.

He seemed healthy enough. He didn't cough. The whites of his eyes showed no reddening.

He said, "Sir, what can I do for you, sir?" *Good old "sir" sandwich,* I thought, *trademark of a fully functional Marine.*

"Have you come into contact with any of the locals?" I asked.

"No, sir." He barked the answer, so I told him, "At ease, Marine."

"Yes, sir." Still too loud.

"Your base is supposed to be isolated, is that right . . ." I looked up his name as I spoke. "Is that right . . . Major Hawkins?"

"No, sir. We do not allow civilians on our base, sir."

I generally like hearing strings of sir sandwiches from my subordinates, but this boy, he took it to an uncomfortable extreme. Hawkins appeared to be in his forties, making him at least ten years older than me.

I said, "Marine, under no circumstances are you to open your gates to anyone not wearing khaki."

"Sir, yes, sir. General, sir, may this Marine inquire about your concern?"

"Just rumors right now. We don't have any solid intel."

"Sir, yes, sir."

"Major, you're not in trouble. A simple 'yes, sir,' will suffice."

"Yes, sir."

"Are you healthy?"

"Yes, sir."

"Are your men healthy?"

"Yes, sir."

"I'm glad to hear that," I said. "All of your men are healthy?"

He hesitated. "Well, General, sir, we had to close supply a few hours early. The corporal in charge called in sick. Nothing major, sir. Just a bug . . . the flu bug, maybe."

"A bug. I see. Has that man been away on leave, maybe recently transferred in?"

"No, sir. He's been on base for three months now. We don't allow our men off base, not in Djibouti. Camp policy is that all liberty is taken on base or out of the country. Corporal Tanner hasn't been on leave yet, sir."

Maybe it is a cold, I thought with a growing sense of relief. It was possible he stepped off base without informing his superiors. I'd known men who went absent without leave; usually there was a woman involved.

I laid my cards on the table, and asked, "Is there any way he's banging some girl in town?"

"The nearest town is fifty miles away, sir. He'd need a vehicle from the motor pool."

That sounded good. I said, "Major, do not allow anyone on or off your base until I personally tell you otherwise. Do you hear me?"

"Are we under attack sir? Should I raise our . . ."

I said, "If the Unifieds were going to attack Djibouti, I think they would have done it by now."

This was good. This was very good. It ensured our survival on some level. If the rest of us died, we'd still have a few hundred clones carrying on the tradition. I would quarantine that base. We would run autopsies, create a vaccine, and inoculate those men.

Hawkins coughed. It wasn't much of a cough, maybe the result of a parched throat.

I asked, "What was that, Major?"

"Sorry, sir, I coughed."

"You coughed? Is that the first time you coughed today?"

"Sir?" he asked, clearly confused.

"DAMN IT MARINE, I ASKED YOU A QUESTION!" I shouted the words. Hell, I screamed them. "IS THIS THE FIRST TIME YOU HAVE COUGHED TODAY?"

The fine Marine on the other end of the conversation jumped at the suddenness of my screaming. He said, "Sir, yes, sir. Sorry, sir. Sir, no, sir, this is not the first time this Marine has coughed, sir. This Marine's throat is slightly hoarse, sir."

I took a deep breath, held it as I calmed myself, and asked, "Does Corporal Tanner receive shipments?"

"Yes, sir; he is in charge of receiving."

I sighed.

It had spread like a cancer; no, more like necrosis. Maybe we could have stopped it with a few amputations had we caught it early on, but by the time we became aware of the danger, our well-oiled circulation system had already spread it too far.

In my mind, I wrote my Corps off as a total loss, like troops in an invasion that have been obliterated. The Air Force and the Army would share our fate. Maybe the Navy stood a chance . . . just a slim chance.

There had been a time when we looped our communications through gigantic satellites armed with broadcast engines. We called those satellites "broadcast stations." Capable of transporting ships to any specified location instantaneously, broadcast stations could also translate and transfer communications across millions of light-years in an instant. We'd had those satellites until just a few years ago. Those had been the trophy years, an era in which I could speak with officers on the other end of the galaxy as easily as I could chat with the aides outside my door.

* * *

I coded my message *URGENT* and sent it to Hauser. It took six minutes and twelve seconds for the message to reach his ship. He responded five minutes later, and six minutes and twelve seconds later, I received his response. At that moment, I missed the old Broadcast Network more than ever before.

In his message, Admiral Hauser asked, "Did I mention what the rescue team found when they entered *Magellan*?"

I wrote, "No," and sent my message off.

It took just under fifteen minutes for my message to reach Hauser and for him to respond. Let me clarify, that wasn't all that we said in our messages, though it was the only part of our conversation I actually cared about. My point was this, my communications with Hauser, who was floating somewhere near Mars, had the snappy rhythm of a world-championship chess match.

He told me that someone had left a hot water spigot open on *Magellan*. *No big deal,* I thought. That showed how little I knew about microbiology. In his message, Hauser said that germs or viruses, whatever that flu was before it entered its victims, thrived in warm, moist environments. The regenerated air in most spaceships is sixty-five degrees and dry, a good atmosphere for killing off germs.

The crew sent to investigate *Magellan* had probably towed the ship back to Earth or docked with a fighter carrier. The corpses would have been placed in climate-controlled body bags and turned over to some unlucky coroner who performed an autopsy.

I said, "They may have kept those germs alive on *Magellan*, but they had other carriers on Earth. The flu has spread through all of my bases. MacAvoy's caught it. The poor son of a bitch looks like he's ready to die."

Hauser sent me a steady stream of meaningless dribble between real messages. My comments about the extent of the outbreak hadn't reached him yet, so he continued boring me with scientific trivia about cultures and sterile fields. He sent me a dissertation explaining the difference between dormancy and death for germs. He wrote about inoculation and said it was too late to inoculate our men. Like General Strait, Tom Hauser considered himself smarter than common ground-pounding clones. Neither of them were as smart as they considered themselves, and us lowly ground-pounders weren't as dumb they thought we were.

MacAvoy might have been as dumb as they thought.

MacAvoy, I mused. *If anyone could have won this war, it would have been you.* Now it looked like he might be the first to die.

"Far as I can tell, every fighter carrier and battleship has been infected," Hauser said in his next message. I'd spent years assigned to U.A. ships; men and supplies shuffled between ships on a regular basis. Hauser added, "Maybe some of the cruisers and frigates are still clean.

"The sick bays are past capacity on the big ships. There haven't been any deaths, yet. I don't know how long it takes. *Magellan* was missing six days before we found her."

Six days. Six days, I thought. Sunny had given me the bug two days earlier; Perry MacAvoy came into contact with it one day ahead of me. *Three days, and he has one foot in the grave.* Was he halfway dead?

"I think I'm coming down with it," I said. "I woke up feeling like an old man. How are you?"

Time passed. Six minutes and twenty seconds passed before he read my question. He answered simply, then six minutes and twenty seconds passed, and I read his response. He said, "Harris, I feel like hell."

13

Nobody died of the flu on August 21, at least, no one that I heard about. Now that I kept alert to it, I noticed a lot of sick clones as I walked through the LCB.

I had two civilian secretaries, both women, both fine. I had one officer, sort of an attaché with civilian organizations, who specialized in running interference for me when politicians came to complain. One of my most overutilized staff members, he'd reported for work that day looking pale. I saw him later that afternoon huddled up with a large mug and a box of mixed teas on his desk. I didn't know the poor guy's name. He was chubby and old for a Marine, making him the perfect man for dealing with angry civilians. He came across as more sympathetic than the young and fit killing machines who manned our bases.

His face looked puffy and pale. He must have been hitting the tissues, too; the bottom of his nose had become red and raw. I walked over to him and read his name tag. He, of course, rose to his feet and snapped to attention.

The guy's name was Chambers, Lieutenant Timothy Chambers. I asked, "Chambers, you feeling okay?"

"Yes, sir. Fine, sir."

"You look like you're battling a cold," I said. "Why don't you call it a day and get you some rest? Maybe you could swing by the infirmary on your way out." I didn't know which base he called home, but it would have an infirmary, and every infirmary had pills and nasal sprays. Nothing could cure him, but they might make him more comfortable.

I raised my voice and spoke to the rest of my staff, "That goes for the rest of you. There's a flu going around. If any of you are under the weather, go home, take care of yourselves." They didn't make me repeat myself.

One of my natural-born secretaries rose to her feet as well. I decided I'd fire her when she returned to work the next day.

I went back to my desk to wait for the autopsy results. I thought I knew what the coroners would find. They'd cut open the *Magellan* corpses and find that those men had all had the flu. Assuming they cut into the bodies quickly enough to take a successful culture, they would incubate the virus, analyze it, and in another few weeks, they might even come up with a vaccine.

On the other hand, an old acquaintance of mine might already have all of that information. I thought about attacking the Unifieds with every able man under my command as I searched for Sunny, but that would only cause them to scatter. This operation called for both a scalpel and a hammer. I would handle the surgical part of the operation, slipping in behind enemy lines and searching for people and files; MacAvoy's troops would handle the blunt-force trauma—smashing rats as they ran for cover.

I needed to find Sunny and any other high-ranking U.A. brass who might be waiting across the Anacostia. This didn't call for an attack so much as an abduction. I would grab them, drug them, and do whatever it took to get everything I needed out of them.

No getting around it, I had mapped out an act of desperation. In another day or two, clones would start dying. They'd die in Washington. They'd die in Hawaii. They'd die in Djibouti. They'd die in space. Unless we figured something out quickly, the entire empire would end.

I met with MacAvoy first. He sat at his desk, a quart-sized pitcher of that foul flu-fighter drink by his side. His mystic sludge hadn't protected him from the ravages of his cold. His face now looked bloodless, and he sniffled after fighting for every breath.

I began the conversation by saying, "If I wake up looking like you tomorrow, I may just shoot myself."

"You're going to look worse than me. I got my flu fighter. I'm going to specking beat this, Harris. You watch. God hasn't made a bug that can specking kill me."

I almost reminded him that it wouldn't be the flu that killed him; it would be a death reflex. Had I said anything, I might have triggered a death reflex. Generally, clones ignored people when dropped hints that they were clones, but in his weakened state, MacAvoy might have been more vulnerable.

I asked, "How is your troop readiness?"

He pulled a gallon jug from the refrigerator in his office and used it to refill the orange goop in the smaller pitcher. The other times I'd seen his flu fighter, it was always in a mug. This time he had it in a glass container. I saw the drink in all of its viscous, speckled, molasses-like glory. He brought the drink to his lips, paused to work up his courage, and guzzled.

"How much of that have you taken?" I asked.

"This is my third pitcher today," he said.

On some level, he knew. MacAvoy had to have figured out that he was a clone. He had to have known it because he had caught a bug that only bit clones. But most likely, he'd only worked it out in his subconscious.

There was something glorious about MacAvoy—even when he was sick and pale and weak, he had a unique majesty. There was something primitive and raw and unafraid that made him great, even if the only reason he wasn't afraid was because he was too stupid to be afraid. He was so convinced of his own invincibility that he never gave in to fear. He never hid his feelings. The man's baldly straightforward approach to combat baffled his enemies. Maybe he'd been lucky all along, but I refused to believe that his luck had finally run out.

MacAvoy coughed and said, "Harris, I have enough healthy clones to bury the specking state of Maryland in synthetic DNA," and grinned. I couldn't help noticing that his drink had left an oily orange mustache across his upper lip. "I can have two full divisions of infantry and artillery ready to move on your command."

"How about bullets?" I asked.

"We have plenty of bullets."

"Shield busters?" I asked.

"Oh. Yeah. Those," he said.

"Have you started making them?"

"We started; I'm not certain how many we have." He raised his hand and coughed into it. He looked down, then wiped his hand clean with a cloth. Almost predictably, his makeshift handkerchief was a standard-issue silicone gun towel.

The poor stiff examined his hand to make sure he'd cleaned all the phlegm from it, then said, "Let me check." Then he picked up an old-fashioned handset, and said, "Sergeant Dex . . . Yes, sergeant, put me through to the factory. Yes, at this hour. I don't care if the plant is closed. Call him at his house."

A moment passed, and someone took the call. MacAvoy said,

"Yes, well, I don't care what time it is. Listen here, have you started manufacturing the rounds I requested?"

"Yes, yes; I am aware of that."

"We always knew it would be a slow process. How many do you have? A hundred thousand? A hundred thousand, that's not very many."

"Yeah. Yes, I understand that."

"Hold on . . ." He hit a button to switch lines, and said, "Hey, Dex, you got any nukes over there? Yeah? Keep one handy; I may need it."

Lowering the handset from his mouth, he said, "Civilian contractor." That explained a lot. Had his soldiers been making those rounds, they would have been at it around the clock.

He and the factory owner exchanged a few pleasantries and MacAvoy lowered the handset. "I have a hundred thousand rounds. If the Unies have more than a hundred thousand men over there, we might have a problem."

Naval Intelligence estimated that they had under twenty thousand troops.

MacAvoy grinned, and asked, "Want to crush the miserable specks?"

He frowned when I answered, "That's not what I had in mind."

"What's the objective?"

"I want to find Sunny," I said.

"Oh for speck's sake, Harris! This isn't about getting one last . . ."

"She's high up in their dirty-work chain," I said, trying to keep my cool. "Why do you think they chose her to infect us, you and me? Do you think she was walking around with that flu for weeks, or do you think she shot herself up with it before the convoy picked her up?

"She probably keeps it in test tubes. She might even have blueprints for brewing up more."

"Can't Tasman get that info from the encryption bandit?" asked MacAvoy.

"If it's in there, it's encrypted," I said. "He hasn't been able to access it."

"Do you really think she'll have anything?" he asked.

"I don't know," I admitted, "but I'd rather be out there killing U.A. soldiers than sitting around here waiting to die."

That sentiment resonated with MacAvoy. He said, "Harris, you don't even know if she went back to the Central District. How do you plan on finding her, a door-to-door search?"

"I want to spread a net," I said. "I'm going to go in alone and ask questions. I'll shake the bushes while you and your men catch everything that comes out the other side."

"You know, Harris, sooner or later, you're going to get yourself killed."

"Sooner," I said. "I'm already dying."

"That's not what Tasman says; he says you're the only one that isn't going to die."

"Sounds lonely," I said. "I'd rather go with the herd."

MacAvoy reminded me of the simple facts. He said, "You won't have a death reflex."

"What exactly do you think the Unified Authority will do once I'm alone? Do you think they're going to let me go? They blame me for the rebellion, for the whole damn war. The ships, the men, the planets; hell, as far as they're concerned, it's probably my fault the aliens came back."

"You could run," said MacAvoy. "Harris, we're all going to die. You don't need to die with us."

There it was again. He knew he would die. On some level, he knew he was a clone; other clones would have died by now. Something had changed him. *Maybe he has a defective death gland*, I thought, and I wondered if that was even possible.

"Get out while you still can. Find someplace to hide. Take a specking Explorer and hightail your ass to another specking planet."

"Another planet?" I asked. "Are you joking? What other planet would you suggest? They're all ash. The only one with people on it is Terraneau. For all we know, the only people there are the same ones killing us with the flu.

"Look, I'd rather die killing the men who killed me than lying in bed. How about it?"

"You're joking, right? Is that a trick question? If I'm going, I'm taking as many of those specks with me as I can. I'm shoving grenades up my ass and farting out pins."

I watched him carefully as he spoke. The color returned to his face. He didn't cough or rub his nose.

"If I get shot tonight, how much time do you think it will shave off my life?" I asked. "A couple of days, maybe." I answered my own question.

"You're one day ahead of me, Perry. Tomorrow maybe I'll look like you. The next day, I'm already laid up in bed, and the Unifieds find me. Then what? I'll be a circus act. They'll try me for war crimes; it'll be a specking circus."

MacAvoy acquiesced, then we brought Hauser and General Strait in on the discussion. The final plan was simple enough. At 19:00, I'd go behind enemy lines. The Unifieds didn't have guard posts or barbed-wire fences. The same roads still ran through their side of town and ours.

As I entered from the west, MacAvoy would surround the insurgents on all sides. I'd make trouble, and if that didn't work, my Marines would come in after me. Once the trouble began, MacAvoy's soldiers would stop and search anyone trying to flee the scene. Strait's fighters would target any jets that entered the atmosphere. Hauser's carriers and destroyers would attack any ships that approached from outside the atmosphere.

Admittedly, we had a weak plan, but everyone acknowledged it as a plan nonetheless. Maybe something would come of it, a virus culture or a blueprint. Maybe I'd spot Sunny and put a bullet through her gorgeous head. Maybe MacAvoy's soldiers would catch Andropov.

As the meeting ended, MacAvoy spoke to the other generals in a conspiratorial voice. He said, "You know, I checked my inventory, and I got a bunch of nukes sitting in my armory."

Strait must have thought he was joking; he said, "Maybe we should light one up."

MacAvoy said, "Did you boys know there are abandoned train tunnels under this building?"

"Train tunnels? What were the Unifieds doing with underground trains?" I asked. The capital had a train system, but it ran aboveground. As far as I knew, the trains in Washington, D. C., had always run aboveground.

"You're thinking modern history, Harris. Who lived here before the Unies? We're talking American-made."

"American-made? Are they still down there?" asked Hauser.

"I went down for a look," said MacAvoy.

"They can't be safe?" said Strait.

"Hell, I'm not looking for a train ride; I want to turn the tunnels into specking missile silos and blow them up.

"If we're all going to die from that specking flu that they gave us, we might as well go out with a big specking bang, right? Give those evil specks a going-away present.

"I say we run this like a specking church raffle; the last man breathing gets to push the button. That's probably going to be you, Harris, which is a real kick in the nuts. You get to flame the Unies, the natural-borns, and the whole backstabbing lot."

MacAvoy grinned, laughed, coughed, drank more flu fighter, and grimaced at the bad taste it left in his mouth.

MacAvoy meant every word of it, but Strait still thought he was joking. He said, "General, maybe you should tie a bow around your devices and call them a going-away present."

I knew MacAvoy well enough to recognize when he was serious. I asked, "How are you going to get them into the tunnels?"

MacAvoy was pale and sweaty, but he had a satisfied grin. Looking more like a lunatic than a man with the flu, he said, "Marine; there are tunnels crisscrossing the whole damn city. My boys have located doorways all over this damn town. Getting bombs into the tunnel isn't the problem. Getting 'em in unseen might be a bitch." He winked at me, and asked, "Anyone else want to leave Tobias a going-away present?"

"Who says we're going away?" I asked.

MacAvoy laughed, and said, "Hoooooahhh, Marine!"

I stifled a cough of my own, and answered, "Hoooorrrrah!"

Strait rolled his eyes and glared at both of us.

14

Back when Ray Freeman was active in his profession, he was a ghost. When he wanted to talk, he found me. It seldom happened the other way around. I never knew where he lived or how he spent his free time. Hell, the entire Unified Authority couldn't locate the man when he hid. Back in the day, the Unifieds once assigned their entire intelligence apparatus to locate him and came up dry.

We lived in an age of miracles, though. Freeman took my call after two tries. I coughed, and said, "Ray."

He asked, "You sick?"

I said, "I've got the flu."

Freeman took that information in with no response. Conversations with him often felt one-sided as he listened carefully, considered every shred of information, and seldom spoke. He never wasted energy on pleasantries. Ask him "How are you feeling?" and he would wait for your next question.

I said, "A lot of people have colds these days, pretty much every clone in the Empire."

"Is the Unified Authority behind it?" he asked.

I sat in my office, comfortable at my desk, not entirely sure that the Unifieds hadn't figured out some way to listen to my communications.

"This version of the flu ends with clones having a death reflex," I said.

Stating that part of the story made me cringe. Tasman had found a list of people the Unified Authority considered primary targets to execute after the "Clone Apocalypse." My name sat at the top of the list. Freeman's appeared just below mine. Neither of us had death glands, but this flu would kill us indirectly; once the clone military complex was out of the way, the Unifieds would come after us. Despite its being every bit as much a death sentence for him as for me, Freeman took the news without flinching.

"How many clones have died so far?" he asked.

"Six."

"Are you sure the Unified Authority is behind it?"

I sighed. "Ray, we captured some of their files. The decryption process is going slow, but the stuff we're getting sounds bad."

"How long before your epidemic turns critical?" he asked.

"There's no way of knowing," I said. "The first victims were on an Explorer we sent to survey Terraneau. She'd been gone six days when we found her. The clones had been dead approximately twenty-four hours. We don't know when the Unifieds captured the ship or how long they waited before they infected the crew."

Freeman went silent. He approached conversations the way chess players approach a match, considering all the angles and the implications. "What does the flight record say?"

"That they broadcasted into Terraneau space," I said. "That's it. It stops after that."

"Death in five days, maybe less," said Freeman. "It all depends how long it took them to catch that Explorer."

"It'd be easy enough to capture an Explorer," I said. "They're slow. They don't have armor or shields. They need an hour to recharge their broadcast generators."

"Antique technology," he said, agreeing with my assessment.

Explorers were tiny little bugs. You could fit twenty of them in the smallest docking bay on a fighter carrier. I said, "If the Unifieds control Terraneau, they might have spotted the anomaly when she broadcasted in."

Freeman didn't respond to my comment. Speculation didn't interest him. He said, "Fire a pulse weapon near an Explorer, and you'll shut her engines down and wreak havoc on the electrical system."

Interesting scenario, I thought. *Magellan* broadcasts into Terraneau space. Broadcasts happen in a blinding bright flash of high-joule electricity that can be spotted from millions of miles away. I imagined *Magellan* emerging from an anomaly, unshielded, unarmed, and unable to broadcast to safety for an entire hour as her generator recharged.

I hadn't memorized the speed charts and top acceleration of Explorers, but I knew they were slow. Unified Authority capital ships topped out at thirty-nine million miles per hour. The Explorer would have been a sitting duck. The Unifieds could have paralyzed her using a pulse torpedo. Her crew would have had no chance—six clones armed with M27s trying to hold up against a destroyer or a battleship; no doubt they'd surrendered.

"Those birds are made out of tissue paper and kite string," I said. "You'd have a hard time detonating an EMP near one without destroying it."

Freeman said, "The point is that you have dead clones."

"Yes, and we don't have time to develop a vaccine. You do

the math; clones are going to start dying tomorrow. We need to capture some high-ranking U.A. officers and see what information they're holding."

"Any officers in particular?" asked Freeman.

"Sunny Ferris," I said.

I heard a noise in the background. Maybe Freeman was in a restaurant or on the street. He wasn't alone. I heard a woman scream something and go silent. Freeman ignored it. "The girl you were dating?"

"The spy I was dating," I said.

"She couldn't have done it by herself," said Freeman.

"No, not by herself," I agreed.

"Do you have any other names? Any other targets?"

"No."

"So you're just going after her?" he asked.

"Yeah."

"You and the Enlisted Man's Army are going after your former lover?"

That, of course, sounded worse than bad. He had misread me. I hoped he had misread me. I said, "Ray, I have their flu. As far as I can tell, every man under my command has been infected. It's too late to stop it from spreading, and we already know the mortality rate; all of my men are going to die.

"It could happen tomorrow, maybe we have an extra day. By the end of the week, every clone in the empire is going to die." I laughed without noticing. It wasn't a nervous laugh or an insane cackle, but it still left me questioning my sanity. "We've lost the war, Ray. The fighting isn't over, but we lost. What would you do?"

Again, he didn't answer my question, and I knew why. If the situation were reversed, Ray Freeman, hit man and mercenary, wouldn't go on a rampage of revenge. He wouldn't try to take as many enemies with him as he could. I was a frontline Marine. I believed in my cause. For me, the fighting became personal. He was a killer for hire. In his mind, he was always the bad guy.

Freeman had the ability to hide even the slightest hint of emotion. When I looked into his eyes, I saw no more soul than I might have seen in the eyes of a shark, but this time he exposed a hint of concern. He said, "Killing her won't save your empire."

"Neither will sitting around waiting to die," I said.

"It won't save your men."

"Maybe they'll go to their graves more easily."

He said nothing.

"They made us, then they abandoned us, then they selected us for target practice. You say I'm doing this because I have a vendetta, and you're right. Do you know why the Unified Authority created a clone army instead of an army of robots—simple economics. Even with food, housing, and education, clones are cheaper and more expendable than robots. They made us because it costs less to manufacture humans than machines.

"Yes, I'm mad, and I want to make them pay. I'm not going to scorch the earth I leave behind, but I want to burn the people who are taking it from me."

Freeman allowed me to finish my rant, but he'd already made his decision. He said, "You're on your own, Harris."

15

The ocular dye turned my eyes green. I shaved my head and darkened my eyebrows to an absolute black that matched the color of the five-inch beard now hanging past my Adam's apple. The intelligence officer who glued the beard to my jaw also used a bleaching agent to lighten my skin.

I wouldn't look like a clone to the casual observer, but the eye color, beard, and whitened complexion wouldn't have fooled a U.A. spy. My height, seven inches taller than the height of a standard-issue clone, offered additional camouflage. At least I hoped it would.

I wore a gun, but not an M27—which was too big and too obvious. Standard-issue firearms stood out, so I chose a Weinstein Industries semiautomatic, a lightweight, sixteen-shot street piece. People who shoot WI-16s don't earn medals for marksmanship. It's a gun for thugs—cheap, disposable, loud, and approximately as accurate as a paper airplane beyond twenty feet—but it had stopping power. Hit your target with a round from a WI-16, and your target would die.

My briefing officer took me to a shooting range so I could get the feel of my little WI-16. The first shot hit low of the heart. I raised the gun and the next shot hit two inches lower. Holding the gun perfectly still, I hit the target wide on either side. Firing a Weinstein Industries pistol, you develop an appreciation for chaos theory.

The briefing officer looked at my weapon disapprovingly, and said, "General, sir, is there a reason you've chosen that particular weapon?"

I held it up, tossed it from my right palm to my left and back again, and said, "I need a civilian model."

"If you want a street gun, sir, I can find a Damon or an O'Donnel. They're cheap, but they won't explode in your face. That Weinstein's more likely to kill you than your target."

I twirled the gun in my hand, closed my fingers around the barrel, and said, "I can still hit people with it. A club is only as good as the man who is wielding it."

The officer asked, "What are you driving, sir?"

I said, "I'm entering a war zone; I want to blend in. I've got an old Nader."

"A Nader!" he said. "What are you trying to do, Harris, get yourself killed? Please . . . please, let me get you a decent gun and decent car."

He had it all wrong. The gun and the car would offer me excellent protection because no one in their right mind would voluntarily choose such crap. Weinstein Industries guns had a nasty reputation for blowing up. Naders were cars that got great mileage, but they topped out at thirty miles per hour and broke down regularly. They were light and small, with tiny engines and recycled aluminum frames. Hit a duck in a Nader, and the duck stood a good chance of walking away from the accident.

No self-respecting Marine would enter enemy territory driving a Nader and packing a Weinstein. For this mission, they were perfect in their imperfection.

I needed to run this mission disconnected; any active communications devices could be detected. The Unifieds had equipment that detected both civilian and military-grade communications equipment when it went hot. If someone spotted me, it would take me longer to call for help, but that was a risk I would need to take.

Once I located a lab, or Sunny, or a computer with information about the flu, I would power up my radio and call in the cavalry. My job was to find the gold mine and protect it while MacAvoy and my Marines closed in around me.

When my briefing officer offered me a wire, I told him, "If I'm going feral, I better play the part." "Feral" was the term we used to describe natural-borns who had been loyal to the Unified Authority, switched to law-abiding EME-ers, only to change loyalties again now that the U.A. had returned. They were like feral dogs, domesticated pets that had returned to the wild.

At this point, I no longer blamed them. They had, after all, returned to the winning side.

The intelligence officer said, "General, you've built your strategy around a flawed stereotype. They're not all like that." In all our jokes, ferals hoarded shitty street weapons like WI-16s, drove crappy cars like Naders, and spent their nights alone with their Ava Gardner movies.

What he didn't know, and I wouldn't tell him, was the identity of the man who provided the gun and the car. I didn't know the guy's name, but he'd been a feral. He died earlier that day. I left his body in a Dumpster.

I said, "If it comes to a fight, I can trade guns and cars with a bad guy. Until then, I'm staying in character."

The officer gave me a hollow-sounding "Yes, sir."

I looked in a mirror. The man staring back at me had a pale complexion, green eyes, a shaved head, and a black beard. He was too tall to be a clone. I inspected my face and clothes and nodded my satisfaction. Not even Sunny would recognize me at a glance.

The WI-16 was small enough to fit under my jacket without leaving a notable bulge. The right people would spot it. They'd see it and know I had come with a shitty gun, but they'd also expect me to come armed.

As my handler and a high-ranking member of the military intelligence community, my briefing officer knew about the flu and its ramifications. He asked, "Do you want to take a cough suppressant? That cough could give you away."

He had a cough, by the way. His cough hadn't graduated to bad or out of control yet, but his voice was scratchy. Thanks to his neural programming, he hadn't yet equated his cough with being a clone.

Most commandos avoid alcohol before going on operations, but in my case, a little medicine wouldn't affect my reflexes. I took the suppressant and thanked the officer, then I walked out to my crappy Nader and drove.

16

Sometimes you sense trouble coming before it arrives. As I crossed the Anacostia on the Capitol Street Bridge, I knew a storm was about to hit. I headed north and east once I crossed the river, working my way past business districts and apartment buildings until I reached Minnesota. There, I crossed an invisible border and entered the area MacAvoy now called the "Unified Central District."

This wasn't the same territory my Marines had invaded two days earlier. *Two days ago.* The thought struck me as absurd. Two days ago we he had the war won. Now I simply wanted to lose it with dignity.

Anyway, I came in from the south, which had evolved into a neutral zone. We controlled it, but we didn't patrol it. We hadn't penetrated as far east as Southern Avenue, which was the border between Washington, D.C., and Maryland. We'd stopped more than a mile shy of that landmark.

In theory, MacAvoy and his army were already in place. They wouldn't come with tanks and artillery, not for this job. They traveled light, guns and checkpoints. They were the net.

The only artillery in this fight would come in from the air. MacAvoy had gunships ready.

My job was to slip into enemy territory, stir up trouble, and locate Sunny and her lab. If the Unifieds smelled an invasion, they'd burn records and smash computers.

If we captured Sunny, maybe we could get some information out of her. If we captured spies, someone might talk. Capture computers or maybe even a lab, and we might rescue the empire.

Southern Avenue took me through residential areas, big houses and lots of malls and churches. We had forced the Unifieds into suburbia. I continued north into the trendy eastern wing of the city, where glass met brick and a new city evolved around the old. Night had fallen. The neon lights in this part of the city showed me it was an adult playground, studded with bars and dance clubs.

I left my car by the curb and strolled across a park with a few trees and bushes but mostly wide-open space. Four- and five-story apartment buildings surrounded the park. I saw the first people in a park just past the clubs. They congregated in the open space surrounded by a few trees, bushes, and past those, four- and five-story apartment buildings.

I left my car by the curb and strolled into the park.

Seeing balconies and roofs on which snipers might lurk, I thought about Freeman and wished he had come. His talents could tip the scales in an operation like this one.

A lot of adults, both men and women, congregated in the park, but not many children. At first I dismissed them as civilians.

Nobody paid attention to me as I crossed the park. Streetlights illuminated the area, but I stayed mostly near the edge of the halo cast by the streetlights. People looking at me would have seen me as a shape, as a shadow. They might have seen that I was bald and taken in my height, not much else.

I spotted a man with a gun. He was dressed like a civilian. He wore a wind jacket and casual slacks. He held an M27 with a rifle stock attached to it—not a civilian then. I wondered how many other soldiers were in the area. The Enlisted Man's Empire only had men in its military, but then military clones only came in one gender. For all I knew, the all-natural-born Unified Authority military recruited men and women.

I could have shot him easily enough. He stood beside a wrought-iron fence, his weapon hanging muzzle down from his right hand. He loitered on the grass, staring up into the skyline, smoking a cigarette. He was young, maybe just twenty-five, and looked fit.

As I walked past him, he dropped his cigarette and stubbed it out with his toe. He turned to look at me but didn't really see me; I was just part of the park.

I didn't think all the people in the park could have been soldiers. Locals still lived in this area. When the fighting started, if it ever did, they would hide in their homes like rabbits hide in their holes. The Unifieds wouldn't kick them out of town, they needed them for protection. If they evicted the innocent bystanders, we'd be free to drop bombs. The bombarding would never end.

I reached the far end of the park and saw my destination, the Lion and Compass, the pub that the U.A. brass had adopted as its new officers' club. They hadn't taken it over officially. Commandeering the bar would have turned it into a target, but the name featured prominently in messages we'd decoded.

I counted six soldiers near the entrance to the bar. They didn't hide their affiliations; they wore BDUs and carried M27s. I knew these guards were for show; there'd be men soldiers dressed like civilians both inside and outside the bar. Not all of the pedestrians were what they seemed.

Other than the guards and some of the usual traffic, the street was quiet and dark. I stepped through the door and entered a loud, vivacious world, brightly lit and crowded.

One thing stood out immediately—the locals didn't view the Unifieds as a conquering army. I saw waitresses and female civilians fraternizing with soldiers. Yes, there were armed men around the room, but the atmosphere was relaxed.

As I stepped through the door, a soldier said, "Hey, you. Yeah you, what's with the gun?" He hadn't noticed I was a synth; I could see it in the way he approached me. He saw me as a criminal, more of a rodent than a threat.

I said, "I just came from the war zone."

"You're still in a war zone. Where'd you come from?" he asked.

"Lower Central."

"Damn, that's practically Clonetown. What were you doing there?" he asked, his voice divulging a grudging respect.

"I live there," I said.

"Your house is still standing?"

"It's an apartment building. I live on 46th. The damage stops at 44th." The addresses were factual even if I didn't live around there; I'd been briefed. The street names said it all. People who lived in that part of town dealt with drugs, gangs, and all-clone patrols. That was the underbelly of the capital.

The soldier gave me a disdainful smile. He was a smoker who might not have shined a blue light laser on his teeth since the war began. His teeth had yellowed to the color of beer. He nodded once, and said, "Here's a little advice. If you reach for that pistol, I will shoot you, he will shoot you, he will shoot you, and so will the guy over there." As he said this, he pointed to soldiers in uniform. He might not have noticed the men in plain clothes, or he might have been holding them in reserve.

"The clones took over your neighborhood; no one blames you

for that, but you're not among friends. You get to keep the gun, but reach for it, and I'll kill you before your finger touches the trigger."

I wondered if I should thank him or just walk away. *What would a thug do?* I asked myself, and decided that street punks don't put much stock in civility. I said, "Get specked, asshole."

"I'll be watching," said the soldier.

I answered, "I heard you the first time," and walked away.

The tables were taken. I ordered a beer at the bar and found an empty stool on which I could sit and drink it.

The soldier had followed me. I saluted him with my beer. He saluted me with his middle finger.

I stepped off my stool, walked over to the guy, and said, "I'll buy you a beer."

He said, "I don't drink with criminals."

I didn't believe his principled stance. He was on duty. There were higher-ranking soldiers on the floor, officers who would notice men drinking on duty.

When I turned to walk back to my stool, I saw that someone else had already claimed it. *For the best,* I thought. Now I had an excuse to mill around and listen in on conversations.

I felt a tickle in the back of my throat that might have become a cough had I not taken that medicine. Thanking my lucky stars that I had taken the drug, I gulped down my beer and ordered another. With that soldier scrutinizing my every move, I pretended to look for someplace to sit.

I heard someone say "Sunny" and stopped.

Two men in civilian dress stood at the bar, men in their thirties. They didn't look like soldiers. Both held drinks, not beers. I mostly looked away from them as I moved in close enough to listen in on them. One of them said something about summer doldrums and humidity, and I quickly realized they weren't talking about the girl; they were talking about the weather.

I heard part of a conversation that might have meant something to me at some other time. There were five men, all clearly officers, not a one of them in uniform. Technically speaking, that made them spies. I was behind their lines, but they had invaded our empire.

A tall, gaunt man with a receding hairline and thin hair said, ". . . more than enough men to take back the east shore. Just because they caught us napping, that doesn't mean they get to move in."

"Be patient," said a short, squat man.

Does he know about the flu? I wondered.

"Patient for what?" asked the first one.

"Right now they have all the tanks and gunships," said the short one. "Once our fleet arrives, the scales will tip in our direction."

"Specking clones," said a third man.

I looked at them and sized them up for their ages and their swagger. They were older, in their forties, probably colonels. Colonels might run smaller bases and watch battles from the sidelines, but they aren't in the know.

I saw a couple kissing. He had his hand on her breast; she had a hand hidden under the table.

That soldier was still following me, still smiling with his beer-colored teeth. Time was running out. *Is it 21:00 or 22:00?* I wondered. I berated myself for not having a better plan, but this was all I had to work with. The boys at Intel hadn't been able to give me names or addresses.

". . . think they figured it out yet?" a man asked his friend as they walked past me. There were three of them.

"That's the point. They won't know till the very end. Even then they won't."

I followed them.

"So what if they figure out that it only infects clones? They don't think they're clones, right? That's the beauty of it. They

145

figure it's just going to affect all of their buddies."

These guys gave off a vibe different from everyone else. They didn't talk like soldiers or civilians. They dressed like civilians: slacks, cotton shirts, loafers. They had long hair by military standards; it touched their ears and collars.

They drank beer from bottles, not from mugs.

Two of them had guns in holsters. I couldn't tell if the third one was armed. He might have been. I could have followed them all night, hoping they would lead me to their laboratory or headquarters. Instead, I decided to persuade them to run, then see where they ran to.

I pulled my useless little WI-16 from its holster and shot the soldier with the yellow teeth. He was five feet away, and I shot him in the face. I meant to hit him between the eyes, but the bullet shattered his forehead instead. So much for Weinsteins.

The back of his head burst open, people screamed and ran, and more shooting followed.

I ditched the Weinstein, tossed it over my shoulder and picked up the dead soldier's M27. I dropped the rifle butt, which would have proved worse than useless in a close-quarters situation.

Somebody near the back of the bar started shooting. Somebody near the entrance started shooting as well. Strangely enough, they didn't shoot at me. That soldier must have been bluffing when he said the other sentries were watching me. They had no clue whom they should shoot.

Now my three intelligence guys, they were more alert. They dropped to the floor like most of the customers, but out came their guns. All three had weapons. One of them jumped to his feet, his pistol out and waving around like an antenna as he searched for the proper target. I shot him.

The guy by the front door finally spotted me and fired. He hit a woman kneeling a few feet from me, and I shot him. Then I spun and fired at the guy at the back of the bar. I hit him three times, but I didn't wait to see if he fell; when trained men are caught unready, their confusion only lasts so long.

Panic had set in at the Lion and Compass. People screamed. Some people ran, others disappeared behind tables and booths. I spotted a man in BDUs running toward the far end of the bar. I shot him in the chest as he dived for safety.

Another of my three intelligence guys tried to shoot from behind a table. I hit him in the arm, the shoulder, and the head. Now I had one U.A. spook left, and that guy started running. Half the bar followed on his heels.

It was a human avalanche, a stampede of two-legged cattle. I sprinted after the guy. He was short, shorter than a standard-issue clone. He blended in with the people around him.

People pushed and jostled as the herd wrestled out to the street. I heard a woman scream and saw her fall. The people behind her trampled the spot where she landed.

Somebody grabbed me from behind. I spun, saw he wasn't armed, and merely knocked his hand away. In the moment I spent dislodging his hand, several people ran into me, knocking me off balance. I stumbled, caught myself, kept pace with the current of people. We ran up the stairs, and through the door, and back into the dusky evening.

Most of the people continued running even after they reached the street. That agent sure as hell did. He'd seen his two buddies dropped; now he sprinted like a world-class athlete. He had his head down and his short legs pumping like pistons in a race car.

I had a clear shot at him, but at that moment, his life meant more to me than my own. If I could catch him, maybe I could get some information. He might lead me to a lab or a computer, with a cure for the flu. I didn't know how much he knew, but I knew he knew something.

He ran. I ran. He reached a street corner and ducked around a building, not pausing to look back in my direction. Did he know I was after him? He seemed alert enough, maybe even smart.

A fleet of sedans screeched to a halt in the distance behind me. More came rumbling down the street and speeding past me. Apparently no one knew what had happened in the bar, just that shots had been fired.

The Unified Authority didn't provide jeeps for its soldiers, but they'd commandeered cars from some of the locals. They had achieved the symbiotic relationship that had always eluded us clones.

The U.A. MPs must have known that several people had run down this street and that there'd been shooting. They could see the crowd around me, but the farther we ran, the more the herd thinned. A couple of men slowed to a stop ahead of me. I streaked past them. One of them yelled, "Hey."

That short spook, the one I was chasing, slid as he tried to round another corner. He might have been fifty feet ahead of me, but I was gaining quickly. I heard shouting behind me. Somebody had finally noticed us running from the scene.

Damn, I wished Freeman had come.

The guy made a sharp turn and started up an alley. That turn helped me more than him. Anything that got me off the street was fine by me.

Not much light in that alley. I heard him stumbling over trash or boxes; it could have been a cat for all I knew. I followed, hitting debris and rolling my ankle, but not injuring myself. No sprain, no break, I kept running. He reached a door, wasted a second opening it, and darted through. I followed. It didn't matter if the building was filled with convalescing patriarchs or armed assassins. I no longer cared. I kicked the door open and ducked to one side. One gun fired at me, and it belonged to my rabbit. He fired three shots into the stone wall on the other side of the alley. Fired in an

148

enclosed hall, those shots sounded as loud as howitzer shells.

I had an M27 and the beginnings of a combat reflex; you better believe I wanted to shoot the bastard. I wanted to dive in low, firing as I leaped. I hoped his friends would come to join him.

I had learned to control my combat reflexes more or less. I drew a steady stream of oxygen in through my nose, spooled the air in my lungs, and exhaled through my mouth. I counted moments and listened to the beat of my heart. *You need him alive*, I told myself. *You need him alive.*

I grabbed the lid from a nearby trash can, clapped it against the door to make a loud noise, then flicked it out, holding it vertically so that he would see the circle instead of the edge. The bastard shot two holes in it and ran.

I heard his footsteps on the tile floor and followed.

The shooting attracted attention inside the building. People stepped out of doorways. Had this been a military barracks, they would have come with guns, but these were locals. They liked the Unifieds more than us clones, but not enough to shoot at me.

Seeing me run past his door, one old man yelled, "Who is he?"

I almost yelled, "War criminal." Instead, I sprinted ahead without speaking a word.

You can shoot him in the leg, I told myself. Maybe not the thigh. Hit the wrong part of a man's thigh, and he'll bleed to death in a matter of minutes. That was the inner, upper thigh. You'd never hit it if you were aiming for it, not on a running man. I needed the bastard alive, and I wasn't aiming for it, which meant he might spin or trip as I shot.

I couldn't take the risk.

He spun and shot at me. We were still in the hundred-foot hall of a small apartment building. The lighting was low, restaurant bright, not office bright. There might have been twenty apartment doors between him and me, some had opened, but when most people saw guns, they closed their doors and hid.

With my combat reflex now in full gear, I saw the world around me so clearly that it seemed to move in slow motion. I saw the bastard plant his right foot, spotted the twitch of his shoulder, and watched as his left shoulder swiveled back. The gun was in his right hand; eons passed as the muzzle lifted and pointed in my direction.

Can't risk killing him, I thought.

He was still aiming wide when the combat reflex got the better of me and I shot at his planted right foot. Good thing I had an M27 instead of a Weinstein; my first shot hit his ankle. The bullet flattened when it hit bone and just about disintegrated everything after that. The guy screamed and dropped, his momentum spinning him around as he hit the floor.

What a quandary I caused for the people living in these apartments. We were both dressed like civilians, both young, and both armed. They hadn't seen the Nader or the Weinstein pistol, and my clothes were as clean as his . . . cleaner, my pants didn't have blood all over them. I might have been the cop and he could have been the criminal for all they knew.

The innocent bystanders had no one to phone for help. Since Unifieds had taken over the neighborhood, they couldn't call for the regular police, and the U.A.P.D. didn't exist. That's what happens when neighborhoods turn into war zones. It isn't fair. War isn't fair.

17

I had caught myself a U.A. intelligence man of some sort. I had no idea what role he played in their organization. I had shot him to stop him from running, but my bullet did a lot more than hobble him; it left the bastard screaming on the ground, his foot attached only by a few thin strips of skin and muscle.

My M27 pointed at his face, I said, "We can take this game in two directions. Either you tell me what I want to know, or I stick my finger up into your ankle and start playing with nerve endings."

Someone yelled, "Hey! What happened here?" I looked up to see two soldiers at the other end of the hall. Good thing I had ditched the Weinstein. Hitting them at a hundred feet with my M27 came as second nature.

Muffled screams came from behind the nearest doors. I scared these people, but that didn't matter to me. By this time, my reflex had hit full stride. Doing violence provided me with a sense of serenity. Compassion was not even an afterthought.

The U.A. spy looked at his ankle and sobbed. He had no fight in him. If he'd held on to his gun, he wouldn't have had the will to shoot me or himself. He sobbed like a little child, rocking back and forth, chanting words that came out in an incoherent wail.

Remaining cold and calm, I said, "You're going to take me to your headquarters."

"Get specked! Get specked! Get specked! Get specked!" he screeched, huffing and puffing and hyperventilating between words as his voice became shriller.

I said, "Wrong answer," and pulled him toward me by his nearly missing foot.

What a noise he made. I regretted that move even before I released him. The guy wailed like a sidewalk siren. It was deafening. His shrieks echoed through the halls. Anyone in the alley would have heard him; he was louder than the gunshots.

"Where are your headquarters?" I repeated.

"Don't, don't, don't," he sobbed. "You specking bastard. You bastard . . ."

I made a theatrical grab for his leg, and he flinched, but he didn't talk, so I flipped him on his stomach and searched him for knives and guns and garrotes. I'd have to carry him to a car if I wanted his help, and I didn't want him slicing my neck or back. Seeing the amount of blood he'd lost, I removed my belt and cinched it around his calf. As I prepared to tighten it, I said, "This is going to hurt," then I yanked the belt tight, tied the slack into a knot, and twisted that knot so tight that it stanched the flow of blood.

He, of course, narrated the entire operation by screaming in my ear.

I took the sorry bastard by the jacket and slung him over my shoulder like a man carrying a gunny sack. As I walked toward the door, I growled, "You lost a foot so far. How much more do you want to lose?"

He only sobbed.

Was I willing to torture him? Under normal circumstances, I rejected torture as an option. Even with the hormones running through me, I knew the difference between hurting people and torturing them. Normal circumstances didn't include my entire nation dying from a manmade flu over the next few days.

I thought about signaling for MacAvoy and my Marines to begin their invasion but decided against it. Not yet. I didn't have the lab. I had a spy, but I got the feeling I'd rendered him worthless.

We got to the front door of the building. Three soldiers stood by on the street by a car they had commandeered. In the daylight, they might have recognized me as a clone, but the light was to my back. They saw my profile, my height, my camouflage. I shot them before they reached for their guns.

"Lucky you, we have a car," I said. I opened the passenger door and flipped him in. He fetched his skull a hard lick against the roof, but he was already in shock and might not have felt it.

I drove a few blocks away, found an empty curb on a mostly dark street, and parked. I looked at my victim and saw that he had gone comatose. "You don't get to sleep through this, pal," I said, and slapped him. His head lolled back and forth, and he stared at me.

I said, "Don't you make me work your leg. Don't you do it. I'll stick my finger right up that wound if I need to." Even then, even with the combat reflex pumping adrenaline and testosterone into my blood to provoke me, I knew I had already crossed a line with that bastard. I'd cross another if I had to, but I didn't want to.

I grabbed his chin, pointed his face at mine, and yelled, "Listen to me! You listen to me! I am going to fill your life with pain in another moment.

"Where is your headquarters?"

"No headquarters," he stammered.

"No headquarters?" I yelled. "Bullshit. Bull specking shit! Where's your lab?"

Still sounding like he was in an eerily dreamy state, he said, "No lab."

"There has to be a headquarters! There has to be a lab!" I slammed my fist into the dashboard of the car, and muttered, "How the speck did Sunny get that shit?"

He seemed to wake out of his stupor. He moaned. Buried in that moan, he repeated the name, "Sunny."

She wouldn't have cooked it up herself, I thought. *She'd have needed scientists and the equipment.* Developing a strain of the flu, a modified virus that would affect an entire population, something like that would require an enormous facility. They couldn't have set up a facility like that in some random suburb.

There are a lot of schools and hospitals and research centers around the capital, I reminded myself. They wouldn't have started from scratch. The Unified Authority probably had a lab in space or maybe on Terraneau. They would have developed the strain there and shipped it to Earth.

Sitting beside me, the pathetic shell of the man slipped in and out of delirium. He sat slumped in his car seat, so limp he could have passed as an invertebrate, and babbled. "Sunny . . . Sunny," and he giggled and sobbed. "Sunny . . . Allison . . . she did it."

"Did what?" I asked. "Who is Allison?"

"That's why you came." He laughed. The dying bastard smiled and laughed and groaned. His teeth chattered. He said, "She killed you."

I said, "Do I look dead?"

"But that's why you're here. She did it."

I didn't like what he was saying; it sounded too specking close to the truth. I asked, "How do you know Sunny?"

He said, "I know Allison. She said you'd all be dead by now."

"Who is Allison?" Realizing that he was trying to tell me something, I asked the question gently.

He must have bitten his lip involuntarily; he had bloodstains on his teeth. He said, "Captain Ewan said she killed you. You're Harris. You're the Liberator. You're Harris."

"Where is Sunny?"

He laughed this dreamy, lazy giggle and seemed to fall asleep. I shook him, slapped him, started to grab for his ankle. He moved a hand to stop me, but he was weak, and I batted it out of my way.

"Where is she?"

"I don't know."

I laid two fingers on the outside of the ankle. I didn't press them into the wound. I didn't squeeze. He needed to know that I could hurt him, and there was nothing he could do about it. "How do you know Sunny?"

". . . know Allison Ewan . . . my boss," he shouted.

"Your boss," I repeated.

"Intelligence," he said, rushing the words as if handing me a bribe.

Not everyone in intelligence is a spy. Spies gathered the data that intelligence analysts interpreted. He might have been the technician who maintained their satellite links. He could have been a saboteur or an interrogator or an assassin. The more I thought about his possible job titles, the less sympathetic I became. Adrenaline and testosterone surged through my system, flooding my thoughts, stimulating my bloodlust; I could barely keep myself together. In another few moments, my combat reflex would wane, and only violence would keep the hormone flowing. The pangs of withdrawal would begin.

"Don't know where she lives. Don't know where she lives.

Don't know where she lives," he chanted.

"Where do you go to meet with her?" I asked.

"Don't know where she lives."

"Meet her," I said. I shook him, grabbed his jacket and drew him toward me, then slammed him back into the seat. "Where do you go to meet her?"

"Never met Sunny. Met Allison," he said.

I sighed. The bloodlust had nearly taken over, but I had regained control of myself. Torturing this man would get me nothing; he was a dead end. If I were going to get anything out of him, he would have spilled it by now.

I reached across the car and opened the far door. That woke the bastard. He asked, "What . . . what are you doing?"

I said, "I'm letting you go," which was the truth, but not the whole truth. Restarting my hunt would be dangerous even without the poor bastard's blood all over my clothes. I planned to let him out of the car, then shoot him.

He said, "You're going to shoot me."

What do you say to that? I couldn't leave him alive, or he'd start screaming. I could have pointed out that he'd just tried to shoot me. Instead, I said, "You can get out, or I can shove you out."

I felt bad about saying that, but in a moment I'd pull the trigger, and the reflex hormones in my blood would surge. Any regrets would be forgotten.

He said, "No. Please."

The boy wanted to live. His foot was shot off, and he was in shock. Pain had clouded his brain, but his survival instinct remained.

He put up his hands, and stammered, "I know where she kept the poison!" and I thought, *God bless the will to survive*.

18

I saw the neighborhood and realized that I had never understood Sunny. The girl I had known lived in a luxury apartment, dressed like a model, attended law school at Harvard, and came from a wealthy family. She was pampered. She was spoiled.

The neighborhood this dying U.A. spook took me to see was a forgotten row of two-story tenements. The war hadn't reached this neighborhood, but it wouldn't make the streets any uglier when it did.

The unending row of apartment buildings butted right against the street, old buildings with dirty concrete steps leading to doors with iron bars over their windows.

By this time, my prisoner had settled down. He still felt the pain from his nearly disintegrated ankle, but he'd fallen into a meditative, almost comatose state.

"You still there?" I asked him.

"Specking clone. I hope you die," he muttered.

You're going to get your wish, I thought. We drifted through streets without streetlights. Light glowed inside some windows, but it wasn't bright, and sometimes it flickered. Some of these people probably used fire to cook.

"Is Sunny in one of these apartment buildings?" I asked.

"Allison," he mumbled.

We'd driven east, away from the bar and the trouble I'd stirred up. We traveled so far east that we might have left the Unified Central District behind. This could have been the free zone, maybe even EME territory.

"Is this Coral Hills?" I asked.

"What?"

"What part of town is this?" I asked. I hadn't ever been to Coral Hills; I just knew of its existence. I said, "Are we in Coral Hills? It's a suburb." Travis Watson was hiding there when he contacted us, and Sunny found the convoy we sent to extract him. The pieces of the puzzle fit together.

I didn't need to ask which building was Sunny's. Up the street, one building glowed more brightly than the others. High-intensity discharge lamps shone down on the street from the roof. Bright, steady light glowed in the windows. The rest of the street looked like it had been removed from the power grid; this building appeared to have its own generator.

Now I had a job ahead of me, and the last thing I needed was an errant hostage. Part of my brain said to kill the bastard. That was the bloodthirsty wing of my brain, the haunted wing in which my ghosts and demons lived. It was also the part of my brain that gave me the best advice.

I said, "I'm not sure what to do with you."

He didn't answer.

"Killing you would be the smart move."

"Please . . ." He whispered the word.

I said, "I could lock you in the trunk."

"What if they kill you?" he asked.

"Good point," I said. "You better hope I survive."

If he made a lot of noise, started beating on the lid and screaming, he'd attract attention. Some good Samaritan would inevitably let him out. *Those damn Samaritans bite you in the ass every time,* I thought. I could tie his hands, but I didn't need to. He'd lost a lot of blood and wouldn't last long. Hell, he could barely keep his eyes open, let alone scream for help. He'd die before I got back, speeding the process would have been humane.

We drove five blocks north, deeper into the darkness. There were houses around us, maybe people watching. I turned off my headlights and coasted on, driving as silently as my stolen sedan was able, until I reached a sheltered spot. I said, "I can hit you or I can shoot you," and then I slammed the butt of the M27 across his head to knock him out.

Killing him would have been kinder.

Kindness. I'd killed this man's friends, shot off his foot, tortured him, kidnapped him, and now I had knocked him unconscious. *He would have killed me,* I reminded myself. He'd even tried. He worked for Sunny. How many people had she murdered?

I stepped around the car and pulled out my limp and barely breathing hostage. I picked him up, loaded him into the trunk, then I drove back onto the main road, around that building, and parked a few blocks away. If any of the locals saw me stash the guy in the trunk of my car, they'd try to rescue him.

This is the part of town where Travis and Emily hid, I thought as I drove. *They must have been somewhere nearby.* Could Rhodes have been visiting Sunny when they caught him? Was she looking for Rhodes when she spotted the convoy?

I found a quiet block and pulled up to the curb. Somebody

entered a doorway and watched me. Maybe he had mistaken me for a burglar. He showed me his knife. I showed him my gun. He stepped back into his building and closed the door.

August in Maryland, the night was humid and the buzz of the cicadas nearly drowned my thoughts. Languid air, so thick you could feel it, coated the street. The cloudy sky filtered beams of moonlight as they shone down on buildings. The alleyways were dark with shadows.

I'd entered a bad part of town. Crates and boxes and junked bikes littered the lanes. Broken glass sparkled in the gutters along the street. Up ahead, Sunny's building glowed like a star, bright white floodlights shining down its dingy walls.

I saw movement.

Silhouettes surfaced and disappeared from the windows. I watched long enough to see a man with a rifle peering down from the roof. He'd go first.

I reached into my pocket and pulled the little signal disc my briefing officer had given me. When I hit that button, I would send a signal to MacAvoy. It would give him my location. My Marines would pour in from the west, and MacAvoy's soldiers would flood in from the east. They would close in on my position. I would only need to secure the building until they arrived, and they would do the rest.

I decided to wait a little longer before sending for MacAvoy.

Sticking to the alleys and watching the skyline, I trotted toward a three-story building that sat kitty-corner to Sunny's. Two days earlier, I had learned that you can't reach the roofs of these buildings using their stairs, so I found my way to the rear of the building and climbed to the roof using a creaking, groaning fire-escape ladder.

Sounds carry across quiet streets at night, but nobody paid attention to me. Maybe the languid air muffled the creaking.

Maybe these people were used to creaking ladders. When I reached the roof, I huddled beside a ledge and waited. If the sniper on the other roof heard me, he'd be on alert. He'd investigate, but hopefully, seeing nothing, he'd lose interest.

In the game of sniping, the prize always goes to players who are patient and alert. I let one minute pass, then another before I crawled toward the ledge that overlooked Sunny's building.

The M27 was a versatile weapon, built for use as both a pistol and a rifle. It had a short barrel, too short for serious sniping. Short barrel be damned, the M27 was accurate to five hundred yards. If I missed this shot, it would say more about me than my weapon.

All the lights on the roof shone down from its edges. To spot my target, I'd need to look past the glare and into the darkness— good cover. I sat behind a ledge, and I waited.

Just when I started to suspect that I had imagined the sniper, the man emerged, dressed in black and carrying a darkened weapon. I spotted his movement first, something I sensed more than saw. When he crept by a skylight, I finally got a fix on him for a moment, but he vanished back into the shadows before I could shoot.

I selected one of the skylights, aimed my M27 in the air above it, and waited for the sniper to step into my bead. Seconds passed. A minute. Something moved near the far ledge of the building, but I ignored it. If I chased phantoms in those shadows, I might lose a real shot.

A few drops of rain fell, just a meaningless sprinkle. They dried as soon as they landed. A moment later, the rain stopped.

A shape appeared above the skylight. I squeezed the trigger, a single shot that sounded like a misfiring engine or possibly a car crash. M27s are not particularly loud, and its echo vanished into the night. No one came to see what happened. Maybe they'd seen the rain and mistaken my shot for thunder.

As I climbed down from the roof, people peered at me through a couple of windows, civilians of all ages and sizes. I stared right back at them. Some of them hid; others pretended to look at their own reflections.

One way or another, the battle would hinge on the next three minutes. I reached into my pocket and signaled my troops, then I sprinted toward the building.

Two men came out of the alley to meet me. They had guns, but they hadn't yet raised them, and I shot them before they identified me. I peered down the alley to make sure they didn't have friends waiting in the shadows. The alley was empty, a long, tight squeeze between two buildings. Most of the windows were dark, but a few were lit. Toward the back of the alley, both buildings had networks of fire escapes. The buildings sat so close to each other that their balconies and ladders looked laced together.

Having eliminated the guards, I leaped the stairs at the front of the building two at a time. The front door was glass; I could see into a hall that led straight through the building. I saw a staircase and mail slots and men rushing through doorways. They fired at me.

The front door splintered; its glass panels shattered into shards and needles. I saw men emerging from distant buildings, aimed my M27 at the lights along the roof, and returned the street to its native darkness.

Gunfire slashed at walls on the other side of the street. I couldn't tell if they were firing at me or at some phantom they'd imagined. A gunman barreled out of a nearby building and fired in my direction; his bullets hit nowhere near me. I sprang from my hiding place, looked through a window, saw men approaching the shattered door they'd shot out, and waited in the shadows. One of the men stepped out to the street. I held my fire until two more came to join him.

The Unifieds returned fire. They weren't shooting to kill me, they only wanted to keep me pinned in the alley. They must have sent people around the building to trap me, but by the time their friends arrived, I had slipped through a gap in a fence.

Only a few seconds passed before one of them found my escape path and followed, but I was gone. They had to move slowly and methodically in case I had set up an ambush; I didn't worry about those clumsy specks ambushing me.

The tenement next to Sunny's was a dilapidated two-story with faux-marble stairs and rugs so threadbare they might as well have been burlap. As I entered the building, a man in combat armor came running into the hall. If he'd looked in my direction, I would have shot him. He didn't. He entered the door across the way without a second glance as I walked up the stairs.

More Marines streamed down the stairs. I froze. These were Unified Authority Marines, shielded combat armor and all. One of them grabbed me by my collar, and said, "Suit up. Some dumb speck attacked the nest."

I nodded and continued up the stairs.

There must have been a couple hundred men living in the building, and from what I could tell, every last one of them was a U.A. Marine. I wondered what would happen if one of them recognized me, but the shaved head and the fake beard did their jobs.

So did MacAvoy's soldiers. I heard gunfire and ran to a window in time to see personnel carriers and Schwarzkopfs round a corner. The trucks were armor-plated and immune to fléchettes.

Soldiers poured out of the backs of the trucks like paratroopers jumping from planes. Seeing the soldiers, the Marines lit up their armor. Unlike the U.A. Marines in their armor, MacAvoy's men wore sturdy BDUs and carried M27s, which should have been useless against shielded armor, but these boys carried MacAvoy's special rounds.

The fléchette cannons fired hair-width fragments of depleted uranium coated with neurotoxins. The ammunition was deadly, but light and inaccurate beyond fifty feet. A good marksman with an M27, on the other hand, could hit targets from a few hundred yards. From what I could see, none of the soldiers on that transport would have qualified for a Marine Corps marksmanship ribbon, but their aim was close enough for paintball.

MacAvoy said he only had a hundred thousand armor-busting rounds, but these boys shot like they had an endless supply. They had their M27s on autofire at walls, windows, and shielded Marines alike.

I didn't waste time watching. Now that the firefight had turned hot, we ran the very real risk that the Unifieds would torch their computers before we got to them.

I sprinted up the stairs to the second floor and entered a hall. The apartments to my right faced Sunny's building. I kicked out the first door. Her building was so close, no more than ten feet away. Looking through the windows, I saw people running, some with guns and some without.

I ran back out to the hall, spotted a couple of U.A. Marines, and stepped out of their way as they jogged to the stairs. Maybe I should have shot them in the back, but MacAvoy's men would massacre them soon enough.

I ran to the last door on the right, kicked it in, and saw what must have been the only two civilians who lived in the building. They sat on the floor in the corner of their apartment, two middle-aged women, huddled and crying. They saw me and screamed. My combat reflex told me to shoot them. It warned me that enemy soldiers would hear them wailing. I ignored my reflex, and they stopped screaming though they continued to hug each other and sob.

I opened the window and stepped onto the fire escape. Below

me, the fighting continued on the street. By this time, some of the shielding on the Marines' armor had failed and a trickle of men in darkened armor fled into the alley for safety. Had they spotted me, they still could have shot at me. Even with their shields out, their fléchette cannons would work perfectly well.

Frankly, MacAvoy's boys scared me more than the Unifieds. The occasional bullet skidded across the buildings, scraping bricks and shattering windows. If I made it through this battle, and the Empire survived the next few weeks, I would have a word with MacAvoy about his soldiers' marksmanship.

I would need to leap somewhere between ten and fifteen feet to land on Sunny's building, then I'd need to climb down the fire escape. It was a bit of a jump. I hoped I landed quietly. I didn't want to attract unfriendly attention.

I climbed up to the roof, took a few steps from the ledge, and jumped. In my adrenaline-fired haste, I sprinted and leaped. I jumped far enough, but not high enough. My feet hit the wall and I landed on my gut.

I threw my legs over the edge and pulled myself to my feet, then climbed down the fire escape to a window near the second-story landing. Somebody spotted me from inside the building as I opened the window. She fired a single shot at me, her bullet punching a neat hole through the glass. I returned fire.

Sunny, dressed casually in slacks and a pullover, disappeared as my bullet shattered the window. I jumped through the empty casing, slid on the shard-covered floor, and ran after her.

I entered the hall no more than two seconds behind her, well in time to see her sprinting down the stairs. I raised my gun. I needed her alive, but saw nothing wrong with shooting her shoulders or arms, then somebody grabbed me from behind and I flipped the bastard over my shoulder and shot him in the head. The blast was exquisite. I had taken this gun from a Unified Authority sentry who'd loaded it with dumdums or possibly hollow-point rounds. The bullet obliterated the man's skull, splashing blood on the floor, walls, and even a portion of the ceiling.

Two more guys came running up the stairs. I shot one before he could aim and hit the other after he'd wasted a shot, then I vaulted over their bodies and dropped onto the last step, skidding forward and hitting my face against the wall. For the first time that evening, I bled. If I'd been thinking about it, I would have wondered why it had taken so long.

My thoughts narrowed, winnowing out everything but my objective, which had now split in two. I wanted to kill Sunny. I wanted to shoot her, to strangle her, to watch her die in my hands. I needed to find the lab, the computers, the files, anything, anything, anything that stored information about . . . I couldn't force any more details. Killing Sunny seemed more important. She'd shot at me. She'd tortured me. She'd humiliated me. And somewhere, a quiet voice in my head whispered, *She murdered you.*

Murdered me? Flu. The flu. Need the lab! Need the files! Save the Enlisted Man's Empire! Clones are going to die tomorrow! My thought fell into line like tumblers in a lock. I heard gunfire, saw EME soldiers entering the front of the buildings, and I stopped. I signaled them to make sure they saw me and recognized me. They would have been briefed. No one fired at me.

Sunny had been in that room when I arrived, I reminded myself. I ran back up the stairs and entered the room. *She was right here, right outside this door,* I reminded myself. I saw nothing significant.

I kicked in the door to the next room and spotted cots and clothing. There were three racks, cases for combat armor, uranium wafers for fléchette cannons.

Same in the next room. The room after that had maps on the walls and computers on the desk. I found a photo—me on a gurney with a tube in my nose. In the picture, my face showed pain.

I saw the desk and the computers and the communications consoles and knew I had found Sunny Ferris's "nest," and my pulse quickened. I darted into the room, frantic, spun, looked for wires, receivers, mines, or bombs. Sunny wouldn't turn her nest over willingly. I checked the lights, the back of the equipment, the desk, both top and bottom, and chair. In my imagination, I saw her laughing and pressing a button, a diode would switch from white to red, and the apartment would explode, maybe the entire building.

I threw the mattresses off the bed. I pulled the pillows apart. Seconds passed, they felt like hours, then I realized, if Sunny were able to destroy the computers, she would have done it by now. I turned and looked at them, and inspected them for damage, but they were fine, unscratched, undented, two of the monitors glowed, words and charts displayed, and I laughed.

Somehow, we had finally caught a break. She'd thought I'd be dead, just like that guy had said. I'd caught her off guard.

An Army major stepped into the room, and said, "General Harris, sir, I have General MacAvoy on the phone."

I said, "Tell him to meet me at the LCB. Tell him, we have our prize."

19

From the air, the silhouette of the eastern suburbs against the dark sky looked like an ancient ruin. Most of the buildings still stood, but entire blocks had been crushed into archways and rubble. MacAvoy's army had begun its assault using M27s with magic bullets before switching to heavy artillery; my Marines had smashed their way in with a bombardment, then chased down the enemy with jeeps and rockets. Strait had sent in fighters as well.

I hated that we had been forced to rely on a hammerblow, but the Unified Authority had indeed forced our hand. Looking at the ruins beneath my helicopter gunship, I tried to estimate how many civilians might have been caught in the fighting. The answer could have been in the millions.

I heard something that should have sounded a mental alarm— my pilot coughed into his headset. He coughed long and hard, practically spat a lung out.

Staring down through the door, I slowly withdrew from an hourlong combat reflex. The hormone in my blood thinned to the point that I regretted the civilian casualties, but I still blamed the Unifieds for every death.

The glow of tiny individual fires lit the streets below. I saw fragments of buildings standing like the walls of fire pits, shielding bonfires from the wind. Long shadows of people moved along the streets—armed soldiers, Marines in combat armor, and traumatized civilians.

I felt alienated from the refugees; it was as if they were ants, and we had chased them from their hill. *When did you become so callous?* I asked myself. What had made me like this? Was it a life spent at war or maybe just the last round of fighting? Was it Sunny?

I thought about the man I had captured in the bar. When I opened the trunk of the car I had left him in, I found him lying in a coma. His foot had come off, but I felt no pity for him. Sure, I handed him and his foot to an Army medic, but I didn't care if the son of a bitch lived or died.

Marines in Jackals patrolled the streets below me. Jackals had heat scanning, making them effective for locating and killing U. A. stragglers.

The gunship on which I rode was part of a trio. Fighters streaked back and forth on either side of us, protecting us from nonexistent enemy jets. Just outside the atmosphere, Hauser's fleet had set up a blockade so tight that the Unified Authority Navy wouldn't have been able to fire a cloaked missile through it.

We flew over the Memorial Bridge, the uncrossable bridge that separated the eastern suburbs from the rest of the capital. Below me, Army engineers searched for bombs and booby traps.

August 22, 2519, the day the war came to an end, I thought. Then I changed the statement into a question. *Could August 22,*

2519, be the day the war finally ended?

I hadn't entered the gunship empty-handed; Sunny's computer sat beside me. We had their computer . . . her computer. If she had the right information, we would no longer need to develop an antidote; we could skip development phase and start manufacturing. We'd simply read their research and bake it right up in our labs.

Peering into the cockpit, I saw a red LED display that showed the time—02:36—a new day had begun. No sunlight showed in the eastern horizon as our convoy reached the Linear Committee Building, but the parking lot and the building shone like a beacon.

The other gunships in the convoy hovered protectively above us as we lowered to the roof of the LCB. At first glance, the landing pad looked clean, but the chop from our blades kicked up a billowing cloud of dust below us. The *WHOOP, WHOOP, WHOOP* of the blades slowed and grew louder as we descended, while men in Army uniforms rushed out to meet us. The moment we touched down, three soldiers ran to our door. They were clones, all the same height and coloring. I inspected the first man closely as he entered the gunship, took hold of Sunny's computer, then handed it to another clone to carry into the building.

I felt this excitement, nothing violent, but a constant current of electricity igniting every ganglion and nerve ending. We had beaten the odds. We were going to win this thing.

The medicine that the briefing officer gave me had run its course. At some point, I had started coughing. It began so subtly that I never noticed; the coughing might even have begun during the firefight. As I climbed down from the gunship, my cough turned *productive*, supposedly a good sign, and I spat a filmy wad of yellow phlegm.

Not very presidential, I said to myself. I was a Marine long before I became a politician. Once we ducked this crisis, I would step down once and for all. I might even hand over my commission. I'd been a lot happier as an enlisted man.

The glare from the lights shining around the outside of the LCB left me squinting. I smelled the sharp scent of gunship fuel in the warm August air, heard the chop of the rotors as her engines powered up, then the wind battered my back as the blades rotated faster. The air flushed around her as the gunship pushed off from the pad.

Entering the building, I found myself in a different world. Bright lights shone down from the ceiling of the LCB, illuminating an empty building. The roof entrance led into a hall that led to a foyer. This was a subfloor of the building, a nearly vacant area reserved for people who came in on helicopters.

The men carrying the computers walked about thirty feet ahead of me.

More people appeared as we reached the foyer. The elevator opened; two Marines and a soldier stepped out. The Marines were my aides; I recognized them though I didn't know their names.

All ants look alike, I mused. I wondered if ants learned to distinguish one colony mate from the next. I wasn't an entomologist, but it seemed like ants probably could tell each other apart. I could tell supposedly identical clones apart.

I was in that kind of a mood, happy, letting my mind wander.

"Welcome back, sir," said Colonel *Whose-it*, my highest-ranking attaché. He saluted. So did the master sergeant beside him. I returned their salutes.

"What was it like out there, sir?" asked the sergeant major.

"This was the big one, the route you wait your entire career to see," I said. We hadn't lost a tank. We killed or captured over ten thousand Unified Authority combatants and lost less than five hundred men.

The soldier waited his turn at attention. He said, "General

Harris, sir, Mr. Tasman and General MacAvoy are waiting for you on the third floor."

We entered the elevator. The elevator doors closed on the bright and empty subfloor and opened to the bright and empty third floor. I had expected swarms of soldiers, maybe even an entire division of intelligence officers and computer technicians.

Maybe we don't need them, I thought.

The men I saw were the walking wounded, pale and bloodless, their backs curved, their shoulders hunched. I heard coughing, saw men with red, swollen eyes. *Is this an office or a hospital,* I thought, but I didn't say it.

We'll get these men fixed up, I told myself. *We'll fix them up rapid, quick, and pronto.* I stepped into the conference room, and the door closed behind me.

Wheelchair-bound Howard Tasman was a ninety-year-old waif of a man; he'd have turned ninety-one in another three months had things worked out differently. The man had lost his entire family, children, grandchildren, and all. He'd lived to see the entire population of his home planet massacred. Veins and arteries showed through the thin, colorless skin of his face, but he looked like he could kick Perry MacAvoy's ass if it came to a fistfight.

MacAvoy sat slumped in a chair, sweating, pale, on the verge of dying. His short hair was wet and clumped as if he'd just climbed out of a shower. On the table beside him sat an enormous pitcher of flu fighter. He looked up at me, his eyes dark and watery, and said, "We've lost over nine hundred men so far."

Nine hundred? His numbers were wrong. I'd heard it was less than five hundred. "Are you sure about that?" I asked.

He said, "Five hundred in the last hour."

The last hour? The fighting ended over an hour ago. "Not possible," I said. "It's just cleanup now. We routed them."

"Harris, 70 percent of my men are incapacitated," said

MacAvoy. "The majority of my men are too sick to stand, and they're starting to die. The first confirmed casualty turned up this afternoon at 16:00."

I digested the news, and my head went numb.

"They died just like those clones Hauser found in space," MacAvoy said. He coughed, licked his lips, and prepared to drink more of his concoction. He clearly hated the damn stuff. He stared at the sludge in his cup, paused to work up his courage, and took a sip. He frowned as he lowered the cup.

"We have Sunny's computer," I said. "We'll make an antidote." I coughed, too. My strength started to fail. My legs turned weak as I walked to a chair.

Tasman finally spoke. He said, "Harris, this isn't a poison, it's a flu. It's an engineered virus. There is no antidote.

"I could have told you that from the start. It's basic biology. You can prevent contamination by inoculating patients with a weak strain to build their immunity, but once they have the virus, there is no way to cure it.

"You might as well send out medical kits with gallons of MacAvoy's drink."

MacAvoy coughed, then took a deep breath to fill his lungs. "I received a message from Tom. He says he's scattering the fleet."

Tom—Hauser—was scattering the fleet. That was bad news. That meant his sailors were dying and that there'd be no one to protect Earth from an invasion. He was scattering his fleet to stop the Unifieds from taking them over. Spread across the solar system, our ships would be harder to locate than inert and in a group.

"What about the computer?" I asked.

"Sunny probably wanted you to have it," said Tasman. "She probably wanted to show you once and for all that your goose was cooked."

"Specking bitch," said MacAvoy. His voice was hoarse,

downright raw. He might have had the same DNA as every other clone, but he'd always been an intense physical specimen. Even now, his five-foot-ten frame looked massive, like a warship listing and about to sink. He had his cigar, the totem he generally carried into battle.

He generally didn't light his cigars during summits and meetings, but he'd fire them up one right after the other during battle. He had his cigar lit now.

"You didn't happen to shoot that bitch, did you?" he asked.

"I saw her."

"Did you kill her?" He brightened as he asked that question.

I shook my head. "She got away."

"Damn, she's going to outlive us," he said.

"What are you going to do?" Tasman asked me.

"I know what they'd do if we had them by the shorts," said MacAvoy. "They'd blow us up, the specks. To hell with the planet; to hell with the people; if they can't get it, to speck with all of it. Blow it all to hell, people and all, that's what they'd specking do."

"We're not going to do that," I said.

MacAvoy removed his cigar and looked at the ember. He said, "You'll be the last man standing, Harris. You get to choose."

Even as I spoke, I could feel the chill spreading through my body like a fog, and along with that fog came aches and stiffness. I felt like my body had aged thirty years since I entered the conference room.

I said, "I'm not scorching the earth."

"That's your call," MacAvoy muttered.

An aide entered the room, a soldier, an Army lieutenant. He looked no more healthy than MacAvoy. He stood at attention, an anemic attention. He only managed to keep his back ramrod straight for a second, then his spine curled, and his shoulders slumped.

"What do you have, Soldier?" MacAvoy growled.

"The latest casualty report, sir."

"Let's hear it?"

"Lewis, Irwin, and Carson are closed, per your orders."

I recognized the names—they were our largest Army installations in the West.

"What is our readiness level?" asked MacAvoy.

"Fifteen percent, sir," said the soldier.

"How many dead at last count?"

The soldier paused, using the moment of silence to brace himself. He said, "We've lost ten thousand, sir. We've lost sixty in this building alone."

What about my Marines? I asked myself. It was an urgent question, but I didn't want to hear the answer.

Tasman repeated his question to me, then he answered it as well. "What are you going to do, Harris? You better find a good place to hide."

MacAvoy looked at me with his red-rimmed, bag-lined, bloodshot eyes, and said something that should not have been able to pass through his lips. He said, "You better run, Harris. This thing isn't going to kill you like the rest of us."

20

Is that part of the flu? I wondered. MacAvoy had all but identified himself as a clone. He'd said, "This isn't going to kill you like the rest of us." He'd included himself in the equation.

I wasn't about to push it. I asked, "What about you?"

MacAvoy took a long drink of flu fighter, frowned, and said, "I'm riding the storm right here."

Tasman said, "General Harris, you're wasting time you don't have. You need to get out of here."

I thought about the day the Unifieds reprogrammed the clones in the Pentagon. Watson had taken Tasman with him. He'd thrown the old cadaver over his shoulder and carried him into the garage. Was that what Tasman wanted now? Did he want me to take him with me?

MacAvoy asked, "Harris, what are you waiting for?"

I said, "I'm going to stay here with you and fight."

MacAvoy laughed at me. He said, "You're such an ass. I'm not going down in a blaze, Harris; I'm staying to spike the cannons."

In ancient warfare, back when cannons fired metal balls instead of lasers and particle beams, soldiers used to drive metal spikes through their cannons before abandoning forts and castles to prevent their enemies from using them.

That was what Hauser had planned for his fleet as well. He would park his ships in every corner of the solar system, maybe even destroy their engines and computers. He and his men would park their ships in the shadows of Mercury and Pluto, and retire to their racks as they died.

"You going to blow up your bases?" I asked.

MacAvoy shook his head. He said, "I'm going to leave the bases and the corpses for Andropov, let him decide what to do with them." He coughed and wiped his nose across his arm, then held up his pitcher of flu fighter, and added, "I got enough of this shit to last me a lifetime, at least my lifetime. I think I'll wait here for Tobias to arrive."

"You going to kill him?" I asked.

With some effort, MacAvoy lifted a general-issue M27. He said, "That's the plan."

Tasman said, "That's stupid."

Howard Tasman was an irritant, a dried-up old husk of a man who was unpleasant to his desiccated core, but his decision to help the clones had landed him in the same boat as the rest of us. Like me, he'd survive the flu, but when the Unifieds found him, they'd execute him.

I said, "I think my Marines are doing better than your soldiers. We had more than enough healthy Marines for the action tonight."

I reached for a nearby communications console and contacted my offices. When my chief aide picked up, I told him to check our bases for casualties. Unlike MacAvoy who'd been keeping a running tally of his casualties, I hadn't been paying attention to sick rates. My aide spent another fifteen minutes tracking down the information. When he called back, he told me that we'd lost over a thousand men. He said that most of our losses were in our West Coast bases. The bases to the east reported equally high rates of influenza but only a few men had died so far.

Apparently, the virus struck first in the West and was working its way east.

MacAvoy sat lifeless in his chair, his back so relaxed it looked like his spine had melted. He dropped the stub of his chewed, gummed, and smoked cigar into a trash can. It clunked on the bottom, and a couple of sparks floated up. Lighting a new cigar he said, "They can have my bases for all I specking care. Maybe Andropov will bury my men with honors. Lord knows they pulled his ass out of the fryer enough times."

He brought up his cigar, clenched it in his jaws, and smiled around it. He coughed. He said, "I might forgive him if he buries my men." He laughed and added, "I might even let him have this building."

"And if he doesn't? Are you going to blow it up?" I asked.

"Blow it up? Are you crazy?" MacAvoy placed both of his arms on the table for support, but his neck still sagged. "I want to debrief the bastard. He won't come if I leave the place in a specking pile."

I looked over at Tasman, and asked, "What about you?"

He said, "Don't you worry about me, Harris; I have it all worked out." Then he smiled, and added, "You know where you need to go. You need to get yourself to Freeman."

Freeman wouldn't help me, not now. He had his own survival to work out. I said, "Maybe I'll stay here. I can help MacAvoy kill our pal Andropov."

I didn't expect Tasman to respond the way he did. He said,

"You're as sick as MacAvoy. You're every bit as infected as he is. Did you know that?"

"He doesn't look like he's dying," said MacAvoy.

Tasman rolled his wheelchair right up to my seat, leaned so that our faces nearly touched, and stared me right in the eye. He said, "Harris, your pupils are almost as wide as your irises. They looked that way yesterday. You're breathing hard." He wrapped one of his withered old claws around my right wrist, and said, "You're pulse is up. I'll wager it has been for days."

"What are you talking about?" I asked, trying to hide my irritation. We had just won the war, and this tired old goat wanted to talk about my pulse and my eye dilation.

He said, "Those are all signs of an adrenal rush. You have a heavy flow of adrenaline running through your blood."

"I just came back from a war zone," I said. "I had a bit of a combat reflex."

"Yes, you did," said Tasman. "I helped program that reflex; I know a little about it. You're still having a combat reflex. You've never stopped having a reflex. The only reason you've got enough energy to stand is because you have so much combat hormone in your blood."

"There are a lot of clones still on their feet," I said, thinking about the soldiers and Marines who had invaded the eastern suburbs.

"The virus is going to run its course," said Tasman. "It's going to get stronger and stronger. In another hour, maybe another day, the hormone isn't going to matter anymore. You need to be someplace safe when that happens. The reflex isn't protecting you from the flu, it's hiding it from you."

Tasman looked me in the eye, and said, "If you don't find Freeman, you're as good as dead. That flu might not kill you, but the Unifieds will. Once you are sick, and your army is dead, killing you will be Andropov's first order of business."

21

I hated the idea of running to Ray Freeman. I'd gone to him twice; he'd turned me down both times. Maybe he was smarter than me; maybe he'd recognized the writing on the wall before I even knew it was there. I tried to call him on my way down to the motor pool. Nobody answered.

I entered the main depot of the motor-pool office and found the place empty, utterly abandoned. An entire fleet of cars sat unguarded. Town cars, jeeps, Jackals, personnel carriers, forklifts, motorcycles, all sitting in neatly lined rows waiting for drivers.

When I entered the office to pull the keys to a town car, I discovered that the motor pool had not been left unattended. The officer in charge lay on the ground just inside the door, alive and somewhat conscious. He stared up at me and mouthed words I didn't understand. I dropped to my knees beside him, and said, "Are you okay, Soldier?"

He said, "I'm sick. It feels like every part of me is breaking." He stared at me. First confusion showed in his eyes, then recognition. He asked, "General Harris? Are you General Harris?"

I touched his head. He had a burning fever; his temperature might have been 110. His skin had turned white, and his sweat-soaked blouse clung to his chest and arms.

I said, "I can help you up."

He shook his head slowly, and said, "General, I think I might be a clone."

I started to lie to him. I started to tell him that he had blond hair and blue eyes, but the death reflex had already begun. He convulsed, a weak tremble ran through him like a jolt of low-wattage electricity. A moment passed and the first drops of blood appeared in his ear.

Feeling cold for not burying the man, I left him where he lay and selected the key to a town car. Weak and alone, I went out to the car and drove away.

I tried to call Freeman again, but he didn't pick up. As I left the motor pool, I considered my options and formed a plan. I would drive to the nearest spaceport. I would commandeer a civilian commuter craft. I knew how to fly the simpler ones. From there, I would fly to safety . . . if there was such a thing as safety.

It was 04:27. The sun wouldn't rise for at least an hour, and the streets were empty. I spotted police cars and EME jeeps as I drove across town. I was in the heart of the capital in the still hours of the morning. No lights shone in the skyscraper windows, but the streetlights shone bright.

A roll of thunder sounded in the distance, and rain sprinkled the street. When I first heard the thunder, I mistook it for artillery and nearly turned to drive east to the battle, the last battle the Enlisted Man's Empire would ever win. What would I have found if I crossed the bridge into Maryland? Would I have found my clones in control, or would I have found a listless, ailing force?

Maybe MacAvoy and Hauser had chosen better than me. Maybe the best we could hope for would be to go down with our ships. I thought about returning to the Linear Committee Building.

MacAvoy had sounded like a lunatic when he talked about *debriefing* Andropov, but I hoped he succeeded. Tobias Andropov wouldn't stop until he knew I was dead. He'd send every man he had to hunt me.

Tasman had been right about the flu's catching up to me. I felt tired and found myself fighting for breath. My vision had blurred enough to stretch bright light into streaks. The warm morning air felt cold to me, so I turned the heat up in my car. A moment later, I felt hot and opened the window.

We once had an enormous joint Army/Navy base just south of the capital, but the Unifieds destroyed it. The closest airfield was a civilian facility just across the Potomac, south and west, across a long bridge.

If I really was as sick as Perry MacAvoy, I needed to get away fast. Just an hour earlier, I would have said I was fine, now my body seemed to melt around me. I wondered about flying. How far could I get? I felt nauseated and wondered if this was a mistake. Mostly, I just felt weak.

I drove across the river on the Curtis Memorial Bridge, then followed George Washington Memorial past the remains of the Pentagon—another casualty of the war with the Unifieds.

The first time I drove through Carmack Gateway Spaceport, it was a thriving, bustling hub with spaceline terminals serving passengers headed to every corner of the galaxy. Now it had airline terminals for travelers who stayed in the atmosphere.

As I rounded the spaceport beltway for a second pass, I spotted a small, poorly lit access road with a sign that said spaceport personnel.

The clock in my car showed 05:16; my time was running out. The first signs of light showed on the eastern horizon.

I followed that little road to a gate with a small guardhouse. The man who came to check my clearance was a natural-born. I handed him my ID, which identified me as General Wayson Harris, EME Marines. I was a full general, not a brigadier or a major general, and I had all four stars on my collar.

The man looked at my picture, then looked at me. He shined a flashlight in my face. Something was wrong. At first, I thought maybe he worked for the Unifieds. Maybe he'd been told to detain me. He finally said, "You don't look much like your picture, General."

He said this as if he thought it was some sort of practical joke.

I had forgotten about the beard, the lightened skin, and eye color. The beard was anything but regulation. I said, "Excuse me one moment," and ripped it from my face—a painful operation.

The guard shined his light on the picture, then on me. This time he said, "Holy speck."

I said, "I can't do anything about the eye color. I'm afraid I'm stuck with green for the next few days."

"You feeling okay, sir? You look sick."

"I'll survive," I said. He didn't know it, but I had just told him a joke.

This guy wasn't an MP; he was just a security guard protecting a facility with no military significance—an employee parking area of a civilian spaceport. He didn't carry a gun. He was just an old man who'd probably been working all night and had never seen anything significant occur during his shift. He didn't know that the world was under new management.

The man ran back to his booth, pressed the button that opened the gate, and let me in.

I parked my town car, pocketed the keys, and tried to climb out of the car. I got as far as lowering my feet to the ground; and then I just sat there. I stared across the branching walkways, long, empty sidewalks lined by bright lights. One walkway led toward the terminals. One led toward the airfield. They both looked so long.

I should have been able to walk. It wasn't as if I had injured the muscles in my thighs and calves. Just a few hours earlier, I had chased a man down. I had jumped from one building to the next. Now I wondered if I had the strength to climb out of my car.

I took a deep breath and did what I had to do. The world seemed to spin around me. When I started walking, the ground started rolling beneath me like the deck of a boat.

I made my way to the walkway and stared at the first lamp ahead of me, changing my focus to the next lamp as I reached the first. Everything was about taking the next step; anything beyond that seemed too far to advance. These legs. How had the muscles in my legs turned so soft?

I'd felt dizzy and weak before this, but I'd always been able to make myself walk another ten miles. That had never been a problem. My arms had never run out of push-ups; I'd always had one more sit-up in my gut. Now I found myself leaning on a lamp to catch my breath as I psyched myself into walking to the next one.

How the speck are you going to fly? I asked myself. I knew the answer. *Sitting down.*

In the sky, layers of peach and violet formed a collage. Clouds so orange they might have caught fire drifted on the horizon.

Day, I thought. I didn't greet that day, not that day, not judgment day. By now the infirmaries on our bases would have too many to take care of. Clones who had trained to be field medics would find themselves overwhelmed by the sheer numbers of the sick. They'd be sick themselves. By the end of the day, the doctors would die along with their patients, turning hospitals into crypts.

A few more steps, then a few more. I reached the unguarded field in which the commuter crafts waited. Rows of small planes stretched out before me. I needed to rest, so I leaned on the gate for support, and caught my breath and searched for something I would know how to fly.

I'd once owned a small plane called a Johnston Starliner. That was more of a corporate jet than a commuter, too big and expensive for an open field like this one. I saw other Johnstons, though, and when I regained enough strength, I stumbled out to have a look at them.

Some of the planes were locked. None of them had keys in them, but that didn't matter. I knew how to make them fly. I'd picked up a trick or two during my mercenary days, when I took time off from the Marines and worked with Ray Freeman.

I found an old Johnston with controls that looked familiar enough, then I switched a few circuits around. Before starting the engine, I checked the fuel. We had a long ride ahead of us, thousands of miles. It didn't have enough gas.

By this time, the lower horizon had turned white, chasing the colors up into the sky. It must have been the middle of the morning, maybe 06:00, maybe 06:30.

The next Johnston I found didn't look like it would fly. Sick as I was, I didn't want to risk my life in a death trap. In the end, I settled on a Johnston Meadowlark, a tiny four-seater with barely recognizable instrumentation, battered seats, and a notice from a mechanic informing me that I owed him $1,750 for replacing my fuel rods.

Early sunlight illuminated the runway. A few stretches of purple and orange still stained the sky, and I had no doubt that I would have spotted the moon if I climbed out of the Meadowlark and looked west.

A few workers walked the runway, checking strobe lights and

power stations. No one had noticed me yet.

The Meadowlark's ignition sat in a tray beneath the yoke. I lowered the tray and examined the circuits. She wasn't new, but the Meadowlark had nothing so prehistoric as wires running through her controls. Sparking the engines involved twisting a couple of circuits until they allowed electricity to run through them. All I needed was a spark, just enough to ignite the engines, which would generate the electricity for the computers, lights, and controls.

A blue-white flash, and the screens on the dash glowed their displays. Bright running lights flashed into view along the nose, attracting the attention of every worker on the scene. The men on the runways stopped, stood, and stared in my direction. A short, chubby man walked out of the control shack, realized that I had taxied out of my parking slip, and started running.

The radio flared to life as well.

"Meadowlark C29-631, this is tower control, you are not cleared for taxi."

I ignored it.

"Meadowlark C29-631, this is tower control, you are not cleared for taxi. Respond Meadowlark C29-631."

The airfield had a tiny runway, just about a quarter of a mile. That would have meant something to me had I had more experience with the Meadowlark, but I'd never even laid eyes on one of these before. I didn't know how quickly it would be able to take off.

"Meadowlark C29-631, stop your plane and shut off your engines."

I heard that last order and thought, *Fat specking chance.*

The commuter runway ran parallel with its much larger commercial cousin.

"Meadowlark C29-631, you are not cleared to enter the commuter runway. You are not cleared for takeoff. We have heavy commercial traffic in the air, C29-631."

Now that he'd mentioned it, I saw the traffic up ahead. Off in the distance, airliners as large as grocery stores sat waiting for clearance. Jets swooped in like gigantic birds of prey, like an owl diving to grab a mouse. Their wheels looked like giant talons.

A wind-breaking wall separated the commuter field from the big birds. I noticed an access road running through a gap in the wall and steered my bird toward that gap. Unless the flu had done something to my depth perception, the Meadowlark would have more than enough room to fit through it.

"Meadowlark C29-631, you are not cleared for takeoff." The flight controller must have paused to watch me. Instead of turning right, toward the northern end of the airfield, I turned left and taxied onto the access road.

"Shit! Shit! The dumb speck is entering the commercial lanes!" he screamed at the other controllers in the tower. Then, to me, he said, "Meadowlark C29-631, you are in violation of commercial space. Stop your engines. Stop your plane now!"

I breezed through the gap between the two runways at a clumsy fifteen miles per hour as I entered lanes reserved for jets. One came streaming by me, looming like a dinosaur, its wings so long and wide I might have been able to hide my plane beneath them. It rumbled past at thirty miles per hour, maybe faster.

As the big jet pulled ahead, dragging its engine noise behind it, I heard distant sirens. I saw police cars and fire trucks headed my way and went full throttle. The bird that had just passed me was going wheels up. Once it did, air control would shut down the runway, and those cars and trucks would surround me. That bird, though, she had gone beyond the point of no return. Racing down the runway at thirty, then forty, and ultimately sixty miles per hour before she lifted from the ground, the commercial jet left winds behind her that would flip cars and trucks on their roofs.

I stayed a hundred yards behind that bird, but it wasn't enough. Winds brushed me left and right; my controls felt tangled. The little Meadowlark bounced in the wake, its wheels never quite leaving the ground. I wasn't generating the speed I needed. If I took off in this whirlwind, I'd only get a few feet off the ground before my plane spun over and toppled.

Behind me and to my right, police cars shadowed me from fifty yards back. They could move faster on the ground than me, and they didn't need to deal with the wake from the jet. They didn't have wings that picked up air currents to make them unstable.

"Meadowlark C29-631, either pull over or get your ass in the air," said a female voice, probably the head controller. She needed the runway, a line of passenger jets and cargo ships had queued in the sky. Taxiing on her runway, I posed a threat to every plane coming or going. She wanted me gone, preferably arrested, but definitely gone.

I didn't want to tell her who I was. The Enlisted Man's Empire still owned the airways for the moment. As president, I probably could have put the other traffic to a halt, but then the Unifieds would know how I escaped. They'd probably figure out that I'd stolen the plane soon enough, but I wouldn't hand them the information.

I hit the gas.

About a quarter of a mile ahead of me, the commercial aircraft lifted off the ground, looking smooth and powerful and graceful. Four lines of white steam rose from her engines in straight lines that evaporated quickly.

I followed, my nose lifting off, dipping so quickly that, for a moment, I thought I might dive into the dirt, then my plane lurched up and almost nearly flipped over. The big bird went wheels up and to the right, so I headed up and to the left. Far above me, I saw more planes, a lot of them, circling like vultures waiting for a meal.

The weather remained clear except for a few hints of wispy clouds. The only noise I heard was the constant growl of the Meadowlark's engine and the warning from the woman running the control tower.

She said, "Meadowlark C29-631, you better never show your face around D.C. airspace again. If we ever find you, we'll send your ass to prison."

I smiled. She was the least of my worries.

22

Under different circumstances, a rogue pilot flying a stolen plane across North America should have expected company. The Washington, D.C., police undoubtedly wanted me for questioning. Well, they wanted a plane thief for questioning though they probably had no clue about the identity of their thief.

And what about the guard who let me in? He had a military town car registered to an EME motor pool. The car was filled with clone fingerprints and clone DNA. The police would find the beard I had worn when I invaded the eastern suburbs. I imagined the U. A. police interrogating the security guard, him telling them that he had seen me, and them reminding him that all clones look alike.

I didn't need to worry about fighters scrambling to intercept me. The pilots who patrolled the airways belonged to the Air Force, an Enlisted Man's Military operation; they were clones. They'd all be confined to their barracks by now. Some would have died already. Some would die shortly.

The sky around me was wide and clean and empty, as clear as a vacuum, and now filled with sunlight. I flew at fifteen thousand feet; all of the bigger birds traveled twenty thousand feet above me. That was good, because I'd switched the Meadowlark on autopilot and started slipping in and out of consciousness.

I spent a lot of time toying with my thermostat when I was awake. No temperature worked for long. Cooler settings soon became too cold, hotter settings, too hot. My shoulders and back hurt, so I shifted in my seat and leaned my head against the window, taking in the panorama below me.

I crossed plains as flat as a living-room floor and carpeted in green. I passed over rivers, and cities, and small towns, and military bases.

My coughing had stopped for the most part. My head hurt, and my sweat glands left me mostly dehydrated. I wondered if I had already outsurvived MacAvoy. I thought about Tom Hauser, out in space, parking his ship and waiting to die. Would he jettison dead sailors or leave them in their racks?

That was the way of the Navy, burial out at sea—even when that sea was an endless vacuum with planets instead of islands. I imagined Hauser alone on a fighter carrier, surrounded by dark decks and empty halls. He'd be like a ghost haunting a castle, roaming passages and reliving a life now over. In my imagination, he was so pale that he became translucent and as pale white as moonlight.

Logic told me that the clone I had conjured in my imagination would already be dead, but logic had little control over hallucinations and delirium. I'd been in the air for several hours now. I'd flown from the East Coast to the West, and now headed south.

I woke up with a string of images in my brain, lifted my head, and looked out of the window and saw a city beside an ocean.

California? I asked myself. *Los Angeles? San Francisco?* My head dropped back against the door of the plane.

The whir of the engine sounded like a giant sucking in air, inhaling all available oxygen, leaving nothing to breathe. The world around me turned from light to dark, and I realized I was in a coffin. I panicked, and cried out, "Don't let me die! I don't want to die!"

There was no one to save me. I was alone out in space, floating through nowhere in a coffin.

As the dreamer of my dream, I could see both inside and outside my coffin. I could see the claustrophobic darkness that surrounded me and the endless expanse on the outside. I floated past giant suns, but the trapped version of me inside the coffin never saw them.

Aaaaung. Aaaung. Aaaung.

The dashboard computer warned me that the plane had reached its destination. I woke up and saw the distant sun. It had crossed over me in my sleep and hovered in the western horizon. It was late in the day in this part of the world.

Below my plane, I saw desert and ocean. The mountains to the east looked like a giant mirage, like an optical illusion.

I knew where I was and forced my eyes to remain open as I landed my plane. I felt so sick, so tired, and sleep strangled my thoughts, but I managed to stop the Meadowlark safely. I opened the door to let in the fresh, dry air. I let it engulf me as I sat, and my thoughts drifted off one more time. The hot air baked my lungs and warmed my aching arms and shoulders.

I wanted water, and I needed to get to town, but my need to sleep was overpowering. Water and safety would have to wait.

23

I had landed in Mazatlan, a recently repopulated area in the geographic territory once known as Mexico. The Unified Authority depopulated the entire region hundreds of years ago, relocating almost all of the residents to colonies in space. For centuries, cities and towns sat empty, their infrastructure slipping into disrepair.

A year ago, the Enlisted Man's Empire repopulated the area with refugees evacuated from Olympus Kri, one of the first planets incinerated by the Avatari aliens. We'd scattered them through most of Mexico and given them nearly unlimited autonomy.

Society hates a vacuum. Without the Unified Authority or the Enlisted Man's Empire pulling their strings, the New Olympians turned to their own leaders—gangsters who had survived the evacuation with their organizations intact.

The gangster who had claimed Mazatlan was Brandon Pugh, a

massive, powerful, ruthless man. Pugh and I weren't friends, but we weren't enemies, either. He'd nearly gotten me killed once, so we had history. Also, I was practically family. Kasara was his niece.

It would have been nice if Pugh and some of his buddies had driven out to meet me and maybe brought me something cold to drink. I would have liked that. They could have brought me a sandwich, too, but I wouldn't have eaten it. *What was the last thing I ate?* I asked myself. It had been a long time ago. I ate something before driving into the eastern suburbs after Sunny.

What had I eaten? That had been a lifetime ago.

What was going on back in Washington, D.C.? Had the last of my clones already died? Death by death reflex was quick, at least they had that. Their bodies tensed as the deadly hormone entered their brains, a sudden twitch, and they died. There must have been some sort of trauma; blood poured out of their ears. I imagined death by reflex to be as fast and as fatal as a bullet through the skull.

I thought of Hauser and MacAvoy. One lost in space, the other practically drowning himself in his mugs filled with a noxious home remedy that wouldn't work. Neither of them would walk away from this. Nor would General Strait, the chief of the Air Force, but I didn't really give a shit about what happened to him.

The airfield was a good ten miles from town, ten miles of arid wind and desert heat. How much of it would I walk? How much of the trip would I spend crawling? Ten miles. Growing up in the orphanage, I used to run farther than that—run, not jog; now it seemed like an unfathomable distance.

I spent an hour sitting in the Meadowlark, trying to persuade myself to leave, but the sun had set, and my head hurt. Sitting and resting made sense, so I sat and rested with my legs hanging out of the door of the plane, the dry air parching my throat, the heat soothing kinks in my shoulder and neck.

I drifted between consciousness and delirium. Sometimes I dreamed. Sometimes I hallucinated, speaking to people whom my conscious mind would have identified as dead.

Sergeant Tabor Shannon tapped me on the shoulder, and said, "What do you think you're doing?"

Shannon was my mentor. He was one of the final Liberators. He'd been in his fifties when I met him. His hair had gone white, but he had the face of a twenty-year-old. He'd been "sentient." He knew he was a clone.

The night I found out I was a clone, we drank ourselves numb. We drank Sagittarian Crash. We drank two, maybe three glasses each and would have kept drinking had the bartender not cut us off. He didn't want us to die at his counter.

I said, "I'm resting." Shannon didn't hear me. He was already gone.

Ava Gardner glided up beside me in his place. She had dark brown hair; hidden in those brown locks was a hint of red that only showed in the right light. She had a cleft chin and ruby lips. She looked at me, and I saw anger in her green eyes. "Oh, no you don't," she said. "You don't get to lie here and wait for it all to end."

"That's how you died," I said.

She said, "That's not what happened. Don't you remember? You murdered me."

"You wanted me to leave you," I said. "You told me to leave you. You said you were tired of living."

She giggled, and said, "Silly, I was already dead by then. That wasn't how you murdered me; that was how you buried me."

"No, that's not true," I said.

Before I could get the words out, she had already gone. Night had set in. The air felt cold. I heard the buzz of insects. The man who stared into my face was big, so big that it had to be Ray Freeman, but he didn't talk like Freeman. He had a high voice, and he spoke in whispers. He said, "Sure he's alive; he's breathing."

I asked, "Where's Ava?"

"Ava who? Did you bring her with you?"

A man with a voice like Ray Freeman said, "He means Ava Gardner."

The whisperer said, "If you find her, let me know."

"I left her on Providence Kri. She wanted me to leave her there. She said she was tired of living."

"What is he talking about?" asked a person who sounded too nervous to be Freeman. Somebody said something like, "Hey, he's saying crazy shit. Is he supposed to be saying crazy shit? Something's wrong with his head."

Someone else came, someone I didn't know. He shined a bright light into my eyes, and said, "Doesn't look like anybody's home."

I didn't know what to say to that. I wanted to go back to sleep, but the man placed his hands on my face and forced one of my eyes open. He shined a bright light into the open eye, then he opened the other eye and repeated the process.

"Are you planning on dying?" asked Freeman. He must have been hiding somewhere behind the guy with the light.

"Got any good reasons for me to live?" I asked.

"Will he live?" asked Freeman.

I saw the outline of a big man, but he wasn't Freeman. In a voice I recognized but could not place he responded, "We're talking a head cold and a little dehydration. For this guy that ought to be a snap; I mean, he survived a bullet in his gut. Give him a day or two, and I bet he's singing in the shower."

Someone said something I didn't understand, then the big man said, "I'm not putting my money on a dead horse; there's no percentage in it."

I said to myself, *That's not Freeman; that's Brandon Pugh. How could I have mistaken him for Freeman?* It didn't matter.

The moment passed, and these ghosts left as well.

My next visitor was Perry MacAvoy. He stood outside the plane glaring in at me. He scowled, pulled his cigar from his mouth, and said, "Stop goldbricking, Harris. Damn waste of synthetic flesh. Five million dead soldiers and you, you damned shit-for-brains Marine, you're taking a breather. I don't know what I ever saw in you."

I said, "Get specked, MacAvoy. What do you want from me?"

"Get your ass off that bed."

"It's not a bed; it's a seat. Do they put beds in Army planes?"

"The Army doesn't use planes. You know that."

"Leave me alone. I'm dying here," I said.

"Dying? You call this dying? What do you know about dying? You don't even have a specking bullet in your lungs, and you think you're dying? This isn't dying; this is sunbathing, princess."

I said, "You're lucky; you're already dead, asshole."

"Are you shitting me, son? You think it's better to be dead?"

"What do you have to worry about? The worst thing that can happen to you already did. As far as you're concerned, it's already over."

"You piece of maggot-ridden sewage waste, how did you get it in your maggot-infested brain that I am done fighting? I'd give my shriveled left testicle to be where you are right now. Shit, I'd give my perfectly good right testicle just to have another shot at those bastards."

I laughed, and said, "They aren't doing you any good; you already lost them. You're dead."

"Dead? You think I'm dead? I'm not dead. I'm going to live forever."

"Get specked," I said.

MacAvoy came and stared me in the eye. He stood so close I could have kneed him if I wanted. He wore a dress uniform with an antique revolver hanging from a holster on his belt. The pistol had a silver finish and a mother-of-pearl grip. The gun was ornate, but it shot real bullets; of that I had no doubt. Officers like Lieutenant General Pernell MacAvoy never wore lipstick, and they didn't sport ornamental firearms.

I asked, "What's with the prehistoric pistol?"

He drew it and aimed it at me. He said, "I use it for shooting cowards, you know, soldiers who run away during the battle. Harris, you ran away." It was MacAvoy who said this, but the voice belonged to Ava.

Did I fall asleep or did I wake up? One way or another, MacAvoy disappeared and so did my world as unknown amounts of time elapsed. I didn't open my eyes, but I knew that a new day had begun when I saw the glow of sunlight through my eyelids.

The air was too cold for Mazatlan. It made my skin prickle.

A soft hand stroked my forehead. I knew it was Sunny's without opening my eyes, so I batted it away. I said, "Bitch, get away from me."

"That isn't very nice."

The other voices had seemed real, but I knew that most of them had come from inside my head. This voice was real, and it didn't belong to Sunny Ferris.

With some effort, I managed to open my eyes. I was in a hospital room. Two armed policemen stood near the door. Kasara sat beside my bed. She had a basin of water and a wet cloth in her hands.

"You've been asleep for a long time," she said.

"How long?" I asked.

"They found you talking to yourself inside your airplane yesterday morning. The doctor said you were badly dehydrated."

She was beautiful. She'd put on some weight since the New Olympian refugees moved to Earth, and she looked healthier. Her eyes were blue and piercing. Her hair was blond and thin.

She said, "You shouldn't have come here, Wayson. You know Brandon. He's not going to protect you."

So the news was out. The world knew that the clone empire was done, even down here, in the New Olympian Territories, even down here, in gangster-controlled Mazatlan.

Four tubes ran into a manifold needle that poked into my forearm. I coughed, and Kasara held up a cup with water, so I could drink from the straw. The water was cool, but it burned when it reached my throat.

"Has he called them?" I asked.

"Those guards aren't there to protect you," said Kasara. "He put them there to make sure you don't leave before the U.A. gets here."

I remembered the words I had heard during a recent delirium, and said, "You don't get any percentage for betting on the wrong horse."

"You play a mean game of possum," she said as she replaced the cup onto the bed tray.

"Your uncle has a loud voice. I heard him in my sleep."

Kasara said, "The Unified Authority has a plane on our airfield." She dabbed at my forehead again. She was tough, but sorrow and sympathy showed in her eyes, even if she concealed it in her voice. She said, "Brandon says you're all alone. The Unified Authority has wiped out the rest of them. Wayson, you're the last clone, the very last one."

I used to be the last Liberator clone; now I'm the last clone, I thought. *No more Liberators. No more general-issue clones. One day, after all of humanity has died, some alien scientist will find my DNA and resurrect me; then I'll be the last human as well.*

24

As a show of his confidence in his New Olympian allies, Tobias Andropov only sent a platoon to arrest me. He could have sent a division and declared martial law in the Territories. By Unified Authority standards, the New Olympian Territories qualified as a lawless state.

Kasara waited with me in the hospital room, taking updates every few minutes and relaying them to me. She sat beside my bed like a wife sitting vigil with her dying husband. We weren't married, but considering the future Andropov had for me, she was sitting vigil.

"How do you feel?" she asked.

I hadn't tried sitting up. I tensed my stomach muscles, made my back rigid, and tried to sit up. My head spun. It felt like someone had attached an air pump to my head and started inflating my brain.

"Did somebody put some drugs in my saline?" I asked.

Kasara said, "I don't think so."

"Then I'm probably sick," I said.

When I first met her, Kasara couldn't chat without flirting. So much had changed in her. She gave my joke a knowing smile and let it pass.

Kasara's phone rang. She listened to what the caller had to say, said, "Thank you," then said, "They're at the capitol building."

"Are they meeting with your uncle?" I asked.

She laughed, and said, "He's not the governor."

"But he's the one who handed me over?" I asked. I knew the answer, but I asked anyway.

"Yes."

The platoon leader's visit to the capitol was just a formality. Andropov knew Brandon Pugh ran Mazatlan.

The door opened. Kasara saw who stepped through, and said, "Speak of the devil."

Brandon Pugh said, "You never told me you were religious."

He came sans bodyguards, though, I supposed, the sentries at the door would have protected him if I tried anything. I wouldn't have tried anything; he was big and strong and menacing, and I was weak as a child. Pugh was powerfully built but heavy, like a professional athlete who has retired and learned to enjoy life.

He stood in the doorway, and asked, "How are you feeling, Harris?"

I said, "Like a dead horse."

When I saw his flummoxed expression, I decided to help him out. I said, " 'I'm not putting money on a dead horse.' "

"Oh, you heard that," he said. "I thought you were down for the count."

"I was. You spoke so loud, I heard anyway."

Pugh turned to one of the guards, and said, "He says I talk too loud," as if it were a joke. The guard laughed. I got the feeling he would have laughed no matter what Pugh told him.

Then he turned back to me, and said, "The doctor says you only got the flu, Harris. A little flu bug isn't gonna kill you."

"The Unified Authority will," said Kasara. She stared at her uncle, her face frozen in anger, her eyes shooting lasers at his. She was skinny and tiny, but she radiated fierceness at that moment. She reminded me of a praying mantis preparing to strike.

Pugh ignored her. He said, "Look, Harris, I didn't have any choice. They tracked your plane here."

"How'd they know it was his plane?" Kasara asked.

Pugh didn't say anything. Kasara did. She said, "Liar."

Pugh said, "Honey, you don't know what's going on right now. All the clones are dead."

"You told me that last night," she said.

"Did I tell you that the Unified Authority Fleet came back from Terraneau? Andropov and his army marched into Washington this morning. It's like the Enlisted Man's Empire never existed.

"Your boyfriend isn't a general anymore; he's a criminal. He's got nowhere to go and no one to help him."

I said, "And there's no percentage in betting on a dead horse."

"I got trouble enough with Andropov without harboring his worst enemy."

I wanted to blame Pugh, but I agreed with him instead. He was a gangster, and from his peculiar perspective, the Unified Authority wasn't the law—it was the biggest gang.

He walked over to the side of my bed and tossed me a thermal pack. I caught it, but it cost me. My arms and shoulders had no strength, and the needle in my arm poked deeper into my flesh.

He said, "I heard you got a fever so I brought you a present. I had one like it back on Olympus Kri, used it when I got sick."

It was a disposable thermal pack, a device our medics carried by the case into battles. At the moment, it wasn't cold. If anything, it was slightly warm.

The viscous gel and radiating marbles inside its sack were designed to absorb and retain temperatures produced by a chemical caplet, be they hot or cold. Pugh had just carried the pack outside, in the hot Mazatlan sun. The gel had leached traces of heat from the air.

Pugh said, "It's disposable; you only get to use it one time."

I knew that. There'd be a small plastic vial, maybe an inch long and a quarter of an inch wide, in the center of the pack. They called it a "stick." Snap the stick, and you initiated a chemical reaction either heating or freezing the gel and the marbles. Packs like this one would stay cold for an hour.

Pugh said, "Give it a good snap, and everything freezes. You only get to use it one time, Harris, then it's trash, so I figure you want to use it when you get real hot. You got a long ride back to Washington."

25

"What are you doing, Brandon?" Kasara asked, sounding more than a little suspicious.

Ignoring his niece, Pugh said, "Harris, I got nothing against you. I hope you make it out of this alive."

We left it at that. For what it was worth, I believed him. He'd been a criminal on Olympus Kri; he planned a life of crime in the Territories, and he couldn't afford the Unified Authority breathing down his neck. Men like Pugh considered themselves businessmen, not outlaws, and preferred to maintain a symbiotic relationship with the law. He wanted the Unified Authority to view him as cooperative, so he handed me over to them. What happened after he handed me over, well, that was my business.

Kasara didn't see it that way. I think she loved me; why, I'm not sure. She didn't understand her uncle's pragmatic motivations. She said, "Maybe I should go with you."

Pugh said, "That's not such a good idea."

I agreed and said so.

"Why not?" she asked.

I didn't know what little surprise Pugh might have hidden into his thermal pack, but he had something up his sleeve. Maybe he'd stashed a grenade among the marble-sized pellets.

Pugh said, "He's not going on a joy ride, honey. Andropov isn't giving your boy the key to the city. For all we know, they might just push him out of the specking plane before it lands."

Kasara turned to me, and said, "They can't do that."

"That's pretty much what I'd have my men do if I had Andropov," I admitted. It wasn't true. I'd captured Andropov before and locked him in jail. He escaped. If I ever caught him again, I hoped I'd have learned from my mistakes.

"I want to go with you," she said.

I said, "No," as forcefully I could, then I coughed up my innards. I made an idiotic pun in my head using the words "phlegm" and "phlegmatic," and I laughed at my own worthless witticisms. This flu would kill me; I didn't want it killing Kasara as well.

I squeezed the thermal pack with my clean hand and felt for a walnut-sized pellet among the pea-sized marbles. Nothing. *What's in there?* I wondered. Pugh saw me squeezing and nodded his approval.

When the Unifieds arrived at the hospital, both Kasara and Pugh received a call. Pugh excused himself. Kasara remained by my bed.

"You should go with him," I told her.

"I want to go with you."

This was my day for puns. I said, "I'm a dead end."

Kasara looked me straight in the eye, her irises focused on mine, and asked, "Do you want me to go with you?"

I said, "No," and I did not look away.

"You killed me," that was what Ava had said in my delirium. It wasn't Ava or her ghost or her angel; the vision I'd had was purely my ego speaking to my id, but I didn't want more lovers calling me from the depths of my subconscious. I liked the idea of dragging as many Unifieds as possible into my grave, but lovers need not apply. Too much had happened for me to go down with a clean conscience, but I wouldn't take any more friends along for the ride.

The Unified Authority military had arrived—ten men in dress uniforms—nine enlisted men and the strangest-looking officer I'd ever seen—Major Joseph Conlon. A prissy wisp of a man wearing white gloves and formal dress greens, Conlon carried the same pearl-handled, nickel-plated revolver that Perry MacAvoy had aimed at me in my hallucination.

Kasara stayed as the Unifieds filed into the room. She asked, "Are you trying to protect me?"

It was a stupid question; of course I was. I said, "Yes."

"What if I don't want you to protect me?"

"What if I don't want you to come with me?"

"For my sake?" she asked.

"For mine," I said.

The major traded a few words with the policemen by the door, and they left. He turned to Kasara, and asked, "Are you his nurse?"

"I'm a friend."

"I see," he said. "Listen, friend, visiting hours are over."

Kasara was dainty, but she had her uncle's mouth. She said, "Who the spe . . ."

Seeing the major's haughty demeanor and knowing that the bastard wouldn't think twice about arresting her, I placed my hand on Kasara's arm, and said, "Go."

Major Conlon glanced at me, then smiled at Kasara. He said,

"See now, friend, the prisoner has given you some very good advice. I'll give you one last chance to take it."

Kasara glared at him and smiled at me, but she knew that she'd been beaten. She kissed me on the cheek and left the hospital room.

Conlon watched her leave, then he said, "You like 'em extra bony, don't you?" His men laughed.

I didn't answer.

He stepped closer to the bed, and said, "I just spent the last year of my life floating in space thanks to you, Harris. I have a wife and two children. They spent the last year alone, again, thanks to you. They didn't know if I died on Terraneau or I survived, all because of you and your specking rebellion.

"Don't cross me, clone. My orders say I need to bring you in alive. They don't say anything about bringing you in with both arms attached and there's nothing about bullet holes or busted ribs.

"You get me, Harris?"

The bastard was only five feet tall and skinny; if he packed 150 pounds I'd have been surprised. He had brown eyes and blond hair and a forehead that spread out like the bow of a boat.

When I didn't answer his question, he glared into my eyes. and I stared straight ahead as if he weren't there. I didn't just ignore him; I pretended he didn't exist.

He said, "Oh, I see, you're a real tough guy. I tell you what, hero; I'm supposed to have a doctor look you over and say you're fit for travel, but seeing what a tough guy you are, how 'bout we skip the doctor. What do ya think?"

He placed a hand on the crook of my arm, pressing his palm over the place where the needle entered my forearm. "What do you think, hero, are you fit for travel?"

Under his grip, the needle dug another half inch into my arm. Normally that kind of pain didn't get to me. Maybe the flu had weakened me. I didn't groan or pull my arm away, but my back tensed, and I exhaled sharply. Gritting my teeth, I said, "Let's skip the doctor."

Conlon said, "Good choice. The medics in these parts are all quacks anyway."

None of the enlisted men made a move as Conlon bullied me. No surprise there, I suppose. Enlisted men seldom question officers. Nothing good ever comes of questioning officers; the officers themselves make damn sure of it. Also, I was the enemy. I was the last clone.

The soldiers didn't bother wheeling me out on a gurney. They had come with a wheelchair with arm cuffs, ankle cuffs, and even a strap that ran around my gut. They wheeled the chair beside my bed and ordered me in. When I tried to stand, my blood rushed to my head, and I promptly fell on my face. Conlon and his detail snickered and applauded as I pulled myself into the seat.

Major Conlon, a poster child for the Napoleon complex, asked me if I planned to wet myself during the flight.

Conlon told me to place my arms on the armrests. I did. Two enlisted men strapped my wrists into place. I lifted my feet onto the pedals, and they strapped my ankles to the chairs. They wound the belt around my diaphragm and cinched it so tight that I had trouble breathing.

After they had fastened a thin strap around my throat, Conlon stepped in front of me, smirked, and asked, "Still feeling like the king of the galaxy?"

There is a world of things that enlisted men watch carefully and officers take for granted. He didn't notice the disposable thermal pack in my hands. He might never have noticed it, but as his men strapped down my arms, one of them tried to pull it out of my hand.

I struggled to hold on to it, and a tug-of-war began.

"What's going on here?" asked Conlon.

"He's got something in his hand," said the soldier.

Conlon looked at it. He asked, "Is that a thermal pack?" then he took it from me and tossed it in his hand. He fondled it, and said, "Still has a stick. Are you saving this for the ride?"

I said, "It could keep me from getting airsick."

He probed the bag with his finger, probably searching for a grenade. Bright or idiotic, Conlon did something I hadn't gotten around to doing. He opened the stem and pulled the chemical stick, then nearly turned the pack inside out as he searched it. He exposed the gel and the marbles and showed them to the other soldiers. "See anything?" he asked.

A few answered, "No, sir."

He seemed to agree. After swishing the marbles and gel around with his fingers, he pronounced the thermal pack, "Harmless enough." He pulled it right side in and dropped it on my lap. His aim wasn't perfect, but he came close to the mark. The pack mostly landed on my left thigh, but some of the weight came down in the crotch.

He said, "Better hold on to it, clone. No one's going to pick it up for you."

And then we left, an eleven-man parade, with the major at the front and me in the middle. We marched out of the hospital. Well, they marched out of the hospital; I rolled out. No one pushed me. My wheelchair had a motor and a little sensor. It followed the sergeant, who followed the major.

People stopped and stared as we filed down the hall. They watched as the soldiers loaded me onto the elevator. When the doors opened to the lobby, I saw a new crowd of spectators. Kasara and her uncle hid in the crowd, watching me carefully, trying to remain inconspicuous.

The U.A. soldiers played to their audience. Major Conlon remained three paces ahead of his men. He strode on without looking back or to the side. His men marched in unison to his footsteps.

The lobby remained nearly silent except for the sound of their synchronized footsteps. A few people whispered. I heard words like "clone" and "execution" and paid no attention to them. I didn't look at Pugh, even as I passed by him. For all I knew, the device on my crotch really was a disposable thermal pack. I would have preferred a grenade, but a regular pack might still prove useful. Anything that held on to temperatures the way that the gel in this pack stored them just about had to be toxic. One sip of that shit, and I wouldn't worry about ropes or firing squads. I could die on my own terms. That idea appealed to me.

Is that why he gave it to me? I wondered. Had he meant it as a suicide kit? That didn't fit his profile.

The Unifieds loaded me into the back of a personnel carrier. We drove to the airfield, where a couple of transports sat waiting. The soldiers wheeled me into the first bird, and we flew toward Washington, D.C.

I sat in the kettle of the transport, a windowless, bell-shaped, metal chamber designed for conveying men into battle. They wheeled me in backward, allowing me to catch a glimpse of the Johnston Meadowlark as the heavy doors at the rear of the transport slowly closed behind me. I wondered if I should have flown somewhere beside Mazatlan and decided it wouldn't have mattered.

26

DATE: AUGUST 24, 2519

I wasn't there when MacAvoy died, but I saw the security feed and filled in the holes with my imagination.

The Unified Authority had an army, but not a large one. Thirty thousand U.A. soldiers landed at Carmack Gateway Spaceport, the very spaceport from which I had stolen the Meadowlark. Most of the soldiers remained in the spaceport, but two thousand men boarded armored personnel carriers and crossed the Potomac on the Curtis Memorial Bridge.

They met no resistance. By this time, the clone virus had run its course. We'd died in our barracks and bases, like so many termites, fumigated in their hives.

The convoy didn't include a single tank or Jackal, just personnel carriers, jeeps, and men armed with M27s. The convoy wound its way east, passing old monuments of ancient presidents. They passed the Lincoln and Jefferson temples, and the George

Washington spike. Then came the war memorials, ancient and modern alike. There'd be new memorials soon enough, one celebrating the sacrifices of natural-borns and their valiant fight against the evil clones.

The convoy turned north on 17th Street. What thoughts entered those soldiers' heads as they passed the ruins of the Pentagon and the National Archive Building, landmarks that their ships had destroyed? Did they blame us? When we invaded, we captured the capital without destroying a single building.

Traffic was light on that day, and the convoy reached the Linear Committee Building just before noon.

The twenty personnel carriers and ten jeeps formed a loose ring around the perimeter. Once the area was secure, three government-issue limousines pulled into the parking lot.

That was when Perry MacAvoy shot off the first of his shoulder-fired rockets.

You have to hand it to MacAvoy; he sent the "Unies" a message just as he promised. Instead of using a handheld rocket-propelled grenade, which would have weighed about three pounds and fired from a foot-long baton, he used a Flaws Rocket, an obsolete weapon used for shooting down gunships. You could destroy a low-gravity tank with a Flaws Rocket; it was also powerful enough to disintegrate a small iceberg. The damn things fired from a five-foot bazooka that weighed twenty-three pounds.

How MacAvoy requisitioned that antique I never found out. I know how he transported it. He no longer had the strength to stand. He'd commandeered one of Howard Tasman's motorized wheelchairs and turned it into a tank by strapping rocket launchers to the armrests. Once he knew Andropov was coming, he drove to a third-floor window that faced the main entrance, and there he had sat and waited for the limousines to arrive.

He was weak; he was dying. He had an oxygen bottle attached

to the back of his wheelchair as well. He sipped flu fighter from a mop bucket.

Knowing that protection protocol called for bodyguard personnel to ride in the lead car and the car in the rear, MacAvoy hit the limo in the middle, then, on the off chance that there had been a fourth car as well, he fired a rocket at the third limousine.

By sheer coincidence, Tobias Andropov was riding in the first car, the one MacAvoy skipped. Having thought that the war was over, he'd absentmindedly stepped into the lead car. It was the junior members of the newly formed Linear Committee who died in cars two and three. Sitting in the first car, Andropov escaped the ambush without a scratch.

Fifteen hundred Unified Authority soldiers stormed the LCB. They ran through the lobby, which was empty, not a clone to be seen. Some soldiers took the stairs; the officers rode the elevators.

They searched the first floor and found hundreds of corpses. Realizing his men would die wherever they went, MacAvoy had summoned his senior staff to the building. Those who had strength enough went there to die, the rest died in infirmaries and barracks. Every soldier died; everyone but MacAvoy.

There must have been magic in that flu-fighter drink. It protected him from the flu, but it didn't make him bulletproof.

The soldiers made their way to the third floor of the LCB. Here they found boxes of bullets and cases of grenades. This was the floor on which Perry made his last stand. It was one very unhealthy clone against fifteen hundred soldiers, but he scared them more than they scared him.

Now that he'd fired both rockets, MacAvoy abandoned the window. He drove his wheelchair out of the office and into the hall. He must have hated riding in that wheelchair. It drove at barely better than three miles per hour. MacAvoy, a man with more adrenaline than patience, kept hitting the accelerator and swearing at the top of his lungs.

He rode the wheelchair down the hall to a spot where he could see all four elevators. The warning bell dinged, a light flashed above the first elevator, and MacAvoy fired a rocket-propelled grenade into the doors as they slid open. The grenade hit and exploded, blowing the various pieces of the elevator into a dozen different directions.

The next door opened. MacAvoy fired an RPG into that one as well. When the third elevator opened, he struck again. The fourth elevator door never opened. Battered by debris from the other elevators, the cable holding the last car snapped.

Despite his cussed nature and the oranges and peppers in his drink, Pernell MacAvoy was nine-tenths dead by this time, but that last tenth, the one that came with a death reflex hadn't yet died. Destroying three elevators filled with officers had returned some of the color to his cheeks, but the man had no strength. Had he been able to stand on his own, he would have rigged the stairwell with explosives. His spirit was willing, but his flesh was cooked, and the best he could do was to connect a single mine to the door. A Unified Authority soldier opened that door, and the mine exploded. The force from that blast sent the door shooting through the air, decapitating the five closest men. The percussion deafened a few hundred more.

The only weapon MacAvoy had left was an M27. He was alone and weak and nearly dead. He pulled out his gun and curled into a coughing fit. He was still coughing when a couple of U.A. commandos finally captured him. Had he not been coughing, he might have shot himself.

A soldier ran up behind him and kicked the wheelchair out from beneath him, spilling him onto the floor. Another man grabbed his M27. A third rolled the dying man onto his stomach and handcuffed his hands behind his back.

Now that they'd caught the dying old clone and taken his weapon, the Unified Authority soldiers became downright brazen. They rolled him on his back, and one soldier kicked his gut. His broken cigar still in his mouth, MacAvoy coughed up blood, then gave the man a cherubic smile.

Security-system cameras captured the moment from several angles, but they didn't record the sounds. Any words spoken were lost. In my mind, I imagined MacAvoy laughing hysterically as he fired his weapons, probably still laughing even after taking that boot to the ribs.

The Unifieds kept a lid on MacAvoy while they secured the building. He was still on the floor, lying in a puddle of flu fighter and blood, when Tobias Andropov stepped out of the stairwell. The two of them had a short conversation, then Andropov's soldiers lifted MacAvoy up to his feet.

He tried to stand, but he had no strength in his legs, so they placed him back in his wheelchair. They pushed the chair beside a wall.

He'd been a clone. As far as they were concerned, that made him less than human. The Unified Authority didn't hold war trials for tanks or jeeps or clones. Only humans had a right to a fair trial, and synthetic humans didn't fit the minimum qualifications.

Lieutenant General Pernell MacAvoy stared into the firing squad as the men aimed the weapons. His smile faded, but he never blinked. The soldiers fired their weapons, and he toppled out of the wheelchair. His jaw must have clenched during that final moment; the cigar remained in place long after his death.

27

Despite the battle, the holes in the parking lot and the destruction of the elevators, MacAvoy apparently left the Linear Committee Building fit for occupancy. The only thing anyone told me about MacAvoy's last stand during my flight to the capital was that he died sitting on his ass. The way they told the story, I imagined him shitting in a latrine with a cigar in his mouth.

I managed to hold on to Pugh's gift. After Conlon dropped it in my lap, I'd spread my thighs wide enough to pinch my legs around it.

It wouldn't have mattered if the thermal pack held a grenade, a bomb, or a gun, I wouldn't have been able to use it during the flight; my guard detail never released my hands. It would have been such poetic justice if the pack had held a grenade, and I had been able to pull the pin—a midair explosion, me taking fifty Unified Authority soldiers and a pilot with me.

Later, after watching the feed of Perry MacAvoy's meteoric swan song, I decided that destroying a mere transport would have paled in comparison.

No one spoke to me as we flew north and east. I sat alone in the dark, my hands cuffed to the armrests, my legs, and chest and neck all strapped in place. The slip around my neck forced me to sit unnaturally straight, causing a crick in my back and neck that damn near drove me crazy. Then there was the needle in my arm. I didn't know what drugs and solutions Pugh's doctors had dripping into my arms, but they ran out halfway to Washington and my aches and pains took on new definition.

I sat there with that empty needle jabbed in my arm, unable to scratch the myriad of psychosomatic itches that formed on my face and neck and back. In truth, I felt lower than I could ever remember. I was sick, but those specking straps kept me sitting at attention for the full three hours.

Transports have a maximum atmospheric speed of two thousand miles per hour. That old Meadowlark I'd stolen flew so slowly that I expected her to drop out of the sky. Flying to Mazatlan in the Meadowlark had taken ten hours, but I had slept through most of it.

I sat facing the ramp and the shadows, so thirsty I thought my throat might tear every time I swallowed. We reached Carmack Gateway and the transport lowered onto a runway. My short flight from Unified Authority justice ended on the same runway that it began, but I had returned weaker and strapped to a wheelchair.

More than anything else, I wanted to drink the gel out of my thermal pack and end everything. Had there been a grenade, I'd gladly have pulled the pin. There'd been a time when my Liberator programming wouldn't allow me to commit suicide, but Sunny had erased that part of my programming during her experiments. Now I would not only have the ability to pull the pin, I genuinely longed for the opportunity.

The MacAvoy of my delirium was right about me. Placed in my position, any respectable Marine would have dreamed about wreaking a little ungodly revenge. Me, I just wanted to die. If I remembered correctly, he had called me "pathetic." Good call.

The doors at the rear of the kettle slowly ground open, revealing Carmack Gateway Spaceport, an open runway, terminals lined by planes, and a vast sea of spectators. It was almost like the long-awaited return of a messianic figure. Hundreds of men in military uniforms surrounded a meter-high dais. Behind them stood a swarm of suit-wearing politicians, both men and women. I also spotted reporters, hundreds of them, pushing to get to the front of the crowd. Mostly, I saw civilians, the natural-born citizens of the Unified Authority, all come to see the galaxy's most notorious terrorist delivered to justice. I was the man of the hour.

Freeman must know about this, I thought. He was the deadliest sniper I'd ever seen. Maybe he would spare me some humiliation. Maybe he'd pick me off as they rolled me down the ramp. He could do it. I'd watched him hit targets from multiple miles away. He had that skill.

The first man to meet me as I came down the ramp was Tobias Andropov, in the flesh. He took three steps forward to greet me, fixing me with a wolf's smile, and said, "The synthetic Spartacus returns without his troops."

The history of Rome. I knew a little something about the history of Rome. I said, "I'd watch your back, Caesar. Of Rome's 150 emperors, only 25 died of natural causes."

He gave me the slightest bow, and said, "Thanks for the warning, Harris, but you will die long before I do."

There was no arguing that point.

Forget the transport filled with peon soldiers, just the sight of Andropov filled me with rage. Something strange . . . with my arms and legs strapped into place and a cord around my neck, my back wrenched straight, and the sun in my eyes, I felt a little healthier than I had in the transport. I didn't feel like dancing or running a marathon, but my brain focused, and my lungs took in more air. The man who had defeated me stood jubilant before me, thousands of people had come hoping to see my execution, and I smiled faintly and relaxed.

Andropov had turned my return into a photo op. He stood heroically at the forefront, overseeing my arrival the way a warden would observe the delivery of a famous criminal. He posed in front of my wheelchair, pointing at me, challenging me, shouting at me.

He said, "Harris, you have been charged with heinous war crimes," but what he meant was, "Lazarus, come forth." I was as good as dead. Had he left me in Mazatlan, I might not have survived. Whatever medicines Pugh's physician had given me, they didn't strengthen me as much as the hormone now surging through my veins.

People yelled at me. They screamed that they wanted me dead. Some pumped their fists in the air. Some had signs that said things like hang the bastard! and death today!

Andropov, the conquering hero, climbed onto a large dais on which sat a podium. He pointed at me, and said, "General Harris says you all owe him a debt of gratitude."

I hadn't said that. I had never said that, never in my life as far as I could remember. That was a specking lie.

Photographers videoed Andropov as he continued. "Having defeated the clones in battle, we have captured their king. In time, we will heal from the wounds he and his kind have inflicted upon us. In time, we will reestablish our galactic empire, we will renew our pangalactic growth and reclaim our place in the stars, but we will never again place our security in the hands of a synthetic horde."

The crowd erupted. The commoners cheered, the reporters applauded, the soldiers hooted and hollered, and the politicians were downright orgasmic. The common crowd wouldn't have known any better, but the soldiers and politicians had to know that this was all bullshit. The Unifieds hadn't beaten us on the battlefield; they'd beaten us in the laboratory. Their flu virus won the war, not their soldiers.

Andropov could have gone on, but anything he said at this point would have been anticlimactic. The quintessential politician, he knew all about the diminishing returns of bluster. Instead of speaking, he lowered his head as if in prayer, and he silently stepped down from the dais.

The tumult that followed . . .

His head still bowed, Andropov looked at me and smiled broadly, then he walked over to Major Conlon and said something, but the deafening noise drowned him out. Conlon shouted, "WHAT?"

Andropov screamed, "GET HIM OUT OF HERE! GET HIM TO THE FACILITY! MAKE SURE NOTHING HAPPENS TO HIM! LOOK AT THEM; I NEED THE CLONE ALIVE!"

The newly returned senior member of the Linear Committee's concern for my well-being wasn't charity; he genuinely needed me. A lot of people had died during the last decade. We'd lost 179 colonies, and our economy had gone to shit. Andropov wanted a scapegoat—an evil genius whom he could blame for everything. He needed a poster boy. You can't haul dead clones into court. As long as I was alive and on trial, Andropov could point at me and blame me for everything. If I died, I'd be a faceless statistic, and blaming the fall of the Unified Authority on a statistic would be a tough sell.

He gazed back at me one last time, and I saw no emotion in his face. He didn't hate me, didn't pity me, and didn't fear me. I was just another vanquished enemy to him, just another head to mount on his wall. My hide would not be the centerpiece in his trophy case.

Andropov was young by world-conqueror standards, forty-six years old. He'd spent more than a year in prison, a guest of the Enlisted Man's Empire. Maybe he planned to let me languish for a year as part of my restitution, but sooner or later I would face a circus-act trial, and my execution would follow.

Seeing that the crowd had become something of a mob, and that that mob wouldn't behave much longer, Conlon acted quickly. He closed his men around me, and they rushed me into an armored personnel carrier. The driver wasted no time. He took us out of Carmack Gateway, taking a runway access road. As we left the spaceport complex, a line of jeeps and tanks fell in behind us.

The personnel carrier didn't have much in the way of windows, just two face-sized bulletproof glass panels on the rear doors. Sitting with a dozen guards around me, I watched the mob shrinking into the distance.

The mob—politicians whom the Enlisted Man's Empire had indulged and left in power in a bid to gain support, a citizenry we had tried too hard to placate. Yes, we had returned to Earth as conquerors; we had defeated their government, but only after they had abandoned us in space.

Conlon, who was so short that he didn't need to duck his head to stand in the back of the personnel carrier, stood beside my chair. He said, "Quite a fan club you have, Harris. If we left you with those people, they would have pulled you apart."

I didn't respond. I had nothing to say.

28

The Unifieds took me to the Naval Consolidation Brig, a well-kept but nearly empty facility on the Maryland side of Washington, D. C. Jeremy Reid, my new warden, was a tall, skinny, white-haired bureaucrat with a soft face and wire-framed spectacles, the kind of cat who can change from stripes to spots depending on who runs the pack. He looked at me, and said, "Wayson Harris, you have been assigned to this facility where you shall remain incarcerated until the Unified Authority elects to execute you properly."

When I answered, "Get specked, asshole," he favored me with a tight-lipped, prudish smile and said, "If you show us proper respect, your short stay with us will go more pleasantly for everyone."

After that, he fell into line with the guards and escorted me into the building, which looked more like a bank with human-sized safety-deposit boxes than an actual prison—a two-story building wrapped around a huge lobby. The place was as empty as a school on the first day of vacation, and immaculate, not just sanitary, like a hospital, but clutter-free, lint-free, dust-free, germ-free, like the reactor room in a nuclear power plant.

Looking across the lobby, I saw that the club chairs were the only things on the floor—two rows of chairs with armrests and straight backs, upholstered in white or green Naugahyde. The floors were done in white linoleum tile; the walls were brick painted a stark white. The bright fluorescent lights left not so much as a shadow in which a speck of dust could hide.

Reid strolled to my wheelchair, and said, "Your cell is on the second floor."

"You run a clean prison," I said.

"It's easy to maintain cleanliness in an unoccupied facility, Harris," he said.

I wondered how long I would live in this sanitarium. For that matter, I wondered how long I would live.

"We had to do some cleaning before we could move you in," Reid confessed, a cheerful ring to his voice. "Some of the old staff, the synthetic men who worked here before the Unified Authority resumed control, died at their stations.

"We buried them in a mass grave out back. It seemed fitting because that was also the way they disposed of their prisoners." Reid had this radiant, smug expression. He was in his sixties, maybe his seventies. He was a weak man, a man who tried to associate himself with other people's triumphs, a worm.

"Very efficient," I said, "killing every enemy and burying them where they fall. Maybe that was where the Enlisted Man's Empire went wrong; we should have been more efficient."

Reid's smug expression disappeared, but instead of taking the bait, he told Conlon, "I'm remanding the prisoner to your custody until he is prepared." He marched off, a skinny, prissy, politician, living proof that adult males can survive without balls.

One of my guards stepped beside me and jabbed his elbow into the side of my head. He whispered, "You know, you're not really the last clone; there are a whole bunch of them on Terraneau."

"Are there?" I asked. I'd had a lot of friends in the battle of Terraneau.

The man said, "Oh hell yes, bunches of them. We reprogrammed them." The man stared at me, his eyes sparkling.

We waited in the gleaming lobby while guards went to the second floor and inspected my room. It was a good thing that this idiot had accompanied me all the way from Mazatlan to the brig. He'd been there when Major Conlon inspected my thermal pack and didn't worry about my holding on to it. Had new guards arrived, they might have confiscated it.

The man asked, "Did you know we kicked your ass on Terraneau?"

"The ass kicking couldn't have been too complete if a bunch of clones are still alive," I said.

He said, "We lost a bunch of ships in the beginning, then our brass invited their brass for a summit."

"A truce?" I asked.

"Not exactly. They fed them a nice meal, then they reprogrammed them. Once their leaders joined our side, the rest of the clones threw in the towel."

"Their leaders," Admiral Jim Holman, the officer in command, wasn't the sanest man I'd ever met, but he was an honorable man. I'd always admired him. He'd known how to run a fleet, and he had a wicked sense of humor.

One mystery solved, I realized. Now I knew how the Unifieds had captured the Explorer without damaging it. The reprogrammed clones must have contacted the Explorer, welcomed the crew to Terraneau, and led them into an ambush.

I looked at the bastard, and said, "Let me get this straight;

your officers invited our officers to a peace summit and reprogrammed them."

"Yeah, that sums it up."

"So much for honor," I said. "You invited them in under a white flag, then you doped . . ." Before I could finish the sentence, the bastard slammed his fist into my jaw. Strapped in at the knees, arms, chest, and neck, made me a sitting target—literally.

Conlon saw it happen and barked, "Thompson!"

Thompson snapped to attention, shoulders back, chest out, eyes straight ahead.

Conlon asked, "Did you just strike the prisoner?"

The bastard answered, "Yes, sir. Sorry, sir."

"Do that again, soldier, and we'll see how tough you are with men who aren't strapped into a wheelchair."

"Yes, sir."

He's out of his mind, I thought. Conlon stood barely five feet. He was short and skinny and weak, and this other guy, Thompson, he looked like a bruiser.

As Conlon walked away, I said, "Ambushing officers under a flag of truce, beating up prisoners in wheelchairs, honor is in short supply."

Thompson glared at me, and whispered, "Keep it up, clone. That little prick won't always be around to save you." He said this so quietly it didn't attract attention, but he wasn't bright enough to stop playing my game. A moment passed, and he said, "Personally I think we should have ordered them to kill themselves after we reprogrammed them."

"As another shining example of U.A. honor?" I asked.

"Watch yourself."

Reid returned. He told Major Conlon, "The room is ready."

Conlon repeated the order to his men and the guards wheeled me up to my new billet. We rolled to an elevator which took me,

Reid, Conlon, and four armed men to the second floor.

Reid said, "We brought in a full staff here just for you, thirty-seven guards. Personally, I don't think we'll need them."

I heard him speaking, but I didn't bother listening to him. I thought about death tolls; mine kept on rising. Along with every man under my command, I had the reprogramming of Jim Holman on my conscience. As far as I was concerned, reprogramming was as bad as death. Holman and his men had become slaves.

"We also have a surgeon on staff," said Reid. "Personally, I consider the guards an unnecessary redundancy, but Mr. Andropov . . ."

My cell was ten feet wide and twelve feet long, with brick walls and no windows. It had a cot, a toilet, and a sink. I spotted it because it was the only cell with an open door and lights.

As we wheeled closer to the door, I saw that what I had mistaken for a cot was more like a gurney. It was too tall for a cot.

"We will keep you on an incapacitation cage," said Reid. "You will be paralyzed, but . . ."

They wheeled me past my cell and down the hall, to the "little shop of horrors"; that was the military term for prison infirmaries. *The Little Shop of Horrors.*

We marched down the open hall past dozens of darkened cells and turned a corner. For the first time that day, I struggled. I pulled at the cuffs and tried to break my legs free.

"Is something wrong?" Jeremy Reid asked.

I couldn't break free. I tried, but I wouldn't have been able to break free even if I'd been healthy.

The corridor snaked on past the cell block and deep into the prison. We passed a doorway that opened to a small holotorium, in which prisoners would have been allowed to watch movies. We passed a staff room, in which guards would have chatted and played games with other guards during their breaks. We passed a doorway that would have led us down to the prison yard in which dead clone guards now rotted in a mass grave.

They had me. Speck it all, they had me.

I struggled, but I had no hope of escape. They would take me into that infirmary, and they would inject me or gas me. Their surgeon would insert two conduction fibers into the spot where my spinal cord met my brain, and I would lie on that table helpless, unable to wag a finger or twitch a toe.

We turned a corner, and I saw a lit doorway. The sanitary scents of alcohol and disinfectant wafted out of the doorway. I struggled against those straps, leaning this way and that, trying to pull my wrists and ankles free, fighting to break the unbreakable strap around my chest.

The entire facility was air-conditioned. The air was cold, not stale but not fresh. The hall was dark except for the dim sunlight coming through the windows and the light from the infirmary . . . the Little Shop. I twisted my chest and shoulders to the left and to the right, but my head and pelvis remained fixed. I wouldn't escape. I couldn't give up.

A man waited for me just inside the infirmary. He wore a surgical gown and carried a six-inch canister with an inhaling mask. The prison butcher came closer and raised the mask. I tried to move away. I tried to turn my head. I tried to hold my breath.

29

I had placed a few prisoners on incapacitation cages during my career, and now I regretted it. This wasn't just storage, it was torture. I knew the electricity would paralyze me, but I didn't realize how it would feel. The electricity made my muscles contract, stiffening my arms, legs, and back. I lay on the gurney with my legs out straight and my arms by my side. It didn't matter that the muscles were tired, I couldn't move them.

I could talk, and I could shut my eyes. I could flare my nostrils, hold my breath, and furl my eyebrows. Everything else was just a memory.

Even above the pain, it was the helplessness that bothered me most. Thompson, the soldier who told me about Terraneau, came in to tell me stories about torturing clones. He brought his lunch in with him one day, placing his sandwich, chips, and apple on my stomach, knowing I couldn't manage enough movement to shake them off.

At some point, one of the guards released a couple of flies in my cell. I heard him enter the cell and unscrew the lid, but he stood behind my table. I couldn't turn to see who did it.

I should have been grateful; he could have brought a wasp or yellow jacket or an entire hive of bees; I wouldn't have been able to stop him. He released a couple of chubby little house flies that buzzed around the cell until they spotted me.

I never saw them except when they hovered over my eyes. They darted in and out of my vision as they explored the room. Eventually, they realized that the only thing of interest was me, and then they approached, circling like sharks.

Every time the surgeon changed my drip, he scrubbed me with some pungent disinfectant which drove the flies from my arms. I had socks on my feet and long pants, but my face was uncovered. They must have landed on my table and on my body, but I couldn't see or hear or feel them. I had no means to shoo them away. I yelled and tried to blow at them when they came near my face, but landing on my stomach or legs and walking around unchallenged, the flies soon realized they had nothing to fear.

Not covered by clothing, my face was the only edible thing in the room. The flies landed on my cheeks and walked over my nose and lips. I blinked my eyes furiously when one of them strolled over my cheek.

At some point, the flies found something more interesting than my face. Eventually, they went away entirely. I don't know if they died of old age or escaped, but they disappeared from my life.

Along with the filaments in my neck, the doctor had plugged an intravenous drip into my arm. Now that I had a U.A. saline drip poking my arm, I realized that the doctor down in the Territories must have placed some kind of narcotic in saline, something that left me drowsy and relatively cheerful as well as hydrating me.

Time passed so slowly.

I tried to sleep. Now that I was nearly rehydrated, I was too healthy to hallucinate. My dreams only came as I slept.

An officer came to visit me, a general. He stepped into the room, made sure I could see him, and started reciting some litany he must have rehearsed a thousand times. He said, "Well, Wayson Harris, conqueror of worlds." Then he stopped, smelled the air, and spoke to someone hiding outside my range of view. He said, "Holy hell! What is that stink?"

That stink was me. Along with cutting off any control of my limbs, the electrical current ended my influence over my bowels. The surgeon didn't bother inserting catheters into my system during my visit to the Little Shop of Horrors, so any extrusions I might have made remained in my pants. Normally, this would have embarrassed me, but seeing how it flustered that pompous U.A. general, I found myself amused.

He tried to fan the air away from his nose. A moment later, he stormed out of my cell.

Now you know what interested the flies more than my face.

30

Thanks to that general, the Unifieds occasionally allowed me to climb off my cage. They gave me ten-minute windows to walk around my cell and cut the current anytime I even hinted about using the latrine.

My "exercise periods" were a joke. The incapacitation cage left me too weak to stand more than a few seconds at a time, but I was getting stronger quickly.

I missed the hydrating formula Pugh's doctor gave me at Mazatlan. That drip left me weak but feeling mended, a pleasant illusion. His medicine hadn't healed me, but it left me feeling relaxed.

Despite everything, I still had managed to keep Pugh's disposable thermal pack. As time passed, it became the focus of my thoughts. I still hadn't used it. I didn't want to use it. Once I did, I would have nothing left.

I began examining it during my "exercise periods." It took a few tries, but I eventually figured the damn thing out.

The moment started with a guard's saying, "Okay, Harris, you have ten minutes."

Steeling my head for a bout of nausea, I climbed from the incapacitation cage and stretched, then I pulled the thermal pack from the spot where I kept it on the sink. Knowing full well that the Unifieds observed my every move, I opened the pack as if confirming that its chemical stick was still intact. I pulled the stick out and inspected it—a tiny cylinder, maybe an inch long, a quarter of an inch in diameter, a clear plastic housing filled with a pearl-colored gas. Still playacting, I fumbled with the chemical stick as I attempted to reinsert it and allowed it to fall into the pack. It sank into the gel and marbles, giving me a chance to examine the pack's insides more closely as I tweezed the stick free.

The marbles looked normal, completely normal, in fact. I certainly didn't find a grenade. Just as I was about to write the pack off as being exactly what it appeared to be, my finger brushed across a strip of cloth running through the gel, which was exactly where it ought not to have been. When the gel froze, that cloth would freeze with it.

As casually as I could, I pulled at the cloth with my fingers. It was like a sleeve, maybe a hilt for an ice pick or something. It was flat and about an inch wide, sewed tight and water-resistant so that nothing soaked in or out of it. As I pinched it between my thumb and forefinger, I found a thin stream of viscous liquid ran through it. I only spent a couple of seconds toying with the sleeve; anything more than that would have attracted unwanted attention.

As I closed the pack up and returned it to its spot on my sink, I tried to figured out what Pugh had given me and why. If that sleeve froze, it would be long and thin like the blade of a knife . . . a liquid knife. That was gel inside the sleeve. When I snapped the stick, the gel would freeze and form a blade. It wouldn't be much of a blade. Like any ice, it would have no tensile strength, but I could use it to kill myself.

As I considered this, I decided that Pugh would have had something else in mind. If he'd wanted me to die, he could have killed me. He'd had plenty of opportunity.

Speaking over the intercom, Major Conlon said, "Okay, Harris, back on your cage."

When he said for me to climb back on my cage, he meant for me to lie down with my head in the center of the table so that the electrical current would run through the diodes in my neck. The first time he told me to get back on the cage, I laughed at him. I expected him to threaten me, and he lived up to my expectations, but not in the way I expected.

He tapped on the window in my door with a silver canister about the size of a coffee mug. He didn't even need to tell me what was in it. I saw the canister and climbed on the table without saying a word.

They couldn't reprogram me, but I hated what that shit did to my head. It felt like waking up from a seizure.

They only had to show it to me once; after that, I became their trained circus animal. Anytime anyone knocked on the door, I climbed onto the incapacitation cage and waited for the electrical current to disable me.

I had no concept of days or time. I had no idea how long I had been in that cell when I finally decoded the thermal pack's secret.

Conlon entered my cell and chatted with me regularly. Was it daily? If so, I spent twenty days in that prison. He visited me twenty times. He began our latest meeting by asking, "How are you doing today, Harris?"

I looked up at him, and said, "I'm being electrocuted. How the speck are you?"

We began every visit that way. That was our handshake.

A patriotic man, Major Conlon wanted to prove to me that my clones had started the war. He blamed us for everything. On this occasion, his topic of choice was New Copenhagen, the final battle of the alien invasion. By the time we stopped the Avatari on New Copenhagen, they had already captured 178 of the 180 colonized worlds.

He asked me, "You fought on New Copenhagen didn't you? I heard the natural-born officers won that battle all by themselves."

I said, "That's interesting."

"That's not how you saw it?" he asked.

"Have you ever seen U.A. officers single-handedly win any other battles?" I asked.

He didn't answer.

I thought about killing him. I couldn't do it at the moment, but sooner or later he'd make a mistake. Maybe he'd walk into my cell without checking to make sure my cage was on. I'd freeze the thermal pack and stab the ice into his heart. I was slowly recovering my strength; with it came thoughts of revenge.

I said, "The Unified Authority sent nine hundred thousand clones to New Copenhagen. Thirty thousand survived. There were ninety thousand officers. Sixty thousand survived the battle. One in thirty clones survived. Two out of three officers walked away.

"If the clones spent the entire battle running away, they didn't do a very good job of it."

Conlon said, "I can verify those statistics."

"Help yourself."

Conlon said, "You fought on the Mogat home world, too."

I asked him how he knew that. Having searched my files, I knew that the Unifieds redacted my military records so that they no longer reflected my involvement in the civil war.

He walked out of the cell without answering.

* * *

Sunny visited me.

I didn't know it was her until after she entered the cell. I'd been sitting on my cage looking at the thermal pack and contemplating my future. Conlon spoke over the intercom. He said, "Harris, back on your cage." I reached to replace the pack on the sink, but he said, "Back on your cage now!"

I placed the pack on the table beside me and lay back so the current could run through me.

I heard the cell door open and thought maybe Conlon had come for another chat. I heard footsteps, and then Sunny Ferris stepped into view. She looked beautiful, her brown hair as lustrous as mink, her blue dress pinching all the right places. I made the mistake of staring into her eyes.

She looked at me and a certain amount of irony and mirth surfaced in her expression. She said, "Wayson Harris, I almost didn't recognize you without your beard."

She was so beautiful. Just looking at her hurt.

"What are you doing here?" I asked.

"I wanted to visit you."

"Delilah visiting Samson in his prison," I said.

"Oh, Wayson, I'm a lot more treacherous than Delilah," she said. "I haven't just plucked out your eyes and cut off your hair, dear, I've caused your entire nation to disappear."

I said, "I know what you did to me in the underwater city. I saw the video feed."

She blushed, and said, "Well that's embarrassing. Still, we had fun. You seemed to enjoy it."

"That's not what I saw. I wanted to kill you."

"You loved me."

We both went silent. I didn't want to speak, but my curiosity got the better of me. I said, "You had a spy in the Linear Committee Building. Who was it?"

"Of course we had people inside the LCB, dear. We had to keep an eye on you."

"Who was it?" I asked.

She didn't answer.

I hoped it was General Strait though I suspected it wasn't. I never liked him. Neither did MacAvoy or Hauser. We almost always left him out of the loop.

"Was it Watson?" I asked. *He's the weasel,* I thought. *I should have seen it from the start. I should have known he was weak from the start.*

Sunny said, "Watson . . . Watson . . . You wouldn't happen to know where we could find him, would you? He's a war criminal, you know. He's wanted for high treason."

"Love him like a son," I said. I was only four years older than him, but he still had some of the youthful misconceptions I'd lost as a teen. He'd seen plenty of war over the last few months; maybe the misconceptions were gone.

I coughed and groaned. Coughing on the incapacitation cage felt like taking a knee to the gut.

She stared down at me, and said, "Wayson, you're falling apart." She stroked her hand across my chest and stomach. I would have recoiled from her if I could have. Beautiful as she was, the sight of her repelled me. How many people had she murdered? Sure, she didn't see them as people; to her they were "synthetics."

Narcissistic, sadomasochist nymph that she was, Sunny must have actually thought that I couldn't resist her charms. She stroked me again, this time starting at my chest and trailing down to my pelvis. She said in a slow, flirtatious whisper, "Wayson, what's wrong? You're usually much more receptive."

She stroked me again, and frustration showed in her expression. Her eyes, narrowed. She pursed her lips.

She was desirable and treacherous, as beautiful as a Venus

or Aphrodite and more dangerous than a sea filled with sharks. Having overseen my brainwashing, she still believed that she owned me, that she understood my every synapse. She laughed, and said, "But you're incapacitated."

I said nothing, but as I looked into her eyes, I saw something I had never noticed before. Sunny was insane. She stared down at me, favoring me with a seductive *come-hither* gaze, thinking that her look of longing would erase every impulse from my brain.

She ran her hand across my face. It was cool to the touch, not cold, but cool. Still battling the flu, I always felt too cold or too hot. At that moment, I felt hot, and her touch soothed me. She placed her hand on my forehead. It felt like a splash of cool water on a summer day.

"You have a fever," she said. "You're hot."

I said nothing.

She ran her fingers along my jaw and down my neck. I hated this woman; she was repulsive. I wanted her and wished she would touch me everywhere. It was as if my brain had been torn into two independent halves, one filled with disgust and hate and sensibility, the other consumed by animal desires. I wanted to kill her. I wished she would lay her body across mine like a satin sheet.

Staring into my eyes, fixing me the way a snake fixes on its prey before it strikes, she climbed onto the gurney. She swung a thigh over my body. We were both dressed, this hadn't yet become sex.

"Shut off the cage," she called to no one in particular, and the electrical current dissolved from my brain.

My shoulders dropped. My arms went limp. My neck and stomach relaxed. My fingers found the thermal pack. I snapped the stick, and the knife became rigid. I grabbed the pack and rammed it into her stomach. The blade cut through the gel and the Mylar, through her clothes and her flesh, and I stabbed it deep into her abdomen. As she sat above me silent and stunned,

I pulled the blade across her stomach, cutting so deeply that the point rolled across her spine. Her blood splashed out readily; it practically fell out of her.

I unzipped her gut quickly, so quickly that the pain hadn't registered until it was already too late for her to scream. Shock showed in her watery blue eyes, and her lips puckered as if forming a question. Sunny fell on me, then rolled from my body. She tried to catch herself as she fell from the gurney, but she had no strength in her arms.

That knife had been my only escape. I might have been able to use it to escape if I had waited for the right moment, and I could certainly have used it to kill myself to deprive Andropov of the pleasure of executing me; instead, I had left myself trapped and helpless, but as I watched Sunny slowly slip from the table, I decided that the pleasure of killing her had been worth whatever came next.

The door of my cell flew open. Conlon ran in first, followed by three enlisted men. He placed his hands under Sunny's arms and propped her up, allowing the other men to grab hold of her. She was still alive, but I had gutted her like a fish; she would not live much longer. Her skin had already turned to the color of whitest marble. Her tropical blue eyes had glazed over, and the color had drained from her lips. Her head lolled as two enlisted men lifted her, the third trying to stanch her bleeding.

"Get her to the infirmary!" Conlon shouted at his men.

One of the men took her in his arms, holding her the way new grooms carry their brides.

As soon as they left the cell, Conlon turned to me, and whispered, "Freeman said you'd do something stupid."

Part II

THE RESCUERS

31

DATE: AUGUST 19, 2519

The call came after midnight, making it August 19. Ray Freeman knew that Harris had captured territory on the east side of the Anacostia, that much had been on the news. He also knew that the attack had been a feint, and that Harris's real objective had been to save Travis Watson. He hadn't yet spoken with Harris and had no idea how that part of the mission had resolved.

Answering the phone before the second ring, Freeman said, "Hello. Who is this?"

The security circuit in his communications console altered his voice so that he sounded like a little girl. When calls came with audio/video connection, his console displayed him as a ten-year-old girl, syncing the voice to the image.

Freeman knew his audio disguise wouldn't stand up to computer analysis, but it rendered his voice unrecognizable to the human ear, and that sufficed.

The man on the other end of the connection said, "Raymond, this is Howard Tasman."

Freeman knew Tasman; he'd protected the neural scientist from U.A. soldiers on Mars. Recognizing the voice, Freeman routed the call through his security equipment and saw that the voice was genuine.

Tasman waited for Freeman to say something. After a few seconds, he said, "Look, Freeman, the Enlisted Man's Empire is about to collapse."

"How do you know?" Freeman asked as he climbed from his bed. He had an emergency kit packed and ready and sitting under his bed. The pack included a few small weapons, a change of clothes, rudimentary surveillance equipment, and money. Working as a mercenary, Freeman had made himself rich.

"We have their computer files."

Along with his emergency kit, Freeman took a pistol and a knife.

"Wayson Harris asked me to decode the files."

Freeman put on pants and a shirt.

"Harris's girlfriend works for the Unified Authority."

"Kasara Pugh?" asked Freeman. His voice betrayed no emotion, neither interest nor surprise.

"Who?" asked Tasman. When Freeman didn't answer, he said, "His girlfriend, Sunny Ferris."

Though he had never met her, Freeman knew the name.

Tasman said, "The U.A. is making its move, and she's involved. Whatever it is, it's already begun."

Freeman considered this. An attack of some sort, why hadn't he heard about it? Harris would have told him.

"Have you told Harris about it?" asked Freeman.

"I wanted to warn you first."

"I'm not part of this war," said Freeman. He was dressed, and he had his kit and his weapon.

Tasman paused and lowered his voice to a whisper. He said, "I found a file that lists Unified Authority targets. I'm on it, so is Watson."

"And I'm on it?" asked Freeman.

"The only person they want more than you is Harris."

Freeman said, "The Unified Authority has wanted me dead for a long time. They'd have killed me by now if they could have found me."

Tasman said, "Ray, I got your number from their files."

32

Before he moved into any of his apartments, Freeman wired them with security systems. He had cameras and listening devices in the walls and motion detectors in the floors and ceilings. Microscopic fibers conducted electrical currents between the windows and the sills around them. The same fibers created circuits between the doors and their jambs. Opening doors or windows would break the currents, setting off silent alarms.

Freeman took other precautions as well. He'd placed miniature motion-sensing robots called "trackers" under his furniture. Little more than a swiveling shaft with an arm and a motion sensor, trackers spotted targets and fired weapons at them. Freeman's miniature trackers fired Taser jacks—highly electrified staples that packed enough voltage to paralyze a grizzly bear.

Freeman kept a safe in the closet in his office. But instead of valuables, it held a canister of toxic gas.

Having spoken with Tasman, Freeman searched his apartment from top to bottom, arming traps, checking cameras, and destroying computers. He wouldn't stay in the apartment, not if the Unifieds knew the location. They might come after him, but they were just as likely to demolish the building with a rocket.

Taking only his weapons and his emergency kit, Freeman left his home, locking the door behind him. He took the elevator to the three-story parking garage. His car waited on the third floor of the garage, but he stepped off the elevator on the second floor, found a sports car with darkened windows and a low roof, and stole it so smoothly anybody watching would have thought he owned it.

He didn't fit in the car, but that was why he'd chosen it. No one would look for a seven-foot giant in a sleek roadster like this Cerulean 750Z. His knees brushed against the dashboard, and the steering wheel pushed against his lap, but if Unified Authority commandos were searching for him, they wouldn't give the car a second glance.

The 750Z's racy engine didn't matter to Freeman. He drove out of the parking structure, headed two blocks west, and ditched the Z in an alley. He used the car as a disguise; now that he was out of the building, he abandoned it.

Large as he was, and hobbled by a slight limp, Freeman glided through alleyways as silent as a ghost, moving slowly, allowing his eyes to adjust between moonlight and shadow.

It took Freeman nearly an hour to travel the two miles to his destination, which was a building beside the one he had just left. By the time he arrived, he had confirmed that no one was following him. He entered through the service entrance.

The building Freeman now entered was nicer than the one in which he lived. It had a more elegant lobby and nicer apartments. Freeman checked the halls, then slipped into the elevator and rode to the thirty-fifth floor.

Freeman unlocked the door and let himself in. This wasn't his apartment; he kept it as a safe house. He had more and better security here than in the apartment across the street.

Freeman entered his nest at 03:37. He didn't need to arm traps or power sensors, the equipment booted the moment he opened the door.

He was tired; but needing information more than sleep, he went to his computer and began looking up police and hospital reports. A battle had just been waged on the outskirts of Washington, D. C. There had been gunfights, casualties, and fires. The hospitals were packed. The police were busy.

Freeman knew about the clone attack, Harris had asked him to join in. That was the clones attacking the Unified Authority; Tasman had said something about the aggression coming from the other direction.

Freeman began checking hospital reports outside the capital area. It didn't take long before he found his answer. Clones were sick. California, Connecticut, Florida . . . hospitals in areas with major military installations reported admitting large numbers of clones.

By 06:00, having found what he needed, he went to sleep. Freeman stretched out on his cot still dressed and holding his pistol. It took him less than five minutes to fall into a meditative state.

At 06:25, the soft buzz of the first alarm woke him. Somebody was attempting to enter the apartment in the building next door. He heard the alarm and rolled off the cot. A second alarm sounded two minutes later, warning him that someone was at the door of this nest as well. Freeman remained calm.

Carrying an S9 fléchette-firing pistol and computerized goggles, he went to the door. The S9 was silent and carried enough depleted uranium to fire one hundred shots. The goggles had been configured to interface with his security cameras.

He looked through the pinhead-sized camera over his door.

Three men stood in the hall, all of them dressed like civilians. Using the goggles, he peered through cameras he had placed around the building, one in the lobby, another overlooking the street.

He spotted two cars idling near the front of the building, each filled with young and athletic-looking men in civilian clothes. Another car waited behind the building.

One of the men outside Freeman's door used a magnetic key to override the main lock. The two old-fashioned bolts Freeman used to latch the door from the inside remained unmoved. Every bit as anxious to interrogate the invaders as they were to collar him, Freeman unlocked the bolts and stepped back from the door.

Several seconds passed before the invaders realized they could open the door, and it swung open. This was the moment. Freeman crouched in a corner, hidden but not protected by his overturned cot. He had his lights off and his S9 was ready. He had his goggles and could see in the dark.

The first man darted into the apartment. Freeman allowed him to pass through the doorway and into the darkened hallway before shooting him through the neck and the head. The other two entered.

Their guns had suppressors; they fired bullets. They shot at the cot, the place Freeman had been.

Using the night-for-day lenses in his goggles, Freeman watched the two men as they split up. *Imbeciles,* he thought. One problem with Unified Authority's special operations was that it had relied on clones for too long. Now that the recruits were natural-borns, and the clones were enemies, the U.A. didn't have any experienced agents or trainers.

The apartment was shaped like a U, with one hallway leading past and into the kitchen to the living room and a second hallway leading to the bedrooms and bathrooms. Hiding behind the computer desk in the living room, Freeman surveyed the situation.

One of the commandos searched the kitchen. He ran a hand along the wall in search of a light switch. The second stood just inside the doorway, his pistol raised and ready.

Freeman shot the one by the door three times, hitting him in the throat, the chest, and the forehead. When his partner came running out of the kitchen, Freeman grabbed him by the throat, lifted him off the ground, and slammed his head and back onto the floor.

Freeman could have killed the man, but he needed him alive. He had questions he needed answered.

33

Freeman stole a truck, drove north to Bethesda, and parked in the visitor's parking lot at Walter Reed Military Medical Center. He knew the hospital would be infested with Unifieds, but that variable was out of his control.

The men guarding Watson would undoubtedly recognize him as well, but that couldn't be helped. He would need to watch for people who were watching him. He'd done that many times throughout his career.

Walter Reed had several buildings, but only one had the kind of security needed to protect an important man like Travis Watson. Looking down from the third floor of the parking garage, Freeman scoured the grounds. He spotted men who might have been commandos near the entrance and all along the street.

Freeman could have picked them off; he'd brought an excellent rifle. But killing those men would only bring reinforcements, and the new commandos would be more alert. He needed them there, assuring their bosses that everything was under control until the absolute final moment, the moment when everything would go cataclysmically wrong.

One thing about hospitals, they had tunnels and service alleys. They had underground loading areas only emergency crews could access. Properly guarding the entire hospital would have required an army. Freeman didn't think the Unified Authority would have that kind of manpower for another day or two.

Lacking men, the U.A. commandos would concentrate their efforts on the entrances to the building and the door to Watson's room. Getting into the building would be easy enough, but Freeman expected to run into trouble when he reached Watson's floor.

Having spent nearly an hour studying the layout of the hospital on his computer, Freeman knew what he needed to do. He took the stairs to the lowest level of the parking structure, a third-level basement compete with generators, heavy equipment, and a labyrinth of service halls. A tall man in a janitor's uniform circled the area aimlessly. He might have been a civilian, but Freeman identified him as a spook.

Killing him would have been easy, but he might have been part of an early-warning system. If he disappeared, his teammates would go on alert.

Freeman waited in the stairwell nearly a minute, giving the man time to walk away. When he opened the door, the man had moved on.

The hall ran endlessly ahead, a dim but thoroughly lit tunnel, too bright to hide in but too dark for reading. The place was a maze, with doorways leading to laboratories and facility closets. The grumble of industrial air-conditioning units and laundry facilities carried through the corridor.

Long and straight, the hall was an assassin's nightmare. There was no place to hide. As he moved through the hall, Freeman saw people walking in his direction, and they could see him. The first people he passed were doctors, but if they'd been Unifieds, there would have been trouble.

Three-quarters of the way down the hall, Freeman passed a gurney with a body bag spread across it. The bag was occupied.

Why place it here? Freeman wondered. *Why not in the morgue?* Like every other hospital, Walter Reed had a morgue; it was right nearby.

The cadaver could only have been a clone. With the Enlisted Man's Empire in control, Walter Reed seldom admitted natural-borns.

Thinking that perhaps this might be an early victim of the Unified Authority's new weapon, Freeman decided to take a quick look at the body. He waited a minute to make sure the hall was empty, then he pushed the gurney down a small branching corridor with few doors and no visible traffic.

Body bags included a chemical stick like the one in Harris's thermal pack. Whoever had placed the corpse in the bag had snapped the stick, freezing the dead man. He lay in his wrapping as stiff as a signpost.

Placing a hand over the man's head, Freeman unzipped the bag. Freezing air rose out of the bag in cotton-fiber swirls that evaporated quickly. Freeman peeled the bag open and searched the body for wounds.

The man had been stripped before he'd been frozen. Freeman noticed that he had the skinny shoulders and softened physique of an older man, possibly a man in his fifties. His muscles hadn't gone to seed so much as lost the sculpted look of youth.

Still looking for a killing injury, Freeman turned the dead man on his side. The frozen body remained rigid. There were no wounds to be found, no bruising, no cuts, no discolorations. The hall was dark, and Freeman would have needed a flashlight to be sure, but he thought he found beads of frozen blood on the dead clone's ear.

Freeman knew all about the death reflex. He rolled the clone onto his back and resealed the bag.

Once he saw that the hall was empty, Freeman rolled the gurney back to the spot where he had found it. Walking on, he passed more gurneys. He turned a corner and found occupied gurneys parked end to end all along the hall that led to the morgue. After checking the hall to make sure he was alone, he pushed through the swinging doors and entered.

The man who met Freeman as he entered the morgue was a clone who looked deathly ill. He was pale. Exhaustion showed on his face. He had swollen, red eyes. Looking surprised that a natural-born giant had entered his domain, the mortician pulled down his procedure mask, and asked, "Who are you?"

"I'm Ray Freeman," said Freeman.

Looking around the morgue, he saw bodies everywhere, some under sheets and some in bags. They were stacked four deep on a couple of examination tables. Little red lights flashed on the handles of the body lockers along the back wall, marking them all as "occupied."

"As you can see, Mr. Freeman, I'm a bit busy," said the clone. He coughed, and muttered, "Damn. I think I might have it."

"Have what?" asked Freeman.

"There's a flu going around," snapped the clone mortician.

Freeman didn't travel in wide circles, but he hadn't seen any signs of a flu epidemic in the civilian world. Cogs meshed in his mind. *The Unifieds have something big,* Tasman had said. Now a flu epidemic had spread among the clones without spreading into the natural-born world. "Is that what killed these men?"

The clone rolled his eyes, and said, "I don't see how this is any business of yours. You shouldn't be here, Mr. Freeman. This is a restricted area."

Freeman responded with his size and his menacing body language. He stepped toward the mortician, then walked around him and examined a corpse that had not yet been flash-frozen. He placed a hand on the dead man's chin and turned it.

"This man appears to have bloodstains on his ears."

"I cleaned him a couple of times; apparently he's still leaking. Sometimes it lasts for hours," said the mortician.

"He had a death reflex?" asked Freeman.

"Who the speck are you?" the clone repeated. "Are you a reporter?"

Freeman didn't answer.

"Are you a doctor?"

Freeman shook his head. He asked, "Am I correct in assuming this man had a death reflex?"

The mortician coughed. He muttered, "Damn cold. My head hurts. My back's stiff. I'm not sure why I reported for work this morning."

Reported for work, thought Freeman. *Not quite military speak, and not quite civilian.* He asked, "What triggered the reflex?"

The mortician shook his head. He said, "I wish I knew. We've lost forty-two clones in the last twenty-four hours, all killed by a death reflex. If you ask me, this qualifies as an epidemic."

Freeman nodded. He asked, "Did they die here?" He looked back at the cadaver, noting the streaks of white in his hair. The dead clone's face had wrinkles around the eyes and the corners of the mouth.

"Yes they did. It's the damnedest thing, they all checked in complaining about flu symptoms. I have the same flu they had. If I didn't know I was natural-born, I'd be really scared about now."

Freeman reached the end of the hall and took the stairs up to the lobby. He entered a cavernous floor space swarming with men who stood five-foot-ten and wore their brown hair cropped short. Their coughing swept in waves around the lobby.

Freeman spotted three civilian men scattered among the clones and they spotted him as well.

The clones were all military men. They stood in razor-straight lines and waited their turns. The civilians were not so constrained. Seeing Freeman, one of them spoke into the discreet microphone in his collar. They all turned and started toward him.

Freeman waded through the sea of clones like an icebreaker pushing through thin summer ice. He didn't pull his gun, and he didn't worry about the U.A. agents pulling theirs; this was a room filled with soldiers. Sick or healthy, the first man to pull a weapon would be mobbed.

Freeman reached an open elevator before the men who were following him could push through the clones. He stepped in and pressed the button for the twenty-ninth floor.

As the elevator doors closed, he watched the natural-borns and practiced his breathing, slowing his heart rate as he pulled his pistol.

The elevator doors opened on the twenty-ninth.

The hall was crowded with patients, nurses, doctors, medics, and orderlies. Hiding his pistol in his pocket, Freeman pushed past medics and patients on his way to a stairwell at the other end of the hall. From his studies earlier that morning, he knew the location of the stairwell, and the short distance between the door and Watson's hospital room.

He took the stairs to the thirtieth floor.

A man with a gun stood peering through the door at the top of the stairs. Freeman shot him in the face with his S9. The fléchette-firing stealth gun used electronics instead of combustion, providing nearly silent operation. Freeman shot the man in the face, he fell to the floor, and Freeman pulled him into the stairwell.

The men in the elevator had done exactly what Freeman had hoped they would do; they had attracted attention. Focused on catching Freeman, they had burst out of the elevator, guns raised and ready. Instead of Freeman, they had stumbled into the clones guarding Watson's floor.

As a former interim president of the Enlisted Man's Empire, Travis Watson was an important man. Harris had posted bodyguards in Watson's hospital suite, outside his door, and watching the elevator. As the guards standing outside the room and the ones by the elevator converged on the Unified Authority commandos, Freeman crossed the short space between the stairwell and Watson's door.

He opened the door and three men pointed M27s at him. Freeman looked beyond the bodyguards into the living room, where Watson sat alone on a couch, his legs stretched straight across the cushions.

Freeman said, "You need to get out of here."

Watson smiled at Freeman, and shouted, "Hey, M, come on out; Ray's here."

34

Freeman raised his hands in the air and let the bodyguards search him. After finding his S9 pistol and his knife, one of the bodyguards started to radio in for help.

"Wait," said Watson. "I can vouch for this man. He's a friend."

Watson had six guards in his room; all of them had the flu. Some were sicker than others. A few coughed sporadically. One never stopped coughing. In the few minutes that Freeman watched him, he vacillated from hot sweats to cold shivers and back.

Freeman said, "Travis, you and I should have a private word."

"What about M?" asked Watson. He sat on a couch dressed in loose pants and a tee shirt, looking more sloppy than casual. He had gained back most of the weight he'd lost while on the lam. The new pounds looked soft.

He showed no signs of having a cold.

Emily looked good. Freeman could tell that she'd been

exercising and probably eating better than Watson as well. She wore a bright blue dress that fit her perfectly. Like Watson, she showed no signs of illness.

Believing that Emily would take the threat more seriously than Watson, Freeman looked at her and said, "This concerns you as well."

"We can't leave," said one of the bodyguards.

"What?" Watson asked.

"They're not allowed to let you out of their sight," said Freeman.

"That's ridiculous," said Watson. "Go get a cup of coffee or something."

The bodyguards didn't move.

Watson's hospital room was like a penthouse suite. It had multiple bedrooms, a kitchen, and an office. Freeman pointed to the office, which had window walls, and asked, "How about if we go in there?"

"How do you know this man?" one of the bodyguards asked.

"He's tight with General Harris," said Watson. "I'd lay heavy odds that Harris was the one who sent him."

"Did General Harris send you?" asked the bodyguard.

Freeman shook his head.

"Nice going," said Watson.

The bodyguard said, "Look, they caught three men with guns coming up the elevators."

"They were chasing me," said Freeman.

"See? He came here to save me," said Watson.

The bodyguards didn't move.

"Guys, this is Mr. Ray Freeman. He may in fact be the most dangerous psychopath in the universe, but he's on our side. If he wanted to kill me, he would have blown up the hospital."

As Watson spoke, Freeman sat on an empty love seat. There were two empty chairs as well, but Freeman was too big to fit in them comfortably, and he'd done enough squeezing into tight spaces the night before.

When the bodyguards still didn't leave, Watson said, "Go! Scat! Be gone with you!"

More serious and more subdued, Emily said, "Ray has saved our lives on more than one occasion, Lieutenant Marks. We'll be safe."

Marks, the highest-ranking bodyguard, glared at Freeman, and said, "You can talk in the office if you need privacy, but we're not leaving."

Emily said, "Thank you, Lieutenant." She led Freeman into the office. Watson followed, shutting the door behind him. He sat on the desk, and asked, "Okay, Ray, what is this about?"

Freeman told them about Howard Tasman's call and the attack on both his nest and his apartment.

Watson whistled.

Emily asked, "Do you think they can do it? Can they beat the clones?"

Freeman leaned forward and fixed her with a facial expression he hoped would come across as concerned instead of menacing. He said, "They already have."

Feeling menaced, mistaking Freeman's glare as a sign that he preferred to speak with Watson, Emily backed away from him.

Freeman asked, "Have you been outside your room?"

Emily didn't say anything. Watson shook his head. "They won't let us near the door."

"So you have no idea what's happening out there?" Freeman asked.

"What's happening?" asked Emily.

"This hospital is like an anthill. There are lines of clones in every clinic and more clones lining up outside the doors. I passed the morgue on my way in. There are so many bodies in the basement that they're stacking them on top of each other."

Emily put a hand on her chest, and said, "That's awful!"

"What's killing them?" asked Watson.

"They have the flu," said Freeman.

"The flu?" Watson sounded unconvinced.

"All six of our guys have the flu," said Emily. "Marks and Whiting have bad coughs."

"All of them are coughing," said Freeman. "I've been watching them since I came in. They're all coughing, some more than others."

"Do you think they have it?" Watson asked. He meant the question more for himself than for Freeman.

"It can't be that contagious," Watson said, brightening a bit. "M and I haven't gotten it."

Emily, who had some emergency training, asked, "The flu isn't going to affect us, is it?"

Freeman shook his head.

"Only clones catch it?"

Freeman didn't answer; it was answer enough.

Emily whispered the word, "Speck." She looked at Freeman, stared into his dark, wide-spaced eyes. She asked, "Are they all going to catch it?"

Freeman nodded.

Watson was a smart guy, but Emily was more alert and more serious. Freeman preferred speaking with her. He said, "The Unified Authority must have created a virus that only infects clones. From what I can tell, it's spread everywhere."

"What about Harris?" asked Watson.

"I haven't spoken to him," Freeman admitted. "His DNA is almost identical to every other clone's. If they caught it, he'll catch it, too."

"What do they die from, the fever?" asked Emily.

Freeman said, "The clones in the morgue died from death reflexes."

"What? How can that . . . That doesn't make sense," said Watson. "They only have death reflexes when they find out they're clones. What are you saying, that the flu makes them realize they're clones?"

Freeman didn't answer. He stood staring through the glass at the clones on the other side. The bodyguards returned his stare. The clone Emily had called "Marks" coughed. Unlike the others, who were in their thirties, Marks had touches of white in his hair and eyebrows.

His eyes still on Marks, Freeman said, "The corpses I saw were old by clone standards, men in their fifties."

"Weakened resistance," said Emily.

"What?" Watson asked.

"As people grow older, their immune systems become weaker," said Emily. "Back when they used to have plagues, the babies and old people died first."

Freeman said, "Maybe it's not a death reflex that kills them. What if the virus attacks the gland, like a viral key that unlocks the hormone?"

Feeling a wave of panic washing over him, Watson said, "But that can't happen to all of them; I mean, how many of them have died so far?"

Freeman didn't answer.

Still struggling, Watson said, "Can it really get all of them? Every single one of them? What about Harris? He doesn't have the gland."

"Not Harris," Freeman agreed. "He doesn't have a death gland."

"But it will kill the rest of them," said Watson, not wanting to believe what he was saying. He turned to look at his bodyguards, and added, "Including them."

"The Unifieds have commandos scattered throughout the hospital," said Freeman.

Emily asked, "Is there any way to save them?" At that same moment, Watson asked a more practical question, "What are we going to do?"

35

The safest way to exit the building would have been to alert the guards and have them sweep the building of unauthorized natural-borns. By doing that, however, Freeman would have tipped his hand. The U.A. officers in charge would have known he was about to make his move.

Freeman, Watson, and Emily needed to slip out of the building without the commandos spotting them.

At Freeman's direction, Watson called the hospital's chief administrator and arranged for a vehicle, clothing, body bags, and a couple of gurneys. Ten minutes later, the administrator delivered the goods.

Freeman explained his idea.

Lieutenant Marks picked up a pair of scrubs, and asked, "Where do I put my gun?"

Freeman said, "You leave it here."

Marks said, "Then I'm not wearing them. I'm on duty; the gun goes where I go."

Emily picked up a body bag, and said, "There is no way I'm letting you seal me in this."

One of the bodyguards coughed, setting off a chain reaction. First he coughed, then three others followed. After watching the clone convulse as he coughed, Watson spread his body bag across the top of one of the gurneys. He opened the flap, and asked, "Don't these bags freeze whatever's inside them?"

Freeman opened the second bag, reached an arm into the top lining, and pulled out a chemical stick the size of a marker pen. He said, "Pull this out." He handed the bag to Emily, who looked at it and shook her head. She said, "I'm not getting in; it'll give me nightmares for the rest of my life."

Watson asked, "And how long do you think that will be, M?"

She looked at him, anger and shock showing in her blue eyes.

"You don't need to do this," said Marks. "We'll keep you safe. You're safer here than you will be on the street." He coughed a deep, wet series of coughs as he finished the sentence.

Emily said, "Ray, promise me you will pull me out of this bag the moment we're safe."

Freeman nodded, though his definition of "safe" didn't necessarily match hers. Safe, as far as he was concerned, might not happen for an entire day, and he would leave her in the bag as long as he needed.

Marks asked, "Can I hide my gun on the gurney?"

Freeman opened a closet, and said, "Why don't you leave your guns in here?" He posed it as a question, but it was an order, and Watson repeated it.

He said, "We're trying to avoid the bad guys, not shoot them. The idea is to get out without letting them know that we're gone."

"But what if . . ." asked Marks.

"You're supposed to be medics. Medics don't carry the guns," said Emily. She looked Marks in the eye, and said, "If you want to keep us safe, you need to do what he says."

Marks and his men grumbled, but they obeyed. They stripped down to their general-issue skivvies and dressed in the loose-fitting scrubs, leaving their guns in the closet along with their uniforms. They sealed Watson and Emily into body bags and loaded them onto the gurneys.

Freeman left the suite first, walking quickly and silently toward the back of the building, where one of the stairwells ran all the way to the basement. He had sixty-six flights of stairs ahead of him, and his leg already hurt. By the time he reached the bottom, he knew he'd be limping.

Dressed in scrubs, Watson's bodyguards looked like every other cloned hospital worker. They wheeled their gurneys into the hallway and immediately blended in, their anonymity offering better protection than their guns could ever have provided.

They followed Freeman's trail, pushing the gurneys into the service elevator at the back of the building, the same elevator the workers used for transporting dead patients to the morgue. When the elevator doors opened, the only people on it were clones dressed in Army uniforms, both of whom worked for Marks. They traded places. The clones in scrubs wheeled their gurneys onto the elevator and the ones in uniform locked themselves in Watson's suite.

Marks pressed the button for the bottom basement, then muttered, "So far so good," in a voice just loud enough for Watson to hear. Marks and his men rode the elevator down to the basement, then rolled the gurneys to the morgue.

The mortician saw them, and asked, "More bodies?"

Marks said, "These ones are special."

The mortician asked, "What? Do they do tricks or something?

You got stiffs for me, stack 'em over there and clear out."

Marks said, "My orders are to wait down here."

"Orders to wait down here," the mortician repeated, not even attempting to hide his irritation. "Somebody gave you orders to babysit stiffs?"

He nearly didn't finish the statement as Ray Freeman pushed in through the door. "You again? Is this the man who gave you the orders? Just who the speck are you?"

"We ready to go?" Marks asked, ignoring the mortician.

Freeman put up a hand to stop Marks. He went to the mortician, and said, "I have orders to take these bodies to Bethesda for examination." He handed over a set of papers signed by the hospital administrator.

The mortician snatched the papers and read them carefully. He said, "I still don't know who you are," and coughed.

Speaking slowly in his rumbling voice, Freeman said, "I'm the one who's going to stuff you into a body bag if I hear that you mentioned my visit to anyone, anyone at all. Do you understand me?"

The clone nodded. He understood.

Freeman and the bodyguards rolled the gurneys out of the morgue and into the garage. Per Freeman's request, an ambulance sat idling. Marks opened the rear door of the ambulance and loaded the gurneys into the back. Freeman climbed behind the wheel. Once Watson and Emily were loaded, Freeman drove out to the street.

36

Stolen cars and ambulances attract attention.

On their way back into the city, Freeman found a small medical clinic on De Russey Parkway. They left the ambulance in the clinic parking lot and hiked four blocks east to a storage facility on Langdrum where Freeman kept an impressively nondescript sedan. Then, with Emily in the passenger seat and Watson in the back, Freeman drove the sedan to the Linear Committee Building.

Using Watson's clearance, they entered the underground parking and took a secured elevator to Howard Tasman's floor. The three of them had just entered Tasman's office when Freeman got a phone call. He said, "This call is from Harris."

"Are you going to tell him we're here?" asked Watson.

Freeman shook his head. He said, "Harris is going to try to save his empire. He has no choice. Do you know what happens when you swim too close to a drowning man? He pulls you down.

"I'm going to put Harris on my speaker so you can hear him, but he can't know we're here in the building. He needs to think you're still at Walter Reed."

Harris was coughing when Freeman answered the call. Freeman asked, "You sick?"

Harris said, "I've got the flu."

Freeman heard this and nodded but said nothing.

Harris said, "A lot of people have colds these days, pretty much every clone in the Empire."

Having just left Walter Reed, Freeman knew more about the flu than Harris did, probably more than Tasman as well. Playing dumb, he asked, "Is the Unified Authority behind it?"

Harris said, "This version of the flu ends with clones having a death reflex."

Freeman asked, "How many clones have died so far?" He knew how many had died up at Reed; at least he knew the tally as it had stood an hour ago. More would have died in the last hour.

Harris said, "Six."

Six, Freeman thought. Harris really didn't understand what was going on yet. Freeman tried to direct him with an innocent-sounding question. He asked, "Are you sure the Unified Authority is behind it?"

"Ray, we captured some of their files. The decryption process is going slow, but the stuff we're getting sounds bad."

"How long before your epidemic turns critical?" Freeman asked.

"There's no way of knowing. The first victims were on an Explorer we sent to survey Terraneau. She'd been gone six days when we found her. The clones had been dead approximately twenty-four hours. We don't know when the Unifieds captured the ship or how long they waited before they infected the crew."

Freeman saw Harris as trying to save a ship that had already sunk. He understood Harris's need to rescue his empire, but he wouldn't buy into it, and he wouldn't accomplish anything by trying to convince Harris that the clone empire was already done. Instead, he played dumb.

He asked, "What does the flight record say?"

"That they broadcasted into Terraneau space. That's it. It stops after that."

"Death in five days, maybe less," said Freeman. "It all depends how long it took them to catch that Explorer."

Harris said, "It'd be easy enough to capture an Explorer. They're slow. They don't have armor or shields. They need an hour to recharge their broadcast generators."

Freeman said, "Antique technology."

"If the Unifieds control Terraneau, they might have spotted the anomaly when she broadcasted in," Harris answered.

"Fire a pulse weapon near an Explorer, and you'll shut her engines down and wreak havoc on the electrical system."

Harris said, "Those birds are made out of tissue paper and kite string; you'd have a hard time detonating an EMP near one without destroying it."

"The point is that you have dead clones," Freeman said.

"Yes, and we don't have time to develop a vaccine. You do the math; clones are going to start dying tomorrow. We need to capture some high-ranking U.A. officers and see what information they're holding."

"Any officers in particular?"

Harris said, "Sunny Ferris."

Tasman had already told Freeman about Sunny, but Freeman hadn't mentioned her to Watson or Emily.

Emily said, "That bitch!"

Freeman tried to cover by asking in a slightly louder voice, "The girl you were dating?"

"The spy I was dating," Harris said.

Glaring at Emily, Freeman said, "She couldn't have done it by herself."

"No, not by herself."

"Do you have any other names? Any other targets?"

"No."

"So you're just going after her?" asked Freeman.

"Yeah."

"You and the Enlisted Man's Army are going after your former lover?"

"Ray, I have their flu. As far as I can tell, every man under my command has been infected. It's too late to stop it from spreading, and we already know the mortality rate; all of my men are going to die.

"It could happen tomorrow, maybe we have an extra day. By the end of the week, every clone in the empire is going to die." As he said this, Harris chuckled. The eerie, out-of-control sound of his laugh scared Emily. She stepped closer to Watson, and he wrapped his arm around her.

"We've lost the war, Ray. The fighting isn't over, but we lost. What would you do?"

Freeman said, "Killing her won't save your empire."

"Neither will sitting around waiting to die," Harris said.

"It won't save your men."

"Maybe they'll go to their graves more easily. They made us, then they abandoned us, then they selected us for target practice. You say I'm doing this because I have a vendetta, and you're right. Do you know why the Unified Authority created a clone army instead of an army of robots—simple economics. Even with food, housing, and education, clones are cheaper and more expendable than robots. They made us because it costs less to manufacture humans than machines.

"Yes, I'm mad, and I want to make them pay. I'm not going to scorch the earth I leave behind, but I want to burn the people who are taking it from me."

Freeman said, "You're on your own, Harris," and ended the call.

As Freeman placed his phone back in his pocket, Emily shouted, "That bitch! That bitch! I knew there was something wrong about her."

In an apologetic tone, Watson said, "Emily and Sunny never got along."

A satisfied smile on his face, Tasman said, "Harris is a Marine. He won't allow himself to go down without a fight, even if the fight won't amount to anything.

"It's like you said, Freeman; he's a drowning man. You'll all drown if you try to save him."

"What if they find an antidote?" asked Watson. He stood at an east-facing window, staring out over the city. He saw plush districts and ruined buildings. Late afternoon, the sun had migrated west, but the day hadn't ended.

Tasman answered, sounding irritable. He said, "It's the flu. You've had the flu before. Did your doctor give you an antidote? Antidotes are for poisons, Watson. This is a virus; there's nothing anyone can do."

Emily stood, and said, "That bitch."

"You're starting to sound like Harris," said Tasman.

"I understand him," said Emily.

Watson asked, "Does Harris know it's over?"

Emily answered. She said, "He's got to know on some level."

"But he's still going after Sunny," said Watson.

"He has to do something," said Tasman.

"It's like he said, 'His men will go to their graves more easily,' " said Emily.

"When the Unifieds take control of the government, they will come after us. The clones won't save us this time. We're on our own," said Freeman.

"Won't they go after Harris first?" asked Watson.

"They'll be looking for all of us," said Emily. "Howard, they'll come after you, too."

"I've already been on the lam," said Tasman. "I'm done with it."

Watson said, "They might not care about Emily. She hasn't done anything."

"Trav, I'm guilty by association," said Emily. "As far as they're concerned, I'm Mrs. Travis Watson; that makes me as guilty as you."

"But Harris isn't just going after Sunny; he's taking all his men," said Watson. "Maybe he'll beat them."

"He'll beat the Unifieds in Maryland," said Freeman.

"What's that supposed to mean?" asked Watson.

"It means that Maryland is just the tip of the iceberg," said Emily. "Trav, they probably have a whole navy waiting somewhere out there in space. They're going to wait for the clones to die, then they'll land."

"There's no way Harris is going to stop them, not in one night," said Tasman. "And once the clones start dying . . ."

"They're already dying," said Watson. "The morgue at Walter Reed is overflowing with dead clones."

"It's overflowing with dead clones?" asked Tasman. "That's even faster than I expected."

Emily walked over to Watson and took his hand; he wrapped his arm around her shoulders.

"What do we do?" asked Watson.

Freeman said, "We'll never be safe, not as long as the Unified Authority is in power. The only way we're going to survive is if we have Harris on our side."

Tasman smiled, and said, "I don't know, Freeman; you're a talented killer."

"I'm a mercenary. I specialize in tactics."

"Then we can't let him go tonight," said Emily. "We have to stop him."

"He'll survive tonight. That's just combat; it's his specialty," said Freeman. "It's the flu that worries me. Harris doesn't like to hide. He's going to want to die fighting."

"So he's screwed, and we're screwed," said Watson.

"Maybe," said Freeman.

"Maybe?" asked Watson.

"There may be someplace we can go to get help," said Freeman.

Tasman's security clearance allowed him to rove freely through the EME's computers. Harris had granted him that access without realizing that he could use it to search EME databases as well as decipher the information on the encryption bandit.

Tasman never considered exploiting that clearance, but Freeman took advantage of it. He used the computers to access a top secret communication between Harris and Tobias Andropov on December 2, 2518, the day that the clones invaded Washington, D.C.

Though the video feed had been recorded from Andropov's point of view, both Harris and Andropov appeared on it. The screen showed Harris sitting by himself in a conference room, but appearances could be deceiving. Freeman had been there as well. He'd made a point of staying out of the camera's range.

Andropov appeared to be alone in his office. Freeman wondered if he'd had somebody hidden with him as well.

The feed was recorded moments before the Enlisted Man's Navy advanced on Earth. Harris and Freeman had just placed the call to a couple of U.A. scientists who had been supplying him with information. They were surprised when Andropov answered the call.

"Hello, Harris. Has your invasion begun?" asked Andropov.

He sat behind an oak desk in the office Harris now used, smirking into the camera.

Seeing Andropov, Harris mouthed the word, "speck," caught himself, and quipped, "I must have the wrong number."

Freeman forwarded ahead through the feed, looking for one particular comment.

Harris said, "Bullshit."

Andropov shrugged his shoulders, and answered, "Think what you want."

Freeman advanced the feed still further.

Andropov shook his head. "You still don't understand. Harris, it doesn't matter how many ships you send here; they're as good as dead.

"You gave us a scare with that device that you used off New Copenhagen; but it won't work this time, not unless you plan on destroying the planet." He paused to smirk.

Looking surprised, Harris repeated the name, "New Copenhagen."

When Andropov mentioned the clones using some kind of weapon near New Copenhagen, Harris and Freeman had both written it off as a mistake. They had used a superweapon of sorts—shield-busting torpedoes that had been developed by the Unifieds for demolishing EMN ships. Harris and an admiral named Holman had fired the torpedoes at U.A. ships patrolling a planet named Solomon. New Copenhagen was in a completely different arm of the galaxy, tens of thousands of light-years away from Solomon.

During the original conversation, Freeman had thought that Andropov had accidentally said New Copenhagen when he meant Solomon. Now he wasn't so sure. He scrolled back and watched the clip again.

A confident, angry Andropov smirked, and said, "You gave us a scare with that device that you used off New Copenhagen; but it won't work this time, not unless you plan on destroying the planet."

Freeman had gone back over that conversation several times in his mind.

"You gave us a scare with that device that you used off New Copenhagen . . ."

Freeman had been at the battle of Solomon. He'd seen Holman hit the U.A. ships with torpedo after torpedo. The stolen torpedoes had been powerful, but it took several shots to destroy the U.A.'s new ships. In the end, Harris and Holman had been forced to retreat.

But those torpedoes weren't the most powerful weapon ever created by the Unifieds. There'd been other weapons, better weapons, weapons that were too expensive, too powerful to deploy. The Linear Committee had created just a few of them at a critical time, a time when practical considerations no longer mattered.

Freeman played the clip one final time.

". . . that device that you used off New Copenhagen . . ."

The weapons themselves would be useless. If they were what Freeman suspected, they were meant for destroying planets, but the men who used them, they could win the war. If he had the right weapons in mind, and the men who commanded them were on New Copenhagen . . . Each of those men was worth an entire division.

37

They could all sense it, that this was the quiet before the storm. Before the hour ended, Harris would enter the eastern suburbs looking for an antidote that the Unified Authority had never developed. If he got the opportunity, he'd execute his girlfriend.

The Enlisted Man's Navy still controlled the solar system. The Enlisted Man's Air Force still patrolled the skies unchallenged. The Unified Authority remained on the run, for now.

The fragile balance of power was about to break.

Freeman drove. Too tall to fit comfortably in the back, Watson sat in the passenger seat. Nobody worried about the Unified Authority tracking them on this errand. For the time being, the Unifieds had their hands full.

Freeman observed the different ways Watson and Emily handled stress. She became silent, not sullen but watchful. He prattled, looking for anything to bolster his confidence.

"Where are we going?" he asked Freeman.

Emily heard the question and slid forward so she could listen more easily.

"Smithsonian Field," said Freeman.

"Smithsonian Field? Where they keep the Explorers?" Watson asked. "Why are we going there?"

Watching the video feed, Freeman had decided a path for himself. He didn't know if Watson and Emily would choose to go with him. He said, "That's the only place I know that has self-broadcasting ships."

"Are we running away?" asked Emily.

Freeman said, "We're looking for allies."

It was six o'clock, and the city was quiet. Night had not yet begun, but the day had ended. Office buildings had shut for the night; restaurants had become busy. Watson spotted a fighter streaking across the sky at the edge of town. They had seen a convoy of personnel carriers parked and waiting in the distance. Other than those brief glimpses, they saw no sign of military activity.

Freeman told Watson and Emily what he knew and what he believed. He said, "After the first invasion, the Unified Authority sent a small fleet of ships to find the Avatari home world."

The term "Avatari" was not commonly used. Emily Hughes knew it because her father had been a senator from a planet that the Avatari had invaded. Watson had heard Harris use the term; otherwise, he wouldn't have known it.

Freeman drove east, crossing the Potomac on the Key Memorial Bridge, then taking the Curtis Parkway east and north, branching off to the Dulles Access Road, then switching onto the Harry Byrd Highway and driving deep into the Virginia countryside.

As the light drained from the sky, and the night sky became as dark as black velvet, Freeman told them about the Japanese population on Ezer Kri, holdouts who had ignored the Unified

Authority's attempts to abolish races. Finding themselves at odds with the U.A. Senate, the Japanese ultimately allied themselves with the wrong side during the galactic civil war. Working with the Morgan Atkins Believers and the Confederate Arms Treaty Organization, the Japanese renovated an enormous fleet of antiquated self-broadcasting warships—the Galactic Central Fleet. When the alliance fell apart, the Japanese escaped in four ships as the Mogats and the Confederates fought for control of the fleet.

After explaining the existence of the Japanese Fleet, Freeman described its final mission. As punishment for having sided with the Mogats, the Unified Authority sent the Japanese Fleet on a top secret mission to locate and destroy the Avatari home world.

Watson said, "Attack the aliens, the ones who destroyed all of our planets? It would have been a suicide mission. There's no way they could have beaten the aliens."

"It's been two years since the Avatari have destroyed a planet," said Freeman.

"Did the Japanese ever return?" asked Emily.

"I'm beginning to think that they did," said Freeman. "I think they came back, but not to Earth."

"It doesn't matter if they came back; we'll need more than four ships to take on the Unifieds," said Watson.

Freeman said, "The ships don't interest me. I'm curious about some of the men who were on them."

"The Japanese?" asked Watson. "What's so special about the Japanese?"

"The SEALs," said Freeman. "During the Mogat War, a U. A. admiral named Che Huang created special clones to serve as Navy SEALs."

"But if they're clones, won't they catch that flu?" said Emily.

"Not if they have different DNA," said Watson. "Even if they do catch it; it won't kill them unless they have death glands."

"They have different DNA," said Freeman. "They'll be as immune as we are.

"Those SEALs were skilled at demolitions, assassinations, and reconnaissance. They would have been able to get you out of Walter Reed without being seen."

"They sound like terrorists," said Emily.

Freeman said, "They're only terrorists when they're fighting against you. They're commandos when they're on your side."

"Is that what we are now? Are we terrorists?" asked Watson.

After Winchester, the Harry Byrd Highway became Highway 50, which connected with Highway 220, which connected to the county route. They stayed on the county route for a couple of hours, eventually turning onto a winding road out to nowhere, but the middle of that nowhere was where they needed to go if they wanted to find Smithsonian Field.

The road took them through a forest.

"What if the SEALs don't want to be found?" Emily asked. "What if they're there, and they don't want visitors?"

"That's possible," Freeman admitted. They had reached the gate of Smithsonian Field. An electric fence surrounded the facility. The clones had placed batteries of rocket launchers in the woods. Security cameras lined the roads. Harris saw the Explorers as a security risk.

"The Unified Authority sent the Japanese to destroy the Avatari and the SEALs to protect the Japanese. If the SEALs see us as a threat to the Japanese, they won't think twice about killing us."

"But you don't think they'll kill us," said Watson.

Freeman allowed the conversation to fade away as he drove up to the gate. He pulled Howard Tasman's security badge from his pocket; the badge emitted a security code.

An intercom device hung down from the gate. The man on the other end coughed for several seconds before speaking. After clearing his throat, he said, "State your business." His voice was reedy and raw.

Freeman said, "Dunkirk, we need an Explorer."

Freeman had called ahead from Tasman's office. After authenticating Tasman's badge transmission, Major Thelonious Dunkirk, the Air Force officer in charge of Smithsonian Field, opened the gate.

38

Emily had no idea how much damage the flu did to clones before it killed them, but she decided Major Dunkirk was on the verge of dying. He was older than most of the clones on active service, probably in his late forties. He was skinny and had a lot of white hair.

His nose was red and swollen along the bottom and running so constantly, Dunkirk dabbed at it with a handkerchief every few seconds. His hair was wet with sweat, and beads of perspiration ran down his forehead.

He waited for them alone in his office, coughing, hacking, slumped over his desk. When they walked in, he raised his head from the desk, looked in their direction, and said, "What about Tasman, is he coming?"

Freeman remained by the door. Watson and Emily stepped closer. Emily said, "You're sick. You need help."

Dunkirk struggled to sit up straight. He coughed, then he coughed again, and his body stiffened. Freeman realized what would happen before Emily or Watson.

Still in his chair, Dunkirk had a coughing fit, loud, deep coughs that sent him lurching forward as if his seat were trying to buck him off. His mouth hung open even after his coughing stopped. For a moment, it looked like he might vomit, but he didn't; instead, he fought for oxygen. He started to stand, then he paused and fell back onto his seat. And his head landed on the desk, smacking face-first, then rolling sideways.

Blood poured from his broken nose. His eyes were open, and his mouth hung slack. After a moment, blood started pooling in his ear. A stream of blood dribbled down, crossing his earlobe and dripping onto his collar.

Emily placed a hand over her mouth, but she didn't scream or cry. She'd seen plenty of death during the relocations to Mars, then Earth. She didn't like it, and she hadn't grown used to it, but it no longer shocked her.

Watson asked, "That's it? That's how they die?"

Freeman didn't answer.

He walked to the computer on the other side of the office and read the screen. As he had hoped, the display showed that an Explorer sat prepped and ready on the runway for Howard Tasman. He said, "We need to go."

We need to go. Watson remembered his bodyguards saying those words or something very similar the day the Unified Authority reprogrammed the clones in the Pentagon. *We need to get going,* he thought. *That's what survivors say.*

Freeman walked out of the office, and Emily followed. Watson spared one final glance at Dunkirk. *Another victim,* he thought, and though he didn't want to admit it to himself, his instinct to survive told him that "he'd better go" before he ended up like the clone. He reached down and closed the clone's eyes, not out of sympathy, but to prove to himself that he wasn't scared.

A lone Explorer sat on the tarmac, a spoon-shaped, silver-hulled bug with lots of windows and retractable wings.

Once he'd made his decision, Freeman no longer wasted energy worrying about risks and consequences. The Explorer was over one hundred years old. It had no shields or guns. If they ran into a Unified Authority ship, they'd be helpless. Having already weighed those possibilities, Ray Freeman wasted no more energy worrying about them.

Watson and Emily were not as committed. As Freeman parked the car, Emily asked, "Who's going to fly that?"

Freeman said, "I will."

"Have you ever flown one?" she asked.

Freeman didn't answer. It was answer enough.

"This isn't a good idea," said Watson.

Freeman said nothing. He unpacked his gear from the car and started toward the Explorer. Watson caught up to him. He walked beside Freeman, and asked, "What if we run into U.A. ships?"

Freeman asked, "What if we do?" and tossed his gear into the Explorer.

"They'll shoot us."

"The Enlisted Man's Navy is out there now. They won't be later. If we run into U.A. ships, they'll probably be busy fighting EMN ships."

He climbed into the Explorer, then turned, and said, "You don't have to come with me. It won't be safe."

Watson followed him into the ship. Emily waited a moment, then she joined them. Freeman closed the hatch and went to the cockpit while Watson and Emily sat in the main cabin.

Though he had never been in the military, Freeman was a qualified transport pilot who also knew how to operate several civilian crafts. He walked to the cockpit and looked at the controls. There was no mistaking the broadcast lever, a red mushroom-shaped button beside a large gauge labeled, broadcast energy level, its digital readout stating, "100%."

Aside from the broadcast equipment, the other instrumentation might as well have been borrowed from a transport. It had the same yoke and gauges. Like transports, Explorers used boosters for vertical liftoffs. Unlike transports, Explorers had retractable wings. Looking around the cockpit, Freeman decided that the ship's computers controlled the wings.

Freeman checked the fuel and saw it was full. He started the boosters. A light flashed, warning him to extend the wings. Freeman tapped the warning light and realized it was an interactive panel when the wings extended.

Freeman flew east and up, quickly leaving the atmosphere behind, rising first through clouds, then through empty atmosphere, and finally emerging in the translucent darkness of space. Somewhere below, Harris and the healthiest of his troops would enter the eastern suburbs looking for Sunny Ferris and seeking to avenge themselves . . . to ease themselves into their graves. Harris's operation was the dead burying the dead; Freeman saw no place for himself in that equation.

As the Explorer rose from the planet, Freeman saw several EME ships looming like great white whales in the distance. The ships were huge, some a full mile from wingtip to wingtip and shaped like wedges. They would be packed with men, some living, some dead, most dying.

Freeman extended an arm to hit the broadcast button and realized he didn't want to touch it. Broadcast engines were among the most sophisticated pieces of technology ever created, and these ones were ancient; if something went wrong, every person aboard the Explorer would die in an instant.

For now, the clones still controlled the area around Earth. Freeman wondered if he would see EME ships when he returned. *We might,* he told himself, *but they'll be filled with Unified Authority sailors.* He reminded himself about the inevitable and pressed the broadcast button.

39

When the Avatari came to conquer the galaxy, New Copenhagen was the only planet on which they'd been defeated. When they returned, they incinerated New Copenhagen first. They raised the temperature on the planet to nine thousand degrees and maintained that temperature for eighty-three seconds.

Even from outside the atmosphere, Freeman and his passengers could see that New Copenhagen still had lakes, seas, and oceans. This wasn't the first time Freeman had visited the planet since its incineration. He'd known what to expect. The only tokens that remained of its forests were ghost trees that rose like spikes from the bare ground. The incineration left no traces of New Copenhagen's once famous meadowlands and left the cities in ruins.

Freeman tried the Explorer's communications gear, sending a message indentifying himself and his ship. For all he knew, the Japanese were orbiting the planet, four battleships armed with a superweapon capable of destroying the Unified Authority's latest ships.

"This is Ray Freeman. I am piloting an unarmed civilian ship. I am searching for Admiral Yoshi Yamashiro of the Japanese Fleet. I am searching for Master Chief Petty Officer Emerson Illych. I have come on behalf of Captain Wayson Harris of the Unified Authority Marines." Freeman had almost referred to Harris as a general, then caught himself. Harris had only been a captain when the Japanese were sent to find the aliens.

Though Freeman had met Yamashiro, he'd never met Illych. He'd heard the name from Harris, who'd been a captain at the time that the Japanese Fleet left to find the Avatari.

Watson and Emily walked into the tiny cockpit as the Explorer approached New Copenhagen. He saw the surface, and asked, "What is that?"

Freeman said, "That is New Copenhagen."

"There is no way anyone lives on that rock," said Watson. "Mars is more habitable."

"It has cleaner air than Earth," Freeman said. He hadn't actually tested the air quality, but scientists had tested the air quality on a similar planet and discovered it was surprisingly high.

"Do you really think the SEAL clones are down there?" Emily asked.

"If they're alive, that's where they are," said Freeman.

"It's a big planet," said Watson. "How do we find them?"

Their ship may have been designed for scientific exploration, with sensors for detecting sources of light, heat, oxygen, radiation, and various chemicals. But Freeman had no idea how to use the equipment, and neither did Watson or Emily.

"Do the computers have a map of the planet?" asked Emily.

"I checked," said Freeman. "They don't."

They approached the planet from outside the atmosphere,

traveling slowly enough to observe its rotation and the distant sun as it showed over oceans and continents. The waters were blue, pristine, primordial. The continents were gray where they had once been green, and brown.

Freeman said, "At nine thousand degrees, forests burn like match heads, rocks explode, and sand melts into glass."

Emily was from Olympus Kri. The Avatari burned her planet a few days after incinerating New Copenhagen. She knew her planet was dead, but she'd never seen what the aliens had done to it.

She watched the scene in shock and horror, her mouth open, her legs weak, her lungs barely taking in air. She spotted twin riverbeds that looked as dry as railroad tracks. "Is this what they did to Olympus Kri?"

Freeman didn't answer.

She said, "I heard there were people here when this happened."

In a rare show of emotion, Freeman said, "My mother was here. So were my sister and her son."

As he spoke, Freeman checked the radar screens for orbiting ships. He searched the horizon as well. He tried the communications console again, identifying himself, invoking Harris's name, and the names of Illych and Yamashiro. No one answered. He steered the Explorer so that she followed the rotation of the planet, staying ahead of the sun, searching the darkness for the glow of lights, knowing their search would probably prove futile. Even if the crews of all four battleships had landed on the planet, the population would be small.

They flew along an equatorial path, the line that would take them over the most major cities. They flew north as they approached a coast that Freeman recognized, and they found the ruins of Valhalla, the largest city on the planet.

Freeman piloted the Explorer low over the planet, just a hundred feet above the wreckage. Traveling slowly, shining searchlights beneath them, they hovered over tall buildings that had melted into sandcastles. They passed neighborhoods that looked like dusty checkerboards. As they approached Lake Valhalla, they saw two roads leading into underwater tunnels.

Freeman said, "There could be people down there."

"Where? Why would they be in those tunnels?" asked Emily.

"Harris and I hid in tunnels like those when the aliens burned Terraneau. The lake water kept the tunnels cool."

"You were on Terraneau?" Emily asked.

"It was Harris's idea; he wanted to get the people out."

"How many did you save?" asked Watson.

"None of the civilian population; they didn't believe us," said Freeman. "We saved a corps of clone engineers, but the people didn't trust Harris. The politicians locked him in jail. We barely got him out in time."

"And they burned," said Watson.

"He went to save the people? He's a hero," said Emily. "I knew he killed people; I didn't know he ever tried to save people."

Freeman asked, "Do you know why I sided with the clones instead of the Unified Authority? I went with Harris because he wanted to evacuate the planets. Andropov didn't care."

"I never heard any of this," said Emily.

"He got the New Olympians off Mars," said Watson. "The rest of his generals wanted to leave you there. Harris was the only one who wanted to bring them to Earth."

"Hey, over there!" said Emily. "Look, there are lights in that building!"

Off in the distance, light shone in a lone skyscraper that stood tall but canted beside the lake. The lower floors glowed, the upper floors remained dark.

Watson said, "There can't possibly be anyone living in there. It wouldn't be safe."

Hovering slowly, Freeman approached the building. Thinking maybe they had found Freeman's SEALs, Watson and Emily became excited. Knowing what the SEALs were capable of doing, Freeman didn't share their enthusiasm. A single rocket would destroy their ship.

He slowed the Explorer and brought her lower, fifty feet off the ground to show his peaceful intentions. Freeman thought about the U.A. ships that the SEALS had destroyed with their "superweapon." He wondered if those ships had come in firing weapons or if the SEALs had destroyed them simply because they had strayed into the wrong part of space.

Calculating odds and consequences came as naturally as breathing for Freeman, as did dismissing fears about the things he couldn't control. He needed the SEALs; what happened next was out of his control.

The building was easily a hundred stories tall. It must have been a marble-and-glass showpiece when the heat went up, but the glass had melted, and the marble had charred to slag.

"What happened to all the other buildings?" Emily asked, seeing the mounds of rubble that marked huge buildings that had once filled entire city blocks.

Freeman knew the answer; he'd seen computer models of what happened. He said, "When you heat the planet, the atmosphere rises from the surface. Once the heat stops, the atmosphere comes crashing down and crushes anything that's left."

Emily didn't say anything, but horror showed on her face.

Watson asked, "What about the people?"

"Cremated," said Freeman. "When we came out of the tunnels on Terraneau, the air was full of ash. It wasn't just burned bodies; it was trees and rubber and anything that burned. Everything burned, then the atmosphere crashed down on the ash and flushed it into the sky."

Emily said nothing. Watson said, "Speck, an entire planet."

Some of the glass remained on the building. It had melted and dribbled down the side like wax running down a candle—rippled and covered in dust. It didn't reflect the Explorer's searchlight.

Freeman landed in a lot not far from the building.

Watson asked, "Do we know there's breathable air out there?"

"I checked," said Freeman

"How can there be any oxygen?" asked Emily. "There aren't any plants."

"There aren't any plants on the surface," Freeman said. "There's algae and seaweed in the oceans and lakes." He tried the radio again, stating his name and that he wanted to speak with Yoshi Yamashiro and Emerson Illych.

No response.

"Do you think there are people in that building?" Watson asked, staring out the cockpit and up at the partially melted tower. "I mean, maybe it's just an old generator that comes on every night."

He made a good point. If the generator were a few floors down in an underground parking facility or possibly some kind of basement, it would have been safe from the heat.

He pressed a button, causing the broadcast generators to start gathering energy, and climbed out of his seat.

"Oh hell," said Watson, pointing out the windshield. People gathered at the foot of the building. Some wore uniforms, some dressed like civilians. Even in the dull light, he could see that some of the people were men and others were women, and that the men were holding guns. Sounding nervous, he said, "Well, now we know there's intelligent life."

Freeman said, "Those aren't the ones you need to be afraid of."

"No?" asked Watson.

Freeman said, "There's something I didn't tell you."

"There are a lot of things you haven't told us," said Emily.

Freeman said, "If the SEALs are here and they're alive, it's because they located the Avatari home world and destroyed it."

"The entire planet?" asked Watson. "That's a lot of destruction."

"Ever wonder why the Avatari burned New Copenhagen and Olympus Kri, but never made it back to Earth?" asked Freeman.

"The SEALs did that?" asked Watson. "Why didn't you tell us that back on Earth?"

Freeman didn't answer. The answer was obvious.

Across the way, two men and a woman left the group and began walking toward the ship. The men wore civilian clothing; the woman wore a uniform.

Freeman stepped into plain sight followed by Watson and Emily. A bright light shone on them.

Freeman squinted. Holding a hand up to shield his eyes from the glare, he could see the silhouettes of the three people. They were short. One of the men was stout, thick with muscle, not fat.

A friendly voice called out, "Freeman-san, I'm very glad to see you. The last I heard, you were lying in a hospital. They thought you might be blind."

40

They sat in a traditional-style Japanese bar. The tables stood a mere two feet off the ground. Tatami mats covered the floor from wall to wall. They had all left their shoes by the doorway.

Freeman said, "We came here looking for Emerson Illych."

"I don't know such a man," said one of Yamashiro's aides.

Freeman said, "He was one of the SEALs assigned to your fleet."

"Illych? The SEAL . . . Ah, yes, yes, yes . . . the SEAL. He was their original leader," said Yamashiro. He turned to the aide, and said, *"Kage no yasha."*

"Oh, *kage no yasha.*" The man nodded.

Yamashiro said, "The master chief died an honorable death. He was one of the first men to die. The Avatari discovered him as he explored the outermost planet in their solar system. His team committed suicide protecting our fleet. They detonated their stealth infiltration pods, destroying the aliens and most of the planet as well."

Freeman had heard the term but had never heard of any being manufactured; stealth infiltration pods were single-man vehicles built around an unstable propulsion system called an impulse engine. *There's the superweapon,* Freeman told himself. From what he had heard, impulse engines generated enough energy to destroy a planet . . . or a fleet of U.A. ships.

This was not the first time Yamashiro had taken Freeman to visit a bar. From what Freeman could see, the man lived on rice wine and cigarettes.

He said, "The reason we came . . ."

Yamashiro held up a hand, and said, "Stop. Stop. Tonight we drink to your welcomed return. Tomorrow, we can discuss business."

Yamashiro, old and stout, with broad shoulders and a thick neck, was a man in his seventies whose hair had turned silver instead of white. He had dark brown eyes and walnut-colored skin, and he stood no taller than five-foot-six, making him a foot and a half shorter than Freeman.

A waitress wearing a silk kimono brought three ceramic cylinders to the table. She bowed first to Yamashiro and the three men on his staff, then to Freeman and Watson. She placed the cylinders in front of Yamashiro, making a show of not looking in Emily's direction, then she bowed and backed away from the table.

Sounding apologetic, Yamashiro explained, "She thinks you are a secretary."

"Why would she think that?" asked Emily.

"She doesn't think you belong at the table," added one of Yamashiro's aides.

"Where does she think I belong?" asked Emily.

"Unfortunately, she believes you should be serving the wine, not drinking it," said Yamashiro.

Emily said, "I'm sorry I asked."

Yamashiro explained, "This wine is special. It's from *Sakura*, our last ship. We only have the rice wine we brought with us. Once this wine is gone, we will switch to beer."

He poured saké from the cylinder and passed the cups around the table.

"I've heard of this stuff. Aren't you supposed to serve it hot?" Watson asked the man to his right. Emily sat to his left. Freeman sat on her other side.

"We always served it hot when we were on *Sakura*. Back then, we had all the saké we needed. Now it is rare, so we drink it cold."

Watson nodded though he didn't understand.

"Where is *Sakura*?" asked Freeman.

"Destroyed. All of our ships were destroyed," said Yamashiro. "They deposited us here, then they went to fight. My son-in-law was in that battle. He was the captain of the ship." Yamashiro's tone and expression revealed the pride he felt in his son-in-law's honorable death.

"Your son-in-law, Takahashi?" asked Freeman, who had met the man eight years earlier.

"Takahashi Hironobu," Yamashiro agreed. "You met him during the Mogat War."

Yamashiro's aide raised his cup, and said, "Takahashi."

All of the people around the table did likewise and repeated the name, then the aide yelled, "*Kampai!*"

The Japanese didn't sip their saké like they might have sipped tea or a glass of fine wine; they threw back their heads and tossed it down their gullets. Watson emulated their example. Freeman tossed his first cup to show his respect, but he wouldn't drink any more. Emily sipped hers steadily, taking less than a minute to drain the small cup.

The man sitting across the table from her nodded his approval.

Yamashiro emptied a *tokkuri* with each round that he poured. He started a second round, pouring saké in everyone's cup except his own. The aide sitting beside Yamashiro poured the saké into his cup.

Freeman remembered the last time he went to a bar with Yamashiro; he and his officers drank specifically to get drunk. It didn't take long. The saké was strong, and they absorbed it like sponges.

Freeman allowed Yamashiro to refill his *ochoko*, but he wouldn't drink the saké.

One of the aides yelled, "*Kampai*," and everybody drank except for Freeman. The man sitting across from him saw this, and asked, "Don't you like saké?"

Freeman ignored him, and asked, "Did all of the SEALs die on that mission?"

Yamashiro said, "That's right, you didn't drink last time, either."

"I don't drink," said Freeman.

No one argued with him as Yamashiro emptied the third *tokkuri* into each of their *ochokos*, then he clapped his hands, and the waitress brought three more *tokkuri*.

Freeman didn't drink any. Emily only sipped at hers, nursing it like a cocktail. Watson, on the other hand, was already getting tipsy. Yamashiro and the other Japanese watched him drink with satisfaction.

Freeman repeated his question. "Did all of the SEALs die?"

Yamashiro looked at the man beside him, and said, "He wants to know about the *kage no yasha*." Then, to Freeman, he said, "Now that we are settled, the *kage no yasha* no longer live among us. They claim they are not fit to eat our food."

* * *

The Japanese didn't live in tents or shacks or partially destroyed buildings, as Freeman suspected; they had an entire city to themselves, complete with apartments and stores.

Beneath the ruins of Valhalla was an underground city, one Freeman would have wanted to have known about during his first visit to New Copenhagen defending the planet, the battle with the Avatari.

The bar had been in the lobby of the building. Once Yamashiro and his men finished drinking, they led their visitors to a steep escalator that ended three hundred feet beneath the building. Halfway down, the walls gave way to a wide, clean expanse with trees, parks, working fountains, and gleaming, marble walkways. There were stores and theaters and a gym.

Watson, who had overestimated his ability to handle saké, looked at the grounds below, and said, "Shit! We're back on Earth."

Yamashiro heard this and smiled.

Emily kept an arm around Watson to make sure he didn't trip on the escalator.

Freeman positioned himself in front of Watson and tightened his grip on its rail. If Watson fell, Freeman would prevent him from rolling.

Yamashiro said, "It was empty when we found it. There were no survivors. We brought generators from our ship, and many of my men are trained engineers. Now it is our city. We finally have our Shin Nippon."

Freeman knew the term; it meant, New Japan.

"But you left family on Earth," said Emily. "I remember after the war, the Unified Authority gave you an island on Earth."

"Furui Nippon," said Yamashiro, as they reached the bottom of the escalator. He stepped onto the floor with such decision that he almost looked sober. Sounding profoundly melancholy, he said, "My daughter. My wife."

"Are they on Earth?"

"Ah, yes, so it is," said Yamashiro.

Freeman and Yamashiro both projected a stoic front. Yamashiro, a man of passions, put away his stoicism when he drank. He shared his inner demons. Freeman kept his demons locked away.

They spent the night in a penthouse with a window that overlooked the entire boulevard. Emily tucked Watson into their bed and went to the living room, where she found Freeman sitting by the window, staring down at the city.

"What are you looking at?" she asked.

He pointed to a loaf-shaped single-story building covered with chrome and flashing lights. The rest of the buildings were dark, but a steady stream of people flowed in and out of that one.

"It looks like a casino," she said.

"It is a casino."

"Why do you care about it?" she asked.

"I don't. I'm looking for phantoms. I haven't found them yet."

"But you think they're coming?" Emily asked. She knew that Freeman meant the SEALs.

Freeman didn't answer.

She said, "You've been right about everything so far."

He said, "I've been wrong about everything."

"You knew we'd find the Japanese."

"I expected twenty thousand people and four self-broadcasting battleships. There are two thousand people here." Freeman took a deep breath. He said, "I thought they'd want to return to Earth. Yamashiro doesn't want to go back; he's just glad to be alive."

"And the SEALs?" Emily asked.

"I was hoping for ten thousand of them. Yamashiro says there were one hundred of them when they landed here; the rest died fighting the Avatari.

"One hundred or one hundred million, it doesn't really matter," Freeman said. "We can only fit fifteen people in our ship."

By New Copenhagen time, it was the first hours of the morning. The plaza below was mostly empty. Janitors swept the walkways. Gardeners worked in the park. Freeman didn't see any policemen. Apparently the citizens of Shin Nippon behaved in an orderly fashion.

"Do you think they'll come with us?"

"Illych might have. He would have come just to save Harris. They were friends."

"We could stay here," said Emily. "I mean, if things are really hopeless, we could stay here. There's room and food. I bet you Yamashiro would let us stay."

"I can't stay," said Freeman.

"You need to save Harris."

Freeman took a long slow breath. He never looked at Emily. The entire time, he stared out the window at the minor galaxy of parks and lights. He said, "I need to be sure that the Unified Authority doesn't win."

"And Harris does?"

"He's already lost," said Freeman. "His empire is gone. His people are gone. I'm not sure what he'll do next. You know he's a Liberator. He has a gland in his brain just like the other clones, only his gland releases a different kind of hormone."

Emily said, "The combat reflex; Travis told me about it. I know Wayson is a Liberator."

Freeman said, "That flu virus will do the same thing to Harris that it did to the other clones. He'll get sick, and when his body has taken too much stress, that gland will release its hormone into his blood system."

"But it won't kill him," said Emily. "It's not poison, it's adrenaline."

"Adrenaline and testosterone," Freeman agreed. "It won't kill him; it should heal him . . . heal his body. That long, steady dose of the hormone is going to do bad things to his brain. He's probably having paranoid delusions already. By the end of the month, he'll be irrational."

41

"The *kage no yasha* no longer live in our city; they say they were sent to protect us, not to eat our food," Yamashiro told Freeman the next morning.

The two of them ate breakfast alone in an immaculate dining hall. White linen cloths covered the tables. The waiters wore white gloves and black suits. Vivaldi's *Four Seasons* played in the background.

"They were skilled fishermen," said Yamashiro. "There are fish in Biwa-Ko. The *kage no yasha* will have created a village near the lake."

"Is Biwa-Ko a lake?" asked Freeman.

"Ah, yes. You will have known it as Lake Valhalla."

They ate a sticky white porridge and drank fruit juice made from powdered concentrate—foods that traveled well on ships. Yamashiro held up a piece of toast, and said, "This toast came from a can.

"We don't have chickens and we don't have cows. Our eggs, milk, and cheese are all made from powder.

"We have enough food to last our two thousand settlers for many decades. How does the old saying go? 'I would trade half of my kingdom for a couple of chickens and some cattle.'"

"I think the saying went, 'My kingdom for a horse.'"

"We have no need for horses," said Yamashiro.

Freeman said, "I know where you can find cows and chickens."

"You may know where we can obtain herds of cows and flocks of chickens, but I think you cannot carry so many animals on one small ship. Perhaps you have selected this ship for reasons of economy," Yamashiro said as he spread marmalade on his toast.

"We're at war," said Freeman.

"The Unified Authority is at war?" asked Yamashiro.

Freeman told Yamashiro about the war between the clones and their makers, including the flu and how quickly it had spread.

Yamashiro said, "Then the war is over."

Freeman said, "There is one clone who won't have a death reflex."

Yamashiro poured himself a cup of coffee and stirred in cream. He said, "Our mutual friend, Wayson Harris. If he is alive, the Linear Committee will have a problem on its hands; he isn't the kind of man who forgives betrayal."

Freeman said, "You've seen how they work; they're traitors and thugs."

Yamashiro put down his spoon, and said, "Maybe, Freeman-san, you are not so safe as well. Maybe they will not forget your indiscretions."

Freeman met Yamashiro's eyes but said nothing.

"Ah . . . so, so, so, this is why you want the *kage no yasha*. You plan to unleash Harris upon the Unified Authority."

Freeman said, "I am not familiar with the term, *kage no yasha*."

"I'm not surprised; it's Japanese. It means 'shadow demon,'" said Yamashiro.

Freeman said, "Yes, the shadow demons." *That describes them,* he thought. "I need to find them."

Yamashiro signaled the maitre d', and said, "There is a man sitting in my office. Tell my secretary to send him down."

He sipped his coffee, and said, "I told you that they did not wish to eat our food and that they went someplace where they could fish. They had one further requirement when they looked for their new home. They wanted to remain close enough to watch over us.

"To this day, they remain our guardian spirits."

42

Jeff Harmer stood five-foot-two. He was three inches shorter than Yoshi Yamashiro, six inches shorter than Emily Hughes, fifteen inches shorter than Travis Watson, and twenty-two inches shorter than Ray Freeman. He was bald and had a charcoal-colored complexion. A thick bone ridge ran above his eyes. His fingers came to sharp points.

Watson didn't bother asking why the Japanese referred to him and his fellow clones as "shadow demons."

Harmer said, "We saw you land. Since we don't have any form of early-warning system, we didn't spot you until you reached the city."

Watson kept his voice and his expression neutral, but his thoughts ran amuck. The SEAL looked like a cross between a human and an animal, maybe an insect. *He's so damn ugly,* he thought. General-issue clones were programmed not to see themselves when they looked in mirrors; Watson hoped

Harmer had the same programming.

Watson asked, "How many of you are there?"

"There are 108 of us." Harmer answered. He had a high voice. It sounded slightly girly but also like the voice of a sociopath.

"A company," said Freeman.

Harmer nodded.

"What kind of company?" asked Emily.

"It's a military term, M," said Watson in an authoritative tone. "Fire teams, platoons, companies, battalions." He hoped he had fooled her; it had taken Harris forever to educate Watson about the chain of command.

"Oh. I should have known that," said Emily.

After a few more moments of pleasantries, Yamashiro said, "Perhaps now would be a good time for you to explain why you have come."

As Freeman didn't speak up right away, Watson said, "How long ago did you leave on your mission?"

Yamashiro answered, "Twenty-five fifteen."

"Four years ago," said Watson.

"Five," Yamashiro corrected.

"While you were hunting the aliens, the Unified Authority discontinued the cloning program," said Watson.

"Why would they do that?" asked Harmer.

"Once the dust settled after the invasion, Congress wanted to know why we lost so many planets. The generals blamed the clones."

"And that led to a war?" asked Yamashiro.

Watson said, "That and the aliens coming back to burn the planets they missed."

"Is that what happened to this planet?" asked Harmer.

Yamashiro said something in Japanese. Harmer answered, also in Japanese. To Watson's untrained ear, the SEAL's Japanese sounded more fluent.

Yamashiro launched into a long explanation in Japanese. Occasionally, Watson heard words he thought he recognized—"-Harris-san," "Unified-u," "kuron" for clone.

Harmer listened carefully, then asked, "Why wouldn't the flu infect me and my men?"

Freeman said, "It was specifically designed to infect standard-issue clones."

"You might catch it, but it won't kill you, not unless you have a death gland," added Watson.

Yamashiro said, "Most unfortunately for Harris, he has similar DNA to the other clones. He is a good man; I am sorry to hear he is in such a situation."

Harmer said, "I met Harris once. He and Illych and I boarded the same dead ship looking for Mogat traps.

"Mr. Freeman, I am sorry to hear about Harris's situation as well, but I don't see how it concerns me. I am not a fan of the Unified Authority, but my mission is to protect the sailors of the Japanese Fleet. We are on New Copenhagen now. Earth politics no longer affect us."

Yamashiro said something in Japanese. Harmer answered. They argued. Freeman watched in silence.

Watson said, "Do you know how we found you?"

Yamashiro and Harmer went silent and turned to listen.

"The Unified Authority Navy sent ships here while they were fighting the clones. You destroyed those ships."

Neither Yamashiro nor Harmer responded.

"The Unifieds know their ships were destroyed while patrolling New Copenhagen space. They don't know you were the ones who attacked their ships, not yet, but they know that someone with a superweapon destroyed their ships here. Once the clones are out of the way, how long do you think Andropov will wait before he sends a fleet here to investigate?"

"Who is Andropov?" asked Yamashiro. Andropov rose to power after the Japanese Fleet had left Earth.

"He was the senior member of the Linear Committee when the Unifieds expelled the clones."

Yamashiro said something in Japanese. Harmer listened but did not respond.

"Once they have Earth, how long do you think it will be before the Unifieds come calling?" asked Watson. "If it's your job to protect the Japanese, you damn well do care what happens on Earth."

Yamashiro said something. When Harmer responded, he spoke in English. He asked, "How many men can you fit on your ship?"

43

Convinced that the Unified Authority Fleet had already moved into Earth space, Freeman weighed his options. Tracking stations could detect the electrical anomaly ships created when they "broadcasted in" from millions of miles away. If he broadcasted in behind Saturn or Neptune, he might escape detection, but it would take several days for them to reach Earth.

After considering the odds, Freeman opted to broadcast in just outside Earth's atmosphere and attempt to land before the U.A. Navy could respond.

Working alone in the cockpit, Freeman made sure the broadcast generator was fully charged. He calculated the broadcast coordinates and inputted them into the broadcast computer.

While Freeman prepared to go wheels up, Harmer and twelve more SEALs loaded supplies and equipment into the back of the Explorer. Watson and Emily watched, wondering how so many people could fit into such a small ship. The SEALs were small, and their equipment was compact; they made it all fit.

As Freeman prepared to launch, Harmer stepped into the cockpit. He waited at the door, a mere five feet behind Freeman, and used an old Navy term. He asked, "Permission to come aboard?"

Freeman said, "Have a seat," then he waited for Harmer to snap the harnesses around the copilot's seat before lifting off.

Harmer asked, "What's the flight plan?"

"We're taking the direct route," said Freeman. "We'll come in close and dive into the atmosphere."

"They're going to spot us," Harmer warned.

"Sure they will," said Freeman. "We stand a better chance hiding once we land than we would in space."

Harmer looked around the ancient cockpit. The walls were mostly glass and metal brackets. There was nothing bulletproof or flakproof about the construction. *A grenade would stop this ship,* he thought. *A hit from a particle gun would blow this thing apart.*

Harmer stared out the window as the Explorer lifted off from New Copenhagen. He took in every detail, committing the shape of the lake and the lay of the hills to memory. He and his fellow SEALs had spent the last fifteen months of their lives in the cavelike ruins of an old hotel, fishing for food and failing miserably as farmers. They'd avoided contact with the Japanese, choosing to hide themselves when well-wishers approached their domain. It had been the happiest chapter of their lives.

The SEALs knew that the Japanese called them "shadow demons." In their hearts, they agreed. They looked like demons, and they were ashamed of it.

The trip was quick. The Explorer rose out of the New Copenhagen atmosphere in a steep ascent, and Freeman initiated the broadcast after they entered open space. Joules of electricity danced on the outer hull of the ship. The lightning that formed around the ship was bright enough to blind anyone who looked at it. Wearing protective goggles, Emily, Watson, and the SEALs watched as New Copenhagen vanished and Earth appeared.

Freeman didn't wait for his eyes to adjust before plunging the Explorer into the atmosphere, fighting friction so fierce that the tiles along the hull glowed orange as embers. Flames formed a skirt around the Explorer's nose. Looking through the windshield, Harmer and Freeman stared into the heart of the flames.

Harmer saw the heat burning at the outside of the Explorer and felt no emotion. Death didn't scare him, not as much as failure. Speaking in a relaxed voice, he asked, "Is this ship rated for this sort of stress?"

Freeman said, "It handles stress better than it handles U.A. torpedoes."

"Fair enough," said Harmer. "Where exactly on Earth are we going?"

They cleared the clouds, and Freeman decelerated. The patch below them was a tapestry of greens and browns and blues. There were mountains and deserts, but mostly there was coastline.

Freeman said, "Harris is weak and in trouble, and he's just about out of friends. He's going to look for someplace to hide until he regains his strength. The only place that fits that description is the New Olympian Territories."

Harmer, who had spent the last six years of his life in an alien galaxy, then marooned on New Copenhagen, had never heard the term, "New Olympian." He decided the territory must be a recently redistricted zone, something that had happened since he had embarked for Bode's Galaxy.

Freeman leveled their descent less than one hundred feet above a stretch of bright blue ocean. Harmer didn't mind flying low, hopefully below the range of ground-based radar systems. It was an old tactic, one that had been around for centuries.

The water beneath the Explorer was royal blue. Not far ahead, the water faded to azure, then turquoise as it reached a white sand beach. Harmer said, "My compliments to Harris; he picked a nice place to hide."

"He came for the gangsters, not the scenery," said Freeman. "The man who runs this place is a criminal named Brandon Pugh. He'll want to help Harris, and he'll cooperate with us."

"Sounds like a helpful fellow," said Harmer. "What makes him so nice?"

They were already over the beach, about one hundred feet above the ground, and flying no more than fifty miles per hour.

Freeman said, "He'll cooperate because he knows that I'll kill him if he doesn't."

They flew over a city, a mixture of ancient stucco and modern architecture. Harmer noted that none of the buildings looked new. The streets were mostly empty of cars, but he saw people. Everything he saw confirmed his hunch, the New Olympians had only recently arrived on Earth.

The civilian airfield was on the other side of town, a modest facility that was too small to accommodate military fighters—a quarter-mile runway with a few small hangars on one end. A lone commuter plane, something small and old, sat at one end of the field.

"Any chance that's Harris's plane?" asked Harmer.

Freeman said nothing.

Harmer commented, "It doesn't look very presidential."

As they hovered near the plane, Harmer said, "It might be abandoned; one of the doors is open." He continued to watch as they passed, and said, "Check that last comment; there's someone sitting in the plane."

Freeman landed the Explorer beside one of the hangars. While he and the SEALs searched the building, Watson and Emily went to speak to the man in the plane.

Finding the building empty, Freeman taxied the Explorer into the hangar. The SEALs waited for the ship to power down, then closed one of the heavy metal doors.

Watson ran back to the hangar, and said, "You're not going to believe this; Harris is sitting in that plane out there. He's unconscious."

Freeman ran to the plane. Harmer went to the Explorer and found a medical kit, then he and his SEALs went to Harris.

They had landed in the middle of the afternoon. The sun was high and hot, and the air was dry. Harmer hoped that Harris had water. *A man could die of thirst out here,* he thought, *especially if he had influenza.*

Emily was next to Harris when Freeman arrived. She said, "He's in bad shape."

Freeman knew nothing about medicine. He looked at Harris, saw the pale skin and chapped lips, and wondered if they had arrived too late.

A SEAL named Warsol approached Harris. Each of the SEALs had specialized in some sort of battlefield training. Warsol was their medic.

"Is he alive?" asked Watson.

"Sure he's alive. He's breathing," said Warsol. At that point, that was everything he knew about Harris's condition. He placed a finger against Harris's throat to check his pulse.

Harris squirmed and tried to raise his head. He asked, "Where's Ava?"

One of the SEALs asked, "Ava who?"

Watson said, "He means Ava Gardner."

The SEAL laughed, and said, "If you find her, let me know."

Harris's head dropped back onto the seat. He seemed to fall asleep.

"What do you think, Warsol?" asked Harmer.

"I think he's real sick."

"I can see that," said Harmer. "Can you pull him through?"

Warsol turned Harris's head to the right, then to the left. He opened Harris's mouth and ran a finger over his tongue. He shrugged his shoulders, and said, "The man's dehydrated."

"I can see that," said Harmer.

Warsol pulled an intravenous hydration kit from his emergency pack. He shoved a needle into Harris's arm, and said, "He'll be a lot happier after I give him a drink."

44

The last time Ray Freeman set foot in Mazatlan, the New Olympians still lived in tents. Over the last few months, they had moved out of those tents into the city.

Freeman knew that Pugh lived in Mazatlan, but he had no idea how to find him. Mazatlan wasn't a big city, but searching it could take days. Unsure if the Unified Authority had monitored his broadcast or tracked his landing, Freeman didn't have time to waste hunting for gangsters.

"Do you know where Pugh lives?" asked Harmer.

Freeman shook his head.

They stood in the hangar, a few feet from the Explorer. It was a small, bare-essentials sheet-metal structure, large enough to hold three civilian commuter craft but too small to hold a second Explorer.

At Warsol's direction, the SEALs carried Harris into the hangar to get him out of the sun. They laid him across the floor of the Explorer, a drip line feeding hydration into his arm.

"I'll send two of my guys to find him," said Harmer. "Naens, Baker, go find Pugh."

"How much time do we have?" asked Petty Officer Samuel Naens.

"You got an hour," said Harmer.

"An hour," Naens repeated. "How are we going to do that? We're ten miles out of town, and we don't even know what the guy looks like or where he lives."

Harmer asked Freeman, "Do you think the Unifieds spotted us when we came in?"

"Don't know."

"Okay, you get three hours," Harmer told Naens.

Naens and Baker slung small packs over their shoulders and trotted out of the hangar. As they reached the door, Naens told Baker, "See, I told you he was reasonable."

Listening to the conversation, Watson realized that he was scared of all of them. Pugh scared him; he was a gangster. Freeman made him nervous. Small or not, friendly or not, the SEALs terrified him.

"What is Pugh going to do for us once we find him?" Harmer asked.

"He'll hand Harris over to the Unifieds," said Freeman.

The SEALs only saw three cars as they headed into town. They ran along the side of the road, never allowing themselves to dip under four-minute miles, inhaling the dry August air through their noses, exhaling through their lightly pressed lips. The sun beat down on their bald heads. Living on New Copenhagen, they'd become acclimated to cooler temperatures. Valhalla was on a more northern latitude, and the planet was slightly farther from the sun.

Baker, who specialized in demolitions, asked, "How are we going to find him?"

Naens, an information-systems specialist, said, "If we find a police station or a library, I can hack into the computers."

"Don't you think they'll notice a little gray man sitting at their computer?" asked Baker. The SEALs looked more humanoid than human. They couldn't just walk into a store and ask for directions.

"Good point," Naens agreed. "Plan B—we start by looking at neighborhoods. If this guy is a gangster, he's going to live where the rich people live."

A half mile from the outskirts of town, they started seeing cars and trucks and hid by the side of the road. Baker said, "We'd be a lot less noticeable if we stole a car."

"What if the owner reports his car is missing?" asked Naens.

"We can make sure he doesn't."

"What if it's a woman?" asked Naens.

"We can make sure she doesn't."

"These people aren't the enemy," said Naens.

"That's a technicality," said Baker. "From what I hear, they're about to become citizens of the Unified Authority."

"They're civilians," said Naens.

"Well, yeah, I'll give you that," Baker admitted. "We'd still be harder to spot in a car, faster, too."

Naens thought about it, and said, "Okay, we can steal a car, but we can't waste time shopping for a nice one."

Heat waves rose from the asphalt and from the barrens along the road. Sparrows and crows flew overhead.

Both SEALs wore discreet communicators clipped to their ears. Naens received a message from Harmer. He asked, "Are you in town yet?"

"Just outside," whispered Naens.

"What are you doing?" asked Harmer.

"Car shopping."

"Look, while you're in town, keep an eye out for soldiers. I want to borrow a uniform if you see one," said Harmer.

"Does it matter if it's clean?" asked Naens.

"Clean is better," said Harmer. "Extra short if you can find it."

Naens said, "I'll let you know."

Most of the buildings on the outskirts of town were empty, but they found a tertiary plant with cars parked around it, almost all of them government-issue. When Baker said he wanted a car with darkened windows, Naens reminded him that they didn't have time for shopping. With no better options to choose from, they settled for the anonymity of a government car.

Car locks and ignition systems posed no problem for Naens or Baker. Under different circumstances, the two SEALs might have stolen two cars, racing to see which one of them could boost his ride first. Fifty-two minutes after leaving the airfield, they entered Mazatlan.

"Where should we look?" asked Baker.

"If he's rich, he'll have a house on the beach," said Naens.

"I'd rather live on a mountain," said Baker.

"That's just plain dumb," said Naens. "When you live on the beach, you can go for a swim anytime you like."

Baker said, "You get a better view from a mountain, and you don't need to worry about flooding or big waves."

Naens drove. He headed west, cut through the city, and followed the shoreline. They drove until they found a row of high-class hotels, most of them closed, then they headed south. They passed stores, businesses, schools, and a police station. They ran out of beach before they found a residential area.

"Okay, your turn," said Naens. "Where do we go?"

Baker pointed to a hilly peninsula that curled into the water. He asked, "How about over there? Those houses are on the beach and on a mountain."

Naens said, "You missed your calling, Baker. You should have been a Realtor."

Baker said, "Thanks. Maybe I'll do that when I retire."

Naens said, "Who are you going to sell to, SEAL clones?"

"I could sell vacation homes to the Japanese," said Baker.

"You think they'd buy a house from the *kage no yasha*?" asked Naens.

"Good point," said Baker. He looked at his reflection in the mirror, didn't like what he saw, and wondered if perhaps he'd find more success building homes than selling them.

The road followed the curve of the peninsula, rising up a slope and around a park with rows of large houses on either side. Here, for the first time, the SEALs saw private cars.

Naens asked, "Do you think we look out of place in this government-issue sedan?"

Baker shook his head. He said, "We should have spent more time shopping." He looked at his watch, and added, "It's been ninety minutes since we left the hangar."

By this time, the sun hung west over the ocean. Night wouldn't settle in for hours, but the air was cooling. Kids played in the streets. Pedestrians walked the sidewalks. The closer they came to the ocean, the bigger the houses became. They passed a house on a hill with several cars parked around it. Men milled among the cars trying to look casual but clearly guarding the area.

"Are those men carrying guns?" asked Naens. "Jeff, my friend, I believe we've found our gangster."

Baker agreed, but he said, "We should drive around some more."

"What, you enjoying the view?" asked Naens.

"They may own the entire block," said Baker. "We should

make sure this is the right house."

Naens turned up a street that led up toward the top of the hill. They parked beside an empty lot and reconnoitered. None of the other houses had a fleet of cars or guards.

Naens contacted Harmer. He said, "We found our man."

"Have you seen him?" asked Harmer.

"I'm looking at his house. He's got guards all around his yard."

"So does the pope," said Harmer.

"Good point. If he comes to the door in mitre and cassock, I promise not to touch him," said Naens.

"I don't think these boys are the Swiss Guard," said Baker.

"Are you sure that's not the mayor's house?" asked Harmer.

"These guards don't look like policemen," said Baker.

"From what Freeman told me, it sounds like they just established this town; maybe they don't have regular police yet."

"Your call, Master Chief, do we hit him or wait?" asked Naens.

"You sure you got the right guy?" asked Harmer.

"I am," said Naens.

"Hit him," said Harmer, who had a policy about trusting his men's judgment.

Naens looked at his watch. Two hours and seven minutes had passed since they had left the airfield. He told Baker, "Keep your eye on the clock. I want to be home before curfew."

Harmer said, "What's the big deal? You're grabbing a gangster; you better beat the clock."

Watson and Emily had waited in the Explorer while Freeman spoke with the SEALs. When Freeman entered the ship to check on Harris, Emily asked, "Are you sure these men know what they're doing?"

Watson added, "I know why you're scary. I know why Harris

is scary. These guys, I think they may be crazy."

Freeman knelt beside Harris, checked his pulse, and felt his forehead without speaking. Then, still looking at Harris, he said, "Watch yourself around them. These clones are scarier than Harris, and a lot more scary than me."

45

Wearing goggles that scanned for electronics and heat signatures, Petty Officer Samuel Naens crouched between a bush and the stucco wall that separated Pugh's mansion from the beach. He flipped his goggles to his forehead and rummaged through his backpack for the tiny Communications Disruption Device he'd packed before leaving New Copenhagen. CDDs "sludged" all open-air communications in a target area, blocking radio and phone signals alike.

Satisfied that the CDD would prevent Pugh's men from coordinating, the diminutive SEAL pulled himself over the seven-foot outer wall in a single fluid motion, landing as silently and gracefully as a cat. He found himself in a shadow-filled corner of the yard, his dark skin blending in with the night.

With the CDD sludging the airwaves, Naens and Baker couldn't communicate, but they had synchronized their responsibilities. Naens's job was to enter the house through the back and disable any guards he located. If he ran into Pugh, he would disable him as well.

Having entered Pugh's backyard, Naens paused behind a tree and searched for dogs. Moments passed, then three black and rust-colored Rottweilers charged around a corner of the house. Naens shot them with tranqs, hitting their necks, silencing them instantly.

One of the guards, a big heavy man, spotted the sleeping dogs and went to investigate. He tried to radio the other guards, but no one answered. Aiming his M27 into the yard, he headed down the hill, and Naens slipped behind him like a cat on the prowl, pressed a foot into the back of the big man's knee, forcing it to buckle, then slipped an arm across his throat and choked him. Naens could have killed the man more quickly and easily, but Harmer had told him not to kill the guards unless absolutely necessary.

Naens dragged the unconscious guard under the deck at the back of the house. He found a door that led to a storage area, picked the lock, and tossed the limp guard and the sleeping dogs inside.

Petty Officer Jeff Baker watched the property from three houses away, hoping that more guards would enter the yard. Slipping past inattentive guards would be easier than subduing them inside the house. Watching the relaxed way in which these men guarded the property, occasionally glancing up and down the street as they chatted, irritated Baker. *Dereliction of duty,* he thought. They were imbeciles. They were dumb thugs who hadn't been challenged for too long. They were ripe for the picking.

Baker stole through one lot, then another, approaching Pugh's home from the south. The sky had the golden glow of the late-afternoon sun. The elongated shadows of the trees stretched the length of the lots he crossed. *A mountain beside a sea,* he thought. *How beautiful.*

He heard the softest yelp and knew that Naens had squelched the dogs. He heard a quiet rustle and knew that Naens had squelched a guard as well. Baker leaped the wall that surrounded Pugh's yard, slipped into the garage through a window, and entered the house from inside the garage.

He crouched and waited in the darkened entryway, blending into the shadows, watching a guard pour himself a glass of water just eight feet away. The man wore a shoulder holster from which hung a pistol.

He could have tranqed the man, but the glass of water posed a problem. Glasses falling on ceramic kitchen tiles made noise and attracted attention. The man was looking away, enjoying the view of the ocean as he drank. Baker waited, poised in the shadows, taking long, slow breaths.

Still staring out the back window, the man lowered his glass. Baker rose to his feet, watched and waited until the gangster placed his glass on the kitchen counter, then the SEAL sprang, covering the distance to target in a single second, reaching a hand over the man's mouth and chin, holding his tranq pistol an inch from the man's spine and squeezing the trigger. The unconscious guard went limp, and Baker gently lowered him to his knees, then scooped him over his shoulder in a fireman's carry and left him curled on the pantry floor.

Killing him would have been easier, he thought, but Baker always followed orders.

He moved over to the living room.

The house wasn't quite a mansion, but it came close. Baker paused to admire the large chandelier that hung over the grand staircase leading to the second floor, then he scanned the living room and the main entrance. He was looking for guards but had enough presence of mind to appreciate the architecture.

The house had two main floors and a lower subfloor that opened onto the backyard.

Baker stole back toward the kitchen and down the dim hallway that led to the bedrooms. He heard a man yell, "What the speck! My phone ain't working."

"Hey, Greg, let me see your phone. I want to see if it works."

A woman stepped out of a doorway. She was skinny and blond with short hair. To Baker, who considered himself only marginally more attractive than most insects, the woman looked beautiful. He slid back, out of the doorway, and hid in the shadows. If the woman stepped into the room, he would "disable" her. He hoped she would stay clear.

The man started yelling again. He said, "Yo, Greg, are you out there?"

"It's me," said the woman. "Greg's not here."

"Where is he?"

She said, "I don't know. Maybe he went outside," as she walked past the door without peering into the room. Baker watched her, gave her a moment, then slipped into the hall. She might have turned into the kitchen or possibly gone up the stairs.

The man was probably Pugh, judging by the command in his tone. He headed down the stairs to the subfloor. That made him Naens's problem.

Baker hid low, remained in the shadows, and waited. He heard the man say, "Hey! Who the speck are you?"

"Brandon, is everything okay?" The woman glided down the stairs, stepped into the hall, and Baker choked her into unconsciousness without leaving so much as a bruise. It only took a moment. He carried her into the pantry and lowered her beside the man . . . Greg.

Three of the men from the front entered the house. One yelled,

"Hey, Brandon, are you having trouble with your phone? Brandon?"

Baker waited until they closed the door behind them, then he tranqed them and dragged them to the walk-in pantry. He thought, *This is a big pantry*. But the floor was filling up. He stacked the men on top of each other and left the pretty woman a respectable space, then he sprinted down the stairs leading to the lower part of the house. Pugh and Naens waited at the bottom of the stairs. Naens said, "Brandon here is an agreeable fellow. When I told him that Ray Freeman and Wayson Harris wanted a word with him, he even offered to drive."

"How did it go upstairs?"

Baker said, "About as expected."

Pugh asked, "How many of my guards did you butcher?"

Baker said, "None."

"You didn't touch them?"

"Sorry, when you said 'butcher,' I thought you meant 'kill.' I knocked out four guards and a woman."

"That would be my niece," said Pugh. "Did you hurt her?"

"Not a scratch on her," said Baker.

"Lucky you," said Pugh. "She's Harris's girl. He wouldn't have taken kindly if she showed up with a black eye."

46

"D'you find any uniforms?" Harmer asked when Naens reported.

They were in Pugh's car, just leaving the neighborhood. The sun had finally set. The streetlights had switched on though the sky was too bright for them to matter. In the way of tropic skies, the horizon was filled with streaks of purple and orange against a glowing red background.

One of Pugh's bodyguards drove. Pugh sat in the passenger seat. Naens and Baker sat in the back. Naens leaned forward, and said, "Excuse me, do you know if the Unified Authority has any installations here?"

"You kidding?" asked Pugh. "Last time Harris and Freeman came through, they massacred the Unifieds and all of their buddies. I ain't seen so much as an ant wearing U.A. colors since."

"Did you hear that? Even the ants are out of uniform," Naens told Harmer.

"Not a problem; we'll borrow a uniform from one of their guards when they arrive."

"Which one of us is changing sides?" asked Baker.

"I am," said Harmer.

Including the times when they'd had to hide, Naens and Baker spent forty minutes running from the airstrip to town. The drive back took ten. Naens identified himself and the car using his headset, and a couple of SEALs opened the gate and let them in.

Pugh asked, "You got guards watching the airstrip?"

"We have guards watching the road, too," said Baker. "I spotted Warsol a half mile back."

Pugh said, "My compliments to your sergeant; he runs a tight ship. So what would have happened if we didn't identify ourselves?"

When neither SEAL answered, Pugh said, "That's what I thought."

They parked in the hangar. The man who met them as they climbed out of the car was neither SEAL nor natural-born. He stood five-two, and his fingers ended in claws, but he had pale skin, blue eyes, and a smooth but macrocephalic brow.

Naens said, "Who are you supposed to be?"

"Major Joseph Conlon, Unified Authority Army," said Harmer.

"Who's that?" asked Baker.

"Some guy Freeman killed back in D.C. I got his ID and papers," said Harmer.

"Too bad you don't have his uniform," said Naens.

"Was Conlon's head shaped like a mushroom?" asked Baker.

"I don't know what he looked like," Harmer admitted. "How do I look?"

"Your head's shaped like a mushroom, and the Army doesn't enlist midgets," said Naens. "Other than that, you look good."

"There's nothing I can do about my forehead; I need to cover up my brow," said Harmer. He sounded defensive.

"In that case, you look good," said Naens.

While the SEALs spoke, Freeman and Watson emerged from the Explorer. They walked over to Pugh. Watson and Pugh were nearly the same height; Freeman had seven inches on both of them.

"Where's Harris?" asked Pugh.

"He's in the plane," said Freeman. Freeman and Pugh knew each other well enough to have a healthy mistrust. Watson had never met Pugh, but he didn't trust him, either.

"Waiting for me to come to him?" asked Pugh, who was both astute and crooked. "First, he sends his goons to grab me, now he's too important to meet my car; things must be going well." He lifted an eyebrow, and said, "Sounds like our boy is king of the world."

Harmer and his SEALs never joined in on the conversation; they didn't believe they had anything to add. Watson had Emily wait in the cockpit. If anything went wrong, he wanted to keep her hidden away and safe.

Pugh entered the ship and saw Harris stretched out on the floor with a drip line attached to his arm. He bobbed his head amiably, and said, "He looks peaceful."

"He should," said Freeman. "The mixture going in his arm is one-tenth morphine."

"Morphine?" Watson asked. "I thought you were hydrating him."

Pugh stared down at Harris, and said, "That explains the smile. Why are you trying to make him an addict?"

"Addiction isn't the problem," Freeman said as he told Pugh about the flu. "He wouldn't have had the strength to fly here if he weren't having a continuous combat reflex.

"You've heard of Volga and New Albatross," said Freeman. Those were former U.A. colonies. New Albatross was a prison colony; Volga was an impoverished backwater world—the colony

Howard Tasman once called home. When the inmates on New Albatross rioted, the Unified Authority sent Liberator clones to restore order. When the citizens of Volga tried to abandon their planet, Liberators were sent to guard the spaceport. Both incidents resulted in civilian massacres.

Pugh knew about both massacres. Everyone knew about them; they occupied a dark place in the public consciousness.

Freeman said, "Massacres happen when the combat reflex goes too long. If we keep him luded long enough, he might come out of this without paranoid delusions."

Harris stirred. He turned his head but didn't open his eyes.

Pugh knelt beside him and pried one of his eyelids up, a trick he had learned for dealing with overdosing lude jockeys. He asked, "Harris, you planning on dying?"

Harris mumbled something incoherent.

Watson said, "We need to get him to a hospital."

"He'll survive," said Freeman.

Pugh said, "All we're talking about is a head cold and a little dehydration here. For a guy like this, that ought to be a snap; I mean, he survived a bullet in his gut last time I saw him."

"Are you going to help us?" asked Freeman.

Pugh answered, "Why would I put my money on a dead horse; there's no percentage in it."

"He's not dead," said Watson.

"What's the difference? He doesn't have his army, and you say the Unies are coming to get him," said Pugh. "That makes him as good as dead."

"Are you a fan of the Unified Authority?" asked Watson.

"Not especially," said Pugh.

"From what I hear, the Unifieds like your enemies more than they like you," said Watson.

"Something like that," Pugh agreed as he rose to his feet.

"If Harris survives this *head cold*, he'll have a score to settle with the Unifieds," said Watson. "If he dies, you have a problem. If he lives, the Unified Authority has a problem."

"He's not the kind of guy who turns the other cheek," Pugh agreed.

Freeman said, "He'll be more effective if he's sane. We need to keep him from having a combat reflex as long as possible."

"I got drugs. I got plenty of drugs," said Pugh. "You want me to set him up?"

"Set him up," that sums it up perfectly, thought Watson.

47

"There's supposed to be a guy there named Franklin Nailor," said Brandon Pugh. "Is he around?"

Pugh knew he wasn't. Nailor was more than dead; he was profoundly dead. Wayson Harris had shot him and hidden him in a trash container in an undersea city that the Enlisted Man's Navy destroyed with nuclear-tipped torpedoes.

"Who is this?" asked the officer on the other end of the line.

"The name's Brandon Pugh; pleased to meet you," said Pugh.

"What is this about?"

The conversation had reached the point when Pugh would draw most on his ability to lie. The Unified Authority had seized control of Washington, D.C., but they hadn't yet declared their victory. Pugh, living in the New Olympian Territories, shouldn't have known that the clones were dead.

"I got a clone I want to give you," said Pugh.

"You wish to give Unified Authority Strategic Command a clone?" asked the officer. He sounded stiff and suspicious.

"Is that where I'm calling? I got this line address from Frank Nailor a few months ago. He told me he was U.A., but he didn't tell me he worked in Strategic Command. I guess he's an important guy."

The officer didn't seem interested in chatting. He said, "Are you calling to report a corpse?"

"No, this one's still alive," said Pugh.

The officer on the other end of the line wasn't in the know. Sounding surprised, he said, "You still have a live one. Let me ask about that."

The next call came ten minutes later. When Pugh answered, the officer on the other end said, "Mr. Pugh, this is Major General Trevor Ormonde. I understand you have a clone in your custody. Is that correct, sir?"

"Hey, General, I'm not exactly 'the police,'" said Pugh. "I don't keep people in my custody."

"As I understand it, you're not the territorial governor, either," said the general, a certain note of dislike in his tone.

"Not me. I'm just a private citizen."

"Okay, Private Citizen, how exactly did you come into the possession of a clone?"

"He came to me," said Pugh. "He flew into my airport."

Something Pugh said seemed to have tweaked the general's imagination. He looked ready to jump out of his chair. "How much do you know about military clones, Mr. Pugh? Would you be able to identify if this clone is a Liberator?"

"I don't know if he's a Liberator, but he says his name is Wayson Harris. Are you boys looking for Wayson Harris?"

Having spent his entire life dealing in drugs and prostitution, Pugh knew when the fish were hooked and how to reel them in.

"Mr. Pugh, according to your files, you have . . . er, an organization," said General Ormonde.

"Yeah, I got an organization; that's how come I know Nailor."

"Do you think your men can keep Harris locked up for the next few hours?"

"For the next few hours, for the next few days, for the rest of his synthetic life, no problem. The man's dying, for crying out loud. We got him in a hospital bed. He wants me to help him hide."

Ormonde said, "You'd better place armed guards around his room. Lock the door from the outside and place armed guards in the hall. Harris is a dangerous man, Mr. Pugh. Don't underestimate him."

Pugh smiled, and said, "He's not causing any problems; we've got him on drugs. Come in a wig, and he'll think you're his mother."

Ormonde sent two transports.

Freeman and Harmer watched from a blind outside the airfield. Freeman watched the scene through a sniper scope. Harmer used field goggles. He asked Freeman, "Did they need two transports to pick up one sick clone?"

Freeman didn't answer.

They watched as fifty enlisted men, eight officers, two Jackals, one jeep, and an armored personnel carrier rolled off the transports. The soldiers organized quickly and boarded the vehicles.

A third transport arrived five minutes later, dropping out of the sky and landing beside them. This one brought soldiers and officers but no vehicles. After the third transport landed, one of the first transports took off.

"Ummmm, now they have an entire company," said Harmer.

"I hope they're from different units. This will go a whole lot easier if they don't all know each other."

Harmer had the flesh-colored face of a natural-born and the gray-tinted body of a SEAL. He sat with his shirt off, waiting for the U.A. uniform in which he would change identities.

Most of the officers and a full platoon remained behind to guard the field. As one of the officers wandered off on his own, Warsol and Jorgensen crept up from behind and snapped his neck. They carried him behind the fuel depot, stripped off his clothes, and stuffed his body into a Dumpster. Baker handed his uniform to Petty Officer Libenson, whose skill set including forgery. Fifteen minutes later, Libenson delivered the uniform to Harmer, having resized it.

Harmer had the face of a natural-born and the uniform of a major in the Unified Authority Army. He wore thick white gloves to cover his fingers.

He asked Freeman, "How do I look?"

Freeman didn't answer, but Naens did. He said, "You're the ugliest natural-born I've ever seen."

"But I do look natural-born," said Harmer.

Naens agreed.

Disguised as Major Joseph Conlon, Harmer prepared to join the Unifieds. He asked Freeman, "Any last words of wisdom to give me?"

Freeman said, "Be careful around Harris; he does stupid things when he's desperate."

Major Conlon slipped through a hole in the fence and walked across the airfield. He approached a sergeant reclining in a jeep, lounging in the sun. "Well now, Sergeant, you look a tad bit too comfortable," said the major. "How about you get your sunbathing ass in gear and drive me to the hospital?"

Woken from his revelry, the sergeant saluted, and apologized. He said, "Sir, my orders were to wait here in reserve."

"Yeah, well, consider yourself called to active duty. I need to get to the hospital rapid, quick, and pronto."

Conlon had beautifully forged orders from Major General Trevor Ormonde instructing him to oversee the transport of the prisoner, but he wouldn't present those orders to the sergeant. He was a major. In the Unified Authority Army, majors didn't explain themselves to sergeants.

The sergeant drove directly to the hospital, arriving ten minutes before the rest of the convoy, which had stopped to visit the capitol. When the transport team arrived at the hospital, Conlon strutted up to the captain in charge and presented his orders.

Having replaced the captain, Conlon led the transport team to Harris's hospital room, where he checked to make sure Pugh had given Harris the special thermal pack that Warsol had built for the occasion. He threatened Pugh's niece and ordered his squad to strap Harris into his traveling chair.

As they left the hospital room, Conlon made a show of inspecting the thermal pack. He took it, tossed it, removed the chemical stick, and added a note as he replaced the stick. The note landed safely on top of the temperature-absorbent marbles, but Conlon wondered if Harris would find it before it sank into the gel.

Even after they arrived at the Naval Consolidation Brig, Conlon oversaw Harris's incarceration. He accompanied Harris to the infirmary, saw the fear in the Liberator's eyes when he realized he was being prepped for an incapacitation cage. He recommended giving Harris "exercise periods" and "latrine privileges" to Reid, the NCB warden.

When Sunny showed up at the prison, Conlon admitted her

into his cell. When Harris nearly sliced her in half, it was Harmer, still dressed as Major Joseph Conlon, who told Harris, "Freeman said you'd do something stupid."

Part III

THE TERRORISTS

48

The power went out, turning my incapacitation cage into nothing more than a table. One moment I lay there with my muscles holding me stiff, the next, my arms, legs, neck, and stomach muscles went limp.

Damn that felt good.

Usually, they warned me before cutting the juice. A tray of food might slide in through the slot at the bottom of my door, then Conlon's voice would speak to me over the intercom saying something like, "Harris, you've got half an hour to eat and take care of your business."

Conlon . . . was he on my side? *Freeman said you'd do something stupid.*

I didn't know what to make of Conlon. The little man strutted around the prison like a king in a palace. The other guards feared the little priss, Lord knows why. Even Reid, the warden, seemed afraid of him.

Now that the current was off, I sat up on the cage like a patient waiting on a doctor's table. I looked around my cell, wondering if someone had cut the power and why. The lights remained on in the hall; only my cell had gone dark.

Somebody retracted the bolt from my cell door. It was a soft sound, not much louder than a coin landing on concrete, but in my ears, it sounded as loud as a gunshot.

I hopped from the table. Having enough strength to hop from the table was new. Maybe my strength had returned, maybe my cell door's opening had cleared the way for a rush of adrenaline.

The hall was empty. Had I not used the thermal pack to kill Sunny, I might have had a weapon to aid in my escape.

Maybe this was a trap; it was almost certainly a trap. Reid or Conlon or maybe a low-level jailer might be waiting outside my door with a gun or a Taser, hoping I'd step outside my cell, prepared to beat me or lynch me as I "tried to escape." This could well have been my punishment for killing Sunny. Maybe Tobias Andropov had authorized it.

The hall was empty. I pulled the door open. This was the first time I'd actually touched the door. It was heavy, maybe two or three hundred pounds of steel and bulletproof glass, but it glided as smoothly as a balloon in an air current.

Someone had left a change of clothes outside my door. Slacks, shoes, socks, a belt, and a casual shirt sat neatly folded. I tore off my prison clothes and dressed myself quickly. It didn't matter much to me if this was an escape or a trap; I wouldn't have minded either.

If I escaped, I would go on a rampage, killing Unified Authority leaders until one of their bullets finally found me. If I died . . . I died. I'd fantasized about killing myself a time or two. That was the one place where Andropov and I agreed—neither of us saw me as fit to live.

I hoped my rescuers had placed a weapon in the clothing. They hadn't.

"You coming?" a man called from down the hall. Apparently, he didn't worry about the Unifieds overhearing him. He didn't whisper, but his voice was soft. I didn't have the strength to run. I crossed the hall as quickly as I could, passing three guards whose throats had been slit.

Conlon met me as I came around the corner. He held a pistol in his right hand.

His right hand . . . He had removed his glove. His fingers were sharp as talons at the ends. With his glove off, I saw the true color of his skin; it was gray, as if he had been sprinkled with coal dust.

"Got an extra pistol?" I asked.

"You won't need it," said Conlon. Only he wasn't Conlon.

He didn't run, but he walked with purpose, and I fell in behind him. We took the stairs down into the lobby and followed a service hall past the kitchen and into the motor pool, where a windowless government delivery van waited, its engine idling. Conlon slid the door open, and I climbed in.

Four SEALs sat crouched in the back of the van. Looking through the gap between the front seats, I saw that Emily Hughes was driving. She waited until she heard the door slide shut, and we pulled away.

Across the van, the SEAL I had come to know as Major Conlon removed his prosthetic forehead. He was even uglier without it, not that I complained. He was a SEAL. I had fought side by side with these vicious little bastards, and I respected them more than any other class of servicemen.

The gray tint of Conlon's skin gave him a cadaverous complexion. The bone ridge above his eyes made him look like an ape.

Having grown up in an orphanage for general-issue clones, I had learned to tell them apart. I didn't know the SEALs as well. I asked, "Is Illych with you?"

Emerson Illych was a SEAL I had known well. He and I had run a couple of operations together.

The man kneeling beside me said, "Illych died."

"Killing aliens?" I asked. The last I had heard, every last SEAL clone had been sent to track the Avatari.

The SEAL nodded.

With the SEALs in charge, breaking out of prison went smoothly. Had I planned the escape, it would have required RPGs, gunships, and a company of Marines. Had Freeman planned it, entire sections of the building would have been destroyed. I specialized in combat; Freeman relied on mercenary tactics. Versed in espionage and guerilla tactics, the SEALs entered quietly, killed the warden, the surgeon, and every single guard, then left the building unnoticed.

49

Freeman's Fortress—a bunker hidden beneath a warehouse registered to a corporation that never belonged to Ray Freeman in the first place. Life went on above us, independent of our presence, unaware of us. If Unified Authority Intelligence tracked signals sent from Ray's computers, they would raid the building above us and find nothing, not even our door.

Freeman's underground nest wasn't huge, but it included housing, equipment, and food.

What he didn't have was men.

Neither did I.

Without a large supply of men, the most we could hope to accomplish was revenge, which sounded great to me, but Travis Watson and Emily Hughes wanted more.

We all sat at the same table, Freeman, Watson, Emily Hughes, and me. Master Chief Petty Officer Jeff Harmer was the only SEAL at the table; the others could have come, but they entrusted

Harmer to look out for their interests.

Emily asked, "What's our endgame?"

I'd heard the term "endgame" before, but I didn't know what it meant. I'd spent my entire life speaking military-ese. "Endgame" didn't fit in my lexicon.

I asked, "What do you mean?"

Freeman translated the term for her. He said, "What are your objectives."

"I want to kill Andropov," I said. Murdering the man who killed my entire species seemed like a reasonable objective.

"Then what?" asked Emily.

"Then he'll be dead," I said.

"What are you going to do once he's dead?" asked Watson.

"Oh, sorry. Once I'm done killing Andropov, I want to start killing senators and generals." It seemed like a logical progression.

"So that's it? You want to kill people?" asked Emily.

"A lot of people," I said hoping to clarify my point.

She turned to Freeman, and said, "He's going to make things worse."

Why is she even here? I wondered. She wasn't a combatant. Okay, yes, she drove the van when the SEALs broke me out of jail. Who else did we have? The SEALs looked like specking space aliens, I had a face like a general-issue clone, Watson was a former president, and Freeman was a seven-foot black man. When it came to being inconspicuous, Emily was the only one of us who could walk down the street without attracting attention.

Freeman's nest didn't have a lot of rooms. We met in the "armory," which contained less gear than I'd expected. Oh, he had rockets and rifles and demolition gear, but all of his vehicles were of the civilian persuasion. Sedans blended in well, but they don't have armor or radar displays.

We were on the Virginia side of the Potomac, which meant that we'd need to cross bridges and risk surveillance cameras every time we entered the capital. Having a vehicle with radar and sludging equipment would have made my travel plans more viable.

"What were you hoping for?" I asked.

Watson, the statesman in our cabal, fielded the question. He said, "I'd prefer for Emily and myself to come through this alive," his frustration coming through loud and clear. I hadn't even been out for a day, and he was already frustrated with me.

"Alive?" I asked.

"I'm a fugitive, Harris. I'm a criminal because I worked for you."

"You applied for the job," I pointed out. "I didn't recruit you."

"I was right out of law school. I applied for a job in a government office, and I ended up as your assistant."

"You also served a brief term as the interim president of the Enlisted Man's Empire," I said.

"And now I'm a traitor and criminal, Harris. If they catch me, they will kill me. I didn't apply for that."

"What do you want me to do?" I asked.

"I want you to fix it."

He was hoping for a messiah, but he got a Liberator clone instead. Raw deal.

Freeman and Harmer remained silent through this. Unlike Emily, who looked both furious and ready to cry, they seemed to find the conversation entertaining.

"Do you have anything to add?" I asked them.

Freeman said nothing. Harmer said, "Personally, I like your plan. It's very straightforward."

I said, "Travis, I'm sorry, but I don't know any way to make things right for you."

"And?" Watson prompted.

I thought about the question. ". . . and maybe the problem will fix itself if we can kill the men who caused it."

"That's you, Wayson! You're the one who caused it," said Emily.

What does she want from me? I wondered. I said, "Emily, I didn't start this war. I was a loyal U.A. Marine."

Harmer said, "It's true, I'll swear it on a five-foot stack of Bibles; the first time I met Harris, he was a U.A. Marine."

Watson glared at Harmer, and said, "Wayson, I am a fugitive. The Unified Authority is looking for me. They want to put me in jail," Watson said, enunciating every syllable as if speaking to an idiot or a child.

I shrugged my shoulders, and said, "Maybe Pugh can hide you." Freeman had already told me about Pugh's role in my arrest by this time.

"Look," I said, hoping to bring them back to the reality of our situation, "there is no way we can beat them. They have a navy and an army." According to Freeman, they didn't have an air force. Apparently, as his last great act of defiance, General Strait disabled every fighter, cargo jet, rocket, and missile under his command. He even erased all of the computers.

Now came the part that cut deep. I said, "The general population won't help us; they never got behind us." The bastards. I asked myself, *How many clones died protecting natural-born lives?* I knew the answer, too. *All of them.*

"I'm sorry, Travis. That's all I have."

Watson and Emily went silent. I couldn't tell if they accepted my apology or blamed me for everything. Maybe they didn't know themselves.

Harmer broke the silence. He said, "I have some good news; the Unified Authority doesn't have much of a navy—six ships."

"How do you know that?" I asked.

"I hacked into their computer system."

"You what?" asked Watson. "They're going to track your signal."

Harmer smiled, and said, "No they won't."

"What about spy ships?" asked Freeman. "They might have stealth cruisers."

"Do they have guns and missiles?" asked Harmer.

I answered, "No."

"Then I'm not worried about them," said Harmer. "We all have our own objectives. Mine is to protect Shin Nippon. I will advance your objectives by accomplishing mine."

"How's that?" asked Watson.

"My men and I came to sink their navy. Once that's done, the Unified Authority won't have a navy or an air force. That will leave their army and their Marines." He turned to face Watson, and said, "You let Harris kill off their army, and they'll fall apart."

I asked, "You want to sink their navy first?"

"That's what we came for, Harris. Once that's done, I'll help you with anything you want."

He made this offer so damned cheerfully, you'd have thought he was offering to help me with gardening instead of assassinations.

"Do you know how you're going to do it?" I asked.

"I have no idea how we can do it," he admitted.

I had a few ideas.

Next I tried to offer an olive branch to Watson. I said, "Maybe you can go to Shin Nippon with the SEALs. You'd be safe."

Watson shook his head, and said, "That's not the life I had in mind."

"Well, Travis what the speck did you have in mind?" I asked.

The meeting ended after that. Emily left the room, storming out without saying a word. Watson chased after her. Harmer went to check on his men.

I didn't think Emily would have gone to hide in the bathroom. She wasn't the crying type.

I went to my rack, a cot in the supply room. As I lay down, I heard her voice through the wall. She was saying, ". . . a complete waste of time. Maybe we should have stayed on New Copenhagen."

I wanted to say something, but I knew it would only make things worse. There was nothing I could say, nothing she wanted to hear from my lips, and maybe she was right.

"We had to get him," said Watson.

"No, Trav, we didn't. We didn't need to rescue him. We don't owe him anything."

"I do."

"No you don't," said Emily. "He's useless. All he cares about is getting revenge."

"Do you blame him?"

"I don't care about him; I care about us. He's going to make things worse for us. He's going to get himself killed, and he's going to take us with him."

Then I heard Harmer. He said, "Miss Hughes, have you ever heard about a planet called Ravenwood?"

Emily said, "I'm sorry, we're having a private conversation here."

Harmer said, "I'll only be a moment."

Emily made a noise that could have been a sigh or a groan.

"Ravenwood was an uninhabitable planet in the Scutum-Crux Arm that the Navy used as a fuel depot, but they also used it as a testing ground. They sent Marines there to defend the planet, then they sent SEALs to kill the Marines."

"Kill them?" Emily asked. "That's barbaric."

"Only one Marine ever survived Ravenwood, and that was Harris. I've seen the feed from the exercise. We sent a squad of SEALs—thirteen men; Harris killed every last one of them."

"So the Unified Authority is barbaric, and Harris is a butcher," Emily said, sounding unimpressed.

"How does that make him a butcher?" asked Harmer.

"He killed thirteen men."

"M, those men were trying to kill him," said Watson.

"And he killed them first," said Emily. "Travis, we'd have been safer without him."

50

Toward the end of the Mogat War, the Unified Authority launched a supership called the *Doctrinaire*, a fighter carrier that was the biggest, strongest, fastest, best-shielded ship in history. The Mogats destroyed the *Doctrinaire* in her first big battle. They found an antiquated self-broadcasting rust tub and broadcasted her smack dab into the middle of the *Doctrinaire*. The resulting wreckage is still floating in space.

The Unified Authority had six self-broadcasting ships that the SEALs wanted demolished, and Smithsonian Field had two thousand self-broadcasting torpedoes capable of doing the job. The fly in the ointment was this, now that the Unifieds had seen us using Explorers, they started paying attention to Smithsonian Field.

"Getting out there will be tough," said Harmer. Using Freeman's computers, he'd tapped into the U.A. satellite-security network. "They have a platoon guarding the facility."

Harmer held his briefing inside Freeman's computer room. As he spoke, he conjured up Smithsonian Field on his computer screen.

There it was—plain to the eye, the administrative office, the underground bunkers that served as hangars, and trucks for transporting troops. "There are rocket batteries along the road. I understand those batteries were your idea, General Harris."

"As a matter of fact . . ." I started to say.

Watson interrupted me. He said, "They were."

"Prudent thinking," said Harmer.

It was prudent thinking. I had foreseen the danger that a fleet of self-broadcasting ships could pose.

All of the SEALs attended this planning session. Apparently rocket batteries didn't bother them. Ignoring the roadside defenses, a SEAL named Warsol asked, "Where are their barracks?"

Freeman answered, "There aren't any barracks on the facility; they send new detachments every eight hours."

Harmer and Warsol grinned at each other. Harmer said, "The changing of the guard."

Using Explorers to torpedo the Unified's self-broadcasting ships was my idea. How we would get to those ships, that was SEAL strategy. They might have been ugly, but those sons of bitches were geniuses, every mother-specking one of them.

The fear of Freeman and me stealing an Explorer probably didn't keep Tobias Andropov awake at night. Why should it? As far as he knew, the only thing we could do with them was escape, and where would we go? He didn't know about New Copenhagen, and we'd sign our own death warrant by flying to Terraneau.

He didn't know about using self-broadcasting birds like torpedoes. Hell, the only people who knew the truth about the *Doctrinaire* were Freeman and me and the Japanese, and he didn't know where to find any of us.

The Unifieds had only assigned a token force to guard Smithsonian Field, just a platoon. Taking the field wouldn't be a lark, but we'd secure it . . . and then the race would begin.

Those old rust buckets at Smithsonian Field, they needed sixty minutes to recharge their broadcast generators. If we got lucky, the Unifieds might not realize that their guard patrol was missing for twenty minutes. It might take them another ten minutes for their gunships to reach us.

Once the shooting started, we wouldn't be able to hold out for more than a minute or two. I had thirteen commandos, a retired mercenary, and two uncommitted civilians on my side. The last thing I wanted was a shoot-out.

Harmer figured a way around the problem.

The detail that guarded Smithsonian was stationed at Fort Belvoir, an Army installation halfway between Washington, D.C., and Smithsonian Field. Dressed as the newly demoted Corporal Joseph Conlon, Harmer planned to infiltrate Belvoir and ride to Smithsonian with a fresh platoon. He would enter the field, slip into a hangar, and start six Explorers charging.

The rest of us would ambush the next shift from Belvoir. We would catch them, kill them, and drive their trucks to Smithsonian Field. Harmer would have the Explorers charged and ready, and that would be that.

The problem is that nothing ever goes as easily as that.

51

Corporal Conlon, our official harbinger of death, drove to the front gate of Fort Belvoir as if he owned the joint. Wearing his linen gloves and prosthetic forehead, and bearing forged orders created by Petty Officer Warsol, Harmer traded salutes with the guards, showed them his orders, and drove onto the base.

Freeman, the SEALs, and I watched from a safe distance, nearly a mile away.

Dressed as Conlon, Harmer drove onto the base at 04:30. The sky was still dark. The changing of the guard occurring at 06:00, Conlon's detail left for Smithsonian Field at 05:15.

For the record, Fort Belvoir looked more like a college campus than an Army base, an abandoned campus at that. Surveying the base from a distant hill, I saw buildings that looked like office complexes and buildings that reminded me of libraries and dormitories. Lights blazed all around the gate and guard shack. Belvoir's streetlights shone like tiny stars.

From our far-off hill, we watched Harmer drive past a semicircular row of five-story admin buildings. By Army-base standards, Belvoir was very deluxe. Most of the Army bases I'd visited were spartan and rough.

Anyway, Harmer didn't stop at the large and dark office complex; he drove to a brick pillbox not far from the motor pool and disappeared into the building. Twenty minutes passed, then lights switched on around the motor pool, and two trucks lined up. Not long after that, a jeep arrived, then a column of men boarded the trucks. If everything had gone according to plan, our boy Conlon left with the trucks.

The time had come to hurry up and wait.

Our ride would leave for Smithsonian Field sometime around 13:00.

There is a bay near Fort Belvoir. The maps call it a bay, but it's really a swamp. I never saw any fish in the bay, but I saw clouds of mosquitoes swarming around it. There were woods and wetlands and small towns. For the most part, we remained in the swamps and the woods, hiding.

The SEALs had survival training and liked the wilds. They explored, slipping in and out of the trees and tracing the streams. They walked into glades and vanished into the shadows. They drilled.

Freeman and I, we sat and watched them, feeling lazy and old. Freeman zeroed his scope, but he didn't shoot. I rested more than anything else. I was a Marine, and Marines learn how to rest whenever the opportunity presents itself. I closed my eyes and tracked the sun through my eyelids. I breathed the air, taking in its mossy stench and loving it. I listened to the rhythm of the water lapping against rocks and logs.

I wondered if perhaps I had beat that flu. My strength hadn't returned, but I didn't cough, not even once. I was anxious for the fight to begin. I imagined rolling into Smithsonian Field, an M27 in my hand. The guards were Marines in my mind; they wore combat armor. They had helmets instead of faces.

I imagined shooting them. I felt good. The air was fresh. The sun dissolved the aches in my limbs and shoulders.

I thought about my men, my empire, my enemies. My daydreams were pretty similar to the hallucinations I had after landing the plane in the New Olympian Territories. I saw many of the same people, but this time they didn't speak to me.

Should I hit Andropov in the Linear Committee Building? I asked myself. The LCB had become a U.A. stronghold. I'd send shock waves through the entire republic if I brought the building down on top of him.

At 11:00, we moved north and east, tracking a creek that ran through the forest and led to the highway. The SEALs trotted along the rock-lined creek like hounds on the scent; Freeman and I could barely keep up with them.

We reached a shady bend where the roadway dipped and tall trees grew. The trees wouldn't hide us from satellite surveillance, but they offered camouflage. There we waited, our heartbeats racing every time we heard a vehicle approaching. Freeman, perched on the high limb of a tree, aimed his rifle when he heard engines or wheels. The rest of us hid along the road. The first vehicle to pass was a jeep. Another jeep passed by about twenty minutes later.

This was a narrow stretch of road—a hairpin turn that would cause drivers to show caution. A row of sturdy trees lined the road, offering good concealment.

I noticed something as I crouched there in waiting—my body still hurt. A dull and ignorable ache had spread across my body, to my shoulders and head in particular. I wasn't coughing, but I supposed my cold hadn't completely gone away. I felt tired but alive, and the sun still felt good on my back.

At 13:23, we heard the growl of big engines. It wouldn't be a jeep this time. Something big was coming around that bend. I rested my finger across the trigger of my M27. Beside me, the SEALs crouched like runners at their starting blocks. With their odd gray skin, they looked like three-dimensional shadows. Determined to do as little damage to the trucks as possible, they opted to use combat knives instead of guns.

We had to be fast. We had to be fast enough to prevent anyone watching the convoy via satellite from becoming suspicious.

The engines grew louder. Birds heard the noise and flew from the trees. Ahead of us, the road sat mostly in shadow, with beams of light shining solid and straight through holes in the canopy of leaves above our heads.

Two trucks. Two personnel carriers. There were twelve of us; each of those trucks would carry anywhere between twenty and thirty soldiers. *What if we made a mistake?* I asked myself. *What if those aren't soldiers? What if they're Marines in shielded armor?*

The first of the trucks appeared at the curve, an army green dragon with a grill at the end of its snout. One of the SEALs flipped a switch, sludging the airwaves in every direction. Freeman fired a single shot that drilled through the supposedly bulletproof windshield and splattered the driver's brains against the back of the cab. The truck continued forward, its front end veering off the road and into foliage and soft ground. The rear of the truck blocked the road, forcing the personnel carrier in the rear to come to a stop.

I saw the SEALs leap from their hiding places and dart behind the trucks, but I lost track of them as I ran to the second truck, threw open the door on the passenger's side. The man riding shotgun was so focused on the stalled truck ahead, he barely glanced in my direction as I opened his door. I fired two shots into his body, grabbed him by the blouse, and slung his corpse to the road. The driver saw me, gave me a *Huh?* reaction, and went for his gun. It would have been easier to shoot him, but I didn't want to spend the next hour sitting on a bloody seat; I grabbed his hand and snapped his wrist, used the injured hand to pull him across the cab, and launched him out onto the side of the street; then I shot him.

While I tossed the bodies of the driver and passenger into the brush where no one would find them, Freeman dropped down from his bough. He pulled the bodies from the first truck and climbed into the cab.

Taking the trucks took no more than ten seconds.

I didn't bother checking on the SEALs; they would come out of this fine. It wouldn't have mattered if the Unifieds had ten soldiers or ten thousand waiting in each of the carriers, at close range, the SEALs would annihilate them.

Freeman backed his truck onto the road and drove on as if nothing had happened. I followed, surveying the damage around me as I drove. When I shot the passenger, my bullet passed through the roof of the truck. I could see the hole, but the guards at Smithsonian wouldn't see it. Freeman, on the other hand, had a mess on his hands. He had a shattered windshield and blood all over the back of his cab. The guards at Smithsonian Field wouldn't need to look too closely to see that.

I flashed my headlights. He must have figured out what I wanted because he drifted along the side of the road, letting me pull ahead of him.

"You back in business?" I asked, using the radio console in

the dashboard to make sure it worked. I wasn't as concerned about Freeman as I was about sludging. Momentary lapses in communications are common; communications dark spots, on the other hand, are a sure sign of trouble.

"I took the turn a little too wide," Freeman said, on the off chance that someone was listening.

So far so good, I thought. We had the trucks, we were back on the road, and the SEALs had turned off their sludging device.

I didn't think anyone was listening. As far as the Unifieds were concerned, this should have been a routine guard change at an unimportant site.

We had a forty-minute drive ahead of us. If I'd been in the back of the truck, I would have spent the time listening in on my men or possibly sleeping.

The ache I had felt before had vanished. I felt good, like I'd never had the flu. *I must be having combat reflex,* I thought. That would be good . . . but I'd always known when I was having a reflex in the past. I wondered why I couldn't tell now.

I let my mind wander as I drove. *How long ago was it?* I asked myself. Was it five days ago that I landed in the Territories too tired and dehydrated to climb out of that Johnston Meadowlark? *Five days ago, maybe six? When did I kill Sunny?* I knew when MacAvoy died—that had just been four days earlier. And ten days ago, the Enlisted Man's Empire seemed to hold an unbeatable hand. Now you could fit the entire empire in the back of two trucks.

No, I thought. *Not in two trucks.* The SEALs didn't belong to the EME; they came to protect the Japanese. Watson and Emily were civilians. I didn't even know if I trusted them. *Travis maybe,* I told myself. I had already decided that Emily wasn't on my side.

What about Freeman? I asked myself.

He might have been on my side, but Ray Freeman was never

really on anyone's side but his own. He was a mercenary; you had to pay him for his loyalty.

I was feeling better though, stronger. My head had cleared.

Freeman and the SEALs broke you out of that prison, I reminded myself. *They didn't need to do that.*

I thought about that. Freeman qualified as an ally at the very least. Then I remembered Harmer telling Emily about Ravenwood. I had killed thirteen of his brother SEALs. Did he tell her that to make her feel safe or to scare her?

We entered that final winding road that led to Smithsonian Field.

Harmer's reasons don't matter, not on this op, I reminded myself. This one was for him. Maybe I was placing my faith in the devil, but I decided I could trust Harmer for the time being.

The gate loomed up ahead, a judgment day made of barbed wire and steel posts. I rolled ahead knowing I had no choice but to trust the SEALs. As far as I could tell, they had no reason to betray me. My enemy was their enemy. My enemy was Freeman's enemy as well.

My enemy is Emily's enemy, I reminded myself. I didn't trust her.

A guard stood at the entrance. He held an M27. His bullets would not penetrate the windshield if he shot at me. Freeman's steel-jacketed rounds had titanium pins for piercing armor. That guard's weapon held general-issue bullets. The rocket battery to the left side of the road was another story. Those rockets would make short work of my armored truck.

I slowed to a crawl and drifted up to the guard, silently praying he kept his eye on me and didn't notice the condition of Freeman's truck. I waved at him to prove my friendly intentions. What he didn't see was that I was balancing my M27 on my lap with the other hand, and held the steering wheel steady with my knee.

52

I never doubted that the SEALs would have their sludging device working by the time we reached the gate. When it came to this kind of op, they didn't make mistakes.

I pulled up to the bar. The guard smiled at me, then recognition showed in his expression. He might not have recognized me so much as recognized that I was a clone.

He turned to look at the guardhouse, and I shot him.

The two guards waiting in the shack scrambled for their guns, but they were too late. I rammed the shack with my truck. The building was made of thin metal and bulletproof glass, and it collapsed like a house of cards. I drove my personnel carrier over the remains of the shack, crushing the men who had been sitting inside it.

The shooting started quickly, bullets hitting my windshield with a loud *thwack*, leaving cracks and divots in the glass. Bullets struck the roof of my cab, ricocheting into oblivion. A screen in the center of the dashboard showed the view from the rear of the truck, and there were my SEALs, leaping like paratroopers. They stayed low as they dashed around me and in through the gate.

Freeman pulled along my left side, blocking the entrance to the field. He cut his engine, ducked beneath his dashboard, and came up with his rifle.

Harmer emerged from one of the subterranean hangars, still dressed in his U.A. BDUs, but no longer wearing his Conlon mask. He emerged, spotted two Unifieds running for their truck, and gunned them down.

Meanwhile, the rest of the SEALs fanned out around the compound. They traveled in teams of two, running to doorways, one man opened the door, one man looked for traps and targets.

Holding my M27, I jumped from the truck and ran toward the offices. I heard shots fired in quick succession and like loud individual claps of thunder—Freeman and his sniper rifle shooting the men in the guard towers. He could kill them through the bulletproof glass and through the armored sleeve that ran around the sides of their towers.

The SEALs fired in three-shot bursts—a drumroll punctuated by a loud bang every time Freeman pulled his trigger.

I spotted a couple of natural-borns disappearing into the closest hangar. I jumped down the ramp and sprinted through the door, not knowing whether I was following two men or twenty.

The hangar was mostly dark, lit only by the sunlight that filtered in through the window slits lining the ceiling. Rows of Explorers gleamed in the dimness, their hulls reflecting the light. They looked like tin cans to me, maybe tin coffins.

I didn't want to shoot around the Explorers; they were so breakable. Bullets penetrated them, grenades tore them apart. I moved ahead slowly, taking in the silence, looking for movements instead of men, listening for footsteps and the click of bullets being chambered.

These birds had batteries, ancient batteries, plastic boxes filled with corrosive chemicals and toxic shit. They had atomic engines. They had liquid-oxygen boosters. A bullet might cause one to explode; an explosion could start a chain reaction.

My heart pounded, my temples throbbed; if I'd ever suffered the flu, the final symptoms had long since exited. I felt good, alive, ready to kill.

Somebody fired a shot. I heard the report, saw the scratch the bullet left on the wall just ahead of me. I spun but didn't fire. The target was gone.

The man ran. His footsteps weren't loud, but they sounded loud in the near silence.

I heard a squeak, spun, and fired, hitting another man as he sprang from his hiding spot among the tool chests and analytical computers. He fell onto a desk and hung there, his head and chest on the desk, his legs dangling to the floor. I couldn't tell if had I killed him, but at least he'd stopped moving.

Footsteps coming from two directions. Was there a third man? I remained hidden and silent, fully aware that they could flank me, possibly on both sides. Maybe they knew Marine tactics—keep your enemy pinned down, then flank him. Shoot him in his hiding hole.

I listened for steps, scrapes, breathing.

"Hey, Harris!" It was one of the SEALs walking down the ramp. I needed to warn him of the threat, so I fired my gun in the air, then I somersaulted from my blind and ducked behind new cover.

The SEAL had been smart. He didn't walk down the center of the ramp. He'd given himself away when he shouted for me, but the moment he realized the fight was still going, he reacted quickly and found cover.

I circled right, crouching beside the shoulder-high wall that separated a parking area for the carts from a mechanic's bay.

"Harris, how many?" the SEAL called.

Looking around an edge, I saw a gun but I couldn't see the man holding it. He wanted to flank me, and he was close; another few feet, and I'd be behind him.

I yelled, "Three," as loud as I could, my voice pounding across the high, cavernous building like a wave. The man with the gun leaped from his cover and tried to dash behind an Explorer for cover. I shot him just as he reached the ship.

"Two," I said.

I was wrong. Several soldiers, possibly as many as ten, fired in my direction. Bullets drilled the partial wall I was using for cover. Bullets struck the wall of the hangar, bouncing off, marking their impacts with sparks. Bullets hit a metal tool chest a few feet ahead of me, making a racket so loud it hurt my ears.

The SEAL stepped out from behind a steel panel. He moved like a squirrel, twitching movements so quick you would miss them if you blinked. He seemed to disappear from the ramp and magically reappear behind the nearest Explorer, his pistol ready, his eyes alert.

The U.A. soldier hiding behind the workbench had the patience of the dead. He made no more noise than a feather floating in a breeze. He moved so glacially slow that he never attracted my attention. One moment I saw empty floor, the next I saw his M27 pointing toward me.

Still crouched behind an Explorer, the SEAL swung his pistol to the left and shot him. The SEAL didn't need to aim; it was as if he'd located the man using telepathy. His one shot hit the soldier in the chest slamming him back first into a wall.

The SEAL tried to sprint to the next nearest Explorer, but his luck ran out. He seemed to fly across the floor, as five single shots rang out. I heard them, each one as distinct as a hammer pounding a nail. *Bang . . . bang . . . bang . . . bang . . . bang.*

One shot struck the right side of the SEAL's chest, and he curled like a boxer recoiling from a hook to his ribs. The next bullet struck his jaw, tearing it away from his skull. The third shot hit his left thigh. The SEAL was still up, still running, still holding his pistol, still unaware that death had already struck. The fourth shot struck the left side of his gut, lifting him off the ground. The fifth bullet hit his right forearm as he fell, and his pistol finally dropped from his hand.

His heart kept beating, flushing blood out of bullet holes, and he curled into a ball like a dying spider.

I found a handhold and pulled myself up the tail assembly of an Explorer. The silly bird didn't open at the back; she had a hatch along the top of her spine. I pulled myself up and kept myself low. I spotted two of the men who had shot the SEAL and shot them.

Three Unifieds tried to circle behind me. I could see them clearly from my elevated vantage point. They crouched in a pack, moving slowly, believing a skein of wires and pipes would conceal them. I might have been able to shoot them, but somebody spotted me and opened fire. Bullets struck the Explorer and passed through her; I had to dive to the ground, or I'd have been shot.

One of the Unifieds decided to follow my lead, the dumb shit. He climbed to the top of an Explorer and ran along her spine, searching for me. He leaped from one ship to the next, landing hard, then scurrying off to the next one as if they were stepping-stones, making so much noise that Beethoven would have heard him.

As he leaped from one Explorer to another, I stepped out from under a retracted wing and shot him in midair. His death did nothing to ruin his trajectory—he reached the next bird, but his legs folded, and he slid down the side of the ship.

Another soldier used that moment to try to sneak behind me.

He stepped out from his cover. I caught him and fired three shots. One of my bullets grazed his arm, sending a spray of blood. He screamed and kept running.

A wounded man, even a dying one, can still shoot. This guy wasn't necessarily dying, either. I would have shot him again . . . tried to shoot him at least, but I was out of bullets.

I watched him for half a heartbeat, taking in the panic in his expression. He was a boy. He might have been twenty-one or twenty-two, and blood gushed through his fingers and streamed down the front of his uniform.

He'd dropped his gun when I shot him. It sat no more than ten feet from me on the polished concrete floor, its trigger and butt pointing in my direction . . . no more than ten very exposed feet away. *Dive for it,* I thought. *Somersault on top of it and skid behind the tail of the next plane.*

A couple of soldiers noticed how much time had passed since I fired my weapon and became emboldened. They stepped into the open. The gun was so close. SO close! But I had to leave it.

"Hey! He went down over there! He's hiding over there!"

I was trapped. I was pinned. I tried to hide between a rolling tool chest and a waist-high brick wall.

"There. Behind there!"

One of the soldiers got too brave for his britches and came looking for me. He stepped around the tool chest, and I tripped him, hit him, took his gun, snuffed out his life. He screamed for help, but he died before any of his friends could arrive.

An officer skidded around the nose of an Explorer. I shot him in the face. Another saw the rapidly expanding puddle of blood on the concrete and ran for safety. I heard the report of a high-powered rifle and saw the body drop; there wasn't much more than neck left above his shoulders.

A squad of SEALs glided into the building as smoothly as

shadows sliding across a well-lit wall. They came too late to help. Freeman had shot the last of enemy.

The battle had lasted ten minutes, longer than it should have. When it ended, we counted up corpses. We had killed forty-seven of theirs; three had either hidden or run away. Master Chief Harmer didn't think they would matter.

With the enemy dead, we shut down the sludging. Now that the fighting had ended, we advanced to the next stage of the mission.

Freeman, ever the stoic, said nothing as he went to the radar shack and started scanning for U.A. warships. He found them one by one, calling their positions to Harmer who relayed them to his men. The navigation coordinates used by broadcast computers come in long strings of numbers, most have twenty digits, but some have more. Freeman shouted them out, then read along as Harmer repeated them to make sure he repeated them correctly.

The SEALs and I had returned to the personnel carriers and grabbed our demolition gear. Whether they spotted our invasion or ignored us entirely, the Unifieds would see what we did next, and they would react. They'd storm the airfield gates. They'd send in their gunships. We didn't care. By the time they arrived; we'd be long gone.

The SEALs placed explosives by the gates and around the fuel depot. I placed my kits in the hangars. I entered the first hangar and saw the blood marking the place where that one SEAL had died helping me and saw no reason to mourn him. I felt nothing. Maybe it was the way our time was ticking away. Maybe not. A lot of people had died in messy ways inside this aeronautical museum. Blood and bullet holes scarred several of the ships.

I rigged explosives along walls and under ships, then I left.

The second hangar was considerably larger. It housed over one thousand Explorers. They sat parked in perfectly straight rows. The hangar walls stood thirty feet high, twenty feet of which were buried underground. From the outside, the building looked like the world's biggest pillbox—long and low to the ground. From the inside, it was so tall and sterile and neat that it reminded me of a cathedral.

I entered, absorbing the absolute silence. There was no blood on these walls. The SEALs had removed six of the planes, leaving a few lines shorter than the ones around them.

I felt like my presence disturbed an inner sanctum, like I was intruding on holy ground. It made no sense. No one had given their lives in this building. These mechanical birds meant nothing. In another few minutes, they would be a thin layer of shattered glass lying beneath a miasma of concrete and steel.

I couldn't deny the sense of reverence. Strange that I would feel more emotion for a den of ancient aerospace ships than for a battlefield in which men had died.

I placed charges on a fueling station, under Explorers, and on the outer walls of the building. When this hangar went up, I wanted to be sure that nothing survived.

Six Explorers sat on the tarmac looking old and innocuous. They were silver birds with retractable wings and lots of glass. They had been designed for scientific exploration, but in another two minutes, they would wage and win a war against powerful foes.

The Explorers sat in two-hundred-foot intervals, which was still far too close together. It couldn't be helped; that was all the room we had to work with.

Looking past the row of planes, I saw that several of the SEALs had gathered in a circle. We'd lost two SEALs taking the trucks, one died helping me in the hangar, two more died capturing the airfield. The surviving members of the squad had collected their bodies and carried them to an empty unused corner of the field.

Using collapsible spades, they buried the bodies among the tall grass and flowers.

The SEALs always buried their own.

Because we hadn't yet finished our mission, Harmer didn't join them. He stood beside me, inspecting the Explorers to make sure they were ready but also watching his men.

"Which men did you lose?" I asked.

He said, "Morris, Hansen, Gomez, Summerland, and Warsol. We're going to miss Warsol; he had valuable skills."

In another moment, he'd send six more men to their deaths. Having started with a band of thirteen, he'd soon be down to two.

Freeman emerged from the radar shack. His limp more pronounced than usual, he walked past us, glaring at Harmer and ignoring me. He entered each of the Explorers, spent about thirty seconds in each, then moved on to the next.

Watching him, I came to understand that feeling of respect I had felt as I placed charges in that hangar. Yes, the Explorers were scientific ships, but the SEALs had other plans for them. In their hands, these ships would become manned torpedoes. They would be weapons of sacrifice and destruction, the men piloting them becoming both the executed and executioner. They were the firing squad, but they had volunteered to fire themselves off like bullets.

"There has got to be a better way to do this," I told Harmer.

Staring straight ahead at the Explorers, he said, "I'm open to suggestions."

Unable to come up with any, I stood mute.

Freeman finished his rounds and came to join us. He stood beside Harmer, towering over him, a mute giant. After several seconds, he asked, "Are you sure your men know how to fly these?"

"I watched you," said Harmer.

He had watched Freeman when they left New Copenhagen. The SEALs were synthetic marvels—able to pick up piloting skills with a glance. They spoke Japanese better than the Japanese. They had eidetic memories; they glance at a map and reproduce it down to the last detail. Harmer had seen Freeman fly an Explorer, then he described the operation to men who hadn't even entered the cockpit, let alone handled the controls. I had no doubt they would execute their final operation with flawless precision.

The funeral ended. *Was that for the five who had fallen or the six who shortly would fly to their deaths?* I asked myself.

The Unified Authority never built autopiloting controls into its broadcast computers. In order for self-broadcasting ships to initiate their broadcasts, there had to be somebody aboard to press the button.

Six SEALs strolled up the runway, calm, at ease, cheerful about what lay ahead. They didn't joke; they would have seen that as disrespectful of their fallen comrades. They formed into a line, and Harmer saluted each of them. He asked, "Are there any questions?" When no one spoke up, he said, "You know what to do."

Master Chief Harmer held up his earpiece for them to see, then clipped it to his ear. His six pilots did the same. Harmer traded one final salute with each of his men, then the six SEALs strode off to their individual Explorers.

If they have earpieces . . . if they can hear him, why can't we set up some sort of remote? I wondered, but I knew the answer. We didn't have time. Even if the SEALs had asked for robot pilots, we wouldn't have had time to make them.

Using the earpiece, Harmer could speak to each of them, and they could speak to each other.

I watched those tiny, ugly bastards trot into their Explorers without so much as a moment of hesitation. They didn't look back or pause before sealing the hatches behind them.

The wind picked up, a long and powerful gust that tore leaves from trees. The chain-link fence that surrounded Smithsonian Field rattled its protest. A few dark clouds rolled over the area, blocking the afternoon sun.

The SEALs didn't have extrasensory perception, but they spoke so softly when they used their earpieces that they appeared to think to each other. All of the Explorers booted up at once. Flames appeared beneath their boosters.

I didn't hear the report of the rifle, but I saw Harmer stumble forward as if shoved from behind. He stood, spoke softly, far too softly for me to hear him, and the six Explorers lifted off the ground at the exact same time and to the exact same height. Their boosters holding them in place, they hovered about eighty feet off the ground, far enough above us that their anomalies were unlikely to reach us.

We stood near the main gate, just a foot or two inside. Harmer's lips moved, giving his pilots the order to broadcast. I covered my face and stared at the ground to protect my eyes. It may have been my imagination, but I thought I felt heat on my head. I thought my hair might have stood on end as well.

The broadcasts themselves were silent, but the anomalies created large pockets of nothingness, and air rushed into those pockets, creating thunder that boomed like a nuclear detonation, and when I opened my eyes, the world was normal, and there was no sign of the anomalies, but Master Chief Harmer lay on the ground. The hole in his back was less than an inch in diameter. The one through his chest was six inches wide with bridges of ribs running across it.

The Unified Authority sharpshooter had hidden himself on the second floor of the two-story control tower. Having seen most of the SEALs boarding the Explorers, he must have decided that the odds had changed in his favor. Not knowing what would happen next, he'd aimed his rifle at the same moment that the Explorers went wheels up. He shot the master chief and just as he turned his sights toward me, the Explorers broadcasted out.

The whiny son of a bitch screamed, "My eyes! My eyes! Oh, shit, I'm blind! I'm blind!"

I would have killed the bastard, but Petty Officer Naens, the last of the SEALs, reached him first. He dashed into the building, and the screaming stopped a few seconds later.

53

Using a hack they learned from the late Master Chief Harmer, Travis Watson and Emily Hughes watched our raid and its aftermath through the Unifieds' satellite network. They didn't offer to play a part in the operation, and no one invited them to join us.

Watson led us into the computer room, and said, "You hit five of their ships. I'm not sure about the sixth; there's no sign of it on the screen."

He pointed to one of Freeman's monitors, a large screen showing radar readings instead of video images. Freeman and Naens went to look. I didn't. I'd been battling annoying aches in my back and shoulders and needed to rest.

Freeman, standing a few feet from the screen, bent at the waist so that he could stare into it. He said, "They might have broadcasted out."

Naens stepped closer and studied what he saw. He didn't have eyebrows. There was no hair on his gray-tinted head. He tapped controls on the screen, bringing up new data, and said, "They didn't broadcast out. Change that. They might have broadcasted out, but they didn't do it in time."

"How do you know that?" asked Freeman.

"Look at the screen," said Naens. "Do you see any Explorers on it? If that ship had broadcasted out, there'd be an Explorer sitting in its place."

"Maybe it flew back to Smithsonian Field," said Emily.

"There's no record of an Explorer," said Naens.

Along with my pains, I felt angry. It wasn't a specific anger, nothing directed at anyone in particular. It was more of a hate-the-world malaise. I needed a nap . . . something to recharge my batteries.

I said, "You should be happy, Emily; a lot of Unifieds died today."

That set her off. Her face flushed so red that her lips almost disappeared, and she said, "I'm not like you; I don't kill people for laughs."

I looked at her and smiled, then I coughed, which ruined the image I had hoped to affect. I started to say, "I don't kill people for laughs," but I realized that I did. Killing the soldiers guarding Smithsonian Field had been entertaining.

I said, "You and Travis better decide what you want. You don't want to be killers, but you don't want to be martyrs. I have news for you, you don't get it both ways. Either get used to killing people or get ready for them to kill you. That's how it works from now on."

I noticed that everyone was staring at me, not just Travis and Emily, but Freeman and Naens. I tried to justify myself. I said, "Honey, a lot of people died, and you just became a whole lot safer. You're not safe, but you're safer. Want to guess what we need to do to make you safe?"

She didn't answer.

No one said anything as I left the room.

54

I slept for a couple of hours. When I woke, I lay still on my rack, taking an inventory of my situation.

Ray Freeman had rescued me; he didn't have to rescue me, but he had. I trusted him.

Naens . . . I didn't even know if "Naens" was his first name or his last, or possibly both. I decided that I trusted Naens, but only because he was a SEAL.

I now trusted Emily Hughes, too. I didn't like her, but I trusted her because she kept her cards on the table, right out where everyone could see them. She didn't approve of me, and that was fine. In a world filled with poisonous snakes, I preferred the ones with rattles on the ends of their tails.

I trusted Watson as well, but it didn't really matter whether or not I trusted him; he posed no danger. He was weak.

My nap left me clearheaded, but I still had aches and pains. At that moment, it seemed like those pains might remain with me for life. I had never been knocked down by a flu virus before and had no idea how long the illness should last. My throat itched.

Naens must have heard me cough. He came into the room as I sat up on my rack. He didn't turn on the lights; the only light in the room was the beam that slanted in through the open door.

I suspect he saw me more clearly than I could see him. The SEALs had genes that gave them catlike sight in the dark.

He asked, "Are you awake?"

"I'm sitting up," I said.

He said, "Yeah."

"I'm sorry about Harmer," I said.

"Mistakes happen when time counts most. We needed to get those ships wheels up; some things were bound to fall between the cracks."

I heard no anger in his voice.

He said, "You kept your end of the deal, Harris. Harmer said you were good for your word. We wouldn't have been able to hit their ships if it weren't for you."

There wasn't anything I could say to that. Using the self-broadcasting Explorers as weapons had been my suggestion; the SEALs hadn't known about using them that way.

"Do you still want to go after their president?" asked Naens.

Hearing the question, I forgot about the ache in my back. The itch in my throat went away.

"It isn't going to be easy," I said. "We just swatted their entire navy. What do you want to bet they placed their ground forces on high alert?"

"Yeah. Too bad we're out of Explorers. Taking down their government would go a whole lot easier if we could broadcast a ship into the Linear Committee Building."

That thought hadn't occurred to me. I wished he had mentioned it one day earlier; it would have made everybody's lives a whole lot easier.

Naens said, "I'm sorry."

I hadn't expected him to apologize. "Sorry about what?" I asked.

"There were supposed to be seven of us helping you; that was the deal, right? You were supposed to help us sink their ships, and we were supposed to help you after that. We didn't live up to our side of the bargain."

"They died in combat," I said. "That means they did their part."

55

DATE: AUGUST 30, 2519

"Andropov knows you're coming after him," Watson said, giving me a searching look as if he'd just unraveled one of the great mysteries of the universe.

We'd all been living in Ray Freeman's hole in the ground for nearly half a week. Life in a can didn't bother me; I'd spent years living on spaceships. Naens didn't seem to care either way. Freeman was indifferent. He'd built this shelter; he would have built it bigger or farther out of town if he couldn't live with it. Emily, who had spent a year living in the Mars Spaceport, didn't like living in a warren, but she knew how to deal with it. Every morning must have felt like a flashback to Mars for her.

When I didn't respond, he just kept on carping. "From what I can tell, he's living in the LCB along with a few thousand U.A. Marines. Marines, Harris, men in shielded armor. He never leaves the building, and neither do the Marines."

"That's good," I said. "If we destroy the building, we take him with it." I hadn't expected Andropov to take up residence in the Linear Committee Building, but it didn't surprise me.

"Can you do that?" Watson asked.

"You planning on using a missile or a bomb?" asked Freeman.

"There's a train tunnel under the buildings," I said. "That opens all kinds of possibilities."

Freeman said, "Think about it, Harris, the U.A. Security Service would never have allowed anyone to dig a tunnel under the LCB; that would have been sending an invitation to the Mogats."

Trusting that MacAvoy really knew what he was talking about, I said, "They didn't dig the tunnel under the LCB; the Unifieds built the LCB over the tunnel. We're not talking recent construction here, this relic dates back to old U.S. times," I said.

"The Americans wouldn't have built a tunnel under their White House," said Freeman.

Watson, the only person in the room who attended a normal elementary school on Earth, said something that every elementary school student learned. He said, "They didn't build it under the White House. They built it three blocks north of the old White House lot."

"How do you know that?" asked Emily.

"Because I've been to the White House. So have you. Your father used to have an office there. It's the Colonial Governors' Hall."

The Governors' Hall was like a pangalactic embassy, the governors of each of the 180 populated planets had offices there. Gordon Hughes, Emily's father, would indeed have had an office there when he was governor of Olympus Kri.

That wasn't historical trivia; it was culture. No wonder Freeman, Naens, and I hadn't known that piece of information; it was out of our realm. We specialized in killing people and breaking things.

"Are you sure those tunnels are still there?" asked Freeman.

I nodded. "MacAvoy found them. He wanted to load them with nukes."

"He wanted to place a nuclear weapon in a tunnel under Washington, D.C.? That would have destroyed the entire city," Emily said, sounding astonished.

"Depends on the size of the nuke," I said.

"You're serious?" asked Emily, who knew damn well that I was.

"You mean about the nukes? That was MacAvoy's idea. I doubt he had a chance to do anything about it. He was pretty sick by the time he mentioned it."

"No, I mean you," said Emily. "You are talking about demolishing the Linear Committee Building, is that correct?"

Fully aware of what would she would say next, I tried to circumvent the storm. I said, "Listen, Emily, if you and Travis are ever going to be safe, we're going to need to kill a lot of politicians, especially the ones at the top. Tobias Andropov isn't the only asshole running things now."

Speaking softly, coldly, as if trying to communicate with a child, Emily said, "There are civilians in that building. There are secretaries and receptionists. Not all of those people are bad."

"I know that," I said.

"They don't all deserve to die," she said.

"That's the problem with war," I said. "A lot of people die." *Why doesn't she see that?* I wondered. It seemed so obvious. "Civilians died when the Unifieds attacked Anacostia-Bolling." Anacostia-Bolling was a joint Army/Air Force base located just south of Washington, D.C. The Unifieds destroyed it without warning; without provocation. "We weren't at war when they destroyed that base."

Emily asked, "What are you saying? Are you planning to go

on killing people until the Unified Authority waves a white flag? Is that when you'll stop?"

Put it in those terms, it sounded stupid, but nearly every military victory had been won by those very means. That was exactly what I had in mind. I said, "Of course not."

Watson said, "But you are planning on evening the score?"

Watson, the law-school graduate, was trying to trap me. I played it obtuse. I asked, "What do you mean?"

"Are you willing to kill civilians?"

"There's a term for it," I said. "They call that 'collateral damage.'"

Emily shouted, "That's perverse!"

I said, "Don't blame me. I didn't coin the term."

Watson asked, "Will you stop when you've killed as many Unifieds as they killed clones?"

Balancing the scales had occurred to me, but I'd dismissed the idea . . . mostly because I no longer had an army to help with the task. I wasn't specifically going after civilians, but I no longer worried about working around them.

"Collateral damage," I thought. The term had a cold, clinical edge to it. It removed the emotion from equations about ending human lives. I looked around the table and asked myself, Who here is collateral? *Is Naens collateral? Is Freeman? Is Emily? Is Travis?*

They all were. I liked them . . . well, maybe not Emily, but I would sacrifice them in a pinch.

"There are hundreds of people working in that building, Wayson," said Watson.

"Seven thousand people," I said. That was how many people we had working there when the clones ran the government. "There were 24,000 people working in the Pentagon when the Unifieds pumped their gas through the vents. There were 150 people working in the Archive Building. There were 52,000 people living on base at Joint Base Anacostia-Bolling.

"Don't tell me numbers," I growled. "I know all of the specking numbers."

Watson flinched when I shouted. Emily didn't. She said, "You say there are seven thousand people there. What do you plan to do about them? Are you going to evacuate the building or are you going to bring the building down on top of them?"

They knew the answer.

Watson stood up, and said, "That's it; I'm out, too."

"You don't want me to kill them?" I asked.

Suddenly sounding tender, Watson said, "There's got to be a limit; even for you."

Emily tried to draw on our old friendship. She and Travis and I had been friends. Sounding very sober and more than a little condescending, she said, "Wayson, for God's sake, think about what you are saying! You are talking about killing thousands of people."

"They killed millions of clones," I said.

"That doesn't make it right," she screamed.

I shouted right back at her. "Synthetic lives are just as valuable as natural-born lives."

Watson asked, "Are natural-born lives as valuable as synthetic lives?"

Silence. Freeman and Naens had nothing to say. Emily and Watson sat red-faced and breathing hard; fear and anger showing in their eyes. They were civilians at heart. Even with their own lives in danger, they didn't have the stomach to fight.

I said, "Let me set the scales for you. The value is twenty million to one. There were twenty million clones serving in the Unified Authority military when Andropov declared war on us.

"Does twenty million to one sound too unreasonable? How about ten million to one? There were ten million clones in the Enlisted Man's Empire when Andropov unleashed his epidemic."

"You're not being fair," said Emily.

"Fair?" I asked. "When the speck did fair become part of this?"

"What are you going to do once you blow up the Linear Committee Building?" asked Watson.

"Maybe I'll blow up the Senate."

"And when it's gone?"

"The Intelligence Agency, military bases, I won't run out of targets."

"And you're going to help him?" Emily asked Naens.

Naens shrugged his shoulders, and said, "Yes."

Screaming now, Emily said, "It's immoral! You're as bad as he is! You're worse than the Unifieds!"

Travis placed a hand on her shoulder, and said, "Emily . . ."

I could see it. In that little glimpse, I saw that he had turned on me. He was too scared to go join the Unifieds, but he'd be deadweight from here on out.

Emily still had some fight in her. She jerked her shoulder out from under his hand, and said, "Wayson, you've lost your mind. You're sick. Your body is fighting off that flu by giving you a combat reflex, and it's making you crazy."

I looked her in the eye, and said, "Bullshit."

And that was it. Emily gave up as well. She said, "Ray, I'm sorry. I can't do this."

He said, "I understand."

"Can't do what?" I asked.

"Fight your war," said Watson. "This is your war now. I'm washing my hands of it. We're washing our hands of it. We're leaving."

"Where are you going to go?" I asked. "I'll let you walk away, but that doesn't mean Andropov will. Where are you going to go?"

Emily started crying. No joke, the girl with the cast-iron soul had actual tears leaking out the corners of her eyes. She said, "It doesn't matter, Wayson. I'll take my chances with Andropov."

Freeman said, "I spoke to Pugh. He says he can hide them."

"That will buy them a little time," I said. "What are they going to do when the Unifieds invade the Territories?"

Freeman must have had an Explorer hidden somewhere or he wouldn't have been able to get the SEALs. I hoped he had a more common bird as well. He'd stand out flying a hundred-year-old self-broadcasting antique.

I asked, "Do you have a plane hidden somewhere?" and he said, "We're going to hitch a ride on a cargo ship."

Watson shook my hand, but he didn't wish me luck. I think he wanted me to fail. Emily hugged me. She kissed me on the cheek. She said, "Wayson, think about what you're doing. You're making a mistake."

I said, "Emily, I'm doing what I have to do."

She didn't answer.

Emily and Travis wouldn't be safe, so Freeman went with them. I hoped he'd return.

56

DATE: AUGUST 30, 2519

He wasn't as skilled as the late Jeff Harmer, but Naens knew his way around computers. He knew how to search and how to find back doors into encrypted information.

Using Freeman's computers, he tapped into networks that had changed owners several times over the years. The Unified Authority built them, then the Enlisted Man's Empire captured them, and now they belonged to the Unified Authority again. Each new owner had built its own level of security on top of past security measures, but when Naens went hunting, he never came up dry.

He checked the computers several times to see if the Unifieds had spotted Freeman or Watson as they traveled south. He looked for information about the sixth U.A. ship, the one that vanished. He looked for any movements suggesting the Unifieds had located us. Now I added a new search to his routine; I had him look for MacAvoy's tunnels.

"Do you think they made it to the Territories?" I asked Naens, as he played with the computer.

"Yes."

"Do you think it or do you know it?"

"I think it."

Freeman might have set up the computer system, but Naens navigated through those computers in ways that Freeman never dreamed of. His fingers were long, round, and sharp; it was as if they had been made for typing. When he typed, his fingers tapped the keys so quickly that it sounded like one long click.

Naens brought up one map of the capital, then another and another—some showed buildings, some showed streets, some showed patterns I didn't recognize. He examined each carefully. I hoped he was looking for MacAvoy's tunnels, but I couldn't be sure.

I excused myself to go look through our inventory.

Freeman had charges and guns, but he didn't have anything big—no missiles, rockets, or bombs. During the final days of the Unified Authority, as the aliens sped through the galaxy incinerating planets, Freeman had developed a new respect for human life. It didn't stop him from killing enemies, but he worried about preserving life. In that way, he wasn't all that different from Watson and Emily.

I wasn't sure I wanted him to return from the Territories. If he came back, he might try to stop me.

I found some grenades and RPGs. He had a couple of rifles and a rack of M27s. He had a complete set of combat armor, something I desperately wanted, but it had been customized for his seven-foot frame. Had I put it on, the knee joints would have been somewhere near the tops of my thighs.

Naens called, "Hey, Harris, I found your tunnels."

I went back to have a look.

Naens sat at the computer studying a three-dimensional wire-frame display. He said, "This wasn't just a train track, Harris; it was a commuter system that went everywhere, even under the rivers." He pointed to thick stripes that he identified as "Potomac" and "Anacostia."

"If you detonated a couple of tactical devices down there, you could destroy all of Washington, D.C.," he said. He meant nuclear weapons. I felt like the ghost of Perry MacAvoy had just tapped me on the shoulder, and this time he wasn't threatening me with a pearl-handled pistol.

I said, "We don't have any nukes."

"Yes we do," said Naens. To the SEALs, an objective was an objective. Once they accepted an operation, they didn't worry over questions about morality.

"Where did you find a nuke?"

"We have three tactical devices; they're already in the tunnels," said Naens. "General Pernell MacAvoy checked them out of the National Armory on August 21."

"MacAvoy," I whispered. "MacAvoy." He'd already placed the nukes in the tunnels by the time he brought up the idea. *Why didn't you pull the trigger?* I asked the ghost with the pearl-handled pistol.

Suddenly, pieces began to fall into place. Now that the Unifieds had control of the armory, they'd know that MacAvoy had checked out a trio of nukes.

The Unifieds hadn't found us because we weren't their top priority. They needed to know what happened to the nukes.

Suddenly, I was glad that Freeman had left with Watson and Emily. If he knew what we were discussing, he might have shot us both.

"How big are the bombs?" I asked.

"Sixty-two megatons apiece," said Naens.

"Big," I said. I'd seen what nuclear weapons can do. I'd fired a few in my time. If we detonated three sixty-megaton bombs under Washington, D.C., the entire Unified Authority would go up in flames. Watson would be safe. So would Kasara.

No more Washington, no more Unified Authority, I thought to myself, and as I thought that, warmth and strength returned to my limbs.

Pugh could become the de facto leader of the New Olympian Territories. Wouldn't that be rich; he'd be in a position to legalize his own organization.

Something somewhere in my psyche nagged at me, warning me not to pull the trigger on MacAvoy's bombs. I didn't know why. All I knew, truly knew, was that the idea sounded glorious. I would take out the bad guys and the people who had turned their backs on me and my kind.

And then I came up with an idea that made absolutely no sense, except in principle, but making sense no longer mattered. I decided that I would kill Andropov . . . I would snap his neck or maybe shoot him right between the eyes. I would have the pleasure of watching him die, then I would detonate my nuclear crematorium, and Washington, D.C., would erupt like a volcano. I'd be in the middle of it, but that was just fine.

"Do you mind dying?" I asked Naens.

"Depends on where and how."

"Underneath the Linear Committee Building," I said. "We kill Andropov, then we set off the nukes."

Naens smiled. I don't know if I'd ever actually seen a SEAL smile before that. It wasn't a pleasant sight. He had a face like a bat—a snout of a nose, tiny dark eyes that looked like black beads, and gray leather skin. He had sharp teeth. He said, "There will be a lot of collateral damage."

"An entire city," I said.

He responded, "The city of my enemy engulfed in flames; now that is a death I can live with."

We started making plans, looking at maps, figuring out details. I liked the idea of waiting a day, but I changed my mind when Ray Freeman called.

He began the chat by saying, "Our friends are safe in their new home."

"Glad to hear it," I said.

"Have you made plans?" he asked.

Have I made plans? Have I made plans? There's no way he can know what we're planning, I thought. But this was Freeman; he might have bugged his own nest. "Sure," I said, giving out as little information as possible.

"Plans involving tunnels?" he asked.

I looked back at the computer. I should have known. He'd bugged his own damned computer, the paranoid bastard. He'd want to know if anyone had accessed it. He had some remote screen that let him see exactly what we were seeing.

"It's just like I said, they're under the LCB," I said, hoping to all hell the bastard didn't notice the three nuclear bombs.

"And you're planning to storm the castle," said Freeman. I heard no suspicion in his voice. I couldn't read his expression.

"Do you want to share in the fun?" I asked, praying to the war gods that he'd decided to stay in the Territories.

"There's a plane leaving the Territories in a couple of hours," he said. "It's headed straight to D.C.

"I wouldn't want you to start the show without me."

When he hung up, I told Naens, "We better get started ASAP."

57

Under other circumstances, I would have preferred to wait for Freeman. He knew the city better than I did. He knew all about explosives, and his rifle would have come in handy as well.

Only, he might have turned that rifle on me. If he were here, he'd fight against us. I hoped he stayed in the Territories; I didn't want to kill my only old friend.

We set out for the tunnels that night.

The nearest train station was only a few miles away. Over the centuries, it had been abandoned, then sealed, and the entrance had been filled with concrete, but according to the records, the station itself had not been touched. It would still be down there, dark and silent, just as forgotten as the men who built it.

There were nearby sewers and pipes. After searching antiquated city plans, Naens located a sewer that nearly intersected with one of the old train system's ventilation shafts.

We'd enter unlit sewers, rappel in shafts that hadn't seen electricity in over three hundred years, then traverse train tunnels so old that even their ghosts would have abandoned them. Now that we had our route to the LCB, I needed gear; I needed a Marine combat visor with its multiplicity of lenses and sensors. Once we entered the LCB, we'd run into an army of guards and soldiers. Cowards like Tobias Andropov surround themselves with protection. If I wanted to kill Andropov, I'd need shielded armor, the armor used by U.A. Marines.

I said, "This job would go more smoothly if I had combat armor."

"Let's go shopping," Naens said. "Shopping," that was SEAL terminology for finding some unlucky Marine and taking the armor off his cold, dead body. I liked working with the SEALs.

Naens and I split up. He went to find the train station while I jumped into the jeep and drove thirty miles south to a place the Unifieds wouldn't think to search for me, Marine Corps Base Quantico.

Night had fallen, by the way. I reached Quantico township at 21:30 and drove through the sleepy little burg unnoticed. If there's one sight the people of Quantico have grown used to, it's jeeps, and I had stolen a jeep.

Quantico township sits like a civilian oasis in a military wasteland. The giant Marine base surrounds the quaint little town on three sides. Driving down those streets, I saw plenty of Marines, but none of them wore combat armor, so I drove on, into the dark woods.

The Marine base in Quantico is big—one hundred square miles that includes expanded living facilities, a golf course, and a cemetery. I'd been to that base many times, but as I viewed it from pine-covered hills to the west, I spotted something new, a freshly turned mound of dirt that was thirty yards long and no more than ten feet wide. I knew what it was and who lay beneath it.

Summer was ending, and fall had not yet begun. A languid breeze filtered through the darkened woods, swinging branches, revealing stars blocked by trees. Below the hills, lights sparkled around the mostly empty Marine base. A few jeeps drove along the roads. Lights shone in some of the barracks. Guards in armor patrolled the perimeter.

I didn't need to make a house call in this case. Once I rang their doorbell, the Marines would send armor my way on the hoof.

The ownership of MCB Quantico might have changed hands, but the operating procedures were static. The Unifieds had placed sensors in these woods. During my brief stint in management, I saw no reason to remove those sensors. I stood beside a three-inch-tall stake at that very moment. The nub at the top of the staff contained a camera and a microphone. I placed my foot on that nub and smashed it.

The loss of a ground sensor would not set off alarms. Deer walked through these woods. So did the occasional poacher. The men monitoring the security station would see that they had lost contact with their sensor, but they wouldn't assume the worst. After all, who would spy on a Marine base?

Still, procedures are procedures; Base Security would send a couple of sentries to investigate. I hoped they'd send a single Marine, and I hoped he'd come wearing armor.

An hour passed before my knight in shining armor appeared. I wanted him to come alone, but the deliveryman arrived with a companion.

They came in a jeep. I watched them through the scope of my rifle . . . well, Freeman's rifle. I could pick one off. If I got lucky, and the second one was dense, he might try to help his buddy before booting up his shields. Once those shields went up though, everything would change.

They parked. Because they wore their helmets, I couldn't tell if they were chatting or kept focused on their work. More likely than not, they would let their minds wander. Why not? Checking a faulty sensor—could orders get more mundane?

The moon was bright enough for me to keep an eye on them while they stood by the road, but the woods were dark, and they disappeared behind trees as they walked. Beams of moonlight filtered through the canopy, silver, slanted rays as faint as mist.

The men didn't carry any weapons other than the fléchette cannons on their right wrists. I'd been hit by fléchettes before. The ammunition the fléchettes were made out of was depleted uranium fragments coated with neurotoxin. A shot through the head or heart would kill you in an instant. A shot through a finger or toe would kill you, too, but it might take a few seconds for the poison to do its job.

The shields were the key. I had to kill both of them before they powered their shields. My rifle wasn't the right tool for the job. The scope helped me see in the darkness, but I could have shot by the light of the moon almost as easily. Rifles are hard to aim at close range, especially in a forest with trees blocking your line of sight.

I let them walk past me, then I slipped away. I trotted to my jeep, which sat hidden behind an alcove of trees.

Working silently, I slid Freeman's rifle into the back of the jeep and pulled out a pistol, an S9. The S9 was made for close combat; I'd have chosen that baby for any kind of close-range combat except hand-to-hand.

Now that I had a weapon, my next trick would be to use it on the delivery boys. I needed to find them and shoot them. I kept my breathing soft and even, watched where I stepped, and moved in a crouch. Step on a branch, and they might hear me. This was a forest; there were a lot of branches on the ground.

I didn't lean against the trees, but I used them to conceal myself as I walked. Those Marines had every advantage. Their helmets hid the sounds of their breathing. Their visors let them see in the dark. The interLink gear in their visors would let them speak to each other without my hearing them.

I circled back and found the place where I'd been hiding. I wanted to ambush them as they returned to their jeep. Time passed slowly, and I began to worry.

Had they already found the broken sensor? How long could I wait? How long should I wait? If they found it, did they dismiss it? Had they already started back toward their jeep?

I took a few steps toward the broken sensor, now more keenly aware of the darkness than I had been before. The moonlight provided a stripe here and a stripe there, but I was more blind than not. I had to walk slowly. They had night-for-day vision. Their depth perception would be limited, but they could see everything around them.

I heard the snap of a dried branch breaking. *Could be an animal,* I told myself, but I knew that it wasn't. They were near. Was I in their path? Would they see me before I spotted them? They didn't know about me, but they could see in the darkness. I was looking for them, but I was nearly blind.

I pressed against a tall pine tree and circled around it, my pistol ready, my breath stuck in my throat. I stepped and stopped, stepped and stopped, moving around the trunk of the tree slow and ready to pounce, like a cat sneaking up on a bird.

I found them. One stood over the sensor, a tall, lanky fellow, just about my size. The other guy was short; I couldn't have fit in his armor. The short one knelt over the sensor.

It would have been good if they separated. The courteous move would have been for the short one to go warm up the jeep while my armor bearer tried to fix the sensor that I had so thoughtlessly smashed.

They stayed together. The guy on his knees gave up on fixing the sensor and they started back to their ride. *Shit,* I thought. I didn't say it. I didn't say anything; I barely allowed myself to breathe.

They moved slowly, and I circled ahead of them, found a tree that was thick enough to hide behind, and waited. Hidden behind the tree, I'd be invisible. Hell, even if they tried to scope the area out using heat vision, they'd only get a trace of me behind this wide trunk. A moment passed, and another, then they stepped into view.

Meaning to shoot the taller Marine in the head, I waited as they approached my position. I kept my S9 low and ready and held my breath. They stepped closer, maybe ten feet away. Closer, just a yard. I'd shoot him through the side of his helmet. There'd be blood in the helmet, but I didn't care so long as the visor still worked. They stepped past me without a sideward glance. I drew in a final breath, brought up my gun, and the son of a bitch looked right at me as I shot. My fléchette hit him square in the face, killing the Marine but also drilling a hole through the front of his visor.

The tall one dropped to the ground and started twitching. His partner surprised me. He reacted like a trained Marine. Instead of ducking for cover or shooting at me, he powered up his shield and fast. He had good reflexes; he had his shield up so fast I never got a shot. An orangish gold envelope of light formed around him, and I ran away.

I didn't know if the man in the shielded armor had had time to raise his wrist cannon or not; I was too busy weaving around trees, sprinting across the forest floor. I leaped a fallen log like a hurdler.

Scrambling through the dark forest didn't go well. I rolled my ankle and brushed my shoulders against trees. I ran too close to a low-hanging branch and it scratched my cheek and neck. Had it been two inches higher, it might have stabbed my right eye.

I ran toward the slanted beams of moonlight, little islets of light surrounded by a sea of near blackness. Was he behind me? Was he shooting? I juked around a stump. I leaped a log; the ground behind it was lower than I expected and my knees buckled under me, causing me to skid on my shins. I landed on pine needles and stones, pine cones crumbled under me, dried branches dug into my legs. If this hurt me, I wasn't aware of it. Looking back, I saw the ghostly glowing figure stalking behind me. He brushed against a fern, and it went up in flames.

He moved like a machine, marching quickly, not bothering to look to the right or the left, storming ahead unafraid. He raised his right arm to fire at me, but I had already dashed around a tree.

Up ahead, a jeep sat alone on the side of the road, its top down, its seats empty. I ran, skipped left, skipped right, passed through a pearly-colored ray of moonlight.

The jeep had no doors. I would have preferred doors. Doors don't stop fléchettes, but they can hide you. I was open, visible, a target. He fired a shot at me. The fléchette drilled through the windshield without shattering it.

I hit the ignition and threw the jeep into reverse despite my nearly overwhelming desire to run, to duck, to hide. I needed to steer.

He was an orange-glowing ghost standing in the red glare of my taillights, confident, unafraid, standing with his arm extended, his wrist cannon pointing toward me, and all I could do was lean farther and farther toward the right as I steered the jeep and hit the gas. The rear of the vehicle hit him hard, like a hammer striking a nail.

It wasn't so much the impact that killed that U.A. bastard as the velocity. I'd seen those shields dissolve entire clips of machine-gun fire, but the jeep was too big to dissolve. It struck the man, and in the split second after the impact, I saw metal turn to steam as I leaped to the ground. I watched as the man and the vehicle rolled backward and bounced across the road. The energy from his shield must have fused him to the back of the jeep, which nearly stalled as it fought its way over a deep rut, but, carried on by its momentum, it continued rolling backward until it slammed into a tree.

Wrapped inside his cocoon of energy, the U.A. Marine was immune to trees and jeeps, but he wasn't immune to momentum. So there he was, riding along on the back of the unstoppable jeep when it hit the impenetrable tree, and though nothing passed through his armor, both his spine and his neck snapped. His helmet flew from his head, and his armor went dark.

I combined the short man's helmet with the tall man's armor, then I climbed into my jeep and drove back to Washington, D.C. My heart pounded hard in my chest, but by this time, I had grown used to it. I had grown used to the rhythm of the pulse thudding in my neck and wrist. My head felt clear, and I knew that I had begun a combat reflex, but really, my head had been clear all day.

I felt fresh and strong and rested.

A thirty-minute drive to D.C., and I wanted to drive it in fifteen. I drove slowly and methodically through Quantico, the township, passing a gas station and small grocery store, but when I left the glare of streetlights behind me and entered the velvety blackness, I mashed the accelerator to the floor. Up ahead, the town of Triangle glowed like a looming sunrise. There was a highway just beyond Triangle, Highway 95, which would connect with Highway 395 and take me all the way to Washington, D.C.

The road to Triangle was dark and lonely, a tree-lined road leading along the golf course and into nowhere. The lights of the base twinkled insignificantly in my rearview mirror. I watched them shrinking into the past and barely had time to register the sedan as I passed it. The car had waited just outside the gate, it was green, and the driver was an MP.

I slowed my jeep to the speed limit and hoped he'd go away, but the MP followed me like a yellow jacket defending its hive. He slowed his car to one mile above the speed limit and followed me for another five or six hundred yards before flashing his lights. If I tried to outrun him, I'd have cars and gunships chasing after me. I slowed, pulled to the side of the road, and came to a stop.

He parked behind me.

I sat stock-still and watched him in the mirror as he approached my car. He carried a computer for scanning tabs and left his gun in its holster. He was natural-born, a boy. He had brown hair and brown eyes but looked nothing like a clone. His smile said he was sorry for bothering me.

He strolled up to my car, and said, "Brother, you are driving way too fast." He paused when he noticed that I still wore my helmet, and his smile faltered. Maybe he realized that he had miscalculated, but he might not have known he would pay with his life. I turned, raised my right arm, and shot him once in the stomach and once in the forehead. The boy died before he hit the ground.

I picked up his body and placed it back in his car, using his safety belt to hold him in place so that casual passersby might think he was resting or chatting on his radio.

I didn't feel bad about killing that kid; he didn't qualify as collateral damage. He was a Marine. He'd taken the oath. Maybe he had parents. Maybe they lived near Washington, D.C., and they and their homes would disappear in the holocaust later this evening; they could go to their graves never knowing their son had died an hour or two before them.

In another hour or two, I would die as well.

I thought about Ava, Ava Gardner, the only woman I had actually lived with, my fallen Hollywood goddess, my movie star. I said, "I'll see you soon enough," and I felt nothing. Her ghost had gone away. She no longer haunted me.

Other ghosts slid from my thoughts as I rolled into Triangle, a good-sized town, a burg with movie holotoriums, restaurants, gas stations, and grocery stores. It was late. The lights turned red at the next block, and I joined a line of cars waiting for green. I looked at the grocery store to my left and saw a woman in a light blue dress carrying a sleeping child.

The child was small, no longer than a cat, and it pressed its face into the woman's shoulder. I had no idea if that child was a boy or a girl. The woman looked tired. She patted the child's head and stroked its back.

The light turned green.

As I drove off, I wondered if my bombs would destroy this town. Probably not. Triangle was thirty miles from ground zero, and my bombs were a few hundred feet underground.

A lot of other children will die. So will their mothers. These thoughts brought no remorse; they were simply an admission of fact. I no longer remembered why I chose to explode those bombs. I didn't bother trying to remember. That was the course I had chosen. I had no interest in changing it.

Night life is as different from life as night light is different from light. Even in the center of the city, with streetlights blaring, billboards glowing, and bright storefronts, no one would ever mistake night for day. A man sat on a street outside a dump of a bar. Couples walked together. A muscular guy in slacks and a tee shirt sat on the trunk of a car; he reminded me of an alley cat surveying its territory.

The ghost of Marianne Freeman glided into my thoughts. She was Ray's sister, a plainspoken woman with the strength of her conviction. I saw her face now, the swell of her cheeks, her brown eyes, her black hair.

I tried to imagine her and Ava, and Kasara and even Sunny, all standing together like sheep in a flock, and I realized something, the ghost of Marianne wouldn't audition for me like the others. Anytime another woman appeared in my imagination, Marianne waved a dismissive hand at me and walked away.

Ava had been the prettiest. Sunny had controlled me more than the others. Kasara had been my first. Only Marianne was sacred to me.

All of them but Kasara had died.

I reached the far side of Triangle and merged onto Highway 95.

58

I approached the capital from the Virginia side, driving toward the George Mason Bridge. I wouldn't need to drive over the Potomac because the entrance to the ruins of a train station was five hundred feet under South Courthouse Road; Naens had entered the ruins of a train station.

I arrived late, at 22:45.

Not much happened along South Courthouse Road at that time of night. The southern end of the street was all houses and apartment buildings, and people had shut down for the night. Lights showed in only a few condominium windows.

This is ground zero, I thought. I imagined people snug in their beds, unaware that Death had just driven past their front door.

The road ended just outside a golf course and I knew precisely where I was. I didn't play golf, but I had visited this facility; it was the Army Navy Country Club. *How ironic,* I thought as I parked my jeep.

I walked the short distance to the nearest manhole and used a pry bar to lift the lid. I dropped the tool down the hole, stepped onto the ladder, then dragged the lid back into place.

I had entered a world of complete darkness and very little sound. The darkness no longer mattered. My visor showed me my surroundings in blue-white tones against a black background. Night-for-day lenses showed me the world without depth, but they did show me the world.

I had entered a long and empty concrete valley. Water trickled down a trench in the middle of the floor. For all I knew, the air around me could smell like roses or shit. I didn't know; the airtight seal around my helmet meant I breathed recirculated air. I could wear this same armor in space or underwater.

I marched ahead.

I didn't know where I was going, but Naens had been here; that much I knew. He had placed virtual beacons, which I saw through my visor. I reached an intersection where the one tunnel met another. A red arrow visible only through a combat visor told me to turn right. A hundred feet farther, a glowing red square marked the hole Naens had blown into the wall.

I peered through the hole; it was like looking down a very narrow elevator shaft. At the top, the shaft ended in darkness. Looking down, the shaft extended so far that I couldn't see the end. The walls were unadorned concrete, riddled with cracks and splotches of moss.

Naens had left a rappel line for me. I attached it to my armor, climbed into the chute, and let myself drop and drop and drop. I passed places where the concrete had shattered over the centuries of disuse. Did I see dirt behind the missing pieces, or was it hollow? Darting past, seeing the world in blue-white and black, I couldn't tell.

Five hundred feet is a long way down. At some point I looked up to see the spot through which I had entered. I didn't find it. The shaft seemed to have formed its own horizon, a spot in which the four walls merged into one like the sides of a needle.

Except for moss and lichens, I saw no signs of life. I had expected to see bats or rats. Perhaps I had descended through skeins of spiderwebs without ever noticing. The walls seemed clean. The drop seemed to go on forever.

I thought about the Enlisted Man's Empire, imagining acres of men on parade, all with the same face and physique and mission, all of them enthusiastic about protecting the nation that had betrayed them.

I looked down and saw a floor. Through my night-for-day lenses, it looked no more than ten feet away. Using the sonar gear built into my visor, I took a sounding. It was still fifty feet below me.

I reached the end of the constriction of the shaft and slid into a wide, domed cavern. The Unifieds had left rows of seats behind, as well as trash cans and booths with incredibly antiquated computer equipment. I saw signs leading to railway tracks on which trains no longer ran and signs leading to exits long ago filled in with concrete.

This wasn't a museum exhibit; it was a tomb. These were the mummified remains of a long-extinct society. A nation known as the United States had used this station during an ancient past in which space travel went no farther than Mars and colonization meant invading other countries. America no longer existed. It had transmogrified into the Unified Authority and converted the world to accept its pangalactic manifest destiny.

There were no spiderwebs down here. Any spiders trapped in this mausoleum had died of starvation three centuries ago and their webs had disintegrated. I walked to a row of seats and ran my finger over the nearest. There was no dust. This train station was dead and sterile.

As I looked around the station, I felt a moment of fear. For just a moment, I thought maybe I had made a mistake. Maybe I had come down too far. Maybe this was a trap. Someone might have sneaked into the sewer behind me, retracted my rappel line, and left me down here trapped like an ant in a jug.

I searched the far wall, then the sides, finally spotting Naens's beacon—a glowing, silver-red line that led up five marble stairs and down a tiled hallway.

"Thank you, Naens," I said out loud. No point thinking the words this time, there was no one around to hear me.

I trotted up the stairs and started down the hall. It was wide, maybe forty feet from wall to wall. Ironically, looking through my night-for-day lenses, the light fixtures on the walls were darker than the darkness. They were round and dark, and they reminded me of eye sockets from which the eyes had been removed. They seemed to stare in my direction in blindness.

Naens's beacon led me to a platform, a gated floor on which passengers had stood and waited to board their rides. In the ancient days, trains had rolled on rails, but these tracks had been built in a more modern period. Instead of traveling on rails, these cars had levitated above magnetically charged trenches. The electricity needed to charge those trenches could have lit a continent in its day. By today's standards, it would have been negligible. The ancients could have run this track for a year on the energy expended during a single broadcast.

I leaped from the platform to the lip along the trench. The jump from the platform to the bottom of the trench would have been about twelve feet, too far a jump to make safely. I jumped eight feet to the track. The drop down the trench would be another four if I decided to take it.

I had miles to cross now. The tunnel led under the Arlington Cemetery, a burial ground for natural-born soldiers with a proper monument for the unidentified dead and only a ten-foot marble obelisk celebrating the millions of cloned military men who had laid down their lives.

I traveled under the Potomac River as well, not that I could tell the difference between when I was under land and when I was under the water. I just remembered it from the maps. Cities and cemeteries, they all looked alike from this vantage point.

The train station had been like a maze, with its branches and hallways. Now that I had entered an actual train tunnel, the maze had ended. This tunnel ran straight as an arrow for miles, with no identifying features to separate one segment from the next.

After half an hour in that tube, I saw signs that I had crossed the river. A walkway appeared on the right side of the track. The walkway led to a platform. I didn't need to brush dust or cobwebs from the sign to read it. The sign said independence ave station.

In few hundred yards, I'd be under "Monument Avenue," passing statues built for soldiers and presidents. There'd be a giant marble needle and museums and monuments that looked like mausoleums. I imagined the ground erupting beneath them, throwing them over like toys left out in a storm. I imagined the water in the Reflecting Pool boiling, then turning into steam, and glass shattering and like ice in a desert. At that very moment, I might have been under the Smithsonian Museum of Military History, the museum that once opened a wing specifically dedicated to clones, then closed it a couple of months later.

Naens left a beacon that led me off the Arlington Line, across 17th Street Station, and onto the City Center Line. I crossed more empty halls and marble floors. Sitting in the center of the floor like a vending machine set on its side was the first of MacAvoy's bombs.

It was seven feet long and four feet wide, wrapped in a smooth rectangular sheet-metal box. Naens's beacon led me right to the bomb, not that I could have missed it, and right to the handwritten note attached to its interface.

> Harris, you're the last man standing. We all knew it'd be you.
> Have a blast. Have a specking-big blast, 186 kilotons of fun.
> If you're wearing armor, the code is 819. If you're hoofing it, just press the button.
>
> MacAvoy

> And Harris, if you can't specking pull the pin, don't feel like too big an ass; I couldn't do it.

Oh, but I could push it. I could set off the bomb. I could destroy this city and all of these people. I'd fantasized about it for the last few hours. I no longer needed to rationalize mass murder to myself, I'd absorbed the idea into my thought stream.

Eight-nineteen, I knew why he'd selected that code, that was the month and year in which the Enlisted Man's Empire collapsed. That was the date that we failed. The bombs were networked, and the network was on the interLink. Using optical commands, I brought up the Link and dialed in the code. Now, with a single wink, I could detonate those bombs. I could do it right there, right then, but I wouldn't.

Perry had said that he would place his bomb under the Linear Committee Building. I was right beneath it, and there was a hidden door that would take me in. I would kill Andropov if I set off the bomb, no doubt about that, but I didn't just want to kill him, I wanted to see him die. I wanted the pleasure of murdering him, not just killing him.

Battle. Combat. My heart was pounding, pounding. My pulse was up. My skin prickled. Somewhere near where I stood was a staircase or a ladder. When I climbed to the top, I would enter the LCB. I would find guards and soldiers, and I would kill them. Some of them would have impenetrable armor just like mine. Maybe Andropov had dressed himself in it as well.

Naens's beacon led away from the platform and the tracks, and there was LCB Station. It looked no grander than any of the others. If anything, it was a tiny bit smaller. The floor was circular, filled with rows of seats and signs showing schedules of trains that no longer ran. There was an abandoned security station, metal detectors, and a bulletproof window through which no guards watched as no passengers stepped through. The darkness, the emptiness. It was outside me and inside me alike.

Naens's beacon led me to an elevator that should by all rights have been dead. I pressed the button, and the doors slid open, revealing a car large enough to carry a 186-kiloton nuclear bomb. Lights shone in the elevator, bright enough that my visor switched from night-for-day to tactical lenses. A small man with a face like a bat smiled up at me. He said, "Harris, I was beginning to worry about you."

59

As the elevator rose, Naens looked up toward my face. He couldn't have seen my face, so he would have been looking at his own reflection or possibly trying to give me the feeling of having him look me in the eyes. After a moment, he said, "You know, if you detonate the bomb, you destroy the building."

Sixty-two-megaton bomb . . . nothing but hollow structure between the device and the parking lot . . . "That stands to reason," I said. "What's your point?"

"We don't need to do this."

"Do what?"

"Raid the LCB."

"I want to kill Andropov," I said.

"That's my point; you'll kill Andropov when you blow up the bomb."

"No, you don't understand. I don't want to kill Andropov; I

want to kill him," I said, trying very hard to sound reasonable and patient. I wasn't feeling either reasonable or patient at the moment. I wasn't calm. I was ready to scream. I was ready to shout. I felt like I had more adrenaline than blood coursing through my veins.

"I don't want him to be dead as a result of something I did. I want to kill him. I want to see him die. I want him to know it was me."

The elevator reached the top and stopped. Naens remained in place as the door opened. He said, "Oh, that makes sense."

The door remained open. Neither of us made a move to step off.

I said, "Travis and Emily aren't in this anymore. They decided to cut and run, right? This isn't about keeping them safe anymore."

"Was it ever about keeping them safe?" he asked.

"That was one of the goals," I said, feeling sheepish. They had helped pull me out of jail, probably stayed the date of my execution, and what had I given them in return? The most I promised them was the possibility of safety as a result of my hunting Andropov.

I felt a stab of guilt, but it didn't outlast the moment. I had placed my enemies before my friends.

As a member of the SEALs, Naens knew all about flying in formation. He was a wingman, not a leader. He and Harmer and the SEALs had come to pull me out of prison, and it was to me that they gave their loyalty in the end even if he didn't approve of my ethics.

Suspecting that he didn't approve, I said, "Let's drop it."

He nodded, and we stepped off the elevator. A moment passed, then he said, "All I'm saying is that if we detonate that device, we win. Why gamble?"

"How are we gambling?" I asked, momentarily intrigued.

"Say we get killed. What happens if you get killed instead of

Andropov? How are you going to set off the device?"

"Did you read the note from MacAvoy?"

"Yes, it has an access code," Naens conceded. "What if your gear gets damaged?"

"I've got shielded armor," I pointed out.

"So do they."

"Drop it," I said, starting to feel more irritated.

"Okay. Sorry."

The elevator didn't take us all the way to Andropov's office; technically, it didn't even take us into the LCB. The building had two basement floors, with three levels of underground parking beneath its basement. The elevator let us out in an abandoned foyer area locked behind an iron door built into the wall at the bottom of the parking garage.

Like the tunnels below, the abandoned chamber at the top of the elevator was completely dark. I surveyed the floor through the night-for-day lenses in my visor. Naens wore goggles he had lifted from Freeman's nest.

Freeman will never know that they're gone, I thought. In another few minutes, the nest would be gone. The street would be gone. The river that separated Washington, D.C., from the state of Virginia might be gone as well. *How much is a megaton?* I asked myself. At first I settled on a thousand tons, but then I reconsidered and decided on a million.

As we walked to the door, Naens said, "Look, this is your operation; you choose the priorities. I'm just saying that operations go south when you add unnecessary details."

"Details like wanting to see Andropov die?" I asked.

"Once you kill him, you're going to set off the device, right? So, he'll be dead, then you'll be dead. I mean, how much time will you have to enjoy the victory?"

I told him, "Drop it," but that would have been too easy. As

409

I approached the door, he took one last shot at convincing me. "Look, Harris, all I'm saying is . . ."

"I need to see Tobias Andropov die for my life to be complete. If I see him die, have the pleasure of doing it with my own two hands, then I die before I set off the bomb, I'll go to my grave a happy man . . . a happy, soulless man."

"Then why set off the device?"

"SPECKING HELL! Naens, let's drop it! I specking want to kill Andropov and then make the Unified Authority pay." I thought about Jim Holman and the clones who had tried to settle on Terraneau—reprogrammed. In my mind, they now lived as slaves. I thought about Ava dying. She didn't need to die, she made the choice, but her collapse had begun with a Unified Authority betrayal. I thought about my brothers, my empire . . . all dead.

If I was right, I would unleash the blast force of 186 million tons of dynamite below the city. Dynamite, of course, was an archaic construct. I had never used it, never learned about it, and had only seen it in funny old movies in which people lit it with a match. *Funny; dynamite no longer exists; matches still do.*

The marble tile floor, made for foot traffic, lay stripped of nearly all furnishings. I spotted the glass-encased display that might have held maps or possibly advertisements, but the benches and trash cans had been removed. Two sets of side-by-side escalators stood as still as stairs in the center of the floor.

Unlike the tunnels, which had been so sterile they reminded me of wrecked ships I'd inspected in deep space, this cavern had a notable sprinkling of dust. I didn't see cobwebs. Until MacAvoy discovered this place, it had been sealed. Maybe an entire ecosystem had been sealed in, but at some point, the rats would have run out of things to eat, then the bugs, then the spiders that ate the bugs.

Thinking he would go first, Naens reached for the door.

I told Naens, "I'll go first. I've got the armor."

The little bastard would have happily taken point even though I was the one in the impenetrable armor. He had a suicidal streak. He wouldn't kill himself, but he didn't care to live.

On most operations, I preferred to work with people who wanted to live. On this occasion, for obvious reasons, Naens's suicidal streak was a welcome addition.

He stepped away from the door as I stepped through, entering a corner of the parking garage populated mostly by armored personnel carriers. Their roofs almost brushed the ceiling. Their wheels were over five feet tall; they looked like limbs. Through my night-for-day lenses, the carriers looked like resting dinosaurs and their tires like stubby dinosaur legs curled in beneath their stomachs.

The bottom level of the garage was filled with personnel carriers. A herd of dinosaurs filled this floor. I lay down on the floor so I could peer beneath the chassis and search for people. I saw no one using my night-for-day lenses, which offered little reassurance, and I saw no one when I scanned for heat signatures.

They'd left the floor unguarded. And why not? They didn't know about the door or the tunnels. As far as the Unifieds were concerned, the bottom floor of the garage was safer than Fort Knox.

A moment passed, and Naens slipped out of the door to join me.

I said, "I don't see any security cameras."

This was his element, not mine. He allowed me to select the strategy, but he would pick our tactics. He pointed to several areas along the ceiling, and said, "There, there, and there."

Scattered lights shone throughout the garage, not enough to make things bright, but my visor had switched to tactical lenses. "I don't see anything," I said.

Naens pulled off his goggles and showed me the insides of his lenses. I held them close to my visor, and still had trouble understanding what I saw—three dark, motionless rectangles. In those rectangles, I saw shadowy forms, which I slowly recognized as armored personnel carriers. The brilliant little bastard had tapped into the LCB security system. Hell, he'd probably done it back in Freeman's nest before we even left for the mission.

I handed the shifty little son of a bitch his goggles, grateful as hell he was on my side, and he led the way through the garage. We weaved between armored transports, avoiding detection as best as possible.

The LCB wasn't especially wide, its underground parking structure stretched out beneath it like the roots beneath a tree. A single hub sat in the middle of the structure with a single bank of ten elevators and two stairwells leading into the building—a good setup for stopping Unifieds from following us down into the tunnels that would also leave us vulnerable on the way in. It was a bottleneck. Lord, I hated bottlenecks.

On the other hand, I didn't need to escape. If worst came to worst, I could explode the damn nukes whenever I wanted.

We walked to the door leading into the hub. Looking through the window, I saw brightly lit emptiness, walls with panels of brushed-steel doors, and nothing more.

"Do you want to take the stairs or the elevator?" Naens asked me.

They're both traps, I thought. *The stairs are a tube; the elevator is a box.* The elevator was better, though. Once inside the elevator, I could press buttons leading to the top, then climb onto the roof of the car.

"Elevator," I said.

Naens nodded. "I'll rig the stairs," he said.

He wasn't only going to rig the stairs. His ambitious objectives included sealing off the upper floor so that I had Andropov all to myself and destroying the lobby so the Unifieds couldn't send in reinforcements. They might send in jets and gunships. The more the merrier. I'd feed them to the nukes once I finished with Andropov.

"Will the stairs still be there if we need them?" I asked.

He shook his head. "If we can get in, so can they," he said. Then he asked, "Did your suit come with a rappel cord?"

I found a cord in one of the compartments, but I wouldn't be able to use it with the shields up. "It does," I said. "Are there cameras on the elevators?"

"Sure there are. I suggest you keep your helmet on for the ride."

It made sense. The camera wouldn't see through my helmet. It might record my virtual dog tag, however, the one that said the name of one of the guys I killed back in Quantico. I didn't tell Naens about riding on the roof of the elevator. On some level, I didn't trust him.

He'd had plenty of opportunity to speck with me if he'd wanted. He could have contacted the Unifieds, and he hadn't. He could have sided with Emily Hughes. Hell, he was a specking SEAL. If he'd wanted to kill me in the tunnels, he could have slipped up behind me and put a bullet through my skull.

The little SEAL didn't bother with packs; he wore a belt and a bandolier, both covered with compartments and cloth loops. I never saw all of the equipment he carried in the compartments, but he carried explosive charges in the loops. The charges had come from Freeman's nest.

Naens said, "Give me three minutes before you get on the elevator."

Three minutes didn't seem like much time.

The thought, *He really does look like a bat*, ran through my mind. He had a small mouth, now drawn tight as he prepared to work, large dark eyes hidden under that thick ridge, and a snout of a nose. His dark, leathery skin offered nearly perfect camouflage in the shadowy garage. You wouldn't spot him without specifically looking for him.

"Is three minutes enough time?" I asked.

"It's enough," he said. His voice remained low and solemn. He took this operation seriously, but it didn't scare him even though he didn't intend to survive. Maybe a stray Unified Authority bullet would find him, maybe he'd die when I set off the nukes, but sure as shooting, he'd die.

He asked, "Do you remember going to the Mogat planet to find Illych?"

I did, but I didn't say anything.

He said, "In case I don't make it back to the tunnels, it's been a pleasure working with you," and he saluted me. It was the oddest thing. Now, at the end, he had suddenly started acting all regulation on me. He waited a moment for me to return his salute. When I did, he spun and headed into the darkness. He was an agile dab of gray on a floor filled with shadows and he vanished into the environment quickly, and I wondered if I would see him again.

I listened for sounds of combat, even boosted the audio in my helmet. I heard nothing. I supposed that meant he had things under control; as a SEAL, he specialized in infiltration.

A few minutes passed, and I called for the elevator.

60

It took less than a minute for my elevator to arrive. The silver doors slid apart, and I walked in. Naens had been right about the cameras in the elevator. How closely people watched them was another story. I entered on the bottom floor, an entirely deserted floor, so I had the car to myself. I pressed the button for the third floor and the top floor—Andropov's suite of offices. I didn't think anyone was watching my car, but if they were, they wouldn't be watching closely. They might see I planned to get out on the third floor and forget about me as I climbed onto the roof of the car.

The doors slid closed, and I felt a slight change in gravity, something so subtle it could have been psychosomatic. I waited a few seconds, then moved to the corner of the lift and turned my attention to the chrome rails that ran along the walls. I planted my right foot onto one rail and used the wall to balance myself as I pushed up to place my left foot on the adjoining rail. At that point, I was too tall for the lift and had to hunch my back as I pushed up on the panel/trapdoor in the ceiling.

The panel flipped open easily enough, and I climbed onto the roof of the elevator and saw the darkened shafts and the moving cars, and I felt my stomach drop. I once went on a tethered spacewalk. I'd once ridden alone in a submarine to the bottom of the sea. Riding on the top of an elevator, staring up a narrow shaft, and seeing cars drop out of the shadows reminded me of just how miniscule I had felt hanging from a leash in space.

The shaft was dark enough that my visor switched to night-for-day lenses, making everything flat and coloring it all in blue-white scale so that the metal skins of the elevator cars blended in with the concrete walls. I crouched and held tightly on to the pipes along the roof of the elevator as the car came to a stop on the third floor. The LCB stood only ten stories tall, making it a midget by Washington standards. The elevators rose and dropped quickly, maybe a floor per second. As I climbed back to my feet, an elevator dropped behind me, again catching me off guard. My car rose three floors, to the sixth, and stopped. *Are they getting on or off?* I wondered.

This time I felt a slight vibration as the car began to move. We lifted one floor, then another, and I lifted the trapdoor and dropped through without pausing to look for passengers. The three men standing in the car hadn't seen me peer in coming from above. I dropped on top of one and caught the other two napping, then I shot them all with the fléchette cannon on my right sleeve.

I'd never used one before, though I understood the point-and-flex muscle mechanics that fired the weapon and prevented accidental discharges. I shot the guy to my right, then the guy to my left, then the one under my knees, hitting the standing men's skulls and the last guy's neck. The fléchettes were tiny, but blood splattered just the same, leaving splash patterns on the walls.

The elevator door opened to chaos.

Naens had begun his work. He wanted to draw the protection away from Andropov and leave them stranded. His plan involved setting charges, which hadn't gone off just yet, but it also involved putting on a show. That much must have begun.

As the senior member of the Linear Committee, maybe the only member after MacAvoy's last stand, Andropov had the floor to himself. Like me, he had kept the floor a wide-open expanse with desks and stations for secretaries and aides. Some workers remained, women in suits and dresses, men in ties and jackets, but most of the population wore combat armor. On a quick scan, I counted about twenty men in armor.

At the far end of the space, the door to Andropov's office sat open and beguiling. It challenged me to approach. Strange as it sounds, until I stepped out of the elevator and spotted that open door and the men guarding it, it had never occurred to me that a bullet or a fléchette or even a lucky knife could cause me to fail my mission.

If one of the Marines killed me before I entered the detonation code, I would fail. Hell, they wouldn't even need to kill me. What if they broke the equipment in my visor? What if someone sludged the air waves?

At that moment, I wondered if maybe I should step back in the elevator and explode my nukes. For all I knew, the Unifieds might have already caught Naens. Even as I considered that possibility, the first of his charges blew, a small explosion that sent a ripple through the building followed by two equally tiny explosions, then the avalanche began.

The entire building quivered as the outer wall on the far side of the building crumbled into scales and flakes. Windows shattered and fell from their casings. The power went out. Computer screens turned dark, so did the light fixtures. Walls slowly disintegrated and slid from the building, revealing gauzy clouds floating across a starlit sky with pale beams of moonlight slanting in through the holes.

My visor switched to night-for-day lenses, but I went back to the tactical view, the unenhanced view. Spotting the Unifieds was easier in tactical, they glowed like golden ghosts.

The next explosion hit with volcanic force, shaking the building from its roof to its underpinnings. Something shook the building once, hitting with the overwhelming force of a hammer striking a nail, one cataclysmic shake, and the stairwell doors launched from the wall on which they were fastened and flew fifteen feet across the floor, trailed by an opaque hedge of dust and smoke.

Things would have gone more smoothly had Naens dialed down the pyrotechnics. Seeing the smoke and the devastation, most of the men guarding the floor raised their shields. Hoping to blend in, I raised mine, then I stepped behind a shoulder-high partition and spotted two guys who had frozen under fire no more than ten feet from where I stood. The bastards were all but sleeping on the job, facing each other as if they weren't wearing helmets and communicating over the interLink, not bothering to raise their shields.

I raised my right arm even with my solar plexus and I shot them low. No one seeing me from the other side of the partition could have known I had done it.

Normally, I aimed for the head; this time, I went for the abdomen. This was U.A. ammo. These fragments had neurotoxin coating them. These targets would die from poison and paralysis before they bled out. Anyway, guys with bleeding holes in their helmets draw unnecessary attention.

Another idiot ran to the blown-out stairwell with his shields off. I let him get past me and shot him in the ass. He stumbled and fell on his face as if he'd tripped, a tiny geyser of blood spurting through his armor.

Naens had warned me that he planned to damage the elevators, but I hadn't grasped his meaning. I shot that third guy, a silent moment passed, and more bombs exploded. Naens must have placed his charges in the bottom of the elevator shaft, turning the shaft into a cannon.

The LCB had two banks of elevators, each holding five lifts. The walls of the shaft withstood the explosions, meaning that the blasts fired the cars up the shafts like bullets in a barrel. The charges went off, the blast fired the elevator cars into space, destroying the roof's structural integrity, and slabs of ceiling came tumbling down, cracking sections of the floor beneath them.

Suddenly, I saw clouds and skyline and pipes and wires where ceilings and walls had been. The north face of the building took the worst damage. A twenty-foot square of roof and ceiling collapsed, slamming into the floor with such force that it crushed men and furniture, and when the cloud of dust cleared, I saw that the floor had twisted and bent to a thirty- or thirty-five-degree angle. Men and debris slid down the floor and disappeared over the edge.

And then somebody shot me. I had my shields up. He couldn't have hurt me with a rocket, at least he couldn't have penetrated my shields, and his fléchettes left nothing but sparks in their wake.

I might not have noticed I'd been shot, but a red icon appeared on my visor warning me that I'd been hit and showing me where it hit me. Only one person shot at me. I had no idea how that person identified me as the enemy or why none of his fellows had caught on.

Slipping behind a partition, I tried to drop to a knee and learned something about my armor. With my shields raised, only the soles of my boots were allowed to touch the ground. The joints over my knees allowed me no more than twenty-five degrees of mobility, then they became stiff.

No wonder they always moved like zombies, I thought. When the fighting started, the Unifieds always marched forward. I'd seen them speed up, but I'd never seen them run. I had always assumed it was because they had shields and felt invulnerable, but that wasn't it. They never ran because they couldn't. They didn't have enough mobility in their legs for a full run.

And me, I couldn't kneel. I suppose I could have tipped over and fallen to the ground like a tree or a bowling pin. Then what? Would I have fused? The only successful strategy we, we meaning the Enlisted Man's Empire, had found for dealing with shielded armor was burying the men who wore it. We toppled a building over on them. We led them into tunnels and collapsed the tunnels. Not a one of them had ever dug himself out. Maybe they couldn't. Maybe their armor had frozen around them, like the walls of a coffin.

I thought about the men we'd buried, trapped—some of them had lasted for weeks before dying. I felt no regret.

The son of a bitch kept shooting me. Every few seconds, the icon flashed in the bottom right corner of my visor, a red silhouette, a white dot marking the spot where his fléchettes struck.

The Marine stood no more than twenty feet from me, his arm up and aimed at me. He could shoot me, but he couldn't hurt me. I could shoot him, but I couldn't hurt him. With our shields up, we had reached an impasse. I broke the stalemate; I lowered my shields. Well, I stepped behind another partition, shut off my shields, and dropped to a knee at the exact same moment. The bastard might or might not have seen me drop my shields, but he didn't shoot.

I sat on the carpeted floor, my back against a desk, hidden by a partition as I rifled through compartments in my armor. I found a pistol. Useless. Rappelling cord. I'd need it later. A half dozen grenades.

Crumbling roof . . . damaged floor. Holding the grenade in my right, I crawled farther, hid behind desks, hid behind partitions. I would need to throw the grenade before I reengaged my shields. If I had the grenade in my hand, the shields would destroy it, maybe even make it explode in my palm.

Where are you, you son of a bitch? Where are you? I pulled the pin, allowed a few seconds to pass, stood, and tossed the pill where I thought the bastard should be. He wasn't there, but there were others, standing, watching, not sure what they should do as I stood, tossed the grenade with a quick flip of my wrist, and brought up my shields at just the right moment.

A lone fléchette hit me from the right side, my stalker, and the grenade exploded, causing an avalanche over the heads of three shielded men. Maybe the floor caved in beneath them, or the percussion sent them flying through holes in the walls. When the smoke cleared, those Marines were absent and unaccounted for, and the chaos I had walked in on seemed like a precision drill compared to the scene I now saw.

A couple of Unifieds dropped their shields and ran toward the nonexistent elevators. I shot them from behind before they changed their minds. I had begun to like these poisoned fléchettes; if I so much as nicked my targets' fingernails, they still died.

I ducked behind a pillar, cut off my shields, dropped to my knees, and hid under a desk. Ten feet from me, the final remains of an outer wall framed a perfect view of monument alley. I saw streets and cars with lit headlights, and colorfully lit fountains and sleepy marble buildings, all ten floors below me, maybe 150 feet down.

The first fléchette missed me by a hair-width. The guy was smart. He didn't look for me, not by hide-and-seek rules at least;

he must have scanned for me using heat vision and spotted me stooped with my shields down under the heavy metal desk. I stood, bringing the desk up with me, balanced on my head, neck, and shoulders, and I sprinted forward. Holes appeared in the desk as he and his comrades fired fléchettes at me, but they didn't have a clear shot and I was an erratic and clumsy, moving target; and then I threw the desk from my shoulders, flexing my muscles as if doing a bench press. My blood was full of adrenaline and testosterone and had been all night, and the desk traveled about four feet through the air and struck the Marine. There was a bright flash and sparks, and the desk seemed to melt in its center, but it was heavy and had velocity and it carried the bastard with it as it fell through the space that had once been a wall.

Now several Unified Authority Marines shot at me, but I already had my shields up. Their fléchettes had about as much impact as mosquitoes slamming into bulletproof glass. When they hit my shields, they didn't just melt; they evaporated. They disappeared so completely it was as if they had never been there.

I stood just outside Tobias Andropov's door, which was closed. At the moment, that simple closed door posed a problem. It didn't even have a lock, for speck's sake, but I couldn't touch the knob without shutting down my shields. I fired a fléchette into the knob. It did nothing; neither did the seven or eight that followed. I thought about kicking through the door, but the joints in my armor fought against me. I couldn't lift my leg high enough.

Meanwhile, a half dozen pricks shuffled around me, shooting me with fléchettes, angling for shots that didn't matter in the slightest, making sure I kept my shields up.

One of them came within a few feet of me, made a point of stepping into my line of sight, and fired shot after shot at my visor. The fléchettes flashed and disappeared, flashed and disappeared, but the guy was eating into my battery life. These shields worked off a small battery that ran out after an hour of nonstop use. Every time something touched my shields, the power surged to fight it off.

Frustrated by the door, I glared at the guy, not that he could see my expression through my visor. He shot me several times. I thought about running at him. *What would happen?* I wondered. We'd probably bounce off each other, might even repel each other like similar poles of a magnet.

Thwack. Another fléchette hit me in the face. *Thwack.* He shot me again. He wasn't hurting me, not even touching me. I wanted to kill him. He was a pest. A nuisance.

Using an optical command, I brought up the code again—819. It would take less than a blink to send it, just a twitch of my eye, and the bombs would explode. All of Washington, D.C., would shake and collapse as the ground below it turned to ash and the air filled with radioactive cinders.

I'll kill them all, I thought, and with that code still up on my screen so that I could initiate the blast at any time, I rushed at the guy with fléchettes in a movement that came as close to running as I could muster.

I closed on him quickly, just three seconds, and he stood there, unmoving, probably stunned as I plowed into him. The blinding electrical flash might have occurred in the world or possibly just my visor. White and gold and yellow spots danced in my eyes, and I couldn't see clearly, but I saw enough to know that my shields had shut off and his shields had shut off as we fell to the floor, and I brought my arm up and pumped five fléchettes into the bastard's gut before we reached the floor. Still partially blinded, I tucked my shoulders, and rolled over his dying corpse and vaulted back to my feet. It took two tries to get my shields back, but they were up before anyone hit me, and the guy I had shot was still down on the ground.

Shoot me again, asshole, I said, maybe out loud, maybe just in my head, and I laughed, and the jagged sound of my laughter sounded bad, even to me, but it didn't stop me. It didn't even worry me. I didn't have time to worry as I ran at the next Marine, bored into him left shoulder first, and fired fléchettes into his chest and stomach. This time I didn't fall with him. Our shields went out the moment we made contact, but I had my eyes shut and balanced myself as I ran into the son of a bitch as if he were a door that I needed to break. We hit, our shields went out, and I restored my shields and shot the bastard as he fell to the ground, and I laughed at the way he dropped and stayed where he fell.

Now that the poor fools saw what I was, they didn't know what to do. I was a cat in a room filled with mice. I was a wolf, and they were small lambs. They didn't know what to do. They had come to protect; I had come to kill and to die. I had nothing that I didn't plan on losing; they had lives they wanted to keep. In the heat of battle, those who worry too much about their lives often lose them.

I was enjoying myself, watching the glowing gold ghosts scatter like small fish. There were only three of them left at this point. It would have only taken two of them to kill me—one to charge and one to shoot. Really, one could have done it though he would have died along with me.

They trotted across the floor as quickly as their armor allowed, weaving through desks and partitions, heading in three different directions. One sprinted toward the elevators. Another dashed to the far end of the building, possibly hoping to hide. I watched him and chuckled as I lowered my shields and pulled a grenade. There I was, offering them my hide, but they were running. And suddenly I understood some of their confusion. They must have been watching the entire fight through night-for-day lenses, and unable to see when I had my shields on and off because night-for-day filtered out ambient glow. They wouldn't have known when to shoot at me.

I threw the grenade sidearm, the way you skip rocks over a lake. It sailed over the tops of several partitions, barely skimming over the top of the last, and exploded in midair. Safely behind my shields again, I watched that partition vanish in a flash of light and a cascade of dust and ceiling tiles and cement. As the cacophony dissolved, I looked for the glow of the man's shields. The area was dark. I found small flames using heat vision, but nothing large enough for a man.

Killing the bastard with the grenade had worked, but it hadn't offered much in the way of satisfaction. I mused at how I had become the cocky hunter stalking after the panicking rabbits. I didn't bother running after them; they had no place to go.

I saw the one who had run to the elevators for safety. He stood by an open shaft, staring into the bottomless empty pit. If he'd packed a cord, he could have rappelled to another floor. He turned, saw me coming, turned back to the hole, and scampered away.

Where are you going? I asked, unaware if I had said the words or only thought them.

In the distance, I saw the flashing lights of a helicopter sliding across the night sky, probably a gunship. I didn't care. *Waste of fuel,* I thought. They couldn't use it, not in this crumbling building, not unless they cared more about killing me than saving Andropov, the man in charge. Andropov had the instincts of a rat; he cared a hell of a lot more about saving his life than ending mine.

Not watching where he set his feet, the man stumbled over a heap of cement and fell onto his knees then his face, and his shields went dark. And there I was, ready for him, holding a five-foot length of jagged-ended pipe that had fallen near him, and I hit him with it. I hit the back of his neck, then his helmet, then his shoulders, then the helmet again, and it cracked, and the cracks spread. And then it caved in and when I hit him again, blood welled out of the crater. I tossed the pipe away, booted my shields, and fired a fléchette between his shoulder blades to make sure he stayed down.

That left one man.

He had hidden in a bathroom. Using heat vision, I saw him quite clearly, cowering against the farthest wall, a faceless orange silhouette, shaped like a man but as scared as a child. I even thought about leaving him, allotting three extra minutes to his life as I killed Andropov, then detonated the nuclear devices . . . the nukes. They no longer scared me the way that they first had. They had become part of my world.

The Unifieds, however, not realizing that they had already lost this fight, sent a gunbird out to kill me. The gunship floated right up to the LCB, stabilized its position no more than ten feet from the outer wall, and started firing chain guns in my direction. Behind my shielded armor, I didn't worry about bullets, not even bullets from a gun that cut men into ribbons. The guns shattered walls and splintered partitions. They hit me like a strong wind, unable to hurt me but shoving me aside.

And then the gunship exploded. The fireball was gorgeous, a luminous twisting, glowing, yellow-and-orange knot that rose and faded but briefly seemed to fill the sky. Naens was alive. The little son of a bitch was alive, and he'd found rockets of some kind.

The chain-gun fire had penetrated the walls of the bathroom, shattering toilets and sinks and pipes from which water gushed out like they were fountains. The U.A. Marine fired three fléchettes at me as I came through the door; they hit me and evaporated, and then he brought his arm to his body and cradled it as if he had broken it and he curled one leg in front of the other, forming a standing version of the fetal position. He didn't even look at me. He stared into an empty stall as I lowered my shields, grabbed a grenade, and pulled the pin. I bowled the pill toward that scared child of a soldier, then I turned and walked out of the bathroom without bothering with my shields, which turned out to be a bad mistake.

He fired at me!

Three tiles shattered as I reached for the door. They coughed little puffs of dust into the air.

I laughed and switched on my shields, but not because of that fainthearted bastard. Moments after I stepped through the door, the grenade exploded. Door and wall burst behind me. The shock wave sent me lurching forward, and I twisted my right leg. I lowered my shields again; I was alone. Almost alone.

The next step I took on my leg sent a shock up my spine, but I hid my wound as I walked to the door of Andropov's office and kicked it aside. Twenty feet ahead of me, behind a desk I had once occupied, sat Tobias Andropov.

61

Andropov wore shielded armor, but he hadn't bothered putting on his helmet. It sat on the desk, and without the optical interface in the visor, the shields did nothing.

I didn't worry about guards or assassins hidden inside this office. Any protection Andropov had, he'd spent outside, trying to keep me out at all costs. He'd known what would happen when I entered. He'd known how that would end.

I said, "I don't know if you knew this, but you're supposed to wear the helmet; it's not going to protect you sitting on a desk."

Andropov was still a young man by politician standards, a man in his forties. He looked soft but trim. His hair was still dark.

His face said it all, his wide-eyed stare, his clenched teeth. He didn't blink.

Even without his helmet, he could still fire the fléchette cannon on the right sleeve of his armor. I'd seen tapes of this man taunting prison guards he knew were about to die. He acted brave when he held the cards. Now, in a cracking voice, he asked, "What do you want me to do?"

Hearing the fear in his voice, I wondered if he had wet himself under the desk.

I said, "You can do whatever you want. You can beg if you want; I don't care."

"Killing me won't fix things," he said. "It won't bring your empire back."

"Nothing will bring it back," I said. "Nothing will specking bring it back."

"I can bring it back," he said.

He looked small behind the desk. He looked like a little boy. Terror makes men into boys. I wondered how many of my men felt terror as they waited for the death reflex to take them. I wondered what tremors ran through Perry MacAvoy's mind as they sat him back in his wheelchair and shot him.

"Did your scientists develop something that resurrects dead clones?" I asked.

"No," he admitted.

I raised my right arm, aimed the cannon at him, and said, "I didn't think so."

He raised his hands, palms forward, fingers up, a show of submission. I reminded myself that a lot of people would still be alive if he'd quit a few weeks earlier. Just six weeks earlier, and Hunter Ritz would still be alive. If he'd stopped three weeks ago, I'd still have a corps of Marines.

His hands still up, he said, "Seven hundred thousand Marines and thirty-two thousand sailors. That's how many there are on Terraneau."

The dumb shit had nothing. He couldn't hurt me; I had my shields up. Even if he had a bomb or a rocket under his desk, the most he could do is send me flying, maybe kill us both, but he wouldn't do that. He wanted to live.

He was weak. He was a politician. He sent people to die; he never faced death himself.

"Reprogrammed clones," I said.

"Cut from the same DNA as the men that you lost."

"Do you have a way of restoring their programming?" I'd gone over that with Tasman. There'd be a high mortality rate if we tried to set them back.

"It shouldn't be a problem," said Andropov.

I fired my first fléchette, hitting the back of his seat just an inch from his face, and said, "I don't believe you."

"We programmed them," he said. "We can reboot them."

"How are you going to get to them?" I asked.

"What do you mean?"

"You don't have a self-broadcasting fleet."

"There are ships . . . cruisers . . . spy ships."

"Cruisers are small," I said. "Spy ships have stealth engines. They're easy to lose, and I don't trust you."

"Damn it to Hell! What do you want?" he shouted. That was when I fired my next fléchette. This one hit near his eye. The sound of the fragment going through the back of his seat made him jump.

He said, "Killing me won't change anything. The Unified Authority still wins."

"You killed my empire; I'm killing yours," I said.

"One man at a time?" he asked. He didn't ask this in a mouthy way. The man was trembling and making no effort to hide it. If he hadn't emptied his bladder when I came through the door, that last fléchette had undoubtedly broken the dam.

"Not exactly," I said. "I'm rearranging the map."

"You're what? What do you mean?"

"I'm erasing Virginia and Maryland," I said.

"You're insane."

I smiled and fired a fléchette into his desk. It may have hit his thigh, possibly his crotch. I hoped it hadn't. I didn't want the fléchette to kill him. I wanted the toxin to do the job.

The fragment was fast, and the pain came slowly. The only signal Andropov sent that the fléchette had hit him was a groan. He moaned and looked down, puzzlement now mixed with the fear in his expression. He must have spotted the little stream of blood spurting up, but he was weak and overcome by shock even before the neurotoxins spread through his system.

He looked up at me. Hate and anger should have shone in his face; instead, I saw fear and surprise. Had he really thought he would talk his way out of this? He didn't speak. He couldn't. He was in shock, paralyzed, dying. Five or six seconds after I shot him, Andropov's head fell to the desk.

He might still have had some life left in him, but not much.

I said, "We both lose our lives and empires." I laughed. I laughed and I laughed, and I couldn't stop myself, and I raised my arm and aimed the tiny cannon and fired fléchettes into that dead man's skull until the top of his head looked like mush.

Then I brought up the code, and I was about to blow up the bombs, but I had a thought. I remembered Naens. He was still alive. He had destroyed the gunship. He was down there, somewhere.

I wanted to thank him. I wanted him to die with honors, to face his death and to know when it arrived. He and I, we would die like soldiers.

During the time I had been chatting with the late Tobias Andropov, several more gunships had arrived. They prowled the air around the building, like cats waiting for a cornered mouse. Those pilots had heat vision. They'd undoubtedly watched me through the walls. The lights on the fronts of their birds searched the ruined floor.

Troops, hundreds of them, thousands of them, had probably surrounded the base of the building. What could they do? Naens had caved walls over the entrances of the building and the parking garage below it.

One of the gunships fired a rocket as I left the office. The gunner who fired it aimed it by me, not at me. They couldn't hit the building with a rocket, not without caving the whole thing in on itself, and Naens had trapped a lot of natural-born Unified Authority personnel in these crumbling walls, so the rocket sailed in through the remains of one broken wall and out through the gaps in another.

Chain guns fired. One gunship hovered over my head, and some stupid bastard tried to jump out. I shot him before he landed, and he toppled onto the floor in a clump. A torrent of bullets hit a desk beside where I stood, mincing it into sawdust and filings. They hit a bookshelf, filling the air with shreds of paper, some of which caught fire.

The flashing icon in my visor warned me that bullets had hit me on every side. *Just you wait right here,* I thought as I reached the elevators, waiting to lower my shields until I stepped into the barrel of the shaft. Even here the bullets followed me.

Chain guns shot through the walls as I lowered my shields and attached my cord to a girder and dropped faster than the elevators had traveled. I dropped two floors at a time, making sure not to stop by doors in which angry Unifieds might be waiting. The explosions had left a few doors open, but from what I could tell, it had launched all of the elevator cars through the roof of the building.

Zipping past open doors, I saw darkness and destruction. Naens's bombs had broken these floors even more than they broke Andropov's floor. I saw bodies and walls demolished into heaps. There was no electricity. Vents as wide as water barrels hung like hoses from holes in the ceilings.

Moments later, I had dropped below the lobby, and three empty levels after that, I unhitched in the garage. The world was pitch-black down here. The sun itself could have followed me into that elevator shaft, and it might not have produced sufficient radiance to light the garage, but I had my night-for-day vision, and I found the small man with a bony ridge over his eyes as I lowered myself to the floor.

"You did a great job," I said.

"Is he dead?" asked Naens.

"If he isn't, he isn't happy," I said.

"Why are you limping?" Naens asked me as I unlocked the cord and walked past him. I headed out of the hub and toward the door to the tunnels.

"I twisted my leg."

"I thought the armor was supposed to protect you."

"It did," I said. "It kept everything out, but it doesn't stop you from twisting your own ankle."

He nodded. I couldn't see his eyes; he was wearing those goggles. Even he would have been completely blind down here without help.

As he followed me, he asked, "Aren't we supposed to be dead by now?"

"I want to watch it happen," I said.

"You want to see the bomb explode?" he asked. "You really are insane."

Those were his last words. He stepped through the doorway, and a single shot was fired. The bullet struck his head, splattering it against a wall. Standing just outside the doorway, I got splashed with a few drops of blood. I raised my shields and stepped over the body.

I yelled, "You shouldn't have shot him, Ray."

Freeman answered, "You won't be able to flip the switch hiding behind a shield."

"I don't need to," I said. "I have remote access."

Freeman went silent. He hadn't considered that possibility. A few seconds passed, and he yelled, "I can't let you set off the bombs."

"I don't see how you can stop me," I said as I searched the tunnels using both night-for-day lenses and heat vision. Neither worked. He was out there, probably hiding behind a thick wall, far out of the range of my fléchettes. He had that sniper rifle. I wanted to set off the nukes, but I hated the idea of killing Freeman.

As long as I kept my shields up, Freeman couldn't hurt me. He couldn't miss me, either. I was a gold-glowing ghost in a universe of black, a human-sized target for a man who could hit a coin from a mile away.

Freeman shouted, "Harris, that flu caused you to have a combat reflex. Your brain is full of hormone. You're not thinking straight."

I crossed the foyer and started down the stairs, which wasn't so easy with my shields up. I had to take each step at its edge so that the backs of my legs didn't rub against the next one up. A couple of hundred yards ahead of me, something moved. I caught a quick glance of the RPG before it struck the stairs.

He wanted to bury me. He wanted to bury me the way I had buried so many Unifieds in shielded armor. It didn't work the way he wanted. Freeman knew everything there was to know about demolitions and sniper rifles, but that RPG he'd fired hit low and wide and did next to nothing.

I shouted, "Try that again, Ray, and I'll set the nukes off from here."

"Then you'll kill me, too, Wayson."

It wasn't Freeman who stepped into the open lobby; it was Kasara. She'd dressed in khaki BDUs like a soldier, but they looked incredibly baggy on her. She had her hair pulled back.

I stopped and stared at her, and I asked, "Why did you come here? You could have been safe. You would have been safe. Once I'm done, you won't ever need to worry about the Unified Authority ever again."

She held a flashlight, a stupid, specking flashlight. It was a civilian-issue flashlight, cheap and small and weak. She took several steps toward me so that we were just a few feet apart.

"I'm not worried about the Unified Authority. Right now, you scare me more than Andropov."

I looked at her and knew that while I didn't love her, I did not want to kill her. I said, "Andropov is dead."

She said, "Wayson, it's not just Unifieds out there; it's children and mothers and grandfathers."

"People who deserve to die," I said.

"Innocent people!"

"Where were they when the Unifieds massacred my people?" I asked. "Where were they when we fought the aliens on New Copenhagen? Where were they when we rescued your people from Olympus Kri? They don't deserve to live. We saved them from Mogats and Avatari."

"And now you want to kill them?" Kasara asked. She was right in front of me now, standing at the base of the stairs, and I had this wild hare of an impulse, I wanted to grab her and to hug her and to allow the joules of condensed electricity that ran through my shields to shock her or burn her like a dried leaf in a fire. *I never loved you,* I told myself.

I saw her face clearly, but her hair and skin were the same damn blue-white color in my lenses. I couldn't see her eyes clearly, they were bathed in shadow. I switched to heat vision, turning her into a vividly colored shadow, and I stepped around her without giving her a second glance.

She yelled, "Wayson!"

I already had the code up—819, the month, the year, the end, and I looked down at the icon that would initiate the explosion. One twitch of my eye . . . the time had come. I . . .

"Freeman, you're sludging the airwaves," I shouted.

He didn't answer.

Now we both knew something about each other's plans. I knew Freeman had a sludging device; he now knew that I had tried to detonate my nukes. I would either need to destroy his device or lower my shields in order to set off my nukes, and he would shoot me the moment I did. That meant that I either needed to destroy Freeman's sludging device, or I needed to destroy him.

I marched ahead, toward the spot from which he had fired the RPG, not as confident as I had been. If he brought the roof down on my head, I would not be able to do a remote detonation.

"Wayson!" Kasara followed after me, calling my name, begging me to stop. "Wayson! Stop, you need help!"

I wanted to turn. I wanted to shoot her, to kill her just like I had killed Andropov, to stand there and watch her die, but I wasn't sure why I wanted to do it. It was an impulse without a root. It was a thought without a cause. I ignored her.

She shouldn't have come, I told myself. *She betrayed me by coming.*

There was an alcove straight ahead. The walls around the alcove were tile over cement, and thick, thick enough to hide a man's heat signature. I aimed my fléchette cannon and stormed ahead, not pausing, confident I would shoot Freeman. He had come. His decision, and the consequences would rest on his head.

I rounded the corner. Freeman was gone, but he had left his sludging device. It sat on the floor, a shoebox-sized device with an antenna, a meter, and a power switch. I shot eight fléchettes into it.

The first shot hit me in the back. The little red icon came up in my visor and with a white dot on my back that froze into place.

I pivoted, aimed my cannon, and the second shot hit me in the chest, and there was Freeman, just out of my accuracy range, holding a target pistol.

I looked down at my chest, saw the goop that he had splattered there. The son of a bitch had shot me with a couple of Perry MacAvoy's shield sappers. "SPECK!" The word erupted from my lips. I aimed my wrist cannon in his direction but slightly high and fired and fired and fired, but he moved behind a wall and my fléchettes vanished and "SPECK!" erupted from my lips again.

I tried to detonate again, but that hadn't been his only sludging device. It might have been a decoy or a backup, but the airwaves were still sludged, and who the speck knew how much juice I had left in my armor, but freshly charged batteries only lasted six minutes when MacAvoy shot them with this shit.

"Wayson, stop! You don't want to do this!" Kasara screamed.

I wanted to shoot her, but I ignored the urge. She'd die in another moment. She'd die soon enough. I turned and walked toward the nukes. They were a few minutes away. I needed to get to them quickly. If my shields went out, Freeman would shoot me.

He yelled, "Harris, it needs to be your choice."

My choice! I thought, and I laughed. My choice? He was sludging the airwaves and waiting to shoot me. I kept my strides long and fast, turning corners, marching through dark halls.

He wanted me to lower my shields, to let him take me. I turned back, saw him poised over a counter, his rifle trained on me. He was thirty feet out of my range. I looked ahead. There was the nuclear device, far ahead. If I pressed ahead, I could still reach it.

"They turned on you as much as they turned on me!" I screamed. "They want you dead, too!"

"That doesn't matter," said Freeman.

"Then what matters? Huh? What the speck matters if that doesn't matter?

"You know what, Ray? More clones died fighting the Avatari, trying to save these bastards . . . the Avatari killed ten times more clones than that specking flu, and they still turned on us. We protected them, Ray. We followed all of their orders. Duty, right? We did our duty. We made all of the sacrifices.

"Does that count for anything?"

A moment of silence, and then a low, calm response, "Not at the moment."

In my mind I saw Hunter Ritz. I saw Sergeant Shannon and Lewis Herrington and Kelly Thomer and Mark Phillips, clones who had died bravely fighting to save natural-borns, and I knew I was letting them down. Freeman had outsmarted me. I wasn't going to avenge them.

Freeman yelled, "Harris, you need to lower your shields. If you don't walk away from this on your own, I'll have to kill you. If you walk away, I can help you, but I won't help you unless you take the first step."

I hated him. I hated Kasara. I hated myself.

There was something wrong with me. I thought about the way I laughed as I killed the Marines guarding Andropov. I thought about my desire to kill millions of civilians. Something was wrong, I knew there was something wrong with what I wanted to do, but I had no idea what.

The nuke sat there, the risk, the gamble, the possibility of fulfilling my only ambition.

"Wayson, we're trying to help you," Kasara said. She was close to me again, running toward me, close enough that I could see the tears on her cheeks. I wasn't moved.

I should have been moved. She cared about me. I didn't know if I ever loved her, but I had certainly cared about her as well.

I turned off my shields and dropped onto a marble bench, fully aware that Freeman would shoot me now that I no longer had shields to protect me. He would execute me; that was the only way he could make sure I never changed my mind.

Freeman had always been careful. Instead of approaching me for the traditional shot to the back of the head, he remained a hundred yards away, out of range. My shields were down, but my wrist cannon still worked.

He yelled, "Now take off your helmet."

It will be a clean shot, I told myself. That is a good way to die, a clean shot through the brain. Quick. No suffering. The best I could ask for.

Fear of death had seldom bothered me, but surrender didn't come easily. I sighed, reached for my helmet, and paused. It would be over in a moment. I thought of my ghosts and accepted that I would soon join them, then I removed my helmet.

I caught a brief whiff of the ammonia saturating the air. I didn't even have time to realize what I had smelled before the world went black.

Part IV

THE BETRAYER

62

DATE: AUGUST 24, 2519

The flu had washed over the Enlisted Man's Empire like a tidal wave. All of the clones were dead except for two Generals—Pernell MacAvoy and Wayson Harris. Howard Tasman had no idea what had become of Harris, but he knew precisely what MacAvoy was doing. The last Army man standing was making his final stand, trying to defend the Linear Committee Building, so sick from the flu that he had to fight from a wheelchair.

Tasman's wheelchair couldn't climb walls or desks, but it could climb stairs. He didn't need a perfect ramp to drive the heavy, six-wheeled chair, tiers would do.

He could hear the battle raging outside. That idiot soldier MacAvoy, the only other man in the entire Linear Committee Building, thought he could fight the entire Unified Authority all by himself.

He'll have to, Tasman mused. *He's the last clone.*

He drilled a hole through the wall of a bookcase, then he looped an electrical cord through the hole. He tied the other end of the cord to one of the armrests on his chair and rolled away. The bookcase was solid teak, with a fine lacquered finish that reflected light in dull streaks.

Shhhuuuurrrre, the sound of rockets fired. The rumbling explosion. The walls of the LCB should have muffled those sounds, but Unified Authority soldiers had shot out so many of the windows.

As he pulled toward his desk, peaceful crashes mingled with the noise from the brewing battle. Books fell from the shelf, and metal figurines and a marble bust. Tasman looked back and saw a set of books with color-coded spines topple to the ground as the shelf teetered. *Books,* he thought.

Books. He hadn't opened an actual book in decades, maybe since he'd been a young man. The old neural-programming engineer didn't know who had stacked these books on the shelves in his office, and he'd never touched them. He didn't need to use them; his computers stored and tabulated any and all information stored in those books.

In his mind, the books had aesthetic value only. He liked antiques, objects that had outlasted their usefulness. *Anything that survives long enough outlives its usefulness,* he thought. The books were old and rare, and probably more valuable in 2519 than on the day they'd been printed.

Some things are more valuable when they are old and useless . . . some things. The bookshelf must have been fastened into the wall. It put up one last fight, causing the wheelchair to skid and stammer, then the heavy shelf fell stiff and stolid to the floor with a *whoosh* and a *thump* that sounded far more muffled than the grenades and rockets outside the building. Tasman dragged it right up to his desk so that it, with his desk, formed the first and last tiers of his staircase.

He drove his wheelchair into the debris field he'd just created and scooped up books and computer parts, a rack made for displaying swords, a box filled with bric-a-brac Tasman didn't own or care about. He picked up anything and everything, and he tossed them onto the upside-down bookshelf.

DATE: AUGUST 18, 2519

Watson had captured the spy, Kevin Rhodes, and used his phone to contact Harris. At first the extraction sounded like a dream, like liberation. Now the dream had become a nightmare.

The battle might have been on the other side of town, but it sounded close, maybe right down the street. Watson had arranged for the battle, but he looked worried. He hid against an inner wall of the apartment, occasionally crawling to the window and peering out at the street.

Kevin Rhodes looked scared as well. Watson and his girlfriend had tied the guy's hands behind his back. To Tasman's eye, the knots looked sloppy. He thought Rhodes might have been able to work his hands free if he tried, but the knots around his legs and ankles looked solid, and he'd have needed a knife to remove the gag and sock from his mouth.

He lay face-first on the old carpeting, looking like the world's largest worm. Awake and alert, Rhodes became more panicked with every explosion. His eyes darted from side to side. He breathed so hard that he reminded Tasman of a woman in labor.

And then there was Emily. Every bang, every crash, even gun chatter caused her to jump. Tasman found it funny. He watched her just for the entertainment value.

She wanted to live. So did Watson. In Tasman's mind, they

had something to live for—youth. Rhodes wanted to live as well. Tasman had no idea why.

"There's something coming up the street!" Watson yelled.

He sounds so damned excited, Tasman thought. He didn't want to admit it to himself, but he wanted to live, too. No, it wasn't that simple. Living didn't matter to him; he had long since given up on life; he just didn't want to die.

"What?" asked Emily. "What do you see?"

"It looks like . . . Holy Hell, it's tanks and trucks! They're coming straight up the road! It's really them! They're going to get us out!"

Emily crawled over for a look at the street. Rhodes didn't move. Their rescue was his death sentence.

"How do we know they're ours?" Emily asked.

Tasman answered. He said, "They haven't shot the building. If the U.A. Army knew we were here, they'd have blown us up."

"Their armor isn't glowing," said Watson.

"No one's shooting at them," said Emily.

As they watched an endless supply of men in armor pouring out of personnel carriers, Watson said, "They look like they're all about the same size." They sounded excited. They hugged each other. They kissed. Tasman half expected them to hump each other right there on the floor; it wouldn't have been the first time he'd seen them do it.

Then there was the knock on the door and an armed escort that led them to an armored personnel carrier. A Marine lugged Tasman down the stairs into the truck. Everyone went into the carrier except for Rhodes. They threw him into the back of a Jackal.

On the far side of the bench, Watson and Emily held each other, but they looked nothing like young lovers. To Tasman, they looked old and stiff, like an ancient couple. He had his arm on her shoulder. She had her hand on his leg. Their hands stayed in one place. They touched, but there was no caress, and they didn't speak.

Watson kept the briefcase with him, holding it beside him as if he would die without it. It sat between him and Emily on the bench, a short, skinny box with the U.A./EME Marines emblem engraved on its face.

The fighting never stopped. Tasman heard it as they loaded him into his seat. He heard it as the convoy drove him away from the building. At some point he heard an enormous explosion, not just a bomb or a rocket, this thing shook the ground like an earthquake. He froze in his chair. Had his plumbing not been hooked into mechanical collectors, he would have needed new clothes.

And then the truck stopped. Trapped in the back, Tasman and the other passengers could not see where they had stopped or why. Emily asked, "Do you think we're at some kind of a base?"

Watson shook his head. "No. If we were that close to a base, I would have tried to run to it for help."

"Maybe they sent a plane for us," Emily suggested.

The back door of the transport opened. Light flooded through the doorway. Tasman placed a hand over his eyes to block it. Squinting behind his fingers, he saw a woman stepping into the carrier. He could not see her clearly, however, until the door shut, and the blinding light went away.

The woman was clean, and her clothes looked freshly laundered, no wrinkles, no tears. Tasman decided she was pretty and young, with dark hair and blue eyes. Surprise showed in her eyes.

She said, "Travis? Emily?"

They looked at her. At first they didn't recognize her. Emily figured it out first. She said, "Sunny." That wasn't a greeting or a question. If anything, it was a label. There was no warmth in Emily's voice.

"Sunny? What are you doing here?"

The woman said, "They captured my apartment building. I hid in a friend's house."

Nobody spoke after that, not for the rest of the ride. Nearly an hour passed before the carrier stopped again. This time it had reached an extraction point.

Sunny, the pretty one in the clean dress, sat and waited while Watson helped Emily out of the back of the personnel carrier. Tasman couldn't get himself out. He was old and mostly crippled; a Marine would need to carry him out. Sunny, the woman with the beautiful brown hair and blue eyes waited with him. She looked at him, gave him the sweetest smile, and said, "Listen up, you dried-up piece of shit."

Silent and scared, Tasman listened.

"We could have killed you on Mars, and we sure as hell can kill you here. The only thing that's keeping you alive is that you're just as worthless to them as you are to us. They can't protect you. They can't save you. Their empire is about to end."

Tasman wanted to say something, maybe ask if she was insane, but he was too scared to speak.

She said, "Do you want to live, Howie? Do you want to stay alive another day? Rhodes had an encryption bandit in that case Watson is holding. If you want to stay alive, you just make sure Harris doesn't see what's on it . . ."

She became quiet.

He wanted to ask what that meant, but a Marine entered the carrier. The woman smiled at both Tasman and the clone Marine who was carrying him. She radiated love and happiness.

They flew to an Army base, then they flew into Washington, D. C., where General MacAvoy met them. He took them to the top floor of the LCB, to Wayson Harris's office. They waited outside while MacAvoy chatted with Harris, then they entered a few minutes later.

Tasman wanted to see how Harris would react when he saw Sunny. Did he know she was an enemy agent? Could he warn Harris?

The old man watched the clone and the girl. She seemed genuinely happy to see him. She kissed him again and again, almost forcing her mouth against his even though he clearly wanted to put on a professional front. Tasman watched him closely, saw the way he stole glances and the overwhelming lust in his eyes. Harris wanted her. Tasman saw something else, too. Harris didn't know that Sunny was the enemy. She was playing with him, but he didn't see it. Maybe he didn't want to see it. Seeing how weak Harris became around her, Tasman wondered if Harris already knew the truth and had chosen to ignore it.

They had a short meeting. Harris wanted to talk business. Sunny kept interrupting, making an emotional scene. Tasman watched how she manipulated him and realized that he had joined the losing team. When the meeting ended, he watched Sunny leave. Her emotions were theatrical.

He wanted to stay and warn Harris, but the Liberator clone wasn't interested in warnings. Harris wanted to chat with General MacAvoy about the battle and the encryption bandit that Watson had taken from Rhodes.

Hearing them speak about the encryption bandit, Tasman began to understand Sunny's play. There must have been vital information in its memory, but Harris and MacAvoy were Neanderthals.

Watching them speak, Tasman no longer knew which side of the war would win. The clones had more men and were better trained, but they had no vision. They were like medieval knights, all gallant and marching around in armor, convinced of their invincibility. The Unified Authority was vicious.

Tasman volunteered to help with the encryption. If the Unified Authority's new weapon was as good as Sunny said, he would hide the information. If the clones could survive it, he would warn them.

Tasman offered to take the information off the bandit, and Harris asked, "Howard, how do you feel about bunking in the Linear Committee Building for the next little while?"

Tasman asked, "Is it going to be safer than the Pentagon?"

Harris said, "You'll be more secure than the gold in Fort Knox."

"Fort Knox is empty. It's been empty for centuries. You said the Pentagon was secure. What makes the Linear Committee Building any safer?"

Harris said, "You'll have me here to protect you."

Deciding that Sunny had been right, the clones couldn't protect him, Tasman said, "Harris, you scare me more than all the rest of them."

Tasman wondered if he had turned himself into a spy.

DATE: AUGUST 24, 2519

The explosions were getting louder. MacAvoy must have set off charges or bombs or grenades inside the building. There was gunfire, lots of it. Tasman did his best to ignore it.

The rise from the floor to the back of the fallen bookshelf was about a foot. Tasman's front wheels brushed against the side of the bookshelf and climbed to the top. The other wheels adjusted and followed. He'd climbed the first tier.

The old scientist was a waif, skin, brittle bones, and no padding between them. His wheelchair weighed hundreds of pounds. The wooden panel that covered the back of the bookshelf groaned, but it held.

His chair leaned back so perilously, he thought it might roll over. The spinning wheels kicked books and plaques to the floor. Then they found traction, and Tasman drove the chair up the dune of books and bits and bric-a-brac on his way to the desk.

* * *

DATE: AUGUST 20, 2519

Breaking into the encrypted data had gone like clockwork. Minutes after moving into his office, Tasman had located the file about the flu. He read it, analyzed it, and realized the clones were finished. Most of the clones had already been exposed. Harris sure as hell was carrying; the only reason Sunny had boarded the personnel carrier was to give it to him personally.

What a bitch, Tasman thought, but he also admired her. She was stronger than Harris. She would destroy him.

That morning, Tasman allied himself with the nation he knew would win the war. Now that he had sided with the Unified Authority, Tasman cared nothing for Harris, maybe even had come to despise him. He began the day by calling MacAvoy and telling him all about Sunny. Then they invited Harris, Tasman practically drooling at the thought of watching the Liberator squirm.

Harris came to meet them.

Tasman didn't say anything about flu viruses or spy networks. Instead, he talked about inventories and accounting. Harris looked impatient. So much the better.

They brought up the underwater cities. Tasman had found video feeds of Harris and his Marines being reprogrammed. They showed the feeds to Harris. He tried to put on a stoic face, but his emotion showed through.

When Sunny's face showed in the screen, Harris asked, "Is that Sunny?"

Tasman said, "You were part of their experiment. When they couldn't reprogram you, they switched to an accelerated form of classical conditioning."

He hid it well, but Tasman enjoyed showing Harris the video of him lying on an operating table. Sunny tortured him first, then they had sex. Even though he knew that there was nothing Harris could possibly have done to stop that, Tasman enjoyed watching him fall apart.

"Wow," said MacAvoy. "Paralyzed one moment and humping like a rabbit the next. Hoorah, Marine!"

Harris said only a single word—"Sunny."

Feeling a little sorry for the fallen Marine, Tasman said, "Harris, you were brainwashed. They molded your subconscious into something they could use. There are hours of her toying with you. Hours of it."

Now the old man felt more trapped than ever. He wanted to clones to win though he knew they couldn't. He didn't want the Unified Authority to win though he knew it would. And he wanted to live though he didn't deserve to.

That was on August 20, back when the clones still believed they would win the war. MacAvoy, the oldest of the commanders, was already starting to show signs that he had the flu. As far as Tasman was concerned, the war was over.

DATE: AUGUST 24, 2519

Tasman's wheelchair screeched and scratched to the top of the mound. It almost rolled back, then it passed from the mound to the top of his desk.

A set of pipes hung exposed above the desk. Tasman took his electric cord and tossed it over the pipes. He held one end, and the other fell down to him. He crossed one end over the other, then he had a knot.

* * *

DATE: AUGUST 21, 2519

In a few hours, Tasman would tell Harris about the flu. He'd waited long enough; the outcome was now inevitable. Every clone on every base and ship would have been infected by now. They'd probably been infected for days.

I couldn't have saved them, he told himself. Warning Harris about Sunny wouldn't have made a bit of difference. Tasman hated himself for having hidden the truth.

The decrepit old scientist was driven by a need to survive. Of late, that instinct often led him to self-loathing.

Tasman began the day by meeting with MacAvoy. He had a vial, something the clones had captured from a Unified Authority spy. This vial didn't contain a virus; it stored chemicals like the ones the scientists had used on Harris and his captured Marines in the undersea city.

Tasman had stayed up all night modifying the order of the chemicals. He knew all about neural programming. He'd been the one who developed the clones and the chemical formulas that the Unified Authority had hijacked to win the war.

Tasman said, "General, I have something you need to see."

He handed MacAvoy the vial and the dumb-ass soldier opened it without giving it a second thought. Having betrayed Harris and MacAvoy, Howard Tasman discovered that he couldn't loathe himself any more than he already had for years.

When the general woke up no more than five minutes later, he looked pale and shaky. He had no idea that the chemicals had just reprogrammed him, but he had a dim awareness of something else. He had become sentient. He knew he was a clone, and he had been programmed in such a way that the realization wouldn't kill him.

Tasman and MacAvoy called Harris to the office. They

discussed the abandoned reprogramming project. Tasman wanted to tell Harris about the flu, almost had the nerve to tell him, then he backed away.

He said, "They have a new weapon. I can't be sure, but I think it's genetic," and he told them about Sunny's involvement without actually mentioning her name.

DATE: AUGUST 24, 2519

Tasman slipped the noose over his head. He aimed his chair toward the far edge of the desk. First he'd betrayed humanity, then he'd betrayed synthetic humanity. He had no one left to betray except himself.

EPILOGUE

Freeman should have killed me the way he'd killed Naens; instead, he'd filled the tunnels with reprogramming chemicals. They didn't reprogram me, but they did put me out. Once I was out, he and Kasara dragged me back through the tunnels. They loaded me into an airplane and flew me back to the Territories.

Now I was under Brandon Pugh's protection. I was also under his influence. Until my body strained out the adrenaline and testosterone circulating in my blood, they planned to keep me luded and happy. Anything to keep me from producing more adrenaline and testosterone.

Three months had passed. They still kept me strapped in my bed, but my dosage was down.

"What are you going to do if I start having another combat reflex?" I asked Freeman when he came in carrying my lunch. I wasn't in a hospital. This wasn't a medical operation. If anything, I was a hostage in a rehab clinic.

He handed my drink to a nurse. They kept me on a liquid diet, mostly because my hands were chained to the rails on the sides of my bed.

"Same thing I'd do to any rabid dog," said Freeman.

"Shoot me?" I asked.

"Shoot you, drown you, poison you . . . permanent solution."

As far as I knew, this was my first lucid day in over three months. I looked around my bedroom. It was a big room. The sun shone in through a rowboat-shaped window. The walls looked like they were made out of plaster or cement. The air was dry. I thought I heard the ocean from a distance. It might have been the ocean, but it could have been dizziness deep inside my head.

I had a needle in my arm. It led to a drip bag that undoubtedly contained Pugh's illicit pharmaceuticals, but it must have held the liquids that kept me hydrated as well.

"Why didn't you shoot me?" I asked. "That would have been your standard MO."

Freeman's expression revealed nothing. He said, "I didn't want to shoot you."

"Why did you shoot Naens? He wasn't the problem. He was helping me."

"I didn't want to shoot him. I didn't have much of a choice. Stopping you was hard enough. I wouldn't have been able to stop both of you."

"Blowing up the city was my idea," I said. "I don't know how he felt about it."

Freeman said nothing.

Bright sunlight shone in through the window. I wished I could climb out of bed and feel it on my skin.

"You should have shot me. It would have made more sense. Naens wasn't wearing shielded armor."

"I had to shoot one of you. I chose him."

The nurse must have been a *Martian*, a New Olympian, a refugee from Olympus Kri. *So many labels, so many locations,* I thought. *The Unified Authority once included 180 planets. How did they ever keep all of that information straight?*

Freeman said, "When the Avatari returned to burn the galaxy, you saved billions of people, Harris. You deserved to live."

"Even if I wanted to kill millions of innocent civilians?" I asked. I wasn't sure that I believed they were innocent. No. I didn't believe they were innocent. I believed that clones had been sent to save them, all of them, and that they had turned their backs on their rescuers. The general citizenry of Earth might not have been guilty of the cleansing, but they were complicit.

I still considered them guilty, but I no longer wanted to kill them. I no longer wanted revenge. Pugh's happy juice must have been good. It was doing its job.

Freeman said, "That was the combat reflex, Harris. That wasn't you."

I didn't agree with him. Then again, I didn't feel like killing anyone. I felt like basking in the warm, warm sun. I felt like swimming in the cool ocean water. I wanted to be hot. I wanted to be cold.

"How long can we stay here?" I asked.

"How long do you want to stay here?" Freeman answered.

"Won't the Unifieds catch up to us?" I had a vague recollection of being in a hospital and Brandon Pugh selling me out. I also remembered hearing he had done that to help me. I was on drugs. I remembered actions more than details.

Freeman said, "The Unified Authority believes you are on another planet. They're not coming after you; they think you're already gone."

"Why do they think that?" I asked.

"Because they tracked an old Explorer ship broadcasting to New Copenhagen."

"Was I on it?" I asked. Maybe this wasn't the territories. Maybe it was New Copenhagen. Maybe these drugs didn't come from Pugh. Maybe they'd come from the Japanese.

"Travis Watson and Emily Hughes were on it," said Freeman.

"Travis can't fly a spaceship," I said.

"I was on it as well," said Freeman. "And then I brought it back."

"Travis and Emily stayed on New Copenhagen?" I asked.

"They felt safer there."

"So we can stay here, or we can go to New Copenhagen," I said; but that wasn't really the trip I had in mind. Freeman had a self-broadcasting ship. The entire universe was open to us, and I knew about a planet where clones still lived. They'd been reprogrammed, but they were synthetic . . . men of my DNA.

Maybe I couldn't free them. Then again, maybe I could. The Unifieds had labs on Terraneau, and the general population was loyal to the Enlisted Man's Empire.

Besides, I was too young to retire.

AUTHOR'S NOTE

In 2007, I wrote *The Clone Elite*, fully convinced that would be the last book in this series. In my author's note, I thanked my readers for sticking with me and I all but told Wayson Harris good-bye. Now, seven years and six books later, I believe that I am finally putting my Liberator clone to bed.

Let me tell you, I have a lot of people to thank. First and foremost, I have the readers who have stayed with me through the Mogat uprising, the Avatari War, the rise of the Enlisted Man's Army, and the return of the Unified Authority. Ten books! Thank you for staying with me.

I want to thank Anne at Ace, who has been kind and long-suffering—I don't think I am a prima donna, but I'm not always good about turning books in right on time. Anne is patient. Anne is sweet. Anne is encouraging. Thank you, Anne.

Anne also had to lay down the hammer on this one. I somehow

thought I had another month to turn this one in when Anne sent me an e-mail letting me know it was late. I begged for time and mercy—three weeks' worth of time to be precise—and she gave me everything she could: a week.

So let me tell you about Christy Petrie, the woman who often pulls me out of the fire. (Yes, "Petrie" as in Ryan Petrie, the mobster Freeman assassinated in *Assassin*. I kill all of my friends in my books. That's how they know I love them.)

With one week to edit, I called Christy and asked if she would mind donating her entire week to me. For the next seven days, I proofed all day and all night, then sent the results to Christy, who proofed all night and all day and got them back to me within hours. She did this for an entire week.

As of this writing, it is 3:36 p.m. on April 28, the day this book is due to the publisher. Christy is correcting the last chapter and the epilogue, then I will go over her edits and turn the book in.

Christy, not only are you an amazing editor, you are an amazing friend. Thank you!

I also want to thank my agent, Richard Curtis. Richard has shepherded my career as I have transformed from a journalist covering video games to a novelist. Like Anne, I also consider him a friend.

Some of you may have been lucky enough to listen to my stories come alive at the hands of GraphicAudio. The company has produced audio dramas based on my books; I admit, they have breathed new life into these stories for me. After I spend three months writing a book and then additional months rewriting the book and then read it again to make changes and then to approve the changes and then to inspect the final layout, I tend to get a bit burned-out.

Ken Jackson and Anji Cornette at GraphicAudio have found a solution for my Harris fatigue; they produce these amazing audio dramas that bring my stories to life all over again. With Jackson as both the voice of Harris and the director, and Elliot Dash playing the role of Ray Freeman, my stories have taken on a new vitality.

I once believed that narrated audiobooks were great and radio plays were an anachronism. I no longer feel that way.

Okay, this already sounds like an Oscars speech. I apologize.

Thanks for reading. I hope you'll try my future projects as well. Submarines anyone?

Steven L. Kent
April 28, 2014

ABOUT THE AUTHOR

Steven L. Kent is an American author, best known for The Clone Rebellion series of military science fiction and his video game journalism. As a freelance journalist, he has written for The Seattle Times, Parade, USA Today, the Chicago Tribune, MSNBC, The Japan Times, and The Los Angeles Times Syndicate. He also wrote entries on video games for Encarta and the Encyclopedia Americana. For more about Kent, visit his official website www. SadSamsPalace.com.

READ ON FOR AN EXCLUSIVE SHORT STORY BY

STEVEN L. KENT

THE SIXTH SHIP
LOST IN A DARK EXPANSE

Lieutenant Alex Chamberlain, the chief weapons officer on the Unified Authority battleship *Barrows* looked up from his screen and said, "Captain, something's going on at Smithsonian Field."

Something is going on, thought Captain Leslie Markham. '*Something is going on' could mean a lot of things, anything from two kids making out on the runway to President Andropov tap dancing on an atomic bomb and eating apple sauce.* She asked, "What kind of activity?"

Barrows was a U.A.N. ship, a self-broadcasting battleship with complement of 900 sailors. She had advanced shields and enough firepower to blow up a small moon. In a fair fight against a dozen obsolete Enlisted Man's ships, *Barrows* would sail away unharmed.

But the Enlisted Man's Empire was gone, extinct, thoroughly wiped out by an engineered flu virus that only one of the clones could resist or withstand. Knowing they were dying, the captains in the all-clone fleet had aimed their ships in every direction and boosted their rockets to maximum acceleration. They died of the flu while their ships scattered outside the solar system like the molecules of a big bang.

"There are six ships on the tarmac," said Chamberlain.

"Ships? Are you referring to Explorers?" asked Markham. They had to be Explorers; the only ships in the facility were Explorers—hundred-year-old self-broadcasting antiques built for charting the galaxy.

"Yes, ma'am."

"Maybe it's a routine cleaning; that field is a museum," said Markham. She'd been briefed on Smithsonian Field. The facility posed no credible security risk. She'd been warned to watch the field in case Wayson Harris, the last of the clones, tried to steal an Explorer, but she didn't take it seriously.

Wayson Harris... one clone, isolated and alone. "They're like ants," Andropov had told his officers. "An ant hill is a problem. Lone ants starve and die."

Having mulled over the situation, Markham added, "Six Explorers, I don't see how that's our problem." *Not with our men guarding the field*, she added in her head. "It's bound to be routine maintenance, nothing more."

"But, Captain, they've charged their broadcast generators," said Chamberlain.

"One of them?"

"All six ships, ma'am."

"Where do they think they're going?" Markham asked herself. She had no idea why Harris would want six ships or how he could use them. If it was Harris, he was alone; that was what Andropov had said. She wondered how a lone man could have moved six ships onto the runway. Still, there was something odd...

Something about the ships triggered a warning in her mind. She felt nervous, but she couldn't put her finger on the reason. She told the officer at the navigation station, "Lieutenant

Carmack, charge our broadcast generator."

"Aye aye, ma'am. Charging broadcast generator, aye."

That can't be Harris down there, she decided. *There's only one of him. Ships don't broadcast unless there's a pilot behind their yoke.* But she couldn't help noticing a telling coincidence. The number six. *Six Explorers... six ships in our fleet.* She dismissed the coincidence but not the paranoia that accompanied it.

"Can you see anything else down there?" she asked the weapons officer.

Barrow was three hundred thousand miles above Earth maintaining a stationary position. Chamberlain, her weapons officer, didn't have a line-of-sight view of Smithsonian Field. That which he saw, he saw through satellites. He said, "There are several people on the runway."

Several people, thought Markham. *It can't be Harris; the latest intelligence reports specifically state that he's alone.*

Engineers, maybe a cleaning crew, thought Markham. She asked, "What are they doing?"

"They're digging holes by the side of the runway."

Six ships charging their broadcast generators, Markham thought. *Men standing by the side of the runway digging holes. Makes no sense.*

"Ma'am, I can't be sure, but it looks like they're placing bodies in the holes."

"Bodies? Human bodies?"

"Yes, ma'am." Three minutes passed and Chamberlain said, "They're filling in the holes, Captain. Now, they're just standing there... in that same spot. It looks like a funeral."

Digging graves... maybe an attack on Smithsonian Field. Six ships. Six Explorers. "What's the charge on our broadcast generator?" Markham asked Carmack, the navigation officer.

"Fifty percent, ma'am."

"How much longer?"

"Another five minutes, Captain."

"What's happening down there?" asked Markham.

"The funeral's over. They're walking up the runway. They're meeting. They're talking. I see nine... no, ten men. They're still talking... now some of them are going to the Explorers."

Six Explorers. Six ships in our fleet. "Mr. Chamberlain, are our shields up?"

"Yes, ma'am," said Chamberlain.

"Are we broadcast ready?" asked Markham.

"Eighty percent... eighty-five percent, ma'am."

"Captain, they've ignited their thrusters," Chamberlain called from weapons.

"How many?" asked Markham.

"All six." Chamberlain sounded calm but curious.

They all seemed so calm, so detached that, just for a moment, Captain Markham questioned her own sanity. She'd have a hell of a time explaining an unauthorized broadcast. She said, "Lieutenant Carmack, log Terraneau as our destination. Prepare to broadcast."

"Terraneau, aye. Destination logged, Captain."

"Get us to Terraneau."

"Captain, they're going wheels up," said Chamberlain, the weapons officer.

"All six?"

"Yes, ma'am."

"Are we set for Terraneau?" asked Markham.

"Terraneau, aye, ma'am."

"Mister Chamberlain, what are those ships doing?"

"Still rising, Captain," said Chamberlain.

"Rising? Do you mean leaving the atmosphere?"

"No, ma'am. They appear to be hovering."

"Hovering?" Markham repeated. *Six Explorers, charged and ready to broadcast... six ships in our fleet. They're lifting just high enough to broadcast.*

"Scan those ships for weapons," she ordered.

"Captain, they aren't carrying weapons," said Chamberlain.

Then they can't hurt us. They're unarmed, unshielded, and defenseless. If they broadcast near us we'll blow them to... If they broadcast into us... The ships aren't carrying weapons because they are weapons. Oh speck! The Explorers are the weapons!

She wanted to warn the other ships in the U.A. Fleet, but she knew it was too late. "Get us out of here! Ensign, broadcast now!" she shouted. She had enough time to think, *if I'm wrong, Andropov will have my hide for this*, and then the broadcast happened, but it did not go smoothly.

It started out according to book—the viewports darkened and the lightning danced outside their ship. As the anomaly began, *Barrows* shuddered and then the lightning vanished and the ship glided into space.

The broadcast itself happened in an instant. Captain Markham looked through the viewport and asked, "Where the hell is Terraneau?"

1

U.A.N. Barrows was long and thin, like the blade of a dagger when viewed from the side. She was twenty-six hundred feet long, four hundred feet tall, and two hundred feet wide. The bridge sat above the point of her nose. Along with navigation and communications stations, the bridge had its own generators and life support systems. Let the rest of *Barrows* crumble, the crew on the bridge would survive.

During the broadcast, something had gone wrong. When the communications officer called the various sections of the ship for damage reports, the only sections that responded were located near the bridge. Weapons tried to run a ship-wide systems diagnosis. The computer reported that the entire ship had gone dark.

Markham sent her chief of security and her engineer on duty to investigate. They left the bridge, entered the nearest elevator, and tried ride down to the engine room on the fifth deck, but they heard two loud thumps and a noise that sounded like chains scraping across a steel floor. The car reached the twelfth deck and stopped, but the doors didn't open.

"Something wrong with the elevator?" asked the chief of security, a large man with a square jaw and rippling muscles.

"Well I sure as speck can't tell from in here," said the engineer. Like her captain, the engineer was a Markham. She and the captain were cousins. The relationship had not landed the engineer any promotions, but it allowed her more latitude when dealing with senior officers.

They tried to pry the door open, but the panels wouldn't give, so they rode up to the thirteenth, where the door automatically opened.

"What a difference a floor makes," joked the chief of security.

The engineer ignored him as she scanned for damage. She didn't see much. Lights flickered somewhere in the distance but the corridor was dark.

The chief of security radioed the bridge. He reported the malfunctioning elevator and the dark corridor.

"We haven't seen any crew members."

Captain Markham replied, "You're going to need to search the entire ship. You might as well begin with deck thirteen."

"Aye aye, ma'am," said the chief of security as he signed off. He didn't like Captain Markham. He considered her a ball-buster. She wasn't dictatorial as ships' captains go, but he'd never served under a woman before. He wanted her to be softer and sweeter than male officers.

He stopped, turned his nose up, and sniffed the air, noting a sharp scent that reminded him of charred popcorn. He took in a breath, considered it, inhaled again, and decided that it wasn't the smell of burned flesh.

He asked the engineer, "You smell something, burned wiring, maybe?"

"Something's burning," the engineer agreed. She shined a flashlight around the outer door of the elevator. The edges didn't line up. The elevator sat skewed in its shaft.

"Is it a fire in electrical systems?" asked the chief of security.

"Something's fried," said the engineer as she dropped to her hands and knees and pressed the torch into the crack between the lift and the wall of the shaft. She considered the damage carefully and said, "Well, the elevator's broken," in an authoritative voice.

"Is that your professional opinion, Ensign Markham?" asked the chief of security.

"No, my professional opinion is that we're lucky we made it out of that lift alive. It's canted nine-degrees off normal and shouldn't be running at all."

"Will it take us back to the bridge?"

The engineer lowered herself to the floor, laid flat on her stomach, and shined her torch in the crack at the bottom of the lift. She said, "It's taken us this far. As long as the pinions hold, we should survive. That's the good news."

"What's the bad news?" asked the chief of security, as he thought, *this bitch is just like her sister*.

"The bad news is that there are two pinions. One is broken; one is cracked."

"So we die if we get back in the elevator?"

Still shining her light through the gap, the engineer said, "Maybe not. The fall might not kill us."

"We're thirteen decks up," said the chief of security.

"True enough," said the engineer, "but there isn't any gravity on the twelfth."

"How can you tell?" asked security.

She signaled the chief of security to join her, then pointed her light into the gap. She said, "You see those steel cables floating like seaweed down there? Those are the counterbalances to this car."

They abandoned the elevator and entered the corridor seeing only by the light of their two torches. They passed a crew's mess, the main galley, and a berthing officers' area. At first glance, everything seemed in order. They didn't see damage or bodies.

The engineer entered the berthing area. It was dark. It was empty—one hundred racks all laid out in rows like shelves in a grocery store.

She whispered, "Where is everybody?"

The chief of security heard the question and grimaced. He walked to the nearest rack, and shined his light in. He turned his light this way and that, shining it on the hollow shelf that normally served as a sleeping station. When the engineer joined him, the chief of security said, "There aren't any bodies."

The engineer asked, "What happened to the sheets and the mattresses?"

The bunks were in stacks of three. The engineer shined her light on the upper bunk and the lower bunk and the stacks to the right and left. None of them had mattresses. She asked, "Did they close this area?"

The chief of security shined his light across the room and said, "That's my rack over there. I was in it three hours ago."

They stood in silence, playing their lights across the rows of racks. The chief of security blew as hard as he could onto the rack, kicking up a cloud of fine gray ash. He asked, "You know that smell in the air?"

The engineer said, "No. No. That's not possible."

"You got any other explanations?"

"I'm just telling you, from an engineering standpoint, disintegrating an entire crew without destroying the ship simply isn't possible."

"Okay. You're the math genius," the chief of security conceded. "You tell me, where'd everybody go?"

The engineer ran her torch across three rows of sleeping stations. She asked, "Are you going to report this?"

"Not yet," said the chief of security. "I still don't have any answers."

As they left the berthing area, the chief of security said, "Maybe they weren't disintegrated. Maybe they were cremated, you know, burned to dust."

"You mean incinerated?" the engineer repeated.

"Yeah, incinerated along with their mattresses."

The engineer shined his torch on the walls, the floor, the ceiling. She went back to the galley and peered inside. She saw cans without labels. There weren't any towels. She picked up a knife. The blade reflected the light from her torch, but the handle was missing. *Was the handle made out of wood or plastic*? she wondered. She noticed that everything that was grounded or conducted electricity was fine. Metal and glass seemed untouched. Everything else was gone.

Incinerated? She wondered if it was possible.

When the chief of security stepped into the doorway, she told him, "There's nothing in the world that could have done this. Not a fire; not even a nuclear bomb."

"How about a broadcast gone wrong?"

They didn't speak after that. They crossed the deck in stunned silence. They passed the rec room. It was dark and empty. The movie screen was missing from the wall.

The chief of security went in to inspect the head. He found the toilets still filled with water. The toilet paper dispensers were empty.

A few hundred yards down the corridor, the walls seemed to have buckled. What had been razor-straight lines now curved and rolled. Above them, white light flashed in lightning-like bursts. Sparks drifted through the air like rain. A huge metal bubble filled the hallway, filling it so tightly that they couldn't squeeze around it.

The engineer said, "I can't imagine what could have done this to our ship."

The chief of security asked, "What if we were hit by another ship?"

When the engineer asked, "What are you talking about?" he shined his light on the floor and the deck to make sure they were solid, then he approached the distortion in the wall. It looked like a break. It looked like a bubble. He rapped his knuckles on a hole and shined his light into it. There were seats inside the distortion. There were computers and flight controls. The lines along the holes were straight and regular.

He said, "Somebody broadcasted this ship into us."

"That's not possible," said the engineer.

"So I hear," said the chief of security. "But here it is."

"Do you know much energy these ships release when they broadcast?" asked the engineer. "There has to be a few billion joules in a broadcast anomaly."

"Is that enough energy to disintegrate crewmen and mattresses?" asked the chief of security.

The engineer considered the power needed to execute a broadcast and answered, "An anomaly inside our hull? That would have disintegrated our whole damn ship."

"Stay here," said the security chief. He squatted beside the strange ship and crawled in through a broken window.

"Hey! What the speck! Where are you going?" yelled the engineer.

"I'm going to have a look around this ship."

2

Captain Markham still didn't know the extent of the damage. The team she'd sent to investigate had just radioed back about the elevator when the alien ship arrived.

The ship looked a bit like a lobster. Her wings curved toward her cockpit like pincers. They ended in cannons instead of claws. There were clusters of cannons on either side of her cockpit. She had rows of weapons just behind her baffles as well.

Captain Markham and Lieutenant Chamberlain watched the ship on a tactical screen as she approached.

Markham said, "She's too small for military use."

"She isn't civilian," said the weapons officer, and he showed her the weapons array.

Captain Markham agreed. She said, "She's a war bird alright. I guess that makes her a frigate, maybe a cruiser."

"If they have frigates and cruisers out here," said Chamberlain. "Can we beat her?"

Chamberlain thought about the question and said, "There's

no telling, ma'am. I don't know anything about her shields or her guns. For all we know, those guns shoot spitballs."

Feeling embarrassed for having asked such a ill-informed question, Captain Markham grunted, "Good point, Lieutenant. Could the clones have made her?" As far as anybody knew, the clones and the humans were the only sentient beings inhabiting the galaxy.

"I don't think she's from the Enlisted Man's Navy," said Chamberlain.

The alien ship circled *Barrows*, traveling slowly, shining some kind of beam up and down her hull. It might have been an X-ray. It might have been a laser. It might have a searchlight or it might have contained an entire battery of scans that shone on the hull of the ship without damaging it.

The alien ship hovered around *Barrows* like a bee examining a flower. It slowly floated from the stern of the ship to the bow, crossed over to the other side and returned to the bow, shining that strange beam the entire time.

Go away. Go away, Markham thought. *If she goes away, she may return with something bigger*, she reminded himself.

The little ship didn't go away. It paused, hung in space near *Barrows*' stern for nearly a minute, and then clamped herself to the side of the larger ship's hull like a tick preparing to burrow into a dog.

Chamberlain, a man of war, said, "Maybe we can overpower them. Maybe we can steal their ship."

Markham nodded and thought, *maybe there's hope*.

A few minutes later, the engineer and the chief of security returned. Captain Markham saw the same expression on their faces and mumbled, "We're specked."

3

"Okay, let's start from the top, where exactly have we landed?" Captain Markham demanded. She sat at the head of the conference table with her bridge officers filling the different positions. The chief of security was present, but her cousin, a lowly ensign, was the highest ranking engineer she could find. Most of the officers present were lieutenants or below.

There was no way of knowing what had become of the rest of the crew. They could be dead. She hoped they were alive and safe and trapped in the back of the ship, but she was pragmatic if nothing else. She knew which hand would fill more quickly if she shat in one hand and wished for riches in the other.

Markham knew that the Explorer had broadcasted into the center of *Barrows*; the chief of security had returned from his mission with photographs of it. She had not yet gone down to inspect the damage herself, but she intended to go after the meeting.

"We have no way of identifying our location, Captain," said

Lieutenant JG Barry Carmack, the highest ranking navigation officer she had left.

"And you don't have any idea where we may be?" asked Markham.

"I know where we aren't, ma'am."

Markham slapped her hand down on the table with a noise like a gunshot. Everybody jumped. "We all know where we aren't, Lieutenant!" she shouted. "We aren't next to Terraneau."

"No, ma'am," Carmack agreed.

"No, ma'am what?" demanded Markham.

"No, ma'am, we aren't near Terraneau."

"I know that. I can see that. I don't see Terraneau when I look through the specking viewport."

"Captain, I can say definitively that we aren't..."

Markham slapped the table a second time. She shouted, "I know where we aren't!"

"Captain, we aren't in the Milky Way Galaxy," said the lieutenant junior grade.

Markham had already raised her hand to slap the table again. She froze and asked, "What?"

"We aren't in the Milky Way, ma'am. I've run an astronomical survey. The stars and formations aren't of the Milky Way. We're in uncharted space."

"You mean this section of the galaxy hasn't been charted," said Markham.

"No, ma'am. We have left the galaxy. If we were in the Milky Way, my computers would have spotted something."

An icy silence filled the room.

"Our astronavigation computers haven't found recognizable planets, stars, formations or nebulae. For all we know, ma'am, we may not be in the same universe. We've entered a *dark expanse*, Captain, someplace unexplored by manned flights or unmanned probes."

Captain Markham listened, considered what her navigator had told her and the many implications. She said, "Lieutenant, I don't claim to understand the workings of broadcast technology, but from what I do know, it sounds as if we don't need to know our current location to fly to a specified planet. Is that correct?"

"Technically..." the navigator began.

Captain Markham raised a hand to stop him. She asked, "Yes or no, Lieutenant?"

"Yes, ma'am; we should not need to know our current location to broadcast to a known one."

"But?" asked Captain Markham.

"Something happened during that last broadcast. I'm not sure what."

"I can tell you," said the engineer.

Leslie Markham turned to Wendy, her cousin. She knew that Wendy was operating way above her pay grade, facing challenges and risks no ensign should be forced to endure. Speaking in a soft voice, she asked, "What can you tell me, Ensign?"

The engineer and the security officer had already discussed their findings with Captain Markham; now, with her permission, they would share the information with the other chiefs. Markham nodded and the engineer said, "Another ship has broadcasted into the center of our ship."

"Say again?" said Alex Chamberlain.

"A small ship broadcasted into our ship as we broadcasted out," said the engineer.

"Bullshit," said the communications officer.

"It makes sense," said Chamberlain, the weapons officer.

"We had our shields up. Nothing gets through these shields," said the communications officer.

The engineer was an ensign, she had a single gold bar on her collar. The communications officer was a full lieutenant. He had a higher rank and two silver bars to prove it. Careful not to overstep her bounds, not convinced her cousin would protect her, the engineer said, "With all due respect, sir, a broadcasting ship wouldn't need to get through our shields; it would materialize inside them, and the shields wouldn't matter. Shields are disabled during the moment of broadcast."

The communications officer asked, "Are you saying that ship struck us as we broadcasted out?"

"Yes, sir."

"The exact moment of the broadcast," said Chamberlain. "They had six self-broadcasting ships on the tarmac. They were using them for weapons, broadcasting them at out our ships. That's why you had us broadcast out, Captain. You knew what they were doing!"

"What who was doing?" asked the engineer.

"Right before everything happened, I spotted men on the tarmac at Smithsonian Field. They must have been clones," said Chamberlain.

"It would appear so," said Captain Markham.

"What are the odds? What are the specking odds?" asked Chamberlain.

"We got lucky, sir," said the engineer.

"How is that?" asked Captain Markham.

"The anomaly from that ship should have caused us to explode. That ship arrived as energy and data at the same moment that we converted into energy and data. Had she arrived a moment earlier, the current and energy from her anomaly would have destroyed us."

"How much damage did we take?" asked Captain Markham.

"Truthfully, Captain, there's no way to know," said the engineer.

"Can you restore radio communications across the ship?" asked Markham.

"No, ma'am; not from the bridge," said the communications officer.

"Can you restore power throughout the ship?"

"For all we know, they have power on the lower decks, Captain," said the engineer.

"Captain, *Barrows* is like a body with a severed spine. She's paralyzed below the neck. She has no feeling. She has no motion. We can't send signals to the other side of the ship and we have no way of knowing if the hull has been breached or the power is out."

"We know that the gravity is out on the twelfth deck," said the chief of security.

Captain Markham took in the message, nodded curtly, and sighed. She asked, "Is there anything else?"

"There's no sign of the pilot," said the chief of security. He almost said, "There's no sign of the man piloting the ship," but he knew from experience that Captain Markham would have made him explain why he assumed the pilot was a man.

"It's entirely possible that the pilot was disintegrated," said the engineer. "There weren't any people on deck thirteen. It's very likely that the anomaly from that collision disintegrated any crew members on that deck."

"He wasn't disintegrated," said the chief of security.

"How do you know?" asked the engineer.

"The pilot of that boat was safe," said the chief of security. "Both anomalies happened outside his boat, and…"

"This is undiscovered territory," said the engineer. "There's no way anyone could predict what happens when you have an anomaly inside an anomaly."

The chief of security continued. "One of the cockpit windows was shattered. The glass was on the outside of the ship which means that whoever broke it, broke it from the inside.

"We need to assume the pilot of that vessel is hostile and..."

Captain Markham interrupted him. She said, "An alien vessel has attached itself to our hull. We don't know their intentions, but we can assume they mean us harm. For now, we need to assume that the pilot of that vessel is hostile and dangerous as well."

"Do we know if the aliens entered the ship?" asked the chief of security.

Markham shook her head and said, "There's no way of telling; we're paralyzed below the neck."

4

Barrows' bridge was one hundred feet long and filled the ship's two hundred-foot width—twenty thousand feet of floor space. The captain's area included a command dais complete with holographic tactical displays, a conference room, and a charting station. Desks, computers, and workstations filled the sprawling area around the captain's dais. All in all, the bridge looked more like a business than the nerve center of a ship. One hundred twenty-three sailors worked on the bridge, more than one tenth of the crew.

Sixty-seven crew members had been on the bridge when Captain Markham ordered navigation to broadcast the ship to Terraneau. Until communications were established with the rest of the ship, Captain Markham would not be able to account for the remaining eight hundred thirty sailors.

Eight hundred thirty-two, she hurled the number at herself as an accusation. She sat on at the conn overlooking—to the best of her knowledge—her entire crew. This bridge remained undamaged and fully staffed. From this perspective, everything looked good.

Wendy, her cousin, approached the dais and said, "Captain, may I have a moment?"

"What is it, Wendy?" Markham asked, choosing to call her cousin by name. As far as she was concerned, the mission was over.

"Captain, except for being melted into the walls around it, that Explorer looked solid. We should be able to use her like a doorway to get to the rest of the ship."

Wendy, can't you know it's over? Captain Markham asked in her head. She said, "There maybe be hostile aliens on the other side of the ship. If that Explorer really is a doorway, the prudent move would be to lock it."

"Captain?" asked the engineer.

Wendy. Wendy. We're cousins. We're friends. We grew up in the same town, Captain Markham tried to send the message telepathically, but her cousin didn't hear. *Formality doesn't matter anymore. Not now. Not in the end.*

Still trying to maintain her command presence for the rest of the crew, she asked, "What about launching the Explorer? Can we break her free?"

"Do you mean like a broadcast?" the engineer asked.

"Yes. I mean a broadcast."

"That would destroy the ship. Everyone would die."

"What about the people on the Explorer?"

"Everyone would die."

"Okay," said Captain Markham. She sighed and asked, "Can we melt the Explorer? Can we seal her to make sure the aliens don't come through?"

"Sealing her up won't be a problem," said the engineer. "I can just pump her full of cold foam."

Cold foam was a compressed chemical compound that expanded by three thousand percent and hardened when it came in contact with oxygen. Engineers pumped it into damaged areas in ships to improve structural integrity.

"Will the aliens be able to cut through?" asked Markham.

"I can't make any predictions, Captain. I haven't seen their technology," said the engineer.

"Yes. Of course," said Markham.

"Captain, may I have permission to speak freely?"

"Yes, Ensign." For the first time in her career, Leslie Markham hated the formalities and protocols of Navy life. This was her cousin, her little cousin. They were friends and family. Would they refer to each other by rank and title to their deaths?

"Three quarters of the crew may be trapped behind that ship, Captain."

"Wendy, we can't risk a rescue," said Captain Markham.

"Captain, the alien vessel is a small boat, maybe fifty hands in her crew. We don't know what's happening in the rest of the ship. For all we know, our crew may have overpowered theirs."

"I can't send a team to investigate. I don't have the manpower."

"Captain, if we seal the Explorer, we cut ourselves off from weapons, transports, and food supplies."

Captain Markham said, "Wendy, we can't send you! What if…"

"What if I die?" asked the engineer.

Captain Markham smiled and thanked her cousin. She called her, "Ensign," and said she'd "think about it."

Leslie Markham was not a beautiful woman. She had short blond hair and green eyes and skin so sallow that it looked like it may never have seen the sun. She stood five-foot-five and weighed one hundred and fifty-three pounds, and had masculine shoulders and sinewy neck.

She'd never been married and had no children, but she'd often been in love. Her most recent lover had been the chief of engineering, a man now lost in the back of the ship.

Markham wanted to send a rescue party, wanted to instruct them to start in the engine room, to find her last love. She thought that would be an appropriate action, but she questioned her own reasoning. She wouldn't risk lives looking for a missing paramour. What if she saved the ship and lost her cousin? How could she ever return home?

They discovered the first of the bodies later that hour.

5

Petty Officer 3rd Class Vince Saban had gone to the bridge's galley, which was really just a break room. It was a nook, a small cabin with a couple of tables, a coffee machine, and a small food service area.

There'd been three sailors in the galley when Saban entered, two men and a woman. Saban traded a few pleasantries and went to look for food while the others left. He had just found a sandwich he liked and sat at the table as the last of the sailors left—PO1 Theresa Kennedy. She remembered him sitting alone, looking off in the distance. She thought he seemed lonely.

That was the last time any crew member saw Saban alive. The next sailor who entered the galley found Saban lying on the floor, mostly hidden by a table. His throat had been slit.

A sailor found the body of Seaman Lori Selwin twenty minutes later. Seaman Selwin had been a weapons technician. She worked in the fore torpedo room, located directly below the bridge.

Selwin died in the corridor outside the torpedo room; at least, that was where the blood trail started. There was a small splash on a wall about five feet off the ground and scattered puddles that suggested she did not go easily. The killing left no large pools of blood, just dribbled spots here and there, the splashes on a couple of walls and splotches on the deck.

Selwin's leg was broken. She had a dislocated shoulder, and a broken neck.

Captain Markham insisted on seeing both of the bodies. She would have placed the bodies in bags, but her corpsmen kept the bags in sickbay, which was in the center of the ship. For lack of any better options, she said a few words over the corpses and jettisoned them into space.

She spoke with her cousin after the funeral. She asked, "Wendy, do you still want take a team to rest of the ship? It could be dangerous."

The engineer looked at the hatch through which they had purged the bodies. She said, "Captain, it can't be any worse than waiting here to die."

6

The search party included eleven men and the engineer. She was the eyes of the operation. The chief of security came as the muscle. He'd drafted seven nonessential sailors into his security service. Three other officers joined the team to assist the engineer.

They were unarmed. The only firearms were on the lowest deck. They carried very few tools. All of the torches and meters were on the fifth deck, near the entrance to the engine room.

They rode the elevator to deck thirteen and climbed off. The three men assisting the engineer carried canisters of cold foam. The canisters weighed thirty pounds. The men assisting the chief of security carried butter knives.

The engineer told the chief of security, "Once we fill that ship with foam, there's no going back."

The chief of security said, "You've got it backwards, pal. We're the ones with the fighting chance. There are weapons and transports in the back of the ship. You saw what happened to Selwin and Saban; it's only a matter of time for anyone on the bridge."

Nothing had changed on deck thirteen. It was still dark and empty, silent as a tomb and sterile as a morgue. As they passed the galley, one of the men said, "Now we know where to go for food." They passed the rec room and one of the men commented about how empty it looked.

A minute later they reached the ship. The security team fanned out along the front of Explorer, their butter knives out and ready as the engineer and her three assistants crawled through the hole into the cockpit.

The engineer showed her men where to place their cold foam canisters and how to prime the detonators. When the cold foam was ready, the security entered. Had it not been for the light of the handheld torches and dials of the detonators, the inside of the Explorer would have been completely dark. Even the emergency lights were out.

They went to the back of the ship. The rear hatch had frozen shut, but there was a ladder leading to an upper hatch. One of the security men climbed the ladder and used a manual override to open the hatch.

The security team left first, followed by the three engineering assistants. The engineer remained behind. She checked each of the canisters, kneeling beside them, reading the data on the detonators.

As she finished examining the canisters, she noticed a shift in the shadows outside the cockpit. She aimed her torch, and there the phantom stood, looking almost human, but not quite. It was short and bald, its skin the color of charcoal.

The creature wore the same basic battle dress uniform worn by Marines and soldiers. It stared through the windscreen at the engineer, moving with the silent grace of a lion or a tiger as it dropped to the ground and entered the broken window at the front of the ship.

The engineer leaped for the ladder and scrambled to the top.

She darted into the airlock, sealed the inner hatch, and pressed the button that detonated the cold foam canisters. She heard the bang of the canisters exploding and the hiss of the foam as she climbed through the hatch.

The chief of security waited for her on the roof of the Explorer. His men stood on the floor below.

The engineer said, "I saw it."

"Saw what?" asked the chief of security.

"I saw the alien."

"Where is it?"

"It's down there... inside the ship."

"Do you think it's in the foam?"

"I don't know."

"So it's Captain Markham's problem," said the chief of security, and he brushed his sleeves as if flicking the problem from his uniform. He asked, "What did it look like?"

The engineer brought her hand to her nose and said, "It's small. About this tall."

"That's pretty short."

"Short and skinny and almost human, but its skin is black. I think it was wearing BDUs."

"You mean a human uniform?" asked the chief of security.

"It looked like regulation battle dress, like what we give our Marines."

They both stared down at the ship. Solidified foam now filled the windows along the roof. Very light gray in color, like cement, the foam seemed to have filled every square inch of the little ship. The engineer said, "It came running into the ship. If it didn't get out, it's dead now."

The way cold foam decompressed and expanded, it wouldn't have encased that creature so much as crushed it.

The chief of security muttered, "I hope it's in there."

"What?" asked the engineer.

"I went out with Lori Selwin a couple of times, nothing serious, but she was a nice girl. If that thing killed her, I hope it died in agony."

The engineer said, "If it's in there, believe me, it did."

As the senior officer, the chief of security brought all of the men into a tight group, just in case that alien had somehow survived the foam. He said, "Look at the man on your right then look at the man on your left. Don't let them out of your sight."

They started walking.

The area was empty and dark. No bodies. No blood. "Looks like the anomaly spread all the way across the ship," said the chief of security.

"Seems to have... on this deck at least," said the engineer.

"You think people may have survived on other decks?"

"*Barrows* is a big ship."

The thirteenth deck was an empty tomb with dusty floors and sterile walls and next to nothing in the way of clutter. That which the anomaly did not affect, it appeared to have left untouched. That which the anomaly destroyed, appeared to have disintegrated to dust. The scent of burning filled the air. The men breathed it until their noses grew numb to the smell.

Two hundred yards down the hallway, they found one of *Barrows'* information systems nerve centers, a location where technicians diagnose the ship's engines, life support, and electrical systems. The room was dark. The computers were dead. When the engineer opened a coffin-sized cabinet supposedly filled with circuitry, she shined torch into the cabinet and found only ash and slag.

"What's that mean?" asked the chief of security.

"Don't expect lights any time soon."

"The air's still running."

The engineer corrected him. "There's still air. That doesn't mean the vents are working. The deck is a half-mile long, and there are only twelve people breathing; it'll be a while before we run out of oxygen."

"The gravity's still working," the chief of security pointed out.

"Good point," said the engineer, wondering if the hardware could have survived the shock that devastated the computers. Broadcast engineering had never been her area of concentration. She knew some of the concepts but didn't understand the theories behind them.

"The gravity wasn't working one deck below us," the engineer said. "At least it wasn't near the bow."

There was a noise. The engineer heard it but paid no attention. The chief of security went silent, shined his light to the floor and whispered, "All of you, lights out... NOW!"

Someone took hold of the engineer, pulling her off balance and then shoving her from behind. She tumbled forward, bumping her face into something unseen and solid. Her head snapped back, and then the person pushed her down by the shoulders and knocked her forward once again.

Though she only saw his thick fingers, and only for a moment, she knew it was the chief of security and that he was trying to hide her in the cabinet. She felt the walls around her on the crown of her head, on her shoulders, against the small of her back, and on her knees. She tried to protest but he closed the cabinet.

Pulling her arms and knees to her chest and squeezing them in tight, emptying her lungs and waiting to inhale, making herself as small as possible, the engineer found enough space to pivot around.

She squirmed, rolled forward, and pressed her eyes against the row of ventilation holes along the side of the cabinet, and saw nothing. She heard men shouting, then screaming, then running. A clucking noise that reminded her of the chatter made by crows filled the air. She heard intelligence in the noise, an intelligence that was both fierce and heartless.

The screaming grew louder and more chaotic. Shrieks. Pleading. Pain. The padding of feet, not boots, soft flesh slapping the metal. She heard this and felt herself drowning in the vibration of heavy steps and the sounds of fighting. With no other choice but to hide, she held her breath as long as she could, and then she heard something far worse than fighting—she heard stillness. No more than a minute or two had passed, and the battle had already ended.

Trapped inside the cabinet, her kneecaps pushed into the dust and the slag, the engineer tried to hold her breath. She heard the wheezing just outside the cabinet, breathing that rattled and hissed. Whatever was out there, it sounded massive, nothing like the lithe, dark-skinned man she had glimpsed outside the Explorer.

The engineer pressed her eyes to the vent, hoping to see flashlight beams or the silhouettes of men. Instead, she saw a turquoise-colored eye with a slit pupil. Claws as wide as railroad spikes stabbed through the metal door of the cabinet, which crumbled like paper as the creature tore it away.

In the low light of abandoned torches, the creature stood eight or nine feet tall. It wore primitive armor that was better suited for a Roman-era gladiator than an astronaut. It had two legs, two arms, two eyes, and mouth, and after that it bore no similarity to a human. The engineer's mind registered the thing as reptile, but it looked like a cat that had been skinned and left out in the sun, its muscles and organs and veins all dried and hardened to leather.

A huge gun hung from the belt that circled the alien's waist, but the creature didn't bother to draw it.

The engineer stared up at the creature, took in the tilt of its head and the way its trifurcated feet spread out on the deck as if they'd been split. The creature clearly knew it had her trapped. It stared at her like a cat preparing to play with a mouse.

The engineer didn't think about what she did next, she simply acted. She reached her hands to the front of the cabinet and wrapped her fingers around the edges. She tightened the muscles in her arms and in her thighs, rolled back, and then with a hard pull, slingshotted herself forward, launching herself like a sprinter in a race, flashing past the creature, vaulting over its scaly tail, and trying to find traction as she skidded across the blood-slicked metal floor.

There were other creatures. The engineer didn't waste moments trying to locate them, but she heard the sounds they made. She heard rattling and clucking, tried to ignore the logic of their sounds, but heard how all of the creatures echoed each other.

Most of them made a different variation of that crow-like cackling noise. On some subconscious level, the engineer realized they were laughing at her. She had become the prey, the fox, the fear-driven animal surviving by instinct instead of thought. Fatigue no longer occurred to her; terror overpowered every other concern.

The blood on the deck was smeared and streaked. Men had been cut down, their bleeding bodies must have been dragged across the floor.

The padding noise accentuated her fear. The alien was chasing her. She heard the thudding, slapping, accelerating footsteps. Her mind was frantic. Fighting for breath, already feeling the muscles tighten in her calves and thighs, she ran up the corridor, darting around corners, losing her way, not caring where she went in the darkness.

She came to a corner where one large hall crossed another, threw her flashlight to the right and sprinted to the left. Behind her, an alien grunted and hissed as it breathed. Its footsteps slowed as it reached the corner. *Go away. Go the other way,* she told it in her thoughts.

Don't be able to see in the dark. Please Lord, don't let it be able see in the dark. Oh, shit, maybe it can smell me! Her thoughts scattered in frantic circles.

The creature stopped. Grunting and snorting as it inhaled, hissing as it exhaled. It made that clucking sound, softly this time, laughing to itself.

I'm blind. I need the flashlight. I need to go back to get the flashlight, she thought, and she almost went to get it. Peering around the corner, looking down the corridor, she saw her torch lying on the floor in a puddle of light and realized what a mistake it had been to throw it away.

7

Nearly an hour had passed since Captain Markham had sent the rescue party to explore the other side of the ship, her ship. She had sent her cousin with a group of unarmed sailors to walk halls and search cabins in a no man's land.

At the time, she had thought that sending Wendy with the team was a mistake; now she wondered if the search party had the safer duty. She looked down at the three corpses. They had died in a group because she had sent them out as a group. The bodies belonged to Petty Officer 3rd Class Wade Korman, Seaman Terrance Ford, and Petty Officer 1st Class Gil Huntsman—good sailors, good men.

Barrows was under siege from within. She had circled the wagons by keeping all available crewmen on the bridge. When Korman and Ford said they needed to go to the head, she'd decided that three men would be safer than two and sent Huntsman to accompany them.

Twenty minutes passed, more than enough time to use the head, enough time to clean it as far as Markham was concerned. Rather than risking another small group, she and sixteen other crew members went to search for her lost sheep, and this was what they found, a heap of broken bodies lying on the floor of the head.

The monster didn't shoot them, which would have been too merciful. Huntsman had two broken legs. One of Korman's eyes was missing. The killer had left a trio of slashes across Ford's throat. All of them had blood on their faces and clothes. Seeing the carnage, Markham believed that the killer had tortured these men. *Bastard*, she thought. *Animal*.

She cleared her throat and said, "If any of you still need to use the bathroom, do it now."

No one responded.

I started with nine hundred sailors, she thought. *Now I have fewer than fifty. Eight hundred thirty-two dead, five murdered, twelve unaccounted for*. Until she received confirmation one way or another, she would consider the search team missing in action.

Captain Markham asked, "Is anybody hungry or thirsty?"

She wasn't. No one spoke up.

One of the crewmen said, "We're going to die out here. That's what's going to happen; we're all going to die out here." He fell to his knees and sobbed inconsolably.

The other sailors stood unmoving, a ring around the dead sailors, staring at the bloody bodies on the floor. A few crewmen whimpered.

Markham gazed down at the panicking sailor. She wanted to kick him, to slap him, to tell him to "man up," to tell him to calm down. She thought about calling him a coward and lying about help coming soon. Ignoring her own urges to collapse to her knees, she put on a stoic face and asked, "Has anyone else given up?"

One of the other sailors patted the sobbing man on the back. Two of them took him by the arms and drew him to his feet. They left the dead sailors on the floor of the head and returned to the bridge.

8

The fire broke out in a weapons locker, in the front weapons array. *U.A.N. Barrows* carried a full complement of Sherman Striker torpedoes, a projectile designed for disrupting the shields of enemy ships.

Sherman Strikers were not particularly concussive torpedoes. They detonated with far less force than standard projectiles. They accomplished their purpose by releasing a potent emission—ionized, electricity-dampening, radioactive particles. Unleashed inside the confines of a ship, the radioactivity would destroy computer systems, short out all circuitry, destroy lights, and eliminate life support and communications systems. None of that destruction would matter, however, as the radiation from a single Striker would pretty much dissolve the crew to liquid.

"What now?" Markham asked the moment the siren sounded.

"There's a fire in the front torpedo room!" Alex Chamberlain reported as he rose out of his chair. As chief weapons officer, he received alert before the others.

"You can't go out there alone," Markham shouted, but she was already too late.

"There are Strikers in that locker," Chamberlain shouted as he reached the hatch. "If those go off, we'll all be dead."

Feeling her control of the situation slipping away, Captain Markham turned to the others and shouted, "Don't just stand there! You heard the man!"

A sailor standing in the communications area asked, "Who should we send?"

"All of you," Markham answered.

The rest of her crew ran to follow.

Captain Markham wondered if they would find Chamberlain or his corpse. She didn't leave with the rest of her sailors. She spun her chair so that it faced hatch, crossed her arms, and waited for Death to enter.

He came quickly. A minute after the rest of the crew left the bridge, the creature that Leslie Markham assumed was the alien saboteur glided into the bridge as silently and smoothly as a shadow.

9

As a weapons officer, Chamberlain knew the way to the locker better than the bridge hands behind him. He knew emergency procedures, had run the drills until every response to every situation had worked its way into his muscle memory. He didn't even need to think to read the signs—white smoke meant burning propulsion; glowing wall panels meant heat emissions; blue warning lights flashed to signal toxicity.

A breach in a Sherman Striker would result in all systems going out. If the main lights and warning lights went out, standard procedure was known as KYAG—short for "kiss your ass goodbye."

He sprinted up the corridor, dodged around a corner, and spotted the open hatch to the torpedo room. That door should have been closed and secured. No one was allowed to enter without authorization.

Though he'd thought he'd been running as fast as he could, Chamberlain found an extra burst of speed when he saw the partially opened hatch. The computers inside the weapons area winked on and off as they peacefully performed their unending calculations. On the far end of the chamber, gray smoke seeped out around the door to the weapons locker.

More crew members clambered in after Chamberlain, grouping behind him, tired from their run and gasping for air.

Chamberlain looked above the door to the locker. Only a white light flashed above the jam, the warning for low oxygen. The other lights, the ones that signaled fires, toxic elements, and radiation, remained dark.

Not stopping to consider the possibility of a trap, Chamberlain clipped an oxygen mask over his eyes, nose and mouth. He grabbed an extinguisher and opened the door. The fire had spread from the torpedo controls to the empty rails used for loading the pills into their tubes. Flames spat and shimmered on the walls and the computers. The fire hadn't reached the torpedoes. It had begun on the opposite side of the narrow locker, thirty feet from the rack on which the Strikers rested.

Chamberlain fired the foam from his extinguisher on the rails first, to prevent the fire from spreading. The blistering heat cut into his senses, making it difficult to breathe and think. Continuing to spray the foam, he worked his way toward the fire, blanketing walls and breakers, smothering the outer limits of the flames.

As other sailors followed his lead, Chamberlain aimed his extinguisher deep into the flames and the fire melted away. First the black-tinged outer flames dissolved and then the yellow insides. For just a moment, Chamberlain thought they'd finally won a battle, and then he saw the ends of wires that had been stripped out of the walls, the wires that ran into the warning lights.

He stood straight and allowed his extinguisher to fall to the floor. *Poison or radiation?* he asked himself. Only then did he notice that the door to the locker had closed.

Still holding his silenced fire extinguisher in his right hand, he pushed through the other crew members and walked to the hatch. He tried to open it, but the door ignored him.

His fingers went numb and the extinguisher dropped from his hands. By the time he turned to look at the sailors who had followed him, some of them had already dropped to their knees and started vomiting.

Death followed quickly.

10

The engineer saw the faintest glow up ahead and recognized it as coming from an emergency stairwell. It wasn't really a stairwell, just an access way, a ladder in a clear plastic tube that connected *Barrows'* many decks. If an alien happened to glance toward the tube, it would spot her.

The stairwell wouldn't protect her, but it was an escape. She was tired and her legs and lungs burned, but she ran to the small hatch and grabbed onto the handle.

Behind her, the alien grunted as it inhaled and hissed as it exhaled. Its feet padded along the metal floor hard and fast. It couldn't have been far away, maybe just around a corner.

The unyielding wheel fought her, stretching the skin of her palms. She squeezed harder, but her sweaty hands slid along the metal.

The alien's breathing grew louder. Its heavy footsteps became faster.

God, please help me! Lord, help me! Oh, Jesus, please help me! She didn't want to look back, but her reflexes overpowered her good sense. She peered over her shoulder and there it was, no more than fifty feet away and nearly invisible in the darkness, but for its tiny eyes gleaming like gems in the glow from the stairwell.

The wheel tipped, then it spun freely and she whipped it all the way to the left. It ran three revolutions and the bolt in the hatch made a loud clank as it slid in its track.

The engineer pulled the hatch open and leaped into the stairwell; she planted her weight on the nearest rung of the ladder running along the side of the wall and slung the hatch shut with all of her strength. The door slammed and she lost her footing. She fell, bouncing off the back wall of the tube and then hitting her forehead on one rung and then another as she started the long fall to the first deck.

Barely conscious and bleeding from her nose and mouth, she fell twenty feet, dropping out of the artificial gravity field surrounding the thirteenth deck and entering the zero gravity of the twelfth. There, she floated like a specimen preserved in a jar of formaldehyde.

Above her, the alien fought with the hatch. A loud bang echoed through the tube when the hatch swung open.

Come on! You have to move! You have to move! She told herself, and then she realized she didn't have the strength and told herself, *It's over.*

She pivoted her body and stared back the way she had come, waiting for death to take her. The monster had her. It would slither down the tube as easily and naturally as... But the alien only peered down at her. Nine feet tall and dressed in armor, it couldn't fit in the tube.

Her head cleared by fear, the engineer grabbed the nearest rung and pulled herself to the ladder. She started climbing down. Two rungs down, she realized she didn't need to climb. She pushed off the ladder like a swimmer pushing off from the side of a pool, and she dropped at a slow even speed, faster than she could possibly have climbed had the gravity been working.

Gliding in zero gravity, the engineer casually dropped three floors. It was controlled. It was soothing. Breathing calmly, her panic slowly started to settle, but the moment ended abruptly. The gravity still worked on deck eight. She noticed the pull of acceleration and stabbed a hand out to catch herself on the ladder as the glide turned into a fall. She wrapped her fingers around a rung, but the pull of weight and momentum were too strong and her fingers never formed a tight enough grip around the rung. She wrenched her shoulder. Her forehead slammed into the wall and one of her feet got tangled in the ladder, and though she was dazed, she had the presence of mind to grab it and hold. on She didn't have the strength to climb, either up or down, so she clung to the ladder, breathing so hard that her bruised ribs sent shockwaves up her spine.

God, please don't let me die now! Not like this! It was a prayer, not a thought. She had become so desperate that she had turned prayer.

A rivulet of blood ran down her forehead, stinging her eyes, mixing with the slick of mucus between her nose and lips. Blood pasted her hair to her cheeks and forehead; a wing-shaped lock of soggy yellow hair hung over her left eye.

She lowered her right foot down one rung, tried to place her weight on it, froze as the jolt of pain ran up her spine. She had hurt her ankle, her hips, and her back. Frustrated, terrified and tortured, she whimpered softly to herself and vowed not to give up.

Then, she looked through the wall. The area was opaque around the tube. She was between decks. The area around her was the floor between deck eight and deck seven. Below her, a corridor stretched ahead like a well-lit tunnel. She could see the floor, the walls, two boots, and the cuffs of two pant legs dangling in the air.

Curiosity temporarily causing her to shelf her pain, the engineer lowered herself down one rung and then another. She kept her eyes fixed on the boots and then the legs, which hung from the overhead like a pair of stalactites.

Now, she could see a blood-soaked kneecap poking out of a tear in the pants. Another rung and she could see more boots and more legs. She tightened her grip around the handles that formed the ladder for security.

Starting to feel light headed, she had stopped breathing. She drew a long quiet breath and climbed down another rung and then another.

They hung from the ceiling. There were dozens of them, maybe hundreds, men and women hanging like sides of beef in a meat locker, their backs arched, their arms and legs dangling lifelessly; they looked like puppets waiting to be strung. Little pools of blood had formed under each body. The engineer saw the scene and understood it; these people were being cured like hams. The aliens weren't bleeding the sailors out like so much kosher meat; they were leaving the blood in, allowing it to gather at the feet.

Dispassionate thoughts—*They do that; alligators and crocodiles store meat*, merged with wild thoughts of survival—*Please, God, don't let them see me! I need to run! God, don't let this happen to me!* Her mental din drowned out any rational thoughts.

Three aliens entered the corridor dragging humans, men she knew, men who had come with her to explore the ship. One of the aliens lifted a man into the air with one hand. It held a short, thick pike of some kind in its other. The creature stabbed the weapon through the man's chest. The end of the pike poked through the back, just below the man's shoulder blades and six-inch spikes emerged from the end of the pike, forming a T.

The alien secured the pike into the ceiling and left the man to hang from it.

The engineer felt a wave of nausea run through her. She didn't scream. Silently, she pulled herself up the ladder, one rung and then another and three more, hiding herself in the structure between the decks.

The deck was nearly soundproof. The engineer couldn't hear the aliens and they probably wouldn't hear her, not through airtight hatches designed to hold out gas and smoke.

Huddled against the ladder, supporting herself in a vertical version of a fetal position, she whimpered and waited.

That first alien, the one that had chased her, was somewhere out there looking for her. It knew she had entered the stairwell. If she didn't move soon, her hiding spot would become a trap.

Reaching tentatively, slowly, silently, she touched a foot to the next rung, lowered her weight onto it, reached a hand to a lower rung, and willed herself to descend. She paused and lowered herself just enough to peer out.

A man hung from the ceiling just a foot from the tube, his head, arms and legs as limp and loose as wet laundry. Little streams of blood ran down the back of his hand and dribbled from the tips of his fingers to the floor.

The aliens had gone away.

Though she tried to stop herself, the engineer looked at the man's face and recognized the chief of security, the man who had saved her life no more than ten minutes earlier. He had a serene expression, maybe from knowing that he had acted honorably in the face of death, maybe just glad that his life was over and his spirit had left *Barrows* behind. Where his spirit had gone, there'd be no pain, no monstrous aliens.

The blood on his face was still wet. He had a faint smile, a Mona Lisa. The engineer couldn't stop herself from staring at him. She saw his leg twitch. She saw bubbles form on his lips as his chest swelled. Blood sprayed from the top and leaked from his back. The man turned his head and returned her stare. What she had mistaken for serenity was the glazed look of a man deprived of all sanity. His mouth opened and she saw blood on his teeth. His tongue lolled. He may have been shouting for help. He may have been screaming in pain or possibly even laughing. She couldn't hear him through the walls of the tube.

The engineer's hands, feet, and brain ceased working as she clung to the ladder and gawked at the man who had so recently traded his life for hers. She couldn't think. The paralysis was absolute, and then she saw something walking through the rows of dangling feet and her survival instinct took over.

She climbed past deck seven, past deck six, and exited the emergency stairwell on deck five. The deck was dark and absolutely silent, but the engineer's brain filled the shadows with hanging bodies and giant lizards.

11

The little man that stepped into the bridge looked human in general, but a few of the details were wrong. His head was a little large; his body looked lithe and athletic.

He wore human clothing. In fact, he wore a Unified Authority battle dress uniform.

His skin had a black tint, like human skin covered in coal dust. The thick bone ridge over his eyes gave him a Neanderthal appearance. He was short, barely over five feet tall. He moved with the assurance of a panther on the prowl, but Captain Markham thought she saw something verging on sadness in his eyes.

Speaking mostly to soothe herself, she asked, "What are you?"

"I'm a petty officer. Senior Chief Petty Officer Jeffrey Baker at your service," said the dark man.

"You can talk," she said. "Are you human?"

"Synthetic."

"You're a clone."

"Yes, ma'am."

"Have you come to kill me?"

"I don't see any other alternative."

"But you don't want to?"

"I need to destroy your computers, anything the aliens might use to find their way to Earth."

"Then I wouldn't be able to find my way home," she said.

"No, Captain."

"I can't let you do that," she said.

He nodded and said, "That complicates things."

"You piloted the Explorer," said Markham, slowly piecing things together.

"I'm not one of the lizards, if that's what you mean," said the dark man.

"Lizards? You mean the aliens that boarded our ship. Are they really lizards?"

"I don't know if they are actual lizards, but they look more like lizards than cats or fish. They're a far cry from human."

"Have you seen them?" asked Markham.

"Yes. I think they came to salvage parts from your ship but right now they're mostly hunting for food.

"I killed most of your crew when I crashed into your ship. The survivors are hanging from the overhead on deck seven. I don't know what became of the team you sent to explore the ship, but they're probably dead by now."

Leslie Markham listened, thought about her cousin and silently apologized to anyone that could read her thoughts.

The dark man took a step toward the dais on which Captain Markham sat. She flinched but she didn't scream. He said, "None of us will make it out of here alive."

"But you're still going to kill me," said Captain Markham.

"You are the captain of the ship; you know too many secrets."

Captain Markham chuckled and said, "I can't lead them back

to Earth. I don't know where we are or how we got here."

"It's not a question of where; it's which," said the dark man. "We're most likely still in the same solar system."

"You don't know what you are talking about. Our computers don't recognize any star patterns. We're in uncharted space."

"They're the same stars we've always seen, but we've never seen them from this dimension," the dark man said as he continued toward her. "Broadcast physics doesn't transfer ships through space; it transfers them through dimensions."

The dark man stood close enough to touch the captain. He reached a hand out slowly as if to show he meant no harm. She watched the hand, tensed as his finger brushed against her shoulder and then her neck. She saw the sympathy in his eyes and relaxed.

He placed the hand on her throat and pressed his thumb across the tracheal rings. Leslie Markham silently passed from consciousness.

12

Senior Chief Jeffrey Baker prided himself on killing as humanely as possible.

He'd come without weapons when he'd broadcasted into *Barrows*. He didn't expect to survive the broadcast, bringing weapons seemed pointless.

The captain looked like she had just drifted off to sleep. *Death comes cordially to those who don't fight it,* he told himself, and he laid her back in her chair as gently as a parent tucking in an infant child.

It was only a matter of time now. Baker was a Navy SEAL, he knew the finer points of sabotage. He had rigged the radiation leak in the weapons locker and trapped the crew so they would die quickly. He'd also arranged for the nuclear reactors in the engine room to implode. At this point, he didn't think a horde of primitive reptilian aliens would have the kind of engineering background they'd need to stop the reactor from destroying the ship. In another five minutes, *Barrows* would explode taking its astronomical charts and navigational data with it.

Just a few more minutes and it will all be over, he told himself.

Having never expected to survive the mission, Baker had no qualms about dying. But when he looked at the display showing the ship's status, he saw something he needed to change.

13

A light shined in the silent distance. The rest of the deck was so dark, that light could have passed as a star shining in unoccupied space.

The engineer saw the light and cautiously approached it. *Drawn like a moth*, she thought to herself. As far as she knew, the only living creatures on this side of the ship were her and the aliens. They were big and cruel and on the hunt.

Some of them were alive, the engineer thought, reminding herself about sailors hanging from the overhead.

She crept forward through the darkness, moving from one hiding place to the next, listening for the pad of feet and wheezing, hissing breaths. Instead she heard nothing except her own heartbeat and breathing.

The light came from an internal observation deck. It shone through a window overlooking the engine room.

The engine room filled the last third of the ship. The area could be accessed through the second, third, and fourth decks. deck five had an observation room in which visitors could sit and watch the grand workings of the ship.

Seeing the engine room, the engineer knew exactly where she was. She'd felt disoriented since before entering the emergency stairwell, but now she knew where she stood. She gazed down into engine room with its maze of catwalks and scaffolding.

Down below her, lizards scurried among the machinery. She could see them, working in the light, dissecting ancillary systems. They removed circuits and wires, panels, piping, gauges. They were vultures, come to pick at the carcass of the ship; she could see that now.

She saw something else, too. Bright red light pulsed from emergency panels at every workstation. Either the aliens didn't see the panels or they didn't care about them.

There was no way those creatures could have known what the light meant, but she recognized the warning. Something had gone wrong with the reactor; it was at the tipping point of a catastrophic meltdown.

She searched the engine room. From what she could see, there were dozens of aliens working at the different stations as if they knew what they were doing. This flash of dizzying unreality sent a chill through her. *How can lizards understand engineering?* she wondered. Watching them, she felt fear and hatred.

The warning light from the reactor no longer scared her; she wanted the ship to explode. She wanted the loathsome, barbaric creatures to die before they started eating sailors. A moment of hate and anger followed by a flash of clarity—she wanted the aliens dead before they ate her. She didn't want to die, but hanging from a ceiling and waiting scared her so thoroughly that dying no longer seemed important.

She tried to remember places she could hide. There was a hanger on deck five. It wasn't far, not from the engine room, and if she managed to reach the hangar, and if there were transports on the launch deck, and if the airlocks would open, maybe she could launch herself into space.

She peered through the window, saw aliens climbing ladders, using tools, looking at circuit maps, and she felt the hope evaporate out of her. Feeling numb and weak, she sank to the floor. *Are they intelligent?* she wondered. *If I were on their ship, would I know what to do?*

As she watched, lizard-like aliens crowded around the reactor. They opened panels. They played with dials. They disconnected cables. Impossible though it seemed, they fixed the reactor and the warning lights stopped flashing.

She heard the breathing before she heard the footsteps, the wheezing, grunting, and hissing. The deck was dark except for the light from the observation area. Terrified that the aliens' slit eyes saw clearly in the dark, she huddled behind a waist-high wall and tried to decide whether she should run or hide. She didn't know if the alien she now heard was the same lizard that had chased her into the emergency stairwell. She didn't know if this lizard had come alone or with an entire hunting party.

Stay? Hide? Run? Fighting wasn't an option. Precious moments slipped away like water leaking between her fingers. She tried to think, but her mind had already become frantic and now she heard the footsteps as the creature slowly approached the observation area.

I can't hide here, not in the light, but if I run...

She climbed to her feet but remained crouching behind the sub-wall, ultimately deciding to crawl to the nearest hallway.

Reaching the corridor, she stood and darted into the darkness, all the while running a hand along the wall until she located a narrow access hall that would lead to a parallel hallway, a smaller corridor used for engineering and maintenance. She tried to silence her breathing, her footsteps, her thoughts, but all of them echoed like sirens in her mind.

In her thoughts, she saw the bridge as a fortress. The rest of the crew was dead, but Captain Markham still had fifty able-bodied sailors in the bridge. If she could just reach the bridge; she'd be safe... if she could find a way back to the bridge. She thought about the dark man she had seen before she set off the cold foam, the short bogey man in BDUs. He no longer seemed scary, not after the lizard-like aliens with their pikes and their armor. He'd seemed almost human.

She reached a break between walls and realized that she'd found the entrance to the service hall. This way was a trap. A bottleneck. It ran between major departments. Once she entered, there would be very few arteries she could use to get out—and just as few that the aliens could use to enter. Unless the alien followed her around this exact corner, it wouldn't be able to find her without retracing her steps.

The engineer turned, she ran, she entered the service hall and kept running. She heard the creature slamming against walls, running quickly, trying to find a way to come after her. She could hear its breathing; it couldn't have been more than a wall or two away, but it was on the wrong side of the wall.

She ran. Fatigue and ache no longer mattered; they'd become concepts, and her mind no longer bothered with them. She couldn't see, but the hallway was straight and empty. Her right shoulder brushed along the wall and she overcompensated; a moment later her left shoulder brushed against a wall.

The bang sounded like an explosion as it echoed through the hall. Somewhere in her subconscious, she imagined the alien slamming an armored shoulder into a wall, trying to break through. The wall must have held.

Barrows was a half-mile long. Having sprinted the length of the ship without knowing it, the engineer ran face-first into a wall, bounced backwards, and collapsed to the floor. As she lay stunned on the deck, she thought, *Get up! I must get up! It's out!*

But she couldn't get up. It was over; she didn't have the strength, and then, in the darkness, she heard padding footsteps on a metal deck. The breathing was loud and rapid, betraying the creature's excitement.

The end, she thought, but as she lay there, the hall lights switched on and she saw the alien, dashing toward her like a javelin thrower ready to cast his spear. She saw its long strides and its tail dragging behind and the mouth gaping open. The creature's teeth were as long as her fingers.

She had willingly given in to death when she couldn't see it coming, but seeing the creature charging toward her, Wendy Markham climbed to her feet. The wall she had struck was the door to the elevator. She tried to open the door, but it wouldn't budge. She looked back, saw the alien was no more than fifty feet away, fumbled for her engineering access card, and ran it through the security slot.

The door opened.

She reached in blindly, felt the nearest rungs of the ladder that ran along the wall of the elevator shaft and took hold of it. She pulled herself in. The shaft was bigger than the emergency stairwell, large enough for elevator cars and large enough for a nine-foot alien in gladiator armor. She knew it would follow her. Maybe it would shoot her this time.

She was already to the next deck when the alien entered the shaft. She looked down and saw it staring at her, following her. Its face was unreadable, but it made that noise that reminded her of crows clucking, and she knew it was laughing at her.

The engineer climbed as quickly as she could, but the alien was faster. She could hear clacking of its armor brushing against the rungs in the wall. As it came closer, its labored breathing seemed to fill the elevator shaft. Its leathery skin creaked as it wrapped its hands around the ladder rungs.

The engineer climbed one deck and then another and then she felt the change, her weight simply disappeared. She kicked off the ladder and took off like a superhero launching into flight. Above her, she saw the base of the elevator. She looked down and saw the alien, still clinging to the ladder. She had reached a dead end. From here, there was no place else to go.

She was faster than the alien, but she'd reached a place from which she would not escape. Unable to stop, she crashed into the bottom of the elevator, turned herself over, and prepared to launch herself back the way she had come. Maybe, if she was fast enough, she could slip past the alien. Maybe it wouldn't reach out and grab her. Maybe it was slow. Maybe it was stupid.

Below her, the creature pushed off the wall and seemed to fill the shaft. It cocked its head back so it could stare up at her, its eyes gleaming in the sliver of light that shined down from the elevator. It chuckled its clucking laugh.

And then it went silent.

The creature moved quickly. It reached for the ladder with blinding speed, but the speed made no difference. Something large and dark, black and green hit the alien hard and fast, and then the alien was gone and the dark man floated where the alien had been.

The dark man grabbed the ladder, looked up at the engineer, and said, "Twelve decks, I doubt that's a far enough drop to kill that creature. We'd better get going." He grabbed hold of the ladder along the wall, pulled himself toward it, and then launched himself so that he glided through the panel he had opened in the elevator floor.

Stopped at deck thirteen, the elevator had a gravity field inside it. With the grace of a gymnast, the dark man pulled himself in up to his chest, and there he stopped, half of his body in the elevator and half dangling out. He hung there for a moment, and then he silently dropped from the elevator car carrying a six-inch-wide cylinder in his hands. The cylinder glowed a dark burned-orange color.

Though she never worked in weapons, the engineer recognized the cylinder as a Hempfield nuclear-tipped torpedo and stifled a scream in her throat. She asked, "What are you doing?"

"I'm destroying the ship," the dark man answered with blithe innocence, as if he saw nothing wrong with killing her and himself. He tucked the weapon under his shoulder, the way one might carry a watermelon or a rolled up rug, and pushed off of the elevator.

"You're going to destroy the ship?" asked the engineer.

"Those things can't have it; they might tap into the computers and find their way to Earth."

"Are you planning on blowing us up?"

The dark man appeared to consider this for only a moment. He said, "Well, I came here to die. I had orders to broadcast my ship into the center of this ship which was pretty much a death sentence.

"Since my orders were to destroy this ship, killing you was pretty much part of the plan. I'm not sure where you'll go if I let you live. This is uncharted territory."

He started climbing down the ladder, the torpedo still tucked under one arm. Carrying the torpedo in zero gravity posed no problem. The "pill" weighed nothing. It weighed eighty-seven pounds in gravity fields similar to Earth's.

Instead of following the dark man down the ladder, the engineer climbed toward the elevator. He paused to smile up at her and said, "I wouldn't go up there if I were you."

"The lizards?" she asked.

"The radiation," answered the dark man. "One of the blue torpedoes sprung a leak. The radiation will have reached lethal levels on the bridge decks by now."

"You did that," said the engineer.

"Obviously."

Apparently uninterested in talking, he continued down the ladder. The engineer followed. "Where are you going?" she asked. He didn't answer.

"Where are you going?" she repeated.

He stopped, looked up at her, said, "Look, I didn't come here to save you."

"Why did you save me," she said.

"An alien got in my way. I moved it aside."

"But..."

The dark man paused and glared up the ladder. He said, "My orders are to destroy this ship."

"Did you kill Leslie?" asked the engineer.

"I killed everybody on the bridge," said the dark man.

The engineer stopped speaking.

The dark man floated down two decks and took hold of the ladder. Speaking in a whisper, he said, "The aliens entered through this deck." He pulled himself from the ladder and tapped a hand against the wall so that he drifted slowly across the shaft to the emergency lever, a chrome-covered handle. Planting his feet along the wall, he pumped the lever and the door slowly opened.

He stopped working and asked, "Do you know how to build a broadcast engine?"

"I've never even worked on one," she answered.

"And you don't know how to get to Earth?"

"I don't know any navigation," she said.

He continued working the crank, opening the door just a foot—a tight squeeze for him and the engineer, too tight for the wide-bodied aliens. He said, "Yeah, you're no threat," then, holding the torpedo above his head as if it were a trophy, he kicked off the wall and glided through partially opened doorway.

The engineer pulled herself to the partially opened hatch, but didn't enter. A moment passed, and then she heard the dark man say, "I'd hurry if I were you, but then, maybe haven't you looked down the ladder?"

14

The engineer looked down the shaft and saw the alien staring back at her. It didn't climb the ladder; this time it clung to the wall, like a spider... like a lizard. Red blood dripped from its snout, its mouth, and ridges along the side of its head. Blood-stained scales surrounded one of its eyes.

Twenty, maybe thirty feet below her, the creature climbed slowly, one of its shoulders seeming to snap in and out of its socket as it crawled up the wall. The alien no longer made that crow-like chuckling noise. Its breathing had become louder. It inhaled long and exhaled quickly, making a spitting noise.

The engineer said, "Oh. Shit."

She placed a hand on either side of the gap in the doorway and pulled herself into the unlit corridor. The dark man floated far ahead of her, pulling himself along the wall. She didn't see him so much as the orange glow of the torpedo he carried under his left arm. In her mind, the dark man seemed to morph into a fighter, a Tomcat or a Harrier, and he carried the torpedo under his wing.

She followed after him, kicking hard off the door to build a good speed and pushing off hatches and handholds to accelerate.

Despite his malformed face and murderous mission, the engineer saw this man as her protector. She trusted him. She wanted his approval. Realizing that she should have feared and hated the scary little man, the bogeyman in BDUs, she wondered if her fears had disguised themselves as trust.

She caught up to him quickly, dragged her hand along the wall to slow herself, and whispered, "It's got a gun. The alien is carrying a gun."

"I saw it."

Thinking the dark man hadn't understood, she said, "We have to run; it's coming after us and it has a gun."

The dark man asked, "Have you see him fire it?"

"The gun? No."

"Neither have I. It could be a gun or something a whole lot worse. They may not be using them because they're too powerful to use inside a ship."

"Too powerful?" asked the engineer. "So powerful they would destroy the ship."

She thought about bombs that might make the ship explode like an over-inflated balloon. She thought about molecular chain reactions disintegrating the bonds between atoms. At a word from this dangerous little man, the gun had gone from a worry to a weapon of mass destruction.

She heard the breathing. It was louder than before. The creature must have caught up to them. It made a bubbling, gurgling sound every time it inhaled.

She thought, *We're going too slow; it's going to catch us; we're going too slow*, but she also thought, *He'll save me. He won't let me die.* She had forgotten about God now. She had forgotten about religion. She had the dark man and she placed her faith in him.

She noticed the glow from the torpedo he kept under his arm. "It's going to see the torpedo!"

The dark man said, "It knows we're here. The question is, does it see us or just the light from the torpedo. Is it going to place more weight on its vision or its sense of smell?"

She not only heard the creature's breathing now, but she also heard crashing sounds. Glancing back, she saw nothing in the darkness.

"It won't catch up to us. It needs gravity for its equilibrium. I watched them when they boarded the ship; they don't do well in zero-G."

The creature's banging and clawing seemed to fill the corridor. Its breathing, however, had faded into the obscure distance.

The dark man said, "It's falling behind. I need to slow down."

"We're slowing down?" the engineer didn't understand.

"I'm going to slow down. You're going to turn right at the next corner and you're going to float straight ahead until you see light in the hall. It's coming from their ship."

"Their ship?" she asked.

"If you can fly their ship, it's yours."

"What if there are aliens on it?"

"That's part of flying the ship."

"What about you?" she asked.

"My orders don't say anything about saving my own skin."

"But…"

"There's your corner, turn," the dark man said as he braced himself along the wall and shoved her down a perpendicular hall. She looked back and saw the orange glow of the torpedo for another second before it disappeared into darkness.

She traveled less than a minute in total darkness, and then she saw the low glow in the distance, a ghostly green so faint that it might have been a mirage. She heard nothing, no breathing, no thrashing. The deck was silent.

The light shone from a hole in the outer wall of *Barrows* like a thin mist that swirled and dissolved into the darkness. She floated to it, through it, and then a gravity field pulled her to the deck as she entered the padded breezeway that ran between *Barrows* and the alien ship. Moist, dank air filled the umbilical connector. The inside of the ship was warm and humid like a swamp.

She entered a ship that was long and wide and devoid of inner walls. She could see both the cockpit, one hundred feet ahead, and the far side of the ship, forty feet away. She saw no chairs, no partitions, no tables. Workstations hung from the overhead like darkened chandeliers, their buttons and screens glowing like stars and planets. Wires and piping ran along the walls and across the deck and overhead giving the ship a cavernous, organic feel.

The overhead was fifteen feet up. In one area, dozens of pipe stems hung from it. Recognizing the stems for what they were, the engineer walked over to look at them. She reached up and tried to touch one, but it was far too high.

She saw one of the pikes leaning against a wall. It was just over two feet long and about three inches wide, a perfect cylinder except for its pointed tip. She needed two hands to lift it; it weighted at least thirty pounds. She remembered the ease with which the alien had pulled and stabbed it into the chief of security—a large and powerful man, but helpless compared to the alien.

The engineer's mind was drifting off from reality, wandering aimlessly. In another few minutes the dark man would detonate his torpedo. The alien might have signaled its shipmates. A dozen aliens might emerge from the breezeway any moment.

She felt hopeless. If they came, there was nothing she could do to protect herself. She asked herself how she had ever convinced herself to even attempt to fly their ship. *I'm not a pilot*, she'd chided herself. *I can't even fly a U.A. starship.*

The aliens were coming. Somewhere from the distance came the sounds of thrashing and banging.

She looked at the pike. It was too heavy to use like a club. As she stared at it, she noticed a rough patch in the smooth bore of its cylinder and ran her thumb over it. Long spikes stabbed out of the sides of the cylinder—the spokes that held dead prey in place as they hung from the ceiling. Running her thumb over the rough patch a second time caused the spikes to retract.

No different than those knives, she thought. She looked at a screen in one of the consoles dangling from the ceiling. She saw a series of lines, some dark and some light. The lines meant nothing to her. As far as she was concerned, they might have relayed anything from engineering data to alien stock market results.

The banging and thrashing grew louder, waking the engineer from her reverie. Still holding the pike, fully expecting to die, she walked to the breezeway. She entered its near total darkness and continued across. Orange light glowed on the far end. She walked to it, past it, and stepped into the weightlessness outside the ship.

In the glow from the torpedo, the alien looked larger and more barbaric than it had in bright light. It struggled in zero gravity, swinging its claws like a drowning man caught in a current. It flailed its tail for balance, striking the walls and the ceiling. Its feet peddled in the air.

The alien held one of the dark man's arms with one of its claws. It swiped at the dark man with the other claw. He dodged the blows and struck back. He was fast and small, and his kicks and punches seemed not to bother the alien.

The engineer could tell that the dark man had already lost the fight. She saw it clearly as she watched the struggle in the orange glow from the torpedo. Not thinking about what she was doing, she moved toward the fight, now holding the pike with one hand because it weighed next to nothing. She could have thrown it all the entire length of the ship if she'd chosen, but instead, she held it above her head like an umbrella as she kicked off a wall and flew toward the fight. She held the shaft of the pike with her left hand and braced the back of it with her right, and she stabbed the point into the neck of alien and uselessly pressed her weightless body against it in an effort to drive it in deeper.

The alien shrieked, whipping its head and snapping its jaws as it strained to free itself. In its struggle, the creature released the dark man and he kicked off a wall, dragging the fighting creature with him, brushing the engineer away as he and the alien hit the floor, driving the pike deeper into the creature's scaly neck. A long stream of blood spurted out of the wound, floating upward, and breaking into beads that looked like drops of crude oil in the orange glow.

"Get flying," said the dark man.

The engineer ignored him, reaching a hand into the melee and causing the spikes to erupt from the creature's neck. The spikes tore fist-sized swatches of meat from the creature. It shrieked and stopped moving.

The dark man glided to the torpedo and said, "You have three minutes and twenty-seven seconds."

"Come with me," she said.

"Three minutes and twenty-two seconds." He said. "My orders didn't say anything about survival."

"Did they say anything about dying?" she asked.

"Three minutes and fifteen," he said, but he left the torpedo and headed toward the breezeway. The engineer followed. As the gravity pulled him to the deck he said, "We're not going to survive this."

She followed him into the ship, noting the glistening areas where blood flowed from his head, his neck, his shoulders, and his back. One of his ears was torn, the top half flapping and bouncing like a leaf in a strong wind.

When she reached the end of the breezeway, the engineer saw a chromed patch on the wall. She pressed it and the door to the breezeway sealed. She didn't know if the breezeway still tethered the alien ship to the side of *Barrows*.

"Two minutes and forty-nine seconds," said the dark man.

The engineer trotted to the console closest to the nose of the ship to see if she could figure out the controls. She looked out through the windscreen and saw stars in the distance, stars in a configuration never seen by man. There'd be no rescue. Even if she figured out how to fly the ship, they would not last long.

The dark man was bleeding badly and would probably die soon. She didn't know where to find food, and if she found it, she wasn't sure that she could eat it. None of that mattered. In another minute the torpedo would explode and her instinct was to survive the moment.

And after that? Well, that didn't matter, either. They were lost in a dark expanse.

AUTHOR'S NOTE

Dark Expanse is a massively multiplayer online real-time strategy game. As RTS games are one of my biggest weaknesses, I constantly remind myself never to type deorc.com into the address bar of my browser. If you share my affliction, I caution you not to open that Pandora's Box as well—unless you have time and a desire for some nostalgic fun.

While this story, most of the characters, and the storyline are entirely original, the aliens were based on my imaginings of a race from within the *Dark Expanse* universe.

THE LOST FLEET
BY JACK CAMPBELL

After a hundred years of brutal war against the Syndics, the Alliance fleet is marooned deep in enemy territory, weakened, demoralised and desperate to make it home. Their fate rests in the hands of Captain "Black Jack" Geary, a man who had been presumed dead but then emerged from a century of survival hibernation to find his name had become legend.

DAUNTLESS

FEARLESS

COURAGEOUS

VALIANT

RELENTLESS

VICTORIOUS

BEYOND THE FRONTIER: DREADNAUGHT

BEYOND THE FRONTIER: INVINCIBLE

BEYOND THE FRONTIER: GUARDIAN

BEYOND THE FRONTIER: STEADFAST

"Black Jack is an excellent character, and this series is the best military SF I've read in some time." *Wired*

"Fascinating stuff… this is military SF where the military and SF parts are both done right." *SFX Magazine*

"*The Lost Fleet* is some of the best military science fiction on the shelves today." SF Site

TITANBOOKS.COM